The MYSTERY series

Volume 3

Other Collections

The Magic Faraway Tree Collection

The Wishing-Chair Collection

The O'Clock Tales

The Magic Folk Collection

The Chimney Corner Collection

Enid Blyton

The MYSTERY series

Volume 3

3 books in 1

EGMONT

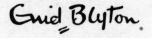

EGMONT

We bring stories to life

The Mystery of the Pantomime Cat first published in Great Britain 1949
The Mystery of the Invisible Thief first published in Great Britain 1950
The Mystery of the Vanished Prince first published in Great Britain 1951
This edition published in 2015 by Egmont UK Limited
The Yellow Building, 1 Nicholas Road
London W11 4AN

ENID BLYTON ® Copyright © 2015 Hodder & Stoughton Ltd
Text copyright for *The Mystery of the Pantomime Cat* © 1949 Hodder & Stoughton Ltd
Text copyright for *The Mystery of the Invisible Thief* © 1950 Hodder & Stoughton Ltd
Text copyright for *The Mystery of the Vanished Prince* © 1951 Hodder & Stoughton Ltd

ISBN 978 1 4052 7570 5

www.egmont.co.uk

54698/4

A CIP catalogue record for this title is available from the British Library.

Printed and bound in Great Britain by CPI Group.

MIX
Paper
FSC   FSC® C018306

The MYSTERY of the Pantomime Cat

Contents

1. AT THE RAILWAY STATION

Larry and Daisy were waiting for Fatty to come and call for them with Buster the Scottie. They swung on the gate and kept looking down the road.

'Nice to be home for the hols again,' said Daisy. 'I wish Fatty would hurry up. We shan't be in time to meet Pip and Bets' train if he doesn't hurry up. I'm longing to see them again. It seems ages since the Christmas hols.'

'There he is!' said Larry, and jumped off the gate. 'And there's Buster. Hello, Fatty! We'll have to hurry or we won't be in time to meet Bets and Pip.'

'Plenty of time,' said Fatty, who never seemed in a hurry. 'Well, it'll be fun to be all together again, won't it? – the Five Find-Outers, ready to tackle the next super-colossal mystery!'

'Woof,' said Buster, feeling a bit left out. Fatty corrected himself. 'The Five Find-Outers and Dog.

1

Sorry, Buster.'

'Come on,' said Daisy. 'The train will be in. Fancy, we've had almost a week's holiday and haven't seen Bets and Pip. I bet they didn't like staying with their Aunt Sophie – she's very strict and proper. They'll be full of pleases and thank-yous and good manners for a few days!'

'It'll wear off,' said Fatty. 'Anyone seen Old Clear-Orf these hols?'

Clear-Orf was the name the children gave to Mr Goon, the village policeman. He couldn't bear the five children, and he hated Buster, who loved to dance round the policeman's ankles in a most aggravating way. The children had solved a good many mysteries which Mr Goon had tried to work out himself, and he was very jealous of them.

'He'll say "Clear orf!" as soon as he spots one of us anywhere,' said Larry, with a grin. 'It's sort of automatic with him. I wonder if there'll be any more mysteries these hols. I feel I could just use my brains nicely on a good juicy mystery!'

The others laughed. 'Don't let Daddy hear you say that,' said Daisy. 'You had such a bad report that he'll wonder why you don't use your brains for

Latin and maths instead of mysteries!'

'I suppose he had "Could use his brains better," or "Does not make the best use of his brains," on his report,' said Fatty. 'I know the sort of thing.'

'You couldn't *ever* have had those remarks put on *your* report, Fatty,' said Daisy, who had a great admiration for Fatty's brains.

'Well,' said Fatty modestly, 'I *usually* have "A brilliant term's work," or "Far surpasses the average for his form" or . . .'

Larry gave him a punch. 'Still the same modest but conceited old Fatty! It's marvellous how you manage to boast in such a modest tone of voice, Fatty. I . . .'

'Stop arguing; there's the train's whistle,' said Daisy, beginning to run. 'We simply *must* be on the platform to meet Pip and Bets. Oh, poor Buster – he's getting left behind on his short legs. Come on, Buster!'

The three children and Buster burst through the door on to the platform. Buster gave a delighted bark, and sniffed at the bottom of a pair of stout dark blue trousers, whose owner was standing by the bookstall.

There was an exasperated snort. 'Clear orf!' said a familiar voice. 'Put that dog on a lead!'

'Oh – hello, Mr Goon!' chorused Fatty, Larry, and Daisy, as if Mr Goon was their dearest friend.

'Fancy seeing *you*!' said Fatty. 'I hope you are quite well, Mr Goon – not feeling depressed at this weather, or . . .'

Mr Goon was getting ready to be very snappish when the train came in with a thunderous roar that made it impossible to talk.

'There's Pip!' yelled Larry, and waved so violently that he almost knocked off Mr Goon's helmet. Buster retired under a platform seat and sat there looking very dignified. He didn't like trains. Mr Goon stood not far off, looking for whoever it was he had come to meet.

Bets and Pip tumbled out of the train in excitement. Bets ran to Fatty and hugged him. 'Fatty! I hoped you'd come and meet us! Hello Larry, hello Daisy!'

'Hello, young Bets,' said Fatty. He was very fond of Bets. He smacked Pip on the back. 'Hello Pip! You've just come back in time to help in a super-colossal mystery!'

This was said in a very loud voice, which was meant to reach Mr Goon's ears. But unfortunately he didn't hear. He was shaking hands with another policeman, a young, pink-faced, smiling fellow.

'Look!' said Larry. 'Another policeman! Are we going to have two in Peterswood now, then?'

'I don't know,' said Fatty, looking hard at the second policeman. 'I rather like the look of Mr Goon's friend – he looks a nice sort of man.'

'I like the way his ears stick out,' said Bets.

'Idiot,' said Pip. 'Where's old Buster, Fatty?'

'Here, Buster – come out from under that seat,' said Fatty. 'Shame on you for being such a coward!'

Buster crawled out, trying to wag his tail while it was still down, in a most apologetic way. But as the train then began to pull out of the station again with a terrific noise, Buster retired hurriedly under the seat once more.

'Poor Buster! I'm sure if I was a dog I'd hide under a seat too,' said Bets, comfortingly.

'It's not so long ago since you always stood behind me when the train came in,' said Pip. 'And I remember you trying to . . .'

'Come on,' said Fatty, seeing Bets beginning to

go red. 'Let's go. BUSTER! Come on out and don't be an idiot. The train is now a mile away.'

Buster came out, saw *two* pairs of dark blue legs walking towards him, and ran at them joyfully. Mr Goon cried out.

'That dog!' he said, balefully. He turned to his companion. 'You want to look out for this here dog,' he told him, in a loud voice. 'He wants reporting. He's not under proper control, see? You keep your eyes open for him, PC Pippin, and don't you stand no nonsense.'

'Oh, Mr Goon, don't say there's going to be *two* of you chasing poor Buster,' began Fatty, always ready for an argument with Mr Goon.

'There's *not* going to be two of us,' said Mr Goon. 'I'm off on holiday – about time too – and this here's my colleague, PC Pippin, who's coming to take over while I'm away. And I'm very glad we've seen you, because now I can point you all out to him, and tell him to keep his eye on you. *And* that dog too.' He turned to his companion, who was looking a little startled.

'See these five kids? They think themselves very clever – think they can solve all the mysteries in the district! The trouble they've put me to – you wouldn't believe it! Keep your eye on them, PC Pippin – and if there's any mystery about, keep it to yourself. If you don't, you'll have these kids poking their noses into what concerns the law, and making themselves regular nuisances.'

'Thanks for the introduction, Mr Goon,' said Fatty, with a grin. He smiled at the other policeman. 'Pleased to welcome you to Peterswood, Mr Pippin. I hope you'll be happy here. And – er – if at any time we can help you, just let us know.'

'There you are! What did I tell you?' said Mr Goon, going red in the face. 'Can't stop interfering! You clear orf, all of you, and take that pestiferous dog with you. And mind you, I shall warn PC Pippin of all your little tricks and you'll find he won't stand any nonsense. See?'

Mr Goon stalked off with his friend PC Pippin, who looked round at the children rather apologetically as he went. Fatty gave him a large wink. Pippin winked back.

'I like him,' said Bets. 'He's got a nice face. And his ears . . .'

'Stick out. Yes, you told us that before,' said

Pip. 'Hey, Fatty, I bet old Mr Goon is going to have a wonderful time telling PC Pippin all about us. He'll make us out to be a band of young gangsters or something.'

'I bet he will!' said Fatty. 'I'd just love to hear what he says about us. I guess our ears will burn.'

They did burn! Mr Goon was really enjoying himself warning PC Pippin about the Five Find-Outers – and Dog!

'You keep a firm hand on them,' said Mr Goon. 'And don't you stand any nonsense from that big boy – regular pest he is.'

'I thought he looked quite a good sort,' said PC Pippin, surprised.

Mr Goon did one of his best snorts. 'That's all part of his artfulness. The times that boy's played his tricks on me – messed me up properly – given me all kinds of false clues, and spoilt some of my best cases! He's a halfwit, that's what he is – always dressing himself up and acting the fool.'

'But isn't he the boy that Inspector Jenks has got such a high opinion of?' said PC Pippin, frowning in perplexity. 'I seem to remember him saying that . . .'

This was quite the wrong remark to make to Mr Goon. He went purple in the face and glared at PC Pippin, who looked back at him in alarm.

'That boy sucks up to Inspector Jenks,' said Mr Goon. 'See? He's a regular sucker-up, that boy is. Don't you believe a word that the Inspector says about him. And just you look out for mysterious redheaded boys dashing about all over the place, see?'

PC Pippin's eyes almost popped out of his head. 'Er – redheaded boys?' he said, in an astonished voice. 'I don't understand.'

'Use your brains, PC Pippin,' said Mr Goon in a lofty voice. 'That boy, Fatty – he's got no end of disguises, and one of his favourite ones is a red wig. The times I've seen redheaded boys! And it's been Fatty dressed up just to trick me. You be careful, PC Pippin. He'll try the same trick on you, you mark my words. He's a bad lot. All those children are pests – interfering pests. No respect for the law at all.'

PC Pippin listened in surprise, but most respectfully. Mr Goon was twice his age and must have had a lot of experience. PC Pippin was very new and very keen. He felt proud to take Mr Goon's place while he was away on holiday.

'I don't expect anything difficult will turn up while I'm away,' said Mr Goon, as they turned into the gate of his little front garden. 'But *if* something turns up, keep it to yourself, Pippin – don't let those kids get their noses into it, whatever you do – and just you send for me if they do, see? And try and get that dog run in for something. It's a dangerous dog, and I'd like to get it out of the way. You see what you can do.'

PC Pippin felt rather dazed. He had liked the children and the dog. It was surprising to find that Mr Goon had such different ideas. Still – he ought to know! PC Pippin determined to do his very best for Mr Goon. His very, very best!

2. A NICE LITTLE PLAN FOR PIPPIN

The Find-Outers were very pleased to be together again. The Easter holidays were not as long as the summer ones, and almost a week had gone by before Pip and Bets had arrived home from their stay with their aunt, so there didn't seem to be much time left.

'Not quite three weeks,' groaned Larry. 'I do hope the weather's decent. We can go for some bike rides and picnics then.'

'And there's a good little show on down at the Little Theatre,' said Daisy. 'It's a kind of skit on Dick Whittington – very funny. I've seen it already, but we might all go again.'

'Oh – is that little company still going?' said Fatty, with interest. 'I remember seeing some of its plays in the Christmas hols. Some of the acting was pretty poor. I wonder if they'd like to try *me* out in a few parts. You know, last term at school . . .'

'Fatty! *Don't* tell us you took the leading part in the school play *again*,' begged Larry. 'Doesn't anyone else *ever* take the leading part at your school but you?'

'Fatty's very, very good at acting – aren't you, Fatty?' said Bets, loyally. 'Look how he can disguise himself and take even *us* in! Fatty, are you going to disguise yourself these hols? Please do! Do you remember when you dressed up as that old balloon woman, and sold balloons?'

'And old Clear-Orf came along and wanted to see your licence,' chuckled Daisy. 'But you had so many petticoats on that you pretended you couldn't find it.'

'And Bets spotted it was you because she suddenly saw you had clean fingernails and filthy dirty hands,' said Larry, remembering. 'And that made her suspicious. I always thought that was smart of Bets.'

'You're making me feel I must disguise myself at once!' said Fatty, with a grin. 'What about playing a little joke on PC Pippin? What a lovely name!'

'Yes – and it suits him,' said Bets. 'He's got a sort

of apple-cheeked face – a nice round ripe pippin.'

Everyone roared. 'You tell him that,' said Pip. 'Go up to him and say, "Dear nice round ripe pippin." He'll be *so* surprised.'

'Don't be silly,' said Bets. 'As if I would! I quite liked him.'

'I wish something would turn up while Mr Goon is away,' said Fatty. 'Wouldn't he be mad to miss a mystery! And I bet we could help PC Pippin beautifully. He'd *like* our help, I expect. He doesn't look awfully clever – actually he might not be so good at snooping about as Mr Goon, because Mr Goon's had a lot of experience, and he's older – PC Pippin looks rather young. I bet we could tackle a mystery better than he could. We've solved a lot now. Six, in fact!'

'We can't possibly expect a mystery *every* hols,' said Larry.

'Let's make up one for PC Pippin,' said Bets, suddenly. 'Just a teeny-weeny one! With clues and things. He'd get awfully excited about it.'

The others stared at her. Fatty gave a sudden grin. 'Gosh! That's rather an idea of Bets, isn't it? Larry's right when he says we can't possibly expect a

13

mystery every hols and somehow I don't feel one will turn up in the next three weeks. So we'll concoct one – for that nice round ripe Pippin to solve!'

Everyone began to feel excited. It was something to plan and look forward to.

'I bet he'll make a whole lot of notes, and be proud to show them to Mr Goon,' said Larry. 'And I bet Mr Goon will smell a rat and know it's us. What a swizz for them!'

'Now this is really very interesting,' said Fatty, feeling pleased. 'It will be a nice little job for PC Pippin to use his brains on, it'll be some fun for us, and it will be *most* annoying for Mr Goon when he comes back – because I bet he's warned PC Pippin about us. And all he'll find is that PC Pippin has wasted his time on a pretend mystery!'

'What mystery shall we make up?' said Bets, pleased that her idea was so popular with the others. 'Let's think of a really good one – that Fatty can use disguises for. I love it when Fatty disguises himself.'

'Let's all think hard,' said Fatty. 'We want to rouse suspicions, first of all – do something that will make PC Pippin think there's something up, you know – so that he will nose about – and find a few little clues . . .'

'That we put ready for him,' said Bets, with a squeal of laughter. 'Oh *yes*! Oh, I *know* I shan't think of anything. Hurry up, everyone, and think hard.'

There was silence for a few minutes. As Bets said, she couldn't think of an idea at all.

'Well – anyone thought of anything?' asked Fatty. 'Daisy?'

'I *have* thought of something – but it's a bit feeble,' said Daisy. 'What about sending PC Pippin a mysterious letter through the post?'

'No good,' said Fatty. 'He'd suspect us at once. Larry, have *you* thought of anything?'

'Well, what about mysterious noises in PC Pippin's back garden at night?' said Larry. 'Very feeble, I know.'

'It is a bit,' said Fatty. 'Doesn't lead to anything. We want to do something that will really get PC Pippin worked up, make him think he's on to something big.'

'I can only think of something feeble too,' said Pip. 'You know – hiding in a garden at night till PC Pippin comes by – and then letting him hear us whisper – and then rushing off in the dark so that he suspects we've been up to mischief.'

'Now, there's something in *that*,' said Fatty, thinking over it. 'That really could lead on to something else. Let's see now. I'll work it out.'

Everyone was respectfully silent. They looked at Fatty as he pursed his mouth and frowned. The great brains were working!

'I think I've got it,' said Fatty, at last. 'We'll do this – I'll disguise myself as a ruffian of some kind – and I'll lend Larry a disguise too. We'll find out what PC Pippin's beat is at night – where he goes and what time – and Larry and I will hide in the garden of some empty house till he comes by.'

He paused to think, and then nodded his head. 'Yes – and as soon as we hear PC Pippin coming, we'll begin to whisper loudly so that he'll hear us and challenge us. Then we'll make a run for it as if we were scared of him and didn't want to be seen.'

'But where does all this lead to?' said Larry.

'Wait a bit and see,' said Fatty, enjoying himself. 'Now, we'll escape all right – and what will PC Pippin do? He'll go into the garden, of course, and shine his torch round – and he'll find a torn-up note!'

'Oooh, yes,' said Bets, thrilled. 'What's in the note?'

16

'The note will contain the name of some place for a further meeting,' said Fatty. 'We'll think of somewhere good. And when our nice round ripe Pippin arrives at the next meeting place, he'll find some lovely clues!'

'Which we'll have put there!' said Pip, grinning. 'Oh yes, Fatty – that's fine. We'll lead PC Pippin properly up the garden path.'

'The clues will lead somewhere else,' said Fatty, beaming. 'In fact it will be a nice wild-goosechase for PC Pippin. He'll love it. And won't Mr Goon's face be a picture when he hears about it all – he'll know it's us all right.'

'When can we do it? Oh, Fatty, let's begin it soon,' begged Bets. 'Can't you and Larry begin tonight?'

'No. We have to find out what PC Pippin's beat is first,' said Fatty. 'And we've got to spot an empty house on his beat. We'd better stalk him tonight, Larry, and find out where he goes. Mr Goon always used to set off about half past seven. Can you manage to come to my house by that time?'

'Yes, I think so,' said Larry. 'We have dinner at seven. I can gobble it down and be with you all right.'

So it was decided that Larry and Fatty should

stalk PC Pippin that night and see exactly what his beat was, so that the next night they could prepare their little surprise for him. Bets was thrilled. She loved an adventure like this – it didn't have the frightened excitement of a real mystery, it was under their control, and nothing horrid could come out of it, except perhaps a scolding from Mr Goon!

Larry arrived at Fatty's house at twenty-five past seven that night. It was almost dark. They were not disguised, as there was no time to dress Larry up. The two boys slipped out of Fatty's house and made their way to the street where Mr Goon's house was. PC Pippin had it now, of course.

The boys could hear the telephone ringing in PC Pippin's front room, and they could hear him answering it. Then the receiver was put down, and the light in the room went out.

'He's coming!' whispered Fatty. 'Squash up more into the bushes, Larry.'

PC Pippin walked down to his front gate. He had rubber on the soles of his boots and he did not make much noise. The boys could just see him as he turned up the street, away from them.

'Come on,' whispered Fatty. 'He's beginning his beat. We'll see exactly where he goes.'

They followed cautiously behind PC Pippin. The policeman went down the High Street, and was very conscientious indeed about trying doors and looking to see if the windows of the shops were fastened. The boys got rather bored with so much fumbling and examining. Each time PC Pippin stopped they had to stop too and hide somewhere.

After about an hour, PC Pippin moved off again, having decided that no burglar could possibly enter any shop in the High Street that night, anyway. He shut off his torch and turned into a side street. The boys crept after him.

PC Pippin went down the street softly, and then went to examine a lock-up garage there. 'Why doesn't he get on with his beat?' groaned Larry, softly. 'All this stopping and starting!'

PC Pippin went on again. He appeared to have quite a systematic method – going up one side of the road and down the other, and then into the next road and so on. If he did this every night, it would be easy to lie in wait for him somewhere!

'It's nine o'clock,' said Fatty, in a low voice, as he heard the church clock strike loudly. 'And we're in Willow Road. There's an empty house over the other side, Larry. We could hide in the garden there tomorrow night, just before nine. Then we could startle PC Pippin when he comes along there. Look – he's shining his torch on the gate now. Yes, that's what we'll do – hide in the garden there.'

'Good,' said Larry, with relief. 'I'm tired of dodging round like this, and the wind's really cold too. Come on – let's go home. Let's meet tomorrow morning at Pip's to tell the others what we've decided, and make our plans.'

'Right,' said Fatty, who was also very glad that the shadowing of PC Pippin was at an end. 'See you tomorrow. Ssssst! Here comes PC Pippin again.'

They squeezed themselves into the hedge and were relieved when the policeman's footsteps passed them.

'Gosh – I nearly sneezed then,' whispered Larry. 'Come on – I'm frozen.'

They went quietly home, Larry to tell Daisy, his sister, that they had found a good place to hide the next night, and Fatty to plan their disguises. He pulled out some old clothes and looked at them. Aha, PC Pippin, he thought, there's a nice little surprise being planned for you!

3. TWO RUFFIANS - AND PC PIPPIN

The five children discussed their plan with great interest the next day. Buster sat near them, ears cocked up, listening.

'Sorry, old thing, but I'm afraid you're not in this,' said Fatty, patting the little Scottie. 'You'll have to be tied up at home. Can't have you careering after me, yapping at PC Pippin, when he comes by our hiding-place.'

'Woof,' said Buster, mournfully, and lay down as if he had no further interest in the subject.

'Poor Buster,' said Bets, rubbing the sole of her shoe along his back. 'You hate to be left out, don't you? But this isn't a *real* mystery, Buster. It's only a pretend one.'

The children decided that Larry and Fatty had better get into their disguises at Larry's house, as it was near to the garden where they were to hide. Then they could sprint back to Larry's without much bother.

'I'll bring the clothes along in a suitcase after tea,' said Fatty. 'Any chance of hiding the case somewhere in your garden, Larry? In a shed or something? Grown-ups are always so suspicious of things like that. If I arrive at your house complete with suitcase your mother's quite likely to want to know what's in it.'

'Yes. Well, there's the little shed halfway down the garden,' said Larry. 'The one the gardener uses. I'll join you there whatever time you say – and we might as well change into our disguises there, Fatty. We'll be safe. What are we going to wear?'

'Oh, *can* we come and see you getting into your disguises?' said Bets, who didn't want to miss anything if she could help it. 'Pip and I could slip out when we are supposed to be reading after supper.'

'Mummy is going to the Little Theatre to see the show there tonight,' said Pip, remembering. 'We'll be quite safe to come and see you disguising yourselves.'

So, at eight o'clock that night, Fatty, Larry, Daisy,

Pip, and Bets were all hiding in the little shed together. Fatty pinned a sack tightly across the tiny window so that no light would show. Then he and Larry began to disguise themselves.

'We'd better make ourselves pretty awful-looking,' said Fatty. 'I bet PC Pippin will shine that torch of his on us, and we'll let him get a good look at our ruffianly faces. Here, Larry – you wear this frightful moustache. And look, there's that red wig of mine – wear that too, under an old cap. You'll look horrible.'

Bets watched the two boys, fascinated. Fatty was extremely clever at dressing up. He had many books on the art of disguising yourself, and there wasn't much he didn't know about it! Also, he had a wonderful collection of false eyebrows, moustaches, beards, and even sets of celluloid teeth that fitted over his own teeth, and stuck out horribly.

He put on a ragged beard. He screwed up his face and applied black greasepaint to his wrinkles. He stuck on a pair of shaggy eyebrows, which immediately altered him beyond recognition. Bets gave a squeal.

'You're horrible, Fatty! I don't know you. I can't

bear to look at you.'

'Well, don't then,' said Fatty, with a grin that showed black gaps in his front teeth. Bets stared in horror.

'Fatty! Where are your teeth? You've got two missing!'

'Just blacked them out, that's all,' said Fatty, with another dreadful grin. 'In this light it looks as if I've got some missing, doesn't it?'

He put on a wig of thinnish hair that straggled under his cap. He screwed up his face, and waggled his beard at Bets and Daisy.

'You look disgusting and very frightening,' said Daisy. 'I'm glad I'm not going to walk into you unexpectedly tonight. I'd be scared stiff. Oh, look at Larry, Bets – he's almost as bad as Fatty. Larry, *don't* squint like that.'

Larry was squinting realistically, and had screwed up his mouth so that his moustache was all on one side.

'Don't overdo it,' said Fatty. 'You look like an idiot now – not that that's much of a change for you.'

Larry slapped him on the back. 'You mind what you say to me,' he growled, in a deep voice. 'I'm

Loopy Leonard from Lincoln.'

'You look it,' said Daisy. 'You're both horrible. PC Pippin won't believe you're real when he sees you!'

Fatty looked at Daisy. 'Do you think he'll see through our disguises then?' he asked, anxiously. 'Have we overdone it?'

'No. Not really,' said Daisy. 'I mean, a policeman sees lots of terrible ruffians and scoundrels, I expect, and some of them must look as bad as you. Ugh, you do look revolting. I shall dream about you tonight.'

'Hey – time's getting on,' said Pip, suddenly looking at his watch. He had been silent and a little sulky because he was not going too. But, as Fatty pointed out, he was not tall enough to pass for a man, whereas he and Larry were. They were both well grown, and Fatty especially was quite burly now.

'Right. We'll go,' said Fatty, and Larry opened the door of the shed cautiously.

'We'll have to go past the kitchen door,' he said. 'But it's all right, no one will hear us.'

The two horrible-looking ruffians tiptoed up the

path and past the kitchen door. Just as they got there, the door opened and a bright beam of light fell on the two of them. There was a loud scream and the door was banged shut.

'Gosh! That was Janet, our cook,' whispered Daisy. 'She must have had the fright of her life when she saw you. Quick, leave before she tells Daddy!'

The two boys scurried away into the road. Bets went home with Pip. Daisy went in at the garden door and heard Janet telling her father in a most excited voice about the two frightful men she had seen. 'Great big fellows, sir,' she said, 'about six feet high, they were – and they glared at me out of piercing eyes, and growled like dogs.'

Daisy chuckled and slipped upstairs. She wasn't at all surprised at Janet's horror. Those two certainly had looked dreadful.

Fatty and Larry made their way cautiously to the empty house. They crossed over whenever they heard anyone coming along the dark streets. Nobody saw them, which was a good thing, for most people would certainly have raised the alarm at the sight of two such extraordinary-looking rogues.

They came to the empty house. They slipped in at the front gate very quietly indeed. There was a side gate as well.

'When PC Pippin comes by, we'll start our whispering here, under this bush,' said Fatty. 'And then when he comes in at the front gate to investigate, we'll sprint out of the side gate. Let him shine his light on our faces, because he can't possibly tell who we are in these frightful disguises.'

'Right,' said Larry. 'Got the torn-up note, Fatty?'

Fatty felt in his pocket. He drew out an envelope. In it was a dirty piece of paper, torn into six or eight pieces. On it, Fatty had written a cryptic message.

Behind Little Theatre. Ten pm. Friday.

He grinned as he took out the torn pieces and thought of the message on them. 'When PC Pippin turns up behind the Little Theatre on Friday we'll see that he finds a lot of clues,' he said to Larry. He scattered the bits of paper on the ground below the bush they were hiding behind. They fell there and lay waiting for the unsuspecting PC Pippin to pick them up later on in the evening!

'Shh!' said Larry suddenly. 'He's coming. I know his funny little cough now, though I can't hear his footsteps. Ah – now I can.'

The boys waited silently until PC Pippin was near the garden. Then Fatty said something in a sibilant whisper. Larry then rustled the bush. Fatty said, 'Ssssst!' and PC Pippin switched on his torch at once.

'Now then! Who's there? You come on out and show yourselves!' said PC Pippin's voice, sounding very sharp indeed.

'Don't run yet,' whispered Fatty. 'Let him get a look at us.'

Larry rustled the bush again. Pippin turned his torch on to it at once, and was horrified to see two such villainous faces peering out at him. What ruffians! Up to no good, *he'd* be bound!

'Run for it!' said Fatty, as the policeman swung open the front gate.

The two boys at once sprinted out of the back gate, and raced off down the road, with PC Pippin a very bad third. 'Hey, stop there! Stop!' he shouted. This was more than the boys had bargained for! Suppose somebody *did* stop them! It would be very awkward indeed.

But, fortunately, no one stopped them or even tried to, though the village butcher, out for a walk with his wife on the fine spring night, did step out to catch hold of them. But when he saw Fatty's horrible-looking face in the light of a street lamp he thought better of it, and the boys raced by in safety.

They turned in at Larry's gate thankfully. They went to the little shed and sank down, panting. Fatty grinned.

'Nice work, Larry! He'll go back there with his torch and snoop round – and he'll find the torn bits of paper and turn up on time for his next clues on Friday. I enjoyed that. Did you?'

'Yes,' said Larry. 'I only wish I didn't have to take off this great disguise. Can't we go round the town a bit and show ourselves to a few more people?'

'Better not,' said Fatty. 'Come on – let's take these things off. Hey – I wish it had been old Mr Goon who came along and spotted us – what a thrill for him!'

Meanwhile, PC Pippin had made his way back to the garden where the two ruffians had been hiding. He was excited. He had never hoped for anything to happen while he was taking Goon's place. And now he had surprised two horrible-looking villains hiding in the garden of an empty house, no doubt planning a burglary of some kind.

PC Pippin shone his torch on the ground under the bush where the two ruffians had stood. He hoped to see some footprints there. Aha, yes – there were plenty! And there was something else too – torn pieces of paper! Could those fellows have dropped them?

PC Pippin took his notebook from his pocket and placed the bits of paper carefully in the flap at the back. There were eight pieces – with writing on them! He would examine them carefully at home. Next he took out a folding ruler and carefully measured the footprints in the soft earth. Then he looked about for cigarette-ends or any other clue. But, except for the bits of paper, there was nothing.

PC Pippin was up past midnight piecing together the bits of paper, making out the thrilling message, writing out a description of the two men, and trying to draw the footprints to measure. He felt very important and pleased. This was his first case.

He was going to handle it well. He would go to that Little Theatre on Friday night, long before ten – and see what he would find there! All this might be very, very important.

4. PLENTY OF REDHEADS - AND PLENTY OF CLUES!

The five children chuckled over the trick they had played on the unsuspecting PC Pippin. Larry had met him the morning after, and stopped to have a few words with him.

Mr Pippin, remembering Mr Goon's words of warning about the five children, looked at him rather doubtfully. This wasn't the dangerous boy though – it was one of the others.

'Good morning, Mr Pippin,' said Larry politely. 'Settled in all right?'

'Of course,' said Mr Pippin. 'Nice place, Peterswood. I've always liked it. You at home for the Easter holidays?'

'Yes,' said Larry. 'Er – discovered any mystery yet, Mr Pippin?'

'Shouldn't tell you if I had,' said Mr Pippin, grinning at Larry. 'I've had a warning about you, see?'

'Yes. We thought you probably would have,' said Larry. 'By the way, our cook had a fright last night. Said she saw two ruffians outside our back door.'

Mr Pippin pricked up his ears at once. 'Did she? What were they like?'

'Well – she said one of them had red hair,' said Larry. 'But you'd better ask her if you want any particulars. Why? Have *you* seen them?'

'Perhaps I have and perhaps I haven't,' said Mr Pippin, annoyingly.

He nodded to Larry and walked off. He was thinking hard. So Larry's cook had also seen a red-haired ruffian. Must have been the same red-haired man that he too had seen that night then. What were they up to? He decided to interview Larry's cook, and did so. He came away with a very lurid account of two enormous villains, six feet high at least, growling and groaning, squinting and pulling faces.

One of them certainly had red hair. Mr Pippin began to look out for people with red hair. When he met Mr Kerry the cobbler, who had flaming red hair, he eyed him with such suspicion that Mr Kerry felt really alarmed.

PC Pippin also came across the vicar's brother, a kind and harmless tricyclist who liked to ride three times round the village each morning for exercise. When Mr Pippin had met him for the third time, and scrutinised him very very carefully, the vicar's brother began to think something must be wrong. Mr Pippin was also surprised – how many more times was he going to see this red-haired tricyclist?

When Larry related to the others that he had met PC Pippin, and told him about the red-haired man seen by the cook, and when Fatty heard from Janet the cook that the policeman had actually been to interview her about him, he chuckled.

'I think a spot of disguising is indicated,' he said to the others. 'A few red-haired fellows might interest our nice round ripe Pippin.'

So at twelve o'clock, a red-haired telegraph boy appeared on a bicycle, whistling piercingly. When he saw Mr Pippin he stopped and asked him for directions to an address he didn't know. The policeman looked at him. Another red-haired fellow! There was no end to them in Peterswood, it seemed.

At half past one, another red-haired fellow

appeared beside the surprised PC Pippin. This time, he was a man with a basket. He had black eyebrows which looked rather odd with his red hair, and frightful teeth that stuck out in front. He talked badly because of these.

'Scuthe me,' lisped the red-haired fellow. 'Pleathe, can you thay where the Potht Offith ith?'

At first PC Pippin thought the fellow was talking in a foreign language, but at last discovered that he was merely lisping. He looked at him closely. *Another* red-haired man! Most peculiar. None of them really looked like the ruffian he had seen the night before though.

At half past two, yet another red-haired fellow knocked at PC Pippin's door, and delivered a newspaper which he said must have been left at the wrong house. Pippin thought it was one that Mr Goon had delivered and thanked him. He stared at him, frowning. All this red hair! Fatty stared back unwinkingly.

Feeling uncomfortable, though he didn't know why, PC Pippin shut the door and went back into the front room. He felt that if he saw one more red-haired man that day he would really go to the optician and see if there was something wrong with his eyes!

And at half past five, when he was setting out to go to the post office, what did he see but an elderly looking man shuffling along with a stick – and with bright red hair sticking out from under his cap!

I'm seeing things, thought poor Mr Pippin to himself, I've got red hair on the brain.

Then a memory struck him. Well! What was it that Mr Goon told me? He warned me against red-haired fellows dashing about all over the place, didn't he? What did he mean? What's all this red-haired business? Oh yes – Mr Goon said it would be Fatty disguising himself! But that boy *couldn't* be as clever as all that! Mr. Pippin began to review all the red-haired people he had seen that day. He thought with great suspicion about the man he had seen three times on a tricycle.

Ah! Wait till I meet the next redhead, said Mr Pippin darkly to himself. If there's tricks played on *me*, I can play a few too! I'll give the next redhead a real fright!

It so happened that the next one he met was the vicar's brother on his tricycle again, hurrying along to catch the post at the post office. Mr Pippin stepped out into the road in front of him.

The vicar's brother rang his bell violently but Mr Pippin didn't get out of the way. So the rider put on his brakes suddenly, and came to such a sudden stop that he almost fell off.

'What is it, constable?' said the vicar's brother, astonished. 'I nearly ran you down.'

'What's your name and address, please?' asked Mr Pippin, taking out his notebook.

'My name is Theodore Twit, and my address is the Vicarage,' said Mr Twit, with much dignity.

'Oh *yes*,' said Mr Pippin. ' "The Vicarage" I *don't* think! You can't put me off *that* way!'

Mr Twit wondered if the policeman was mad. He looked at him anxiously. Mr Pippin mistook his anxious look for fright. He suddenly clutched at Mr Twit's abundant, red hair.

'Ow!' said Mr Twit, and almost fell off his tricycle. 'Constable! What does this mean?'

Mr Pippin had been absolutely certain that the red hair would come off in his hand. When it didn't, he was horrified. He stared at Mr Twit, his pink face going a deep red.

'Do you feel all right, constable?' asked Mr Twit, rubbing his head where Mr Pippin had snatched at his hair. 'I don't understand. Oh – thank goodness, here is my sister. Muriel, do come here and tell this constable who I am. He doesn't seem to believe me.'

Mr Pippin saw a very determined-looking lady coming towards him. 'What is it, Theodore?' said the lady, in a deep, barking kind of voice. Mr Pippin took one look at Muriel, muttered a few words of shamed apology, and fled. He left behind him two very puzzled people.

'Mad,' said Muriel, in her barking voice. 'Mr Goon was mad enough, goodness knows – but really, when it comes to this man snatching at your hair, Theodore, the world must be coming to an end!'

It so happened that Miss Twit went to call on Fatty's mother that evening, and when Fatty heard her relate the story of how that extraordinary Mr Pippin had tried to snatch at dear Theodore's red hair, he had such a fit of the giggles that his mother sent him out of the room in disgust at his manners. Fatty enjoyed his laugh all to himself, with Buster gazing at him in wonder.

So old PC Pippin is on to that trick, is he? thought Fatty. Right. It must be dropped. Hope he doesn't associate me with the red-haired ruffian he saw last night, though. He won't turn up at the Little Theatre and find his precious clues if he thinks it's a trick.

The five children had had a meeting that day, which was Thursday, to decide what clues they would spread for Pippin at the back of the Little Theatre. There was a kind of verandah there, under cover, where all kinds of clues might be put.

'Cigarette-ends, of course, to make PC Pippin think other meetings have taken place there,' said Fatty.

'Yes – and matches,' said Larry. 'And what about a hanky with an initial on it – always very helpful that, when you want clues!'

'Oh yes,' said Daisy. 'I've got an old torn hanky and I'll work an initial on it. What shall I put?'

'Z,' said Fatty, promptly. 'Might as well give him something to puzzle his brains over.'

'Z!' said Bets. 'But there aren't any names beginning with Z, surely?'

'Yes there are – Zebediah and Zacharias, to start

40

with!' grinned Fatty. 'We'll have old PC Pippin hunting round for Zebediahs before he's very much older!'

'Well, I'll put a Z on then,' said Daisy. 'I'll get my needle and thread now. What other clues will you leave?'

'A page out of a book,' said Pip. 'Out of a timetable or something.'

'Yes. That's good,' said Fatty, approvingly. 'Any other ideas?'

'What else do people drop by accident?' wondered Daisy. 'Oh, I know what we could do. If there's a nail or anything there, we could take along a bit of cloth and jab it on the nail! Then it would look as if whoever had been there for a meeting had caught his coat on the nail. That would be a very valuable clue, if it was a real one!'

'Yes, it would,' agreed Fatty. 'And we'll take a pencil and sharpen it there – leave bits of pencil-shavings all over the place. Gosh, what a wonderful lot of clues!'

'We must also leave something to make PC Pippin go on with the chase somewhere else,' said Larry.

'Yes. What about underlining a train in the timetable page that we're going to throw down?' said Pip. 'We're going to chuck one down, aren't we? Well, if we underline a certain train – say a Sunday train – old PC Pippin will turn up for that too!'

Everyone giggled. 'And Fatty could dress up in some disguise, and slip a message into PC Pippin's hand to suggest the next place to go to,' said Daisy. 'We could send him over half the country at this rate!'

'Wait till Mr Goon gets a report of all this,' said Fatty with a grin. 'He'll see through it at once – and won't he be mad!'

Soon all the clues were ready, even to the pencil-shavings, which were in an envelope.

'When shall we place the clues?' said Bets. 'Can I come too?'

'Yes. We'll all go,' said Fatty. 'I don't see why not. There's nothing suspicious about us all going out together. We can go on our bicycles and put them in the car-park at the back of the Little Theatre. Then we'll pretend to be looking at the posters there, and one of us can slip up to the verandah and drop the clues. It won't take a minute.'

'When shall we go?' asked Bets again. She always wanted to do things at once.

'Not today,' said Fatty. 'There's a bit of a breeze. We don't want the clues blown right off the verandah. The wind may have died down by tomorrow. We'll cycle along after tea tomorrow, about six.'

So the next day, about ten to six, the five set off, with Buster as usual in Fatty's bicycle basket. They cycled round to the back of the Little Theatre and came to the car-park there. A good many children were there already, getting bicycles from the stand.

'Hello!' said Fatty, surprised. 'Has there been a show here this afternoon?'

'Yes,' said a boy nearby. 'Just a show for us children from Farleigh Homes. They let us in for nothing. It was very good. I liked the cat the best.'

'The cat? Oh, Dick Whittington's cat, you mean,' said Fatty, remembering that the show that week was supposed to be a skit on the Dick Whittington pantomime. 'It's not a real cat, is it?'

'Course not!' said the boy. Daisy, who had already seen the show, explained to Fatty.

'It's a man in a cat's skin, idiot. Must be rather a small man – or maybe it's a boy! He was very funny, I thought.'

'Look – there go the actors,' said a little girl, and she pointed to a side door. 'See, that's Dick Whittington, that pretty girl. Why do they always have a girl for the boy in pantomime? And that's Margot, who is Dick's sweetheart in the play. And there's Dick's master – and his mother, look – she's a man really, as you can see. And there's the captain of Dick's ship – isn't he fine? And there's the chief of the islands that Dick visits.'

The five children gazed at the actors as they left the side door of the Little Theatre. They all looked remarkably ordinary.

'Where's the cat?' asked Bets.

'He doesn't seem to have gone with them,' said the little girl. 'Anyway, I wouldn't know what he was like, because he wore his cat-skin all the time. He was awfully good. I loved him.'

A teacher called loudly, 'Irene! Donald! What are you keeping us waiting for? Come on at once.'

The car-park emptied. Fatty looked round. 'Now,' he said, 'come on! The coast is clear. We'll all go and look at these posters and talk to one another – and then when we are sure no one is watching us, I'll slip up to the verandah and drop the clues.'

It was most annoying, however, because one or two people kept coming to the car-park, and for some reason or other walked across it. Fatty finally discovered that it was a short cut to a newsagents in the next street.

'Blow!' he said. 'We'll have to hang about till it shuts. It's sure to shut soon.'

It was boring having to wait so long and talk endlessly about the posters. But at last the shop apparently did shut and nobody else took the short cut across the car-park. It was now getting dark. Fatty slipped up the three steps to the verandah.

He threw down the clues – cigarette-ends and matches – torn hanky with Z on – pencil-shavings – page torn from a timetable with one Sunday train underlined – and a bit of navy blue cloth which he jabbed hard on a nail.

He turned to go – but before he went, he took a look in at the window nearby. And what a shock Fatty got!

5. PC PIPPIN ON THE JOB

A very large, furry animal was inside the window, looking mournfully up at him – or so it seemed. The eyes were big and glassy, and gave Fatty the creeps. He recoiled back from the window, and almost fell down the verandah steps.

'What's up?' asked Larry, surprised.

'There's something peculiar up there,' said Fatty. 'Horrible big animal, looking out of the window at me. I could just see it in the faint reflection cast by that street lamp outside the car-park.'

Bets gave a little squeal. 'Don't! I'm frightened!'

'Idiot, Fatty! It must be the cat-skin of Dick Whittington's cat,' said Larry, after a moment. Everyone felt most relieved.

'Well – I suppose it was,' said Fatty, feeling very foolish. 'I never thought of that. The thing looked so lifelike though. I don't think it was just a *skin*. I think the actor who plays the cat must have still been inside it.'

'Gracious. Does he *live* in it then?' said Daisy. 'Let's go and see if it's still there, looking out of the window.'

'We'll wait here,' said Bets to Daisy.

'*We'll* go,' said Larry. 'Come on, Fatty, come on, Pip.'

The three boys stepped quietly up the verandah steps, and looked in at the window. The cat was no longer there, but as they stood watching, they saw it come in at the door of the room and run across on all fours to the fireplace. An electric fire was burning, and the boys could distinctly see the cat pretending to wash its face, rubbing its ears with its paws, in exactly the same way as a cat does.

'There it is!' said Fatty. 'It's seen us! That's why it's acting up like this. It thinks we're children who came to see the show, and it's still pretending to be Dick Whittington's cat. Gracious – it gave me a start when I first saw it at the window.'

'Meeow,' said the cat loudly, turning towards the window, and waving a paw.

'I somehow don't like it,' said Pip. 'I don't know

why. But I just don't. I know it's only somebody inside the skin, but it looks too real for me. Let's go!'

They went back to the girls. It was not quite dark, and the church clock struck seven o'clock as they went to fetch their bicycles from the stands.

'Well – we've planted the clues,' said Fatty, feeling more cheerful as he undid Buster from where he had tied him to the stand. 'Hey, Buster, old chap – good thing you didn't spot that cat. You'd have thought you were seeing things – a cat as big as that!'

'Woof,' said Buster, dolefully. He didn't like being left out of the fun, and he knew something exciting had been happening. He was lifted into Fatty's basket, and then the five cycled slowly home.

'I wonder when PC Pippin will go along,' said Fatty, as he dismounted at his gate. 'He'll be sure to get there long before ten, so that he can hide before the meeting takes place – and there won't be a meeting after all! Only plenty of clues for him to find.'

'See you tomorrow, Fatty!' called Pip and Bets. 'Good-bye, Larry and Daisy. We'll have to hurry or we'll get into trouble.'

They all rode away. Fatty went indoors, thinking of the way the cat had looked at him through the window. That really had given him a jolt! 'If I were Bets I'd dream about that!' he thought. 'I wonder if PC Pippin's going to hide himself on the verandah somewhere. If he gets a glimpse of that cat, he'll get the fright of his life.'

PC Pippin did not go to the verandah until about half past eight. He meant to be there in good time for the meeting, whatever it was. He had been very thrilled indeed to find the message about the meeting at ten o'clock behind the Little Theatre, when he had pieced together the torn bits of paper.

Mr Goon would be pleased with him if he could unearth some mystery or plot, he was sure. Pippin meant to do his best. He had already snooped round the back of the Little Theatre the day before, to see where he could hide on the night. He had discovered a hole in the verandah roof through which he could climb, and then he could sit on the windowsill of the room above, and hear everything.

Pippin arrived at the verandah as the clock on the church chimed half past eight, exactly an hour and a half after the children had left. He had his torch with him, but did not put it on until he had made sure that there was nobody about anywhere. There was a glow in the room behind the verandah. Pippin looked into the room. He saw that the glow came from an electric fire. In front of it, lying as if asleep, was what looked like a most enormous cat. PC Pippin jumped violently when he saw such a big creature.

He couldn't believe his eyes. *Was* it a cat? Yes – there were its ears – and there was its tail lying beside it on the hearth-rug.

PC Pippin gazed into the window at the great, furry creature outlined by the glow of the fire. It couldn't be a gorilla, could it? No, people wouldn't be allowed to keep a gorilla like that. Besides, it looked more like a cat than anything else.

PC Pippin was just about to give a loud exclamation when he stopped himself in time. Of course! It must be Dick Whittington's cat – the one that acted in the skit in the pantomime. He hadn't seen it himself, but he had heard about it. Funny the cat keeping its skin on like that – because there was really somebody inside it. You'd think he'd want to take the hot skin off as soon as he could!

Pippin wondered if the meeting, whatever it was, would take place if there was that cat in the room nearby. But perhaps the meeting would be in the car-park. In that case, would it do much good him climbing on the verandah roof? He wouldn't hear a thing.

Pippin debated with himself. He cautiously switched on his torch and flashed it round the verandah floor. And he saw the clues!

His eyes brightened as he saw the cigarette-ends, the matches, and the pencil-shavings. Somebody had been here before – quite often too, judging by the cigarette-ends. The verandah must certainly be the meeting-place. Perhaps the cat was in the plot too. That was certainly an idea!

Carefully Pippin picked up the cigarette-ends, the matches, and even the pencil-shavings. He put them all into envelopes. He then found the torn timetable page, blown against the side of the verandah, and was extremely interested in the underlined Sunday train.

He looked round and found the handkerchief with Z on it, and wondered if it could be the letter

N sideways. Pippin could not for the life of him think of any name beginning with Z, not even the ones the children had thought of!

Then he spotted the bit of navy blue cloth caught on a nail. Aha! Oho! *That* was the most valuable clue of all. Find somebody with a hole in a navy blue coat and you were getting somewhere!

Pippin took another cautious look into the window of the room at the back of the verandah. The great cat was still lying in front of the electric fire. Very strange – especially if you considered that the cat wasn't really a cat but a human being inside a cat-skin – or a furry skin of some sort. As he watched, Pippin saw the cat move a little, get more comfortable and apparently settle itself to sleep again.

'Funny creature,' thought Pippin, still puzzled, but very much relieved to see the cat move. 'I sort of feel that if a mouse ran across the room, the cat would be after it – though I know it's not a real cat!'

He decided that it was about time he climbed up through the hole in the verandah roof, and sat on the windowsill of the room above. The men might come any moment now – one of them might be early – you never knew! It wouldn't do for him to be seen.

With all his clues safely in his pocket, PC Pippin heaved himself up through the hole in the roof. He felt his way to the windowsill and sat down on it. It was hard and cold, and much too narrow to be comfortable. Pippin resigned himself to a long and uneasy wait.

He had not been there more than a few moments when he heard a very weird sound. PC Pippin stiffened and listened. It sounded to him very like a groan. But where could it be coming from? The room behind him was in black darkness. There was nobody near him out of doors as far as he knew – and if it was the cat before the fire making a noise, how could he *possibly* hear that? He couldn't!

The noise came again, and Pippin felt most peculiar. There he was, sitting on a narrow windowsill in the dark, waiting for rogues to meet down below – and groans sounding all round him! He didn't like it at all.

He listened, holding his breath. The groan came again. It was *behind* him! PC Pippin suddenly felt sure of that. Well, then, it must be in the *room* behind him! PC Pippin felt round the window, meaning to open it. But it was shut and fastened from inside.

Pippin remembered his torch. He took it from his belt and switched it on, so that the light shone into the room behind. Its beam swung slowly round the room – and then came to rest on something very surprising.

A man was sitting at a desk. He had fallen forward, his face on his outstretched arms. Beside him was a cup, overturned in its saucer, the spoon nearby on the table. PC Pippin stared in horror.

Then the beam picked out something else. A big wall-mirror was standing on the floor, reflecting the light of the torch. A large hole showed in the wall nearby, the place from which the mirror had been removed. A safe had been built in behind the mirror – but it was now empty, and the safe-door was swinging open.

'Thieves! A robbery!' said PC Pippin, and rose to the occasion at once. He doubled his hand in folds of his big handkerchief and drove his fist through the window! PC Pippin was on the job!

6. A MYSTERY BEGINS

The five children knew nothing about PC Pippin's exciting night, of course. Pip and Bets were asleep in bed when he smashed the window at the back of the Little Theatre, and Larry and Daisy had been told they could listen to the nine o'clock news, and then go to bed. Fatty had been in his room trying out a wonderful new aid to disguise – little pads to put inside the cheeks to make them fat!

I'll try these tomorrow, thought Fatty, with a grin. I'll put them in before breakfast and see if anyone notices.

Fatty went to bed wondering if PC Pippin had found the clues he had spread about the verandah, and how long he had waited for the mythical meeting. Poor old Pippin – he might have waited a long time!

If Fatty had only known what was happening he

would never have gone off so peacefully to bed that night – he would have been snooping round the Little Theatre, looking for *real* clues! But all he had done was to play a trick on PC Pippin that had placed that gentleman right on the spot – the very spot where a burglary had taken place not so long before. Lucky Pippin!

Next day at breakfast, Fatty put in his new aid to disguise – the cheek-pads that forced out the soft part of his cheeks and made him look plump. His father, buried behind his paper, didn't seem to notice any difference. But his mother was puzzled. Fatty looked different. What was it that made him look strange? It was his cheeks! They were quite blown out.

'Frederick – have you got toothache?' his mother suddenly asked. 'Your cheeks are very swollen.'

'Oh no, Mummy,' said Fatty. 'My teeth are quite all right.'

'Well, you don't seem to be eating as much as usual, which is very strange, and certainly your cheeks look swollen,' persisted his mother. 'I shall ring up and make an appointment with the dentist.'

This was really very alarming. Fatty didn't want

the dentist poking round his mouth and finding holes in his teeth. He felt quite certain that even if there wasn't a hole, the dentist would make one with that nasty scrapey instrument of his.

'Mummy – do believe me – not one of my teeth has holes in,' said Fatty, desperately. 'I ought to know.'

'Well, then, why are your cheeks so puffed out?' asked his mother, who never could leave a subject alone once she had really started on it. She turned to his father. 'Don't *you* think Frederick's cheeks are swollen?'

His father glanced up in an absent-minded manner. 'Might be,' he said. 'Eaten too much.' Then to Fatty's relief he went on reading his newspaper.

'I'll ring up the dentist immediately after breakfast,' said Fatty's mother.

In desperation, Fatty put his hands to his mouth and removed two cheek-pads – but instead of being pleased that his cheeks were now no longer swollen, his mother cried out in disgust. 'Frederick! How *can* you behave like that! Removing food from your mouth with your fingers! What *is* the matter with you this morning?

You'd better leave the table.'

Before Fatty could explain about the cheek-pads, his father gave an exclamation. 'Well, well! Listen to this in the paper. "Last night it was disclosed that the manager of the Little Theatre, in Peterswood, Bucks, was found drugged in his office, and the safe in the wall behind him was open, the contents having been stolen. The police already have one suspect in their hands." '

Fatty was so astounded to hear this that he absent-mindedly put his cheek-pads into his mouth, thinking they were bits of bread, and began to chew them. He simply couldn't believe the news. Why, he and the others had actually been hanging round the Little Theatre half the evening, and they had seen nothing at all – except the pantomime cat!

'Could I see the piece, Dad?' asked Fatty, wondering why the bread in his mouth was so tough. He suddenly realised that it wasn't bread – ugh, how horrible, he had been chewing his cheek-pads! And now he didn't dare to remove them again in case his mother accused him of disgusting manners once more. It was very awkward.

'Don't talk with your mouth full, Frederick,' said his mother. 'And of course you can't have your father's paper. You can read it when he has finished with it.'

Very fortunately at that moment the telephone rang. The maid answered it and came to fetch Fatty's mother. So Fatty was able to remove the half-chewed cheek-pads and put them into his pocket. He decided never to wear them again at mealtimes. He glanced longingly at his father's paper. Ah – he had folded it over again and the bit about the robbery was on the back, but upside down. Fatty managed to read it two or three times. He began to feel very excited.

Would it be a mystery? Suppose they hadn't got the right suspect? Then the Five Find-Outers could get on to it at once. Fatty felt that he couldn't possibly eat any more breakfast. He slid away quietly from the table before his mother came back. His father didn't notice him go.

Fatty flew off to Pip's at once. Larry and Daisy would be along soon, for they had planned a meeting there. Pip and Bets had a fine big playroom of their own, where they were not often disturbed, and it made a very good meeting place.

Pip and Bets had heard nothing of the great news. Fatty told them, and they were amazed. 'What! A robbery committed last night at the Little Theatre! Did it happen while we were there?' cried Pip, in excitement. 'Here's Larry, with Daisy. Larry, heard the news about the Little Theatre robbery?'

Larry and Daisy had heard all about it. They knew even more than Fatty because Janet, their cook, knew the woman who cleaned the Little Theatre, and had got some news from her, which she had passed on to Larry and Daisy. Larry said Janet felt certain that the robbers were the two ruffians she had seen the other night in the beam of light from the kitchen door!

'To think we were all there last night, mooching round, hanging about and everything!' groaned Fatty. 'And we never saw a thing. We were so busy preparing clues for old PC Pippin that we never saw anything of a real crime that must have been going on almost under our noses.'

'Janet says that Mrs Trotter, the woman who cleans the Little Theatre, told her that last night the police found the manager stretched out across his office desk, his head on his arms, asleep from some drug – and behind him was his empty safe,' said Larry. 'It was one that was built in the wall, hidden by a big wall-mirror hanging in front of it. She said the police must have discovered the whole thing not very long after it was done.'

'The police! I suppose that means PC Pippin,' said Fatty. 'Gosh – to think we planted him there on that verandah, surrounded by a whole lot of false clues – and there he was right on the spot when a real robbery was committed! It's absolutely maddening. If only we'd snooped round a bit more, *we* might have hit on the mystery ourselves. As it is, we've presented it to the police – or rather to PC Pippin – and they will get in straight away, and solve the whole thing.'

There was a doleful silence. It did seem very bad luck.

'I suppose PC Pippin will think all those cigarette-ends and hanky and so on are real clues now – clues to the real robbers, I mean,' said Bets, after a long pause.

'Gosh! So he will! He'll be right off on the wrong track,' said Fatty. 'That's awkward. Very awkward. I don't mind playing a silly trick on either Mr Goon or PC Pippin – but I wouldn't want to do anything that would prevent them from catching the burglars. Those clues of ours will certainly confuse them a bit.'

'You mean – they'll start looking for people whose names begin with Z, and they'll go and watch that Sunday train?' said Daisy. 'Instead of going on the right trail.'

'Yes,' said Fatty. 'Well – I think I'd better go and see PC Pippin, and own up. I don't want to set him off on the wrong track – make him waste his time solving a pretend mystery when he's got a real one to see to. Blow! It will be very awkward, having to explain. And I bet he won't give me any information either, because he'll be so annoyed with me for playing a trick on him. We could have worked nicely with old PC Pippin. We never could work with Mr Goon.

Everyone felt very glum. To think they had gone and spoilt a perfectly super *real* mystery by making up a stupid pretend one!

'I'll come with you to explain,' said Larry.

'No,' said Fatty. 'I take the responsibility for this.

I'd like to keep the rest of you out of it – if PC Pippin takes it into his head to complain about us, my parents won't take a lot of notice – but yours will, Larry – and as for Pip's parents, they'll go right off the deep end.'

'They always do,' said Pip. His parents were very strict with him and Bets, and had been very much annoyed three or four times already when Mr Goon had complained to them about the children. 'I don't want our parents to know a thing. Mummy already said she's glad Mr Goon is away because now perhaps we won't get into any mischief these holidays, and make Mr Goon come round and grumble about us.'

'I'll go and see PC Pippin now,' said Fatty, getting up. 'Nothing like getting a nasty thing done at once. I do hope Pippin won't mind too much. Actually I think he's rather nice. He'll be thrilled at getting a case like this when Mr Goon is away.'

He went out, with Buster close at his heels. He whistled loudly to show that he didn't care about anything in the world. But actually Fatty did care quite a lot this morning. He felt guilty about all those false clues. He could have kicked himself for spoiling his chance of working with PC Pippin. Mr Pippin wasn't like Mr Goon. He looked sensible, and Fatty felt sure he would have welcomed his help.

He came to Mr Goon's house, in which PC Pippin was now living while Mr Goon was away. To his surprise, the door was wide open. Fatty walked in to find PC Pippin.

There was a loud voice talking in the front room. Fatty stopped as if he had been shot. It was Mr Goon's voice. *Mr Goon*! Had he come back then? Was he going to take over the mystery? Blow!

Fatty stood there, wondering what to do. He wasn't going to confess to PC Pippin in front of Mr Goon! That would be very, very foolish. Mr Goon might even take it into his head to go and tell Inspector Jenks, the children's very great friend – and somehow Fatty felt that the Inspector would not approve of the little trick they had played on the unsuspecting PC Pippin.

Mr Goon was evidently very angry. His voice was raised, and he was going for poor PC Pippin unmercifully. Fatty couldn't help hearing as he stood in the passage, undecided whether to go in or out.

'Why didn't you send for me when you first saw those rogues under that bush in the garden? Why didn't you tell me about the torn-up note? Didn't I tell you to let me know if anything happened? Turnip-head! Dolt! Soon as I go away they put in a dud like you, who hasn't even got the sense to send for his superior when something happens!'

Fatty decided to go – but Buster decided differently. Aha! That was the voice of his old enemy, wasn't it? With a joyful bark Buster pushed open the door of the sitting-room with his black nose, and bounded in!

7. GOON - PIPPIN - AND FATTY

There was a loud exclamation from Goon. 'That dog! Where did it come from? Clear orf, you! Ah, you'd go for my ankles, would you?'

Fatty rushed into the room at once, afraid that Mr Goon would hurt Buster. Pippin was standing by the window, looking very crestfallen indeed. Goon was by the fireplace, kicking out at Buster, who was dancing happily round his feet.

Goon looked up and saw Fatty. 'Oh, you're here too, are you?' he said. 'Setting your dog on me again! What with having to deal with that turnip-head over there, and this dratted dog, and you, it's enough to make a man retire from the police force!'

To Fatty's horror, he caught up the poker and shook it at Buster. Fatty ran to Mr Goon and twisted the poker out of his hand. The boy was white with fury.

'See?' said Goon, turning to Pippin, who was also looking rather white. 'See that? You're a witness, you are – that boy sets his dog on me, and when I protect myself, as I've a right to do, the boy comes and assaults me. You're a witness, Pippin. Write it all down. Go on. I've been after this pest of a boy and his dog for a long time – and now I've got him. You saw it all, didn't you, Pippin?'

Fatty now had Buster in his arms. He could not trust himself to speak. He knew Mr Goon to be a stupid, ignorant man with a turn for cruelty, but Mr Goon had never shown his real nature quite so openly before.

Pippin said nothing at all. He stood by the window, looking scared and very much taken aback. He had been shouted at by Mr Goon for half an hour, blamed for all kinds of things, called all kinds of names – and now he was supposed to take out his notebook and put down a lot of untruths about that nice dog and his master.

'Pippin! Will you please write down what I tell you?' stormed Goon. 'I'll have that dog destroyed. I'll have this boy up before the court. I'll . . .'

Buster growled so fiercely that Goon stopped.

'Look here,' said Fatty, 'if you're going to do all that, I think I'll put Buster down and let him have a real good go at you, Mr Goon. He may as well be hanged for a sheep as for a lamb. He hasn't bitten you, as you very well know – but if you're going to say he has, well then, he jolly well *can*.'

And Fatty made as if he was going to put the barking, struggling Buster down on the floor!

Goon calmed down at once, and tried to get back control of himself. He turned in a dignified way to Pippin. 'I'll tell you what to put down. Come on now, stir yourself – standing there like a ninny!'

'I'm not going to put down anything but the truth,' said Pippin, most surprisingly. 'You tormented that dog with the poker – might have injured him for life. I don't approve of behaviour of that sort, no, not even from a police officer. I like dogs – they never go for *me*. I wouldn't have that dog destroyed for anything. And all the boy did was to take the poker from you to stop you hitting his dog! A good thing he did too. You might have killed the dog – and then where would you be? In a very awkward position, Mr Goon, that's where!'

There was a dead silence after this unexpected

and remarkable speech. Even Buster was quiet. Everyone was most surprised to hear this speech from the quiet PC Pippin, and perhaps Pippin himself was most surprised of all. Goon couldn't believe his ears. He stared at Pippin with his mouth wide open, and his eyes bulged more than ever. Fatty was thrilled. Good old PC Pippin!

Goon found his tongue at last. His face was now a familiar purple. He advanced to Pippin and shook a fat and rather dirty finger under his nose.

'You'll hear more of this, see? I'm back again and I'm in charge of Peterswood now. *I'll* take charge of this new case – and you'll have nothing to do with it whatever. Nothing. If you thought you'd get a good mark for it from the Inspector, you can think again. I'll make a bad report out on you and your behaviour – thinking you'd manage it by yourself and get all the praise – not letting me know anything. Gah!'

Pippin said nothing, but looked thoroughly miserable. Fatty was very sorry for him. Goon was enjoying ticking off Pippin in front of Fatty. It gave him a sense of power, and he loved that.

'You hand me over all them clues,' said Goon.

'Every one of them. Aha! Frederick Trotteville would very much like to know what they are – wouldn't you? But you won't know! You'll never know!'

Pippin handed over to Mr Goon all the false clues that Fatty had put on the verandah! They were in envelopes or paper so Fatty could not see them – but he knew very well what they were! In fact, he could have given Mr Goon quite a lot of information about them. He grinned to himself. Right! Let Mr Goon have them and work on them. Much good would they do him! Served him right for being so beastly to PC Pippin.

'See what happens to people who work against me, instead of with me?' said Goon to Fatty, spitefully. 'I shan't let him have anything to do with this new case – and you kids won't neither! I'll manage it myself. Pippin, you can do my routine work for the next two weeks, and keep your nose out of anything else. I don't want your help – not that a turnip-head like you could help a fellow like me. Don't you come mewling to me with any of your silly ideas – I just don't want to hear them.'

He put away all the clues in a box and locked it.

'Now I'm going along to interview the manager of the Little Theatre,' he said. 'Oh yes, I know *you've* interviewed him already Mr Clever – but I don't care what you've got out of him – it won't be anything worthwhile. Well, you get down to that writing I ticked you off about – and just remember this – I shan't forget your insubordination this morning over that there pestiferous dog. Yes, real insubordination – refusal to perform your rightful duties when commanded. Gah!'

Mr Goon made a dignified and haughty departure, walking ponderously down the path to his front gate, and shutting it sharply. Fatty, Buster, and Pippin were left together in the little sitting-room. Fatty put Buster down. He at once ran to Pippin and pawed eagerly at his legs, whining.

Pippin stooped down and patted him. He looked so miserable that Fatty wanted to comfort him.

'He's thanking you for sticking up for him,' he said. 'Thanks from me too, Mr Pippin. Awfully decent of you.'

'He's a nice dog,' said Pippin. 'I like dogs. I've got one of my own, back home. Mr Goon wouldn't let me bring him here.'

'I bet you think just about the same of Mr Goon as I do – as we all do,' said Fatty. 'He's a beast. Always has been. He'd no right to speak to you in that way, you know.'

'I thought I was on to such a good case,' said Pippin, sitting down and taking out his fountain pen to write. 'I was going to send for Mr Goon this morning, of course – but he saw a notice in the paper and came tearing back, accusing me of not having told him anything. Now I've had to give him all my clues – and he'll use them instead of me.'

Fatty considered things carefully. Should he confess to PC Pippin now that they were not real clues? No – Mr Goon had them – let him mess about with them! Fatty thought that possibly PC Pippin might feel he ought to tell Mr Goon they were false clues, if he, Fatty, confessed to him that they were – and that would spoil everything. Mr Goon would go and complain to their parents, they would be forbidden to try and solve this mystery, and PC Pippin would be hauled over the coals by Mr Goon for being so stupid as to be taken in by false clues.

It would be very nice indeed if Mr Goon would

busy himself with those clues, and leave the way clear for Fatty and the other Find-Outers to go to work! PC Pippin might help them. That would be better still.

'Mr Pippin, don't take any notice of what Mr Goon says to you,' said Fatty, earnestly. 'I am sure that Inspector Jenks, who is a great friend of ours, wouldn't allow him to speak to you like that, if he knew.'

'The Inspector told me about you and the others,' said Pippin. 'He's got a very high opinion of you, I must say. Said you'd been no end of a help in solving all kinds of mysterious cases.'

Fatty saw his chance and took it. 'Yes – that's true – and, Mr Pippin, I shall be on to this case too – and probably solve it! I should be very proud if you would help us – it would be nice to present the Inspector with another mystery correctly solved. He'd be thrilled.'

Pippin looked up at the earnest Fatty. Fatty was only a boy in his teens, but there was something about him that made people respect him and trust him. Brains? Yes. Character? Plenty! Cheek? Too much. Pluck? Any amount. Pippin saw all this as he looked at Fatty and sized him up. Well – if Inspector Jenks liked this boy and admired him, then he, Pippin, was quite prepared to do the same – very willing to, in fact, seeing that it looked as if Fatty was not going to work with Mr Goon! Pippin couldn't help thinking it would be very nice indeed to help this boy to solve the mystery – what a blow for Mr Goon that would be!

'Well,' he said, and paused. 'Well – I'd like to help you – but wouldn't I have to tell Mr Goon anything we discovered?'

'But, Mr Pippin, didn't you hear him tell you that he didn't want your help?' said Fatty. 'Didn't you hear him say you weren't to go to him with any of your silly mewling ideas – whatever *they* are! You'd be disobeying his orders if you told him anything.'

This seemed a very sensible way out to Pippin. Yes – he certainly would be disobeying orders if he went and told Mr Goon anything now. On the other hand, surely it was his duty to work on the case if he could. Wasn't he the one to discover the robbery?

'I'll help you,' he told Fatty, and the boy grinned with pleasure. 'I guess if the Inspector has let you meddle in other cases, he'd say you could meddle in this one too. Anyway – I'd like to pay Goon back for some of the beastly things he said to me.'

'Hear, hear – very human and natural of you,' said Fatty, agreeing heartily. 'Well now, Mr Pippin, I'll lay my cards on the table – and you can lay yours there as well. I'll tell you all I know, and you can tell me all *you* know.'

'What do *you* know?' said Pippin, curiously.

'Well – I and the other four were round the back of the Little Theatre from about half past five last night till seven,' said Fatty. 'Just snooping about you know – looking at the posters and things.'

'Oh, you were, were you?' said Pippin, sitting up and taking notice. 'Did you see anything interesting?'

'I looked in at the window at the back of that verandah,' said Fatty. 'And I saw the pantomime cat there – at least, I feel sure that's what it must have been. It was like a huge furry cat. It came to the window and stared at me – gave me an awful scare. I saw it in the reflected light of the street lamp. Then, when Larry and Pip and I looked in later, we saw it sitting by the fire, pretending to wash itself like cats do. It waved its paw at us.'

Pippin was listening very earnestly indeed. 'This is most interesting,' he said. 'You know – there doesn't appear to have been anyone at all in the Little Theatre when the robbery was committed – except the pantomime cat! Mr Goon wants to arrest him. He's sure he doped the manager and robbed the safe. Would you believe it – the pantomime cat!'

8. PIPPIN'S STORY - AND A MEETING

Fatty's brains began to work at top speed. 'Go on,' he said. 'Tell me all you know. What time were you there, Mr Pippin – what did you see – how did you discover the robbery and everything? My goodness, how lucky you were to be on the spot!'

'Well, actually I was after two rogues I'd seen under a bush the other night,' said Pippin, and Fatty had the grace to blush, though Pippin didn't notice it. 'I thought they might be meeting at the back of the Little Theatre, and I was hiding there. I got there at half past eight, and when I looked into the room at the back of the verandah – where you saw the cat – I saw him too. He was lying fast asleep by the fire. Funny to wear a cat-skin so long, isn't it?'

'Yes. Must be an odd fellow,' said Fatty.

'Well – he *is* odd – odd in the head,' said Pippin.

'I saw him this morning, without his cat-skin. He's not very big, except for his head. He's about twenty-four, they say, but he's never grown up really. Like a child the way he walks and acts. They call him Boysie.'

'I suppose he got dropped when he was a baby,' said Fatty, remembering stories he had heard. 'Babies like that don't develop properly, do they? Go on, Mr Pippin. This is thrilling.'

'Well, I saw the cat asleep by the fire as I said,' went on Pippin. 'Then, when the clock struck nine, I reckoned I'd better hide myself. So I climbed up through a hole in the verandah roof and sat on the windowsill of the room above, waiting. And I heard groans.'

'Go on,' said Fatty, as Pippin paused, remembering. 'Gosh, weren't you lucky to be there!'

'Well, I shone my torch into the room and saw the manager lying stretched out on his desk, and the empty safe in the wall behind him,' said Pippin. 'And I smashed the window and got in. The manager was already coming round. He was doped with some drug. I reckon it had been put into his cup of tea. The safe was quite empty, of course. It's being examined for fingerprints – I got an expert on the job at once – and the cup is being examined for drugs – just a strong sleeping-draught, I expect.'

'Who brought the manager the cup of tea – did he say?' asked Fatty, with interest.

'Yes – the pantomime cat!' said Pippin. 'Seems pretty suspicious, doesn't it? But if you talk to Boysie – the cat – you can't help thinking he'd got nothing to do with the whole thing – he's too silly – he wouldn't have the brains to put a sleeping-draught into a cup of tea, and he certainly wouldn't know where the safe was – or where to get the key – or how to find out the combination of letters that opens the safe door, once the key is in.'

'It's very interesting,' said Fatty. 'Who was in the Little Theatre at the time, besides Boysie?'

'Nobody,' said Pippin. 'Not a soul! All the cast – the actors and actresses, you know – had gone off after the free show they'd given to the children of the Farleigh Homes, and we can check their alibis – find out exactly where they were between the time of their leaving and eight o'clock. The deed was done between half past five and eight – between the time the show was over and the time the manager had drunk his cup of tea, and fallen unconscious.'

'I see. And you've got to check the whereabouts of all the people who might have gone back and done the robbery,' said Fatty. 'Yes. But what's to prevent a stranger doing it – I mean, why should it be one of the actors?'

'Because whoever did it knew the best time to do it,' said Pippin. 'He knew where the safe was. He knew that the manager had put the takings there the day before and hadn't taken them to the bank that day, as he usually did. He knew where the key was kept – in the manager's wallet, not on his keyring – and he knew that the manager liked a cup of tea in the evening – and into it went the sleeping-draught!'

'Yes – you're right. No stranger would have known all those facts,' said Fatty, thoughtfully. 'It must be one of the cast – either an actor or an actress. It's strange that Boysie took in the tea, though, isn't it? Do you think he helped in the robbery?'

'I don't know! He says he doesn't remember a thing except feeling very sleepy last night and going to sleep in front of the fire,' said Pippin. 'That's certainly where *I* saw him when I looked into the room. He even said that he didn't take in the cup of tea to the manager, but that's nonsense, of course – the manager says he certainly did, and he wouldn't be likely to be mistaken. I think Boysie is scared, and said he didn't take in the tea to try and clear himself – forgetting he is quite unmistakeable as the pantomime cat!'

'Yes – it looks as if Boysie either did the whole thing or helped somebody else,' said Fatty. 'Well, thanks very much, Mr Pippin. I'll let you know if we spot anything. And remember – don't give anything away to Mr Goon. He won't thank you for it!'

'I shan't open my mouth to him,' said Pippin. 'My goodness – here he is, back again – and I haven't even begun this report he wants! You'd better clear out the back way, Frederick.'

Goon loomed up at the front gate, looking most important. He was talking to the vicar, solemnly and ponderously.

Fatty tiptoed out into the hall and made for the kitchen, with Buster in his arms. He meant to go into the back garden, hop over the fence at the bottom and make his way to Pip's. What a lot he had to tell the others!

He heard Mr Goon's loud voice. 'Do you know what the vicar tells me, Pippin? He tells me you were rude to his brother yesterday – snatched at his hat or something! Now, I really do think . . .'

But what Goon really did think Fatty didn't wait to hear. Poor PC Pippin! He was going to get into trouble over his curiosity about redheaded people now! Fatty couldn't help feeling very, very sorry!

If we'd known Mr Pippin was so decent we'd never have thought up all those tricks, said Fatty to himself, as he made his way to Pip's, where he knew the others would be anxiously awaiting him. Still – I can make it up to him, perhaps, by solving this peculiar mystery. The Mystery of the Pantomime Cat. Sounds good!

Larry, Daisy, Pip, and Bets had become very impatient indeed, waiting ages for Fatty. He had been gone for an hour and a half! What in the world could he be doing?

'Here he is at last,' called Bets from the window. 'Rushing up the drive with Buster. He looks full of importance – bursting with it. He must have plenty of news!'

He had. He began to relate everything from the very beginning, and when he got to where Mr Goon had threatened Buster with a poker, Bets gave a scream, and flung herself down on the floor beside the surprised Scottie.

'Buster! Oh, Buster, how *could* anyone treat you like that! I hate Mr Goon! I do, I do. I know it's wrong to hate people, but it's worse *not* to hate cruel people like Mr Goon.'

Buster lay down on his tummy, wagging his plumy tail with pleasure at all this loving fuss. In fact, he was so thrilled that he hung his red tongue out and began to pant with joy.

'I wouldn't be a bit surprised if Bets took a poker to Mr Goon if she thought he was going to hurt Buster,' said Fatty. 'She may be frightened of him herself – but she'd be all pluck and no fright if she thought he was going to hurt anyone else! I know Bets!'

Bets was so pleased at this speech from Fatty. She went red and buried her face in Buster's neck. Fatty patted her on the back.

'I felt like banging Mr Goon on the head myself

when I twisted the poker out of his hand,' he said. 'Oh my goodness – you should have seen his face when he found that I had the poker and he hadn't!'

'Go on with the story now,' said Pip. 'It's getting more and more exciting. Gosh, I wish I'd been there.'

Fatty went on with his tale. The children squealed with laughter when they heard that Mr Goon had demanded all the false clues, and had been solemnly handed them by PC Pippin.

'He'll meet that Sunday train. Fatty!' chuckled Pip, 'can't we meet it too?'

'Oh *yes*,' begged Bets. 'Let's. Do let's. Mr Goon would be awfully annoyed to see us all there. He'd think we knew the clue too.'

'Which we do,' said Larry. 'Seeing that we thought of it!'

'Yes – it's an idea,' said Fatty. 'Quite an idea. I've a good mind to disguise myself and arrive on that train – and arouse Mr Goon's suspicions and get him to follow me.'

'We could all follow too,' suggested Bets. 'We really must do that. It's tomorrow, isn't it? Oh Fatty, wouldn't it be fun?'

'Go on with the tale,' said Daisy. 'Let's hear it

to the end before we make any more plans. It'll be dinnertime before Fatty's finished.'

Fatty then told the rest of the tale to the end. The children were very glad to hear that PC Pippin had stuck up for Buster and Fatty. They all agreed that PC Pippin was very nice indeed. They were thrilled to hear about the pantomime cat, and the two girls wished they had been brave enough to peep into the verandah room and see him the night before.

'Do you think he did it all?' asked Bets. 'If he took in the tea, he must have done it. He may be cleverer than we think.'

'He may be, Bets,' said Fatty. 'I shall have to interview him. In fact, I thought we all could – together, you know, just as if we were children interested in him. He may be on his guard with grown-ups. He wouldn't be with children.'

'Yes. That's a good idea,' said Larry. 'Gosh, what a thrill this is! To think we put our clues in the very place where all this was going to happen – and managed to put a policeman there too, so that he would discover the crime. It's extraordinary.'

'Well – we must set our wits to work,' said Fatty. 'We've only got just over two weeks to solve the mystery – and Mr Goon is on the job too – hampered by a few false clues, of course! But we've got PC Pippin to help us. He may learn a few things that it's impossible for us to find out.'

'How are we going to set to work?' asked Larry.

'We must make a plan,' said Fatty. 'A properly set-out plan. Like we usually do. List of suspects, list of clues, and so on.'

'Oooh yes,' said Bets. 'Let's begin now, Fatty. This very minute. Have you got a notebook?'

'Of course,' said Fatty, and took out a fat notebook and a very fine pen. He ruled a few lines very neatly. 'Now then – SUSPECTS.'

A call came from the hall. Bets groaned. 'Blow! Dinner already! Fatty, will you come this afternoon and do it?'

'Right,' said Fatty, 'Half past two everyone – and put your best thinking-caps on! This is the finest mystery we've had yet!'

9. PIPPIN IS A HELP

Fatty thought hard during his lunch. His mother found him very silent indeed, and began to wonder about his teeth again. She looked at him closely. His cheeks seemed to have subsided – they were not very swollen now!

'Frederick – how is your tooth?' she asked suddenly.

Fatty looked at his mother blankly. His tooth? What did she mean?

'My tooth?' he said. 'What tooth, Mummy?'

'Now don't be silly, Frederick,' said his mother. 'You know how swollen your face was this morning. I meant to ring the dentist but I forgot. I was just asking you how your tooth was – it must have been bad because you had such a swollen face. I think I'd better ring up the dentist, even though your face *has* gone down.'

'Mummy,' said Fatty desperately, 'that wasn't toothache – it was cheek-pads.'

Now it was his mother's turn to look at him blankly. 'Cheek-pads! What *do* you mean, Frederick?'

'Things you put in your cheeks to alter your appearance,' explained Fatty, wishing heartily that he had not tried them out on his mother. 'A – a sort of disguise.'

'How very disgusting,' said his mother. 'I do wish you wouldn't do things like that, Frederick. No wonder you looked so awful.'

'Sorry Mummy,' said Fatty, hoping she would talk about something else. She did. She talked about the extraordinary behaviour of Mr Pippin who had snatched at Mr Twit's hair, or hat, she didn't know which. And she also told Fatty that the vicar had complained about it to Mr Goon, now that he was back again to take charge of this new robbery case at the Little Theatre.

'And I do hope, Frederick,' said his mother, 'I *do* hope you won't try and meddle in *this* case. Apparently Mr Goon is well on the way to finding out everything, and has a most remarkable collection of clues. I do *not* like that man, but he certainly seems to have been very quick off the mark in this case – came straight back from his holiday, found all these clues, and is on the track of the robber at once!'

'Don't you believe it,' murmured Fatty, half under his breath.

'What did you say, Frederick? I wish you wouldn't mumble,' said his mother. 'Well, I don't suppose you know a thing about this case, so just keep out of it and don't annoy Mr Goon.'

Fatty didn't answer. He knew a lot about the case, and he meant to meddle in it, for all he was worth, and if he could annoy Mr Goon, he was certainly going to. But he couldn't possibly tell his mother all that! So he sank into silence once more and began to think hard about all the suspects.

He would have to find out their names and who they were and where they lived. It was pretty obvious that only one of the theatre people could have committed the crime. One of them had come back that night, let himself in quietly, and done the deed. But which one?

Fatty decided he must go to Mr Pippin and get

the list of names and addresses. He would do that immediately after his lunch. So, at a quarter to two, when he left the table, Fatty rushed off to see if Mr Pippin was available. If Mr Goon was at home, it was no good. He couldn't possibly ask PC Pippin anything in front of Mr Goon.

He walked by the sitting-room window of the little cottage belonging to Mr Goon. Pippin was there, facing the window. Goon was also there, his back to it, writing at the table. Fatty tiptoed to the window and tried to attract Pippin's attention. Pippin looked up, astonished to see Fatty winking and beckoning outside. He turned round cautiously to see what Mr Goon was doing.

When he turned back again he saw, held up to the window, a piece of paper on which Fatty had written,

MEET ME IN HIGH STREET TEN
MINUTES' TIME.

Pippin grinned and nodded. Fatty disappeared. Goon heard the click of the gate and turned round.

'Who's that coming in?' said Goon.

'No one,' said Pippin, truthfully.

'Well, who was it going out then?' said Goon.

'Can't see anyone,' said Pippin.

'Gah! Call yourself a policeman and you can't see who opens a gate in front of your nose,' said Goon, who had eaten too much lunch and was feeling very bad-tempered. Pippin said nothing at all. He was getting used to Mr Goon's remarks.

He finished what he was doing and then got up. 'Where are you going?' asked Goon.

'Out to the post office,' said Pippin. 'I'm off duty at the moment, Mr Goon, as you very well know. If there's anything wants doing, I'll do it when I come back.'

And in spite of Goon's snort, Pippin walked out of the house and up to the post office. He posted his letter and then looked for Fatty. Ah, there he was, sitting on the wooden bench. Pippin went up to him. They grinned at one another and Buster rubbed against Pippin's trousers.

'Come into that shop over there and have a lemonade,' said Fatty. 'I don't want Mr Goon to see us hob-nobbing together.'

They went into the little shop, sat down, and

Fatty ordered lemonades. Then, in a low voice, Fatty told Pippin what he wanted.

'Do you know the names and addresses of the actors and actresses at the Little Theatre?' he asked.

'Yes,' said Pippin, at once. 'I got them all last night. Wait a bit – I think they're in my notebook. I don't believe I gave them to Mr Goon. He's been out interviewing the whole lot, and I expect he got the names from the manager – same as I did.'

'Oh – he's interviewed them already, has he?' said Fatty. 'He can get going when he likes, can't he?'

'Yes,' said Pippin. 'He's found one of them has a name beginning with Z too – you know one of the clues was an old handkerchief with Z on it. Well, see here,' and he pointed to one of the names in the list he was now showing to Fatty, 'the name of Dick Whittington, the principal boy – who's acted by a girl – is Zoe Markham. Looks as if Zoe was out on that verandah for some reason or other – at a meeting of the crooks, perhaps.'

Fatty was horror-stricken. To think that there was actually somebody with a name beginning with

Z! Who would have thought it? He didn't know what to say. At all costs, he would have to clear Zoe somehow. Fatty wished very heartily for the hundredth time that he and the others hadn't started PC Pippin on a false mystery complete with false clues.

'Has Zoe got an alibi – someone to swear that she was somewhere else between half past five and eight o'clock?' asked Fatty, looking worried.

'Oh yes. They've all got alibis,' said Pippin. 'Every one of them. I interviewed them myself last night, the whole lot – and Mr Goon gave them the once-over again this morning. Alibis all correct.'

'Mysterious, isn't it?' said Fatty, after a silence. 'I mean – it *must* be one of those theatre people, mustn't it? Nobody else had so much inside knowledge as to be able to give the manager a cup of tea, and then take down the mirror, find the key, work out the combination, and open the safe.'

'Don't forget it was the pantomime cat who took in the cup of tea,' said Pippin.

'Yes. That's stranger still,' said Fatty. 'Anyone would think he'd done the job.'

'Mr Goon thinks so,' said Pippin. 'He thinks

all that business of the cat saying he doesn't understand, and he doesn't remember, and bursting into tears is put on – good acting, you know.'

'What do *you* think?' asked Fatty. Pippin considered. 'I told you before. I think Boysie's a bit funny in the head – never grown up, poor fellow. You know, I've got a cousin like that – and he wouldn't hurt a fly. It's a fact, he wouldn't. I don't see how he could possibly have done all that. I'm sorry Mr Goon's got it into his head that Boysie's done the job – he'll scare the poor chap into fits.'

'Well – it's quite possible that somebody hid in the kitchen somewhere when Boysie was making the tea, and popped something into the cup when Boysie wasn't looking,' said Fatty.

'Yes. There's something in that,' said Pippin. 'But we still come back to the fact that it can only have been done by one of the theatre folk – no one else knows enough to have done it – and they all have alibis – so there you are!'

'Can I have their names and addresses?' asked Fatty. 'I'll copy them down.' Pippin handed over his notebook. Fatty looked through the pages with interest. 'Gosh – are these your notes about where they said they were between half past five and eight o'clock last night?'

'That's right,' said Pippin. 'Take them along with you, if you like. Save you a lot of trouble! They've all been interviewed twice, so you can take my word for it they won't say anything different the third time – that's if you were thinking of interviewing them, Frederick.'

'We're making out a plan,' said Fatty, stuffing the notes into his pocket. 'I don't quite know what it will be yet. I'll tell you when we know details. Thanks very much, Mr Pippin.'

'If you ever see a villainous-looking tramp with red hair, let me know, will you?' said Pippin. 'I mean – you get about a lot on that bike of yours – and you might happen on the fellow – and his mate with him. The ones I saw under the bush that night in Willow Road, I mean.'

'Er – yes – I know the ones you mean,' said Fatty, feeling extremely guilty at this mention of the red-haired villain. 'I'll certainly let you know if I see him again. But I don't think he had anything to do with this robbery job, you know.'

'Ah, you can't tell,' said Pippin, finishing his glass of lemonade and standing up. 'If ever I saw wickedness in anyone's face, it was in that red-haired fellow's. I wouldn't care to be seen in *his* company. I'll walk a little way with you, Frederick – it's a nice day. Your dog all right?'

'Yes thanks,' said Fatty. 'Takes a lot to upset a Scottie like Buster!'

'That properly turned me against Mr Goon, that did,' said Pippin, as they walked down the High Street – and round the corner they bumped straight into Mr Goon! He glared at them both, and Buster flew round him delightedly.

'Buster, come here,' ordered Fatty, in such a stern voice that Buster felt he had to obey. He put his tail down and crept behind Fatty, keeping up a continuous growl.

'You be careful of the company you keep, Pippin,' ordered Mr Goon. 'I warned you against that boy, didn't I? Always interfering and meddling, he is! Anyway, he can't interfere in *this* case much! Cast-iron, that's what it is! I'll be making an arrest any time now!'

Mr Goon walked on, and Pippin and Fatty looked

at one another with raised eyebrows.

'It's that pantomime cat he's going to arrest,' said Pippin. 'I saw it in his eyes! And before he's finished with that poor cat he'll make him confess to things he didn't do. He will!'

'Then I'll have to see that he doesn't,' said Fatty. 'I must set the old brains to work IMMEDIATELY!'

10. THE SUSPECTS AND THEIR ALIBIS

At just half past two, Fatty walked into Pip's drive for the second time that day, and was hailed by Bets from the open window.

'Hurry up, Fatty! We want to make our plan!'

Fatty hurried, grinning at Bets' impatience. He went up the stairs two at a time, and found the other four waiting for him round the table.

'Ha! A conference!' said Fatty. 'Well – I've got some information here which we'll study together. Then we'll really get going.'

He told the children quickly what PC Pippin had told him, and then got out the notebook with names, addresses and particulars of alibis in. The word 'alibi' was new to Bets, and had to be explained to her.

'Is it anything to do with lullaby?' she asked, and the others roared.

'No, Bets,' said Fatty. 'I'll tell you what an alibi is. Suppose somebody smashed this window, and your mother thought it was Pip – and Pip told her he was with me at the time, and I said yes, he certainly was – then I am Pip's *alibi* – he's got his alibi, because I can vouch for his being with me when the window was smashed.'

'I see,' said Bets. 'And if somebody said that at just this moment you had hit Mr Goon on the head, and we said no, you couldn't have, because you were with us – we'd *all* be alibis for you.'

'Quite right, Bets – you've got the idea,' grinned Fatty. 'Well – I've got a list of the alibis of all the suspects here – which will be very, very useful. Listen and I'll read out the names of the suspects first, and then I'll tell you their alibis and what we know about them.'

He read from PC Pippin's notes.

SUSPECTS

Number one. Pantomime Cat, *otherwise known as Boysie Summers. Was in theatre at the time in question. Took manager a cup of tea before eight o'clock. Says he didn't, but*

admits he had a cup of tea himself.
Says he went to sleep most of the evening.

Number two. Zoe Markham, who plays the
part of Dick Whittington. Says she left theatre
with other members of the cast, and went to
her sister's, where she played with the children
and helped to put them to bed. Her sister is
Mrs Thomas, and she lives at Green House,
Hemel Road.

'I know her!' said Daisy. 'She's awfully nice. She's got two dear little children. One's having a birthday soon, I know.'

'Hey,' said Larry suddenly. '*Zoe* Markham! I hope Mr Goon doesn't connect up the Z for Zoe with the Z on that old hanky of Daisy's – the one we used for a false clue.'

'I rather think he has,' said Fatty. 'We'll have to do something about that, if so. Well – to continue . . .'

Number three. Lucy White, who plays the
part of Margot, Dick Whittington's sweetheart.

> *Says she went to call on Miss Adams,*
> *an old age pensioner who is ill, at address*
> *11 Mark Street. Sat with her till nine o'clock,*
> *and helped her with her knitting.*

'Miss Adams is a friend of our cook's,' said Larry. 'She used to come and help with the sewing. Nice lady.'

> *Number four.* Peter Watting, *who plays the*
> *part of Dick's master. Elderly, and rather*
> *obstructive. Would not answer questions readily.*
> *Said he was out walking with suspect number*
> *five at the time.*

> *Number five.* William Orr, *who plays the part*
> *of the captain of Dick's ship. Young man, affable*
> *and helpful. Says he was out walking with Peter*
> *Watting at the time.*

'Then those two are alibis for each other,' said Larry, with interest. 'What's to stop them from *both* going back to the theatre and doing the robbery, and then giving each other an alibi?'

'That's a good point, Larry,' said Fatty. 'Very good point. PC Pippin doesn't seem to have worked that out. Wait a bit – here's another note about it. "Suspects four and five (Peter Watting and William Orr) further said they had gone for a walk by the river, and had called at a teashop called "The Turret" for some sandwiches and coffee. They did not know the exact time".'

'Bit fishy, I think,' said Pip. 'Wants looking into.'

Number six. Alec Grant, *who plays the part of Dick's mother. Usually takes women's parts and is very good at them, a fine mimic and good actor. Says he was giving a show at Hetton Hall, Sheepridge, that evening, from six to ten – acting various women's parts to an audience of about one hundred.*

'Well! That rules *him* out!' said Larry. 'He's got a hundred alibis, not one.'

'Yes. It certainly clears *him*,' said Fatty. 'Well, here's the last suspect.'

Number seven. John James, *who plays the*

part of the king in the play. Says he went to
the cinema and was there all the evening,
seeing the film called, You Know How It Is.

'Not much of an alibi either,' said Pip. 'He could easily have popped in, and popped out again – and even popped back in again after doing the robbery. Poor alibi, I call that.'

'Well now,' said Fatty, 'I imagine that Mr Goon will check all these, if he hasn't already – but he's such a mutt that I expect he'll miss something important that *we* might spot. So I vote we all check up on the various alibis ourselves.'

There was a deep silence. Nobody felt capable of doing this. It was bad enough to interview people – it was much worse to check an alibi!

'I can't,' said Bets, at last. 'I know I'm a Find-Outer and I ought to do what you tell me, Fatty, but I really *can't* check an ali–alibi. I mean – it sounds too much like a *real* detective.'

'Well, we may be kids, but we're really good detectives all the same,' said Fatty. 'Look at all the mysteries we've solved already! This is a bit more *advanced*, perhaps.'

'It's very advanced,' groaned Larry. 'I feel rather like Bets – out of my depth.'

'Don't give up before you've begun,' said Fatty. 'Now, I'll tell you what I propose to do.'

'What?' asked everyone, and Buster thumped his tail on the ground as if he too had a great interest in the question.

'There are three things we must do,' said Fatty. 'We must interview Boysie, and see what *we* think of him – and we'll interview him all together, as we suggested before.'

'Right,' said Larry. 'What next?'

'We'll see every other suspect too,' said Fatty.

There was a general groan.

'Oh *no*, Fatty – six people! And all grown up! We can't possibly,' said Daisy. 'What excuse could we have for seeing them even?'

'A very good excuse indeed,' said Fatty. 'All we've got to do is to find our autograph books and go and ask for autographs – and we can easily say a few words to them then, can't we?'

'That's a *brilliant* idea,' said Pip. 'Really brilliant, Fatty. I must say you think of good ideas.'

'Oh well,' said Fatty, modestly, 'I've got a few

brains, you know. As a matter-of-fact . . .'

'*Don't* start telling us about the wonderful things you did at school last term,' begged Pip. 'Go on with our plan.'

'All right,' said Fatty, a little huffily. 'The third thing we must do is, as I said, check up on the alibis – and if we think hard, it won't be so difficult. For instance, Daisy says she knows Zoe Markham's sister, who lives near her, and she also says one of the children is having a birthday soon. Well Daisy, what's to stop you and Bets from taking the child a present, getting into conversation with the mother, and finding out if Zoe *was* there all that evening? Zoe's sister wouldn't be on her guard with two children who came with a present for her child.'

'Yes – all right, Fatty, I can do that,' said Daisy. 'You'll come too, won't you Bets?'

'Yes,' said Bets. 'But you'll ask the questions, won't you Daisy?'

'You've got to help,' said Daisy. 'I'm not doing it all!'

'Now, the next suspect is Lucy White who went to sit with Miss Adams, an old age pensioner,' went on Fatty. 'Larry, you said she was a friend of your cook's, and used to come to help with the sewing. Can't you and Daisy concoct some sort of sewing job you want done, and take it round to her – and ask a few questions about Lucy White?'

'Yes, we could,' said Daisy. 'I'll pretend I want to give Mother a surprise for Easter, and I'll take round a cushion cover I want embroidering, or something. I've been there before, and Mary Adams knows me.'

'Splendid,' said Fatty. 'That's two alibis we can check very easily indeed. Now, the next one – well, the next two, actually, because they are each other's alibis – Peter Watting and William Orr. Well, they apparently went to a place called "The Turret" and had coffee and sandwiches there. Pip, you and I will call there and also have coffee and sandwiches tomorrow morning.'

'But it's Sunday and I have to go to church,' objected Pip.

'Oh yes. I forgot it was Sunday,' said Fatty. 'Well, we'll do that on Monday or Tuesday morning. Now, suspect number six is Alec Grant, who was apparently giving a concert at Hetton Hall to about a hundred people. Seems hardly necessary to check that.'

'Well, don't let's,' said Larry.

'The thing is – a really good detective always checks *every*thing,' said Fatty. 'Even if he thinks it really isn't necessary. So I suppose we'd better check that too. Bets, you can come with me and check it. We'll find someone who attended the show, and ask them about it and see if Alec Grant really was there.'

'Right,' said Bets, who never minded what she did with Fatty. She always felt so safe with him, as safe as if she was with a grown-up.

'That only leaves one more,' said Fatty, looking at his list. 'And that's John James who says he went to the cinema all evening.

'Yes – and we thought it was a pretty poor alibi,' said Pip. 'Who's going to check that one up?'

'Oh – Larry and I could tackle that, I think, or you and Larry,' said Fatty.

'But how?' asked Larry.

'Have to think of something,' said Fatty. 'Well, there you are, Find-Outers – plenty for us to find out! We've got to see Boysie, got to get autographs from all the cast and have a look at them – and got to check up on all the alibis. Pretty stiff work.'

'*And*, Fatty, we've got to meet that train tomorrow and lead old Mr Goon a dance,' Bets reminded him. 'Don't let's forget that!'

'Oh no – we really must do that,' grinned Fatty. 'I'll use my new cheek-pads for that.'

'Whatever are those?' said Bets in wonder, and screamed with laughter when Fatty told her. 'Oh yes, do wear those. I hope I don't giggle when I see you.'

'You'd better not, young Bets,' said Fatty, getting hold of her nose and pulling it gently. 'Now what time's that train we underlined?'

'Half past three tomorrow afternoon,' said Pip. 'We'll all be there, Fatty. What will *you* do – go to the next station, catch the train there, and arrive here at half past three?'

'I will,' said Fatty. 'Look out for me. So long, everyone. I've just remembered that my mother told me to be home an hour ago, to meet my great-aunt. *What* a memory I've got!'

11. TREAT FOR MR GOON

Fatty worked out the timetable for putting the plan into action that evening. They couldn't do much the next day, Sunday, that was certain. Daisy had better buy a present for Zoe's sister's child on Monday and take it in with Bets. The next day, perhaps she and Larry could go and see Miss Adams and find out about Lucy White.

He and Larry would go to 'The Turret' on Monday and have coffee and sandwiches and see if they could find out anything about Peter Watting and William Orr. They could leave Alec Grant till last, because it really did seem as if his alibi was unshakable, as it consisted of about a hundred people. He would not dare to give an alibi like that if it were not true.

I can't think how to find out about the last fellow's alibi – what's his name? – John James, said Fatty to himself. Can't very well go and talk to a cinema and ask it questions! Still, I'll think of something.

He paused and looked at himself in the mirror. He was thinking out his disguise for the next day – something perfectly reasonable, but peculiar, and with red hair so that it would attract Mr Goon's attention. He would wear dark glasses and pretend to be short-sighted. That would make the children want to laugh.

We'll go and see Boysie – what a name – on Monday morning, thought Fatty, drawing a line round both his nostrils to see what effect it gave.

Gracious! Don't I look bad-tempered! Grrrrr! Gah!

He removed the lines and experimented with different eyebrows, thinking of his plan the whole time.

We'll all go and ask for autographs after the afternoon performance at the Little Theatre on Monday, thought Fatty. And dear me – why shouldn't we *go* to the performance and see everyone in action? It mightn't tell us anything – but on the other hand, it might! That's a jolly good idea. Well – Monday's going to be pretty busy, I can see, what with interviewing and asking for autographs and checking up alibis. Now, what about that train tomorrow? Shall I speak to Mr Goon when I see him or not? I'll ask him the way somewhere!

He began to practise different voices. First, a deepdown rumble, modelled on a preacher who had come to his school to preach one Sunday, and who had been the admiration of everyone because of his extremely bass voice.

He tried a high falsetto voice – no, not so good. He tried a foreign voice – ah, that was splendid.

'Please, Sair, to teel me ze way to Hoffle-Foffle Road!' began Fatty. 'What you say, Sair? I not unnerstand. I say, I weesh to know ze way to Hoffle-Foffle Road. HOFFLE-FOFFLE!'

There came a knock at his door. 'Frederick. Have you got Pip and the others in there with you? You know I don't like them here so late at night.'

Fatty opened his door in surprise. 'Oh no, Mummy – of course they're not here. There's only me!'

His mother looked at him and made an

exasperated noise. 'Frederick! What have you done to your eyebrows, they are all crooked! And what's that around your eye?'

'Oh – only a wrinkle I drew there for an experiment,' said Fatty, rubbing it away hastily. 'And you needn't worry about my eyebrows, Mummy. They're not really crooked. Look.'

He took off the eyebrows he was wearing, and showed his mother his own underneath. They were not at all crooked, of course!

'Well, what will you think of next Frederick?' said his mother, half-crossly. 'I came to say that Daddy wants you to listen to the next bit on the radio with him – it's about a part of China he knows very well. Are you *sure* you haven't got anyone else with you here? I did hear quite a lot of voices when I was coming up the stairs.'

'Mummy, look under the bed, behind the curtains and in the cupboard,' said Fatty generously. But she wouldn't, of course, and proceeded downstairs – but stopped in a hurry when she heard a falsetto voice say, 'Has she gone? Can I come out?'

She turned at once, annoyed to think there was someone in Fatty's room after all – but when she saw Fatty's grinning face, she laughed too.

'Oh – one of your voices, I suppose,' she said. 'I might have guessed. I cannot think, Frederick, how it is that you always have such good reports from school. I cannot believe you behave well there.'

'Well, Mummy,' said Fatty, in his most modest voice, 'the fact is, brains *will* tell, you know. I can't help having good brains, can I? I mean . . .'

'Shh!' said his father, as they walked into the sitting-room. 'The talk's begun.'

So it had – and a very dull talk it proved to be, on a little-known part of China which Fatty devoutly hoped he would never have to visit. He passed the dull half hour by thinking out further plans. His father was really pleased to see such an intent look on Fatty's face.

The Find-Outers were finding the time very long, as they always did when something exciting was due to happen. Bets could hardly wait for the next afternoon to come. How would Fatty be disguised? What would he say? Would he wink at them?

At twenty-five past three, Larry, Daisy, Pip, and Bets walked sedately onto the platform. A minute later, Mr Goon arrived, a little out of breath, because he had had an argument with PC Pippin, and had had to hurry. He saw the children at once and glared at them.

'What you here for?' he demanded.

'Same reason as you, I suppose,' said Pip. 'To meet someone.'

'We're meeting Fatty,' piped up Bets, and got a nudge from Larry.

'It's all right,' whispered Bets. 'I'm not giving anything away, really – he won't know it's Fatty when he sees him – you know he won't.'

The train came in with a clatter and stopped. Quite a lot of people got out. Mr Goon eyed them all carefully. He was standing by the platform door, leading to the booking-office, and everyone had to pass him to give up their tickets. The four children stood nearby, watching out for Fatty.

Bets nudged Pip. A voluminous old lady was proceeding down the platform, a veil spreading out behind her in the wind. Pip shook his head. No – good as Fatty was at disguises, he could never look like that imperious old lady.

A man came by, hobbling along with a stick,

his hat pulled down over his eyes, and a shapeless mackintosh flung across his shoulders. He had a straggling moustache and an absurd little beard. His hair was a little reddish, and Mr Goon gave him a very sharp look indeed.

But Bets knew it wasn't Fatty. This man had a crooked nose, and Fatty surely couldn't mimic a thing like that.

It looked almost as if Goon was about to follow this man – and then he saw someone else – someone with much redder hair, someone much more suspicious.

This man was evidently a foreigner of some sort. He wore a peculiar hat on his red hair, which was neatly brushed. He had a foreign-looking cape round his shoulders, and brightly polished, pointed shoes.

For some peculiar reason, he wore bicycle clips round the bottoms of his trousers, and this made him even more foreign-looking, though Bets didn't quite know why it should. The man wore dark glasses on his nose, had a little red moustache, and his cheeks were very bulgy. He was very freckled indeed. Bets wondered admiringly how Fatty managed to produce freckles like that.

She knew it was Fatty, of course, and so did the others, though if they had not been actually looking for him, they would have been very doubtful indeed. But there was something about the jaunty way he walked and looked about that made them quite certain.

The foreigner brushed against Bets as he came to the exit. He dug his elbow into her, and she almost giggled.

'Your ticket, sir,' said the collector, as Fatty seemed to have forgotten all about this. Fatty began to feel in all his pockets, one after another, exclaiming in annoyance.

'This tick-ett! I had him, I know I had him! He was green.'

Mr Goon watched him intently, quite ready to arrest him if he didn't produce his ticket! The foreigner suddenly swooped down by Mr Goon's feet, and shoved one of them aside with his hand. Goon glared.

'Here. What are you doing?' he began.

'A million apologeeze,' said the stranger, waving his ticket in Goon's face, and almost scraping the skin off the end of the policeman's big nose. 'I have him – he was on the ground, and you put your beeg foots on him. Aha!'

Fatty thrust the ticket at the astonished collector, and pushed past Goon. Then he stopped so suddenly that Goon jumped.

'Ah, you are the pliss, are you not?' demanded Fatty, peering at Goon short-sightedly from his dark glasses. 'At first I think you are an engine-driver – but now I see you are the pliss.'

'Yes. I'm the police,' said Mr Goon gruffly, feeling more and more suspicious of this behaviour. 'Where do you want to go? I expect you're a stranger here.'

'Ah yes, alas! A strangair,' agreed Fatty. 'I need to know my way to a place. You will tell me zis place?'

'Certainly,' said Mr Goon, only too pleased.

'It is – er – it is – Hoffle-Foffle House, in Willow Road,' said Fatty, making a great to-do with the Hoffle-Foffle bit. Goon looked blank.

'No such place as – er – what you said,' he answered.

'I say Hoffle-Foffle – you say you do not know it?

How can zis be?' cried Fatty, and walked out into the road at top speed with Mr Goon at his heels. Fatty stopped abruptly and Mr Goon bumped into him. Bets by this time was so convulsed with laughter that she had to stay behind.

'There isn't a house of that name,' said Goon exasperated. 'Who do you want to see?'

'That ees my own business – vairy, vairy secret beeziness,' said Fatty. 'Where is zis Willow Road? I will find Hoffle-Foffle by myself.'

Goon directed him. Fatty set off at top speed again, and Mr Goon followed, panting. The four children followed too, trying to suppress their giggles. Hoffle-Foffle House was, of course, not to be found.

'I will sairch the town till I see zis place,' Fatty told Mr Goon earnestly. 'Do not accompany me, Mr Pliss – I am tired of you.'

Whereupon Fatty set off at a great pace again, and left Mr Goon behind. He saw the four children still following, and frowned. Little pests! Couldn't he shadow anyone without them coming too? 'Clear orf!' he said to them, as they came up. 'Do you hear me? Clear orf!'

'Can't we even go for a walk, Mr Goon?' said Daisy pathetically, and Mr Goon snorted and hastened to follow 'that dratted foreigner,' who by now was almost out of sight.

Mr Goon, in fact, almost lost him. Fatty was getting tired of this protracted walk, and wanted to throw Mr Goon off, and go home and laugh with the others. But Mr Goon valiantly pursued him. So Fatty made a pretence of examining the names of many houses, peering at them through his dark glasses. He was getting nearer and nearer to his own home by this time.

He managed to pop in at his front gate and scuttled down to the shed at the bottom of the garden, where he locked the door, and began to pull off his disguise as quickly as he could. He wiped his face free of paint, pulled off his false eyebrows and wig, took out his cheek-pads, straightened his tie, and ventured out into the garden.

He saw the four children looking anxiously over the fence. 'Mr Goon's gone in to tell your mother,' whispered Larry. 'He thinks the suspicious foreigner is somewhere in the garden and he wants permission to search for him.'

'Let him,' grinned Fatty. 'Oh my, how I want to laugh! Sh! Here's Mr Goon and Mummy.'

Fatty strolled up to meet them. 'Why, Mr Goon,' he began, 'what a pleasant surprise!'

'I thought those friends of yours had gone to meet you at the station,' said Mr Goon suspiciously.

'Quite right,' said Fatty politely. 'They did meet me. Here they are.'

The other four had gone in at the gate at the bottom of the garden, and were now trooping demurely up the garden path behind Fatty. Goon stared at them in surprise.

'But – they've been following *me* about all afternoon,' he began. 'And I certainly didn't see you at the station.'

'Oh, but Mr Goon, he *was* there,' said Larry, earnestly. 'Perhaps you didn't recognise him. He does look different sometimes, you know.'

'Mr Goon,' interrupted Mrs Trotteville, impatiently, 'you wanted to look for some suspicious trespasser in my garden. It's Sunday afternoon and I want to go back to my husband. Never mind about these children.'

'Yes, but,' began Mr Goon, trying to sort things

out in his mind, and failing. How *could* these kids have met Fatty if he wasn't there? How dare they say they had met him, when he knew jolly well the four of them had been trailing him all that afternoon? There was something very peculiar here.

'Well, Mr Goon, I'll leave you,' said Mrs Trotteville. 'I've no doubt the children will help you look for your suspicious loiterer.'

She went in. The children began to look everywhere with such terrific enthusiasm that Mr Goon gave up. He was sure he'd never find that red-haired foreigner again. *Could* it have been Fatty in one of his disguises? No – not possible! Nobody would have the sauce to lead him on a wild-goosechase like that. And now he hadn't solved the mystery of who was coming by that half past three train! He snorted and went crossly out of the front gate.

The children flung themselves down on the damp ground and laughed till they cried. They laughed so much that they didn't see a very puzzled Mr Goon looking over the fence at them. *Now* what was the joke? Those dratted children! Slippery as eels they were – couldn't trust them an inch!

Mr Goon went back home, tired and cross. 'Interfering with the law!' he muttered, to PC Pippin's surprise. 'Always interfering with the law! One of these days, I'll catch them good and proper – and then they'll laugh on the other side of their faces. Gah!'

12. ZOE, THE FIRST SUSPECT

The next day, Monday, the Five Find-Outers really set to work. They all met at Pip's as usual. They were early, half past nine – but, as Fatty pointed out, they had a lot to do.

'You and Bets must go and buy a birthday present for that child – Zoe Markham's niece,' he said. 'Got any money?'

'I haven't any at all,' said Bets. 'I owe Pip for a water pistol, and it's all gone to pay for that.'

'I've got a little, I think,' said Daisy.

Fatty put his hand into his pocket and pulled out some silver. He always seemed to have plenty of money. He had aunts and uncles who treated him well, and he was just like a grown-up the way he always seemed to have enough to spend.

He picked out a few pound coins. 'Here you are, Daisy. You can get a little something with that.

When's the child's birthday?'

'Tomorrow,' said Daisy, 'I met her little sister yesterday and asked her.'

'Good,' said Fatty. 'Couldn't be better! Now you go and buy something, you and Bets, and put a message on it, and deliver it to Mrs Thomas, Zoe's sister. And mind you get into conversation with her and find out exactly when Zoe went there on Friday night, and what time she left.'

'How shall we get her talking though?' said Daisy, beginning to feel nervous.

Fatty looked sternly at poor Daisy. 'Now I really can't plan everyone's conversation! It's up to you to get this done, Daisy. Use your common sense. Ask what the mum herself is giving the child – something like that – and I bet she'll take you in to see the present she's bought.'

'Oh yes – that's a good idea,' said Daisy, cheering up. 'Come on Bets – we'll go and do our bit of shopping.'

'I'm going to see PC Pippin for a few minutes, if I can,' said Fatty. 'I want to find out one or two things before I make further plans.'

'What do you want to know?' asked Larry.

'Well – I want to know if there were any fingerprints on that wall-mirror, which had to be lifted down to get the safe open, at the back of it,' said Fatty. 'And there might have been prints on the safe too. If there were, and the job was done by one of the actors or actresses, we might as well give up our detecting at once – because Mr Goon has only got to take everyone's fingerprints, compare them with the ones on the mirror or safe – and there you are! He'd have the thief immediately!'

'Oh, I hope he won't!' said Bets, in dismay. 'I want to go on with this mystery. I want *us* to solve it, not Mr Goon. I like this finding-out part.'

'Don't worry,' said Fatty, with a grin. 'The thief wouldn't leave prints behind, I'm sure! He was pretty cunning, whoever he was.'

'Do you think it *was* Boysie, the pantomime cat?' asked Daisy.

'No – not at present, anyway,' said Fatty. 'Wait and see what we think of him when we see him. Oh, and Larry, will you and Pip go along to the theatre this morning and get tickets for this afternoon's show? Here's the money.'

And out came the handful of money again!

'It's a good thing you're so *rich*, Fatty,' said Bets. 'We wouldn't find detecting nearly as easy if you weren't!'

'Now, let's see,' said Fatty. 'We've all got jobs to do this morning, haven't we? Report back here at twelve, or as near that as possible. I'm off to see PC Pippin, if I can manage to get him alone. Come on, Buster. Wake up! Bicycle basket for you!'

Buster opened his eyes, got up from the hearth rug, yawned and wagged his tail. He trotted sedately after Fatty. Bets went to put on her coat, ready to do the bit of birthday shopping with Daisy. Pip and Larry went to get their bicycles, meaning to ride down to the Little Theatre to get the tickets.

Fatty was just wheeling his bicycle from Pip's shed. He called to the other two. 'Pip! Larry! Don't just buy the tickets – talk to as many people down there as you can! See if you can find out anything at all.'

'Right, Captain!' grinned Larry. 'We'll do our best.'

Off went all Five Find-Outers – and Dog – to do a really good morning's detection work. Bets and Daisy walked, as Bets' bike had a puncture. They were soon down in the town, and went to the toy-shop there.

'Jane's only four,' said Daisy. 'She won't want anything too advanced. It's no good buying her a difficult game or puzzle. We'll look at the soft toys.'

But there was no soft toy they could afford – they were all much too expensive. Then Bets pounced on a set of doll's furniture, for a doll's house.

'Oh, look! Isn't it sweet! Let's get this, Daisy. Two tiny chairs, a table and a sofa – lovely! I'm sure Jane will love it.'

'How much is it?' said Daisy, looking at the price. 'We can just about manage it if I add some of my own.'

'I'll give you some of my pocket money next week,' said Bets. 'Oh, I do like these little chairs!'

Daisy bought the doll's furniture, and had it wrapped up nicely. 'Now we'll go home and write a message on a label, and take it to Jane's mother,' said Daisy. So off they went, and wrote the label. 'Many happy returns to Jane, with love from Daisy and Bets'.

Then they set off once again to call on Mrs

Thomas, Zoe's sister. They came to the house, a small pretty one, set back from the road. They stopped at the gate.

Daisy was nervous. 'Now, whatever shall we do if Mrs Thomas isn't in?'

'Say we'll come again,' said Bets promptly. 'But she will be in. I can hear Jane and Dora playing in the garden.'

'What shall we say when the door is opened?' asked Daisy, still nervous.

'Just say we've got a present for little Jane, and then see what Mrs Thomas says,' said Bets, surprised to see how nervous Daisy was. '*I'll* manage this if you can't, Daisy.'

That was quite enough to make Daisy forget all her nervousness! 'I can manage it all right, thank you,' she said huffily. 'Come on!'

They went to the front door and rang the bell. Mrs Thomas opened the door. 'Hello Daisy!' she said. 'And who is this – oh, little Elizabeth Hilton, isn't it?'

'Yes,' said Bets, whose name really was Elizabeth.

'Er – it's Jane's birthday tomorrow, isn't it?' began Daisy. 'We've brought her a little present,

Mrs Thomas.'

'How kind of you!' said Mrs Thomas. 'What is it?'

Daisy gave it to her. 'It's just some doll's furniture,' she said. 'Has she got a doll's house?'

'Well, isn't that strange – her daddy and I are giving Jane a doll's house tomorrow!' said Mrs Thomas. 'This furniture will be *just* right!'

'Oh – *could* we see the doll's house, please?' asked Bets at once, seeing a wonderful chance of getting into the house and talking.

'Of course,' said Mrs Thomas. 'Come in.'

So in they went and were soon being shown a lovely little doll's house in an upstairs room. Daisy led the talk round to the Little Theatre.

'You sister Zoe Summers acts in the show at the Little Theatre, doesn't she?' she said innocently.

'Yes,' said Mrs Thomas. 'Have you seen any of the shows?'

'We're going this afternoon,' said Bets. 'I do want to see that pantomime cat.'

'Poor cat!' said Mrs Thomas. 'Poor Boysie. He's in a dreadful state now – that awful policeman has been at him, you know – he thinks Boysie did that robbery. I expect you heard about it.'

Just as she said that, a tall and pretty young woman came into the room. 'Hello!' she said, 'I thought I heard voices up here. Who are these friends of yours, Helen?'

'This is Daisy and this is Elizabeth, or Bets – that's what you are called, isn't it?' said Mrs Thomas, turning to Bets. 'This is Zoe – my sister – the one who acts in the show at the Little Theatre.'

Well! *What* a bit of luck! Daisy and Bets stared earnestly at Zoe. How pretty she was – and what a smiley face. They liked her very much.

'Did I hear you talking about poor Boysie?' said Zoe, sitting down by the doll's house, and beginning to rearrange the furniture in it. 'It's a shame! As if he could have done that job on Friday evening! He hasn't got the brains – he'd never, ever think of it, even to get back at the manager for his unkindness.'

'Why – is the manager unkind to Boysie?' asked Bets.

'Yes – awfully impatient with him. You see,' said Zoe, 'Boysie is slow, and he's only given silly parts like Dick Whittington's cat or Mother Goose's goose and things like that – and the manager shouts at him till poor old Boysie gets worse than ever. I couldn't bear it on Friday morning, when we had a rehearsal – I flared up and told the manager what I thought of him!'

'Did you really?' said Daisy. 'Was he angry?'

'Yes, very,' said Zoe. 'We had a real shouting match, and he told me I could leave at the end of this week.'

'Oh dear,' said Daisy. 'So you've lost your job then?'

'Yes. But I don't mind. I'm tired and I want a rest,' said Zoe. 'I'm coming to stay with my sister here for a bit. We shall both like that.'

'I expect you thought it served the manager right, when he was drugged and robbed that night,' said Daisy. 'Where were you when it happened?'

'I left at half past five with the others,' said Zoe, 'and came here. I believe old Mr Goon thinks I did the robbery, with Boysie to help me!'

'But how could he, if you were here all evening?' said Bets at once. 'Didn't your sister tell Mr Goon you were here?'

'Yes – but unfortunately I went out at a quarter to seven, after I'd put the children to bed, to go to the postbox,' said Zoe. 'And my sister didn't hear me come back ten minutes later! I went up to my bedroom and stayed there till about a quarter to eight and then came down again. So, you see, according to Mr Goon, I could have slipped down to the Little Theatre, put a sleeping-draught into the manager's cup of tea, taken down the mirror, opened the safe and stolen the money – all with poor Boysie's help! *And* Mr Goon has actually found a handkerchief – it isn't mine, by the way – with a Z on it, on the verandah at the back of the theatre – and he says I dropped it when Boysie let me in that night. What do you think of *that*?'

13. LARRY AND PIP ON THE JOB

The two girls were full of horror – especially at the mention of that unfortunate handkerchief. Daisy went scarlet when she remembered how she had sewn a Z on it in one corner, never, ever thinking that there might be anyone called Zoe.

They both stared at poor Zoe, and Bets was almost in tears. Daisy wanted to blurt out about the handkerchief and how she had put the Z on it – but she stopped herself in time. She must ask Fatty's permission first.

'Mr Goon was most unpleasant,' said Mrs Thomas. 'He cross-examined me about Zoe till I was tired! He wanted to see all the navy coats in the house too – goodness knows what for!'

The two girls knew quite well! Mr Goon had got that bit of navy blue cloth that Fatty had jabbed on a nail for a false clue – and he was looking for a coat with a hole in it to match the piece of cloth! Oh dear – this was getting worse and worse.

'He also wanted to know what kind of cigarettes we smoked,' said Zoe. 'And he seemed awfully pleased when we showed him a pack off "Players"!'

Daisy's heart sank even further, and so did Bets'. It was 'Players' cigarettes whose ends Fatty had scattered over the verandah. Who would have thought that their silly, false clues would have fitted so well into this case – and, alas, fitted poor Zoe so well!

Bets blinked back her tears. She was scared and unhappy. She looked desperately at Daisy. Daisy caught the look and knew that Bets wanted to go. She wanted to go herself also. She too was scared and worried. Fatty must be told all this. He really must. He would know what to do!

So the two of them got up and said a hurried good-bye. 'We'll be seeing you this afternoon,' said Daisy to Zoe. 'We're coming to the show. Could we have your autograph, all of us, if we wait at the stage door?'

'Of course,' said Zoe. 'How many are there of

you? Five? Right – I'll tell the others, if you like, and they will all give you their autographs. Mind you clap me this afternoon!'

'Oh, we will, we really will,' said Bets fervently. 'Please don't get arrested, will you?'

Zoe laughed. 'Of course not. I didn't do the robbery, and poor Boysie had nothing to do with it either. I'm quite sure of that. I'm not really afraid of that nasty Mr Goon. Don't worry!'

But the two girls did worry dreadfully as they hurried away, longing for twelve o'clock to come, so that they could tell Fatty and the others all that they had found out.

'We did very well, actually,' said Daisy, when they got to Bets' playroom and sat down to talk things over. 'Only we found out things we didn't like at all. That *handkerchief*, Bets! I do feel so guilty. I'll never, ever do a thing like that again in my life.'

Larry and Pip came along about ten to twelve. They looked pleased with themselves.

'Hello girls! How did you get on?' said Pip. 'We did very well!'

So they had. They had biked down to the Little

Theatre, and had gone to the booking office to book the seats for the afternoon's show. But the office was closed.

'Let's snoop round a bit – because if anyone sees us, we can always say we've come to buy tickets, and we were looking for someone to ask,' said Pip. So they left the front of the theatre and went round to the back, trying various doors on the way. They were all locked.

They came to the car-park at the back of the theatre. A man was there, cleaning a motorbike. The boys had no idea who he was.

'That's a fine bike,' said Pip to Larry. The man heard their voices, and looked up. He was a middle-aged man, rather stout, with a thin-lipped mouth and bad-tempered lines on his forehead.

'What are you doing here?' he said.

'Well, we actually came to buy tickets for this afternoon's show,' said Larry. 'But the booking office is shut.'

'Of course it is. You can get the tickets when you come along this afternoon,' said the man, rubbing vigorously at the shining mudguards of the motorbike. 'We only open the booking office on Saturday mornings, when we expect plenty of people. Anyway, clear off now. I don't like loiterers – after that robbery on Friday I'm not putting up with anyone hanging around my theatre!'

'Oh – are you the manager, by any chance?' said Larry at once.

'Yes. I am. The man in the news! The man who was doped and robbed last Friday!' said the manager. 'If I could only get my hands on the one who did that job!'

'Have you any idea who did it?' asked Pip.

'None at all,' said the manager. 'I don't really believe it was that idiot of a Boysie. He'd never have been able to do all that. Anyway, he's too scared of me to try tricks of that sort – but he might have helped someone else do it. Someone he let in that night, when the theatre was empty!'

The boys were thrilled to hear all this first-hand information. 'It said in the paper that Boysie – the pantomime cat – brought you in your cup of tea – the one that was drugged,' said Larry. 'Did he, sir?'

'He certainly brought me in the tea,' said the manager. 'I was very busy, and only just glanced up to take it – but it was Boysie all right. He was still in his cat-skin so I couldn't mistake him. Too lazy to take it off. That's Boysie all over. I've even known him go to bed in it. But he's funny in the head, you know. Like a child. He couldn't have done the job by himself, though he must have had something to do with it – he's so easily led.'

'Then – somebody might have come back that night – been let in by Boysie – your tea might have been drugged – and taken up by Boysie to you as usual, so that you wouldn't suspect anything,' said Larry. 'And as soon as you were asleep, the one that Boysie let in must have crept up to your room, taken down the mirror, got the key from wherever you keep it, and opened the safe – and got away before you woke up.'

'That's about it,' said the manager, standing up to polish the handlebars. 'And, what's more, it must have been one of the cast, because no one knows as much about things as they do – why, whoever the thief was even knew that I didn't keep the safe key on my keyring – I always keep it in a secret pocket of my wallet. And only the cast knew that, for once, I hadn't put Thursday's takings into the bank, because they saw me coming back in a temper when I found out the bank was closed!'

The boys drank all this in. Some of it they already knew, but it sounded much more exciting and real to hear it from the lips of the manager himself. They didn't like him – he looked bad-tempered and mean. They could quite well imagine that he would have a lot of enemies who would like to pay him back for some spiteful thing he had said or done to them.

'I suppose the police are on the job all right,' said Pip, taking a duster and beginning to rub the spokes of the wheels.

'Oh yes. That constable – what's his name? – Mr Goon – has been practically *living* here this weekend – interviewing everyone. He's got poor Boysie so scared that I don't think he really knows what he's saying now. He shouts at him till Boysie bursts into tears.'

'Beast,' muttered Pip, and the manager looked at him in surprise.

'Oh, I don't know. If Boysie did it, he's got to get it out of him somehow. Anyway, it doesn't hurt him to be yelled at – only way to get things into his thick head sometimes!'

The motorbike was finished now, and shone brightly. The manager ran it into a shed. 'Well, that's done,' he said. 'Sorry I can't give you your tickets now. You'll get them easily enough this afternoon. There are never many people on Mondays.'

The boys went off, delighted at all they had learnt. To get the whole story from the manager himself was simply marvellous. Now they knew as much as Mr Goon did! It was certainly very, very mysterious. The pantomime cat *had* taken the drugged cup of tea to the manager – and if he hadn't put the sleeping-draught into it himself, he must have known who had done it – must even have let them in. He might even have watched while the thief took down the mirror and robbed the safe. Things looked very black for Boysie. Larry and Pip could quite well imagine how Mr Goon must have shouted and yelled at him to try and make him tell the name of the robber.

'Come on – it's a quarter to twelve. Let's get back,' said Larry, who was bursting to tell his news. 'I wonder how the girls have got on. They had an easy job, really. And so had Fatty – just got to question PC Pippin, and that's all.'

'I like this detecting business, don't you?' said Larry, as they cycled up the road. 'Of course, it's more difficult for us than for Mr Goon or PC Pippin – all they've got to do is go to anyone they like and ask questions, knowing that the people *must* answer the police – and they can go into any house they like and snoop around – but we can't.'

'No, we can't. But, on the other hand, we can perhaps pick up little bits of news that people might not tell Mr Goon,' said Pip. 'Look out – there's Mr Goon now!'

So it was – a frowning and majestic Mr Goon, riding his bicycle, and looking very important. He called out to them as he came near.

'Where's that big boy? You tell him if I see him again this morning, I'll go and complain to his parents. Poking his nose where he's not wanted! Where is he?'

'I don't know,' said Pip and Larry together, and grinned. What could Fatty have been doing now?

'You don't know! Gah! I bet you know where he's hiding, ready to pick Pippin's brains again. Does he think he's on this case too? Well, he's not.

I'm in charge of this. You tell him that!'

And with that, Mr Goon sailed off, leaving Larry and Pip full of curiosity to know what in the world Fatty had been doing now!

14. MORE NEWS - AND A VERY FAT FACE

Fatty had had rather a hectic morning. He had biked down to the road where Mr Goon lived, and had looked into the front room of the police cottage as he passed by. Only PC Pippin was there. Good!

Fatty leaned his bicycle against the little wall in front of the house, leaving Buster on guard. He then went down the front path, and knocked on the window of the room where PC Pippin was sitting, laboriously making out reports on this and that.

Pippin looked up and grinned. He opened the door to Fatty and took the boy into the front room.

'Any news?' said Fatty.

'Well,' said Pippin, 'there's a report on the safe and the mirror – about fingerprints. Not a single one to be found!'

'Then whoever did the job was wily,' said Fatty. 'Looks as if that rules out the pantomime cat!'

Pippin was about to speak again, when he heard Buster barking. They both looked out of the window. Mr Goon was just dismounting from his bicycle, looking as black as thunder. Buster parked himself in the middle of the gateway, and barked deliriously, as if to say, 'Yah! Can't come in! Woof, woof! Can't come in! Yah!'

'You'd better go,' said PC Pippin, hurriedly. 'I've a bit more news for you but you must go now.'

As Buster now showed every sign of being about to attack Mr Goon, Fatty hurriedly left the house and ran up to the front gate. He picked Buster up and put him in his bicycle basket.

'What you doing here?' blustered Mr Goon. 'I've warned Pippin against you, Mr Nosey Parker. You won't get anything out of *him*! He's not on this case. He doesn't know a thing – and he wouldn't tell you if he did. Clear orf! I'm tired of that cheeky face of yours.'

'Don't be rude, Mr Goon,' said Fatty, with dignity. He hated his face being called cheeky.

'Rude! I'm not rude – just truthful,' said Mr Goon, wheeling his bicycle in at the gate. 'I tell you. I don't want to see that fat face of yours any more today! I'm a busy man, with important things to do. I won't have you noseying around.'

He went in, pleased to think that Pippin had heard him treat that boy the way he ought to be treated. Aha! He, Mr Goon, was well on the way to solving a very difficult case. Got it all, he had – and for once, Frederick Algernon Trotteville was going to have his nose put out of joint. Him and his fat face!

With these pleasant thoughts to keep him company, Mr Goon went in to fire off a few sharp remarks to Pippin. Fatty, anxious to have a few more words with Pippin, rode up the road a little way, and then leaned his bicycle against a tree, putting himself the other side of the trunk so that he might watch unseen for Mr Goon to come out and ride off again. The policeman had left his bicycle against the wall of his cottage, as if he meant to come out again in a little while.

Fatty stood and brooded over Goon's rude remarks about his face. Goon thought he had a fat face, did he? All right – he'd show him one! Fatty slipped his hand into his pocket and brought out two nice new plump cheek-pads. He slipped one into each cheek, between his teeth and the fleshy part of the cheek.

At once, he took on a most swollen, blown-out look.

Mr Goon came out of his house in a few minutes and mounted his bicycle. He rode slowly up the road. Fatty came out from behind his tree to show himself to Mr Goon.

'You here again?' began Goon, wobbling in rage. 'You . . .'

And then he caught sight of Fatty's enormously blown-out cheeks. He blinked and looked again. Fatty grinned, and his cheeks almost burst.

Mr Goon got off his bicycle, unable to believe his eyes, but Fatty jumped on his and sailed away. He waited in a side road, riding up and down, till he thought Mr Goon must have gone, and then cycled back to Pippin.

'It's all right,' said PC Pippin, from the window. 'He's gone to send a telegram and after that he's going to the theatre car-park to snoop round again, and then he's got to go to Loo Farm about a dog. He won't be back for some time.'

Fatty had now taken out his cheek-pads and looked quite normal again.

'I won't keep you more than a few minutes,' he told PC Pippin. 'I know you're busy. What other news have you?'

'Well, there *was* a sleeping-draught in that cup all right,' said Pippin. 'A harmless one, but strong. Traces of it were found in the cup. So that's proved all right.'

'Anything else?' enquired Fatty. 'Has the money been traced?'

'No. And it won't be either,' said Pippin. 'It was all in used notes and coins.'

'Any idea yet who did the job?' asked Fatty.

'Well, I've seen Mr Goon's notes, and if you want a *motive* for the robbery – someone with a spite against the manager – any of the company would do for the thief!' said Pippin. 'Mr Goon wasn't going to tell me anything, as you know, but he's so proud of himself for finding out so much, that he gave me his notes to read. Said it would do me good to see how an expert got to work on a case like this!'

Fatty grinned. 'Yes – the sort of thing he *would* say. But what do you mean – all the company had a spite against the manager?'

'Mr Goon interviewed the manager, and got quite a lot out of him,' said PC Pippin. 'Now – take Zoe Markham – she had a row with him that morning and got the sack. And now Lucy White – asked him to lend her some money because her mother was ill, and he raged at her and refused. And here's Peter Watting and William Orr – they want to do a series of decent straight plays here instead of this comic stuff, and the manager laughed at them – told them they were only fit for third-rate comedy stuff. Said that third-rate people would have to be content with third-rate shows.'

'I bet they were angry,' said Fatty.

'Yes. They were furious apparently,' said Pippin. 'Almost came to blows. Threatened to harrass him if he called them third-rate again. As a matter of fact, they are quite good, especially William Orr.'

'Go on,' said Fatty. 'This is interesting. Who else has a grudge against him?'

'John James wanted a rise in his salary,' said Pippin. 'Apparently the manager had promised him this after six months' run. So he asked for it and was refused. The manager said he never promised him anything of the sort.'

'Nice amiable chap, this manager,' said Fatty with a grin. 'Always ready to help! My word, what a way to run a company! They must all hate him.'

'They do!' said Pippin. 'Even poor Boysie, the pantomime cat, detests him. Now let me see – is that the lot? No – here's Alec Grant. He wanted permission to go and act in another show on the days he's not on here – and the manager wouldn't let him. There was an awful row about that apparently – so, you see, there are plenty of people who would very much like to pay the manager back for his spiteful treatment of them!'

'What about their alibis?' asked Fatty, after a pause to digest all this.

'All checked,' said Pippin. 'And all correct, except that there's a query about Zoe Markham, because she went out of her sister's house that evening, and nobody saw her come back; she says she went straight up to her room. So, what with that fact and the Z on the handkerchief found on the verandah, Goon's got her and Boysie down as chief suspects now!'

This wasn't very pleasant. PC Pippin bent over his papers. 'Well,' he said, 'that's all I can tell you for the present – and don't you let on I've told you either! You'd better go now – and don't forget to let me know if *you've* got anything interesting up your sleeve.'

'I haven't at the moment,' said Fatty soberly. 'Except that I hope Mr Goon was tired after his afternoon walk yesterday!'

Pippin looked up at once. 'What – trailing that redheaded foreigner! You don't mean to say he was *you*!'

'Well – I thought Mr Goon might as well meet *somebody* off the three thirty train!' said Fatty. 'You'd have thought he would have been a bit suspicious of redheads by now, wouldn't you, PC Pippin?'

And with that Fatty went off whistling on his bicycle, thinking hard. A thought struck him. He put his cheek-pads in, and rode off to the post office. Goon might still be there.

He was. Fatty sidled into the nearby phone kiosk as Mr Goon came out of the post office. The policeman saw someone grinning at him from the kiosk and stopped. He gazed in horror at Fatty, whose cheeks were now as enormous as when Goon had seen him a short time before.

Fatty nodded and grinned amiably. Goon walked off puzzled. That boy! His face seemed fatter than ever. He couldn't be blowing it out with his breath, because he was grinning. He must have some disease!

Fatty shot off on his bicycle, taking a short cut to the car-park behind the theatre. He took his bike to the shed, and bent over it. In a moment or two, Goon came sailing in on *his* bicycle, and dismounted to put it into the shed. He saw a boy there, but took no notice – till Fatty turned round and presented him with yet another wonderful view of his cheeky face.

Goon got a shock. He peered closely at Fatty. 'You got toothache?' he enquired. 'Talk about a chubby face!'

He disappeared into the theatre, and Fatty rode off to Loo Farm. He waited there for ten minutes, sitting on his bicycle behind a wall. When he spotted Goon coming along, he rode out suddenly, and once again Mr Goon got a fine view of a full moon face shining out at him.

'Now you clear orf!' yelled Mr Goon. 'Following me about like this! You with your fat face and all. You go and see a dentist. Gah! Think yourself funny, following me about with that face?'

'But Mr Goon – it looks as if you're following *me* about,' protested Fatty. 'I go to use the phone, and you are there! I go to the car-park and you come there too. And I call at Loo Farm and, hey presto, you come along here as well! What are you following ME for? Do you think *I* did the robbery at the Little Theatre?'

Mr Goon looked in puzzled distaste at Fatty's fat face. He couldn't make it out. How could anyone's face get as fat as that so suddenly? Was he seeing double?

He decided not to call at Loo Farm while that boy was hanging round with his full moon face. Mr Goon rode away down the road defeated.

'Beast!' he murmured to himself. 'Regular beast, that boy. No doing anything with him. Well, he don't know how well I've got on with this case. Give him a shock when he finds it's all cleared up, arrests been made, and sees the Inspector giving me a pat on the back! Him and his fat face!'

Fatty looked at his watch. It was getting on for twelve. He'd better go back and join the others. What news had they been able to get?

He rode up to Pip's house. They were all there, waiting for him. Bets waved out of the window.

'Hurry *up*, Fatty! We've all got plenty of news! We thought you were *never* coming!'

15. AT THE SHOW AND AFTERWARDS

The children sat down in Pip's big playroom, a bag
of chocolates between them, supplied by Larry.

'Well – it looks as if we've all got something to
report,' said Fatty. 'Girls first. How did you get on,
Daisy and Bets?'

Taking it in turns to supply the news, Bets and
Daisy told their story. 'Wasn't it *lucky* to see Zoe
herself?' said Daisy. 'She's sweet, she really is. *She*
couldn't possibly have done the job, Fatty.'

'But isn't it awful about the hanky with Z on?'
said Bets. 'And oh, Fatty – she smokes the same
kind of cigarettes as our cigarette-ends were made
of – "Players"!'

'Well, Mr Goon will probably find that most of
the others smoke them too, so we needn't worry so
much about that,' said Fatty. 'I'm sorry about that
hanky business, though. *Why* did we put Z on that

silly hanky!'

'Don't you think we ought to tell Mr Goon that – I mean, about us putting the hanky down for a false clue?' said Daisy, anxiously. 'I can't bear Mr Goon going after poor Zoe with a false clue like that – it's awful for her.'

'It can't *prove* anything,' said Fatty, thinking hard. 'If it *had* been hers, she might have dropped it any old time, not just that evening. I don't see that Mr Goon can make it really *prove* anything.'

'Neither do I,' said Larry. 'We'll own up when the case is finished – but I don't see much point in us spoiling our own chances of solving the mystery by confessing to Mr Goon.'

'All right,' said Daisy. 'Only I can't *help* feeling awful about it.'

'I must say you two girls did very well,' said Fatty. 'You got a lot of most interesting information. What about you, Larry and Pip?'

Then Larry and Pip told of their meeting with the manager, and related in great detail all he had said to them. Fatty listened eagerly. This was fantastic!

'Well – that was fine,' he said when the two boys had finished. 'I feel there's absolutely no doubt at all now that it was Boysie who took in the doped tea. Well – if he *did* do the job – or helped somebody to do it – he certainly made it quite clear that he was in it, by taking the tea to the manager! I suppose he didn't realise that the remains of the tea would show the traces of the sleeping-draught. It's the sort of thing someone like Boysie would forget.'

'Well – we shall see him this afternoon,' said Daisy. 'I forgot to tell you, Fatty, that we arranged with Zoe to meet all the members of the show after it has finished this afternoon, for autographs. So we shall see Boysie as well.'

'Very good,' said Fatty pleased. 'You all seem to have done marvellously. I consider I've trained you really well!'

He was completely pummelled for that remark. When peace had been restored again, Larry asked him how *he* had got on – and he related all that Pippin had told him.

'It's funny that every single member of the show had a grudge against the manager, isn't it?' he said. 'He must be a beast. He did just the kind of things that would make people want to pay him back. Motives sticking out everywhere!'

'What are motives?' Bets wanted to know.

'Good reasons for doing something,' explained Fatty. 'Understand? The show people all had good reasons for getting back at their manager – motives for paying him back for his beastliness.'

'It's a very interesting mystery, this,' said Larry. 'Seven people could have done the job – all of them have good motives for getting even with the manager – and all of them, except Boysie, and perhaps Zoe, have good alibis. And we don't think either of those would have done the job! Zoe sounds much too nice.'

'I agree,' said Fatty. 'It's a super mystery. A proper Who-Dun-It.'

'What's *that*?' said Bets at once.

'Oh dear,' said Pip. 'Bets – a Whodunit is a mystery with a crime in it that people have got to solve – to find out who did it.'

'Well, what's it called a Whodunit for then?' said Bets, sensibly. 'I shall call it a Who-Did-It.'

'You call it what you like,' said Fatty grinning. 'So long as we find out who-dun-it or who-did-it, it doesn't matter what we call it. Now – what's the next step?'

'We'll all go to the show this afternoon, watch everyone acting, and then go round and collect autographs, speak to all the members of the show, and take particular notice of Boysie,' said Larry, at once.

'Go up top,' said Fatty. 'And tomorrow we go after the rest of the alibis. Larry and Daisy will go to see Mary Adams, to find out if Lucy White's alibi is sound – and Pip and I will see if we can test Peter Watting's and William Orr's. We shall have to find out how to check John James too – he went to the cinema all evening – or so he said.'

'Yes – and Alec Grant's,' said Daisy. 'He went to Sheepridge and gave a show there on his own.'

'Silly to check that really,' said Pip. 'So many people heard and saw him. Anyway, it will be jolly easy to check.'

'There's Mummy calling us for dinner,' said Pip. 'I must go and wash. What time shall we meet this afternoon? And where? Down at the theatre?'

'Yes,' said Fatty. 'Be there at a quarter to three. The show starts at three. So long!'

They were all very hungry indeed for their meal. Detecting was hungry work, it seemed! Fatty spent a long time after his meal writing out all the things he knew about the mystery. It made very interesting reading indeed. Fatty read it over afterwards, and felt puzzled. So many suspects, so many motives, so many alibis – how in the world would they ever unravel them all?

At a quarter to three, all the Find-Outers were down at the Little Theatre. A young boy was in the booking office, and sold them their tickets. They passed into the theatre and found their seats. They had taken them as far forward as they could, so as to be able to observe the actors very closely.

They were in the middle of the second row – very good seats indeed. Someone was playing the piano softly. There was no band, of course, for the show was only a small one. The stage curtain shook a little in the draughts that came in each time the door was opened. The children gazed at it, admiring the marvellous sunset depicted on the great sheet.

The show began punctually. The curtain went up exactly at three o'clock, and the audience sat up in expectation.

There were two plays and a skit on Dick Whittington's Pantomime. In the first two plays,

Boysie did not appear, but he came in at the last one, and the children shouted with delight as he shuffled in on all fours, dressed in the big furry skin that the boys had seen through the window on Friday night.

He was very funny. He waved to the children just as he had waved to the three boys when they had peered in to see him on Friday night. He capered about, cuddled up to Zoe Markham (who was Dick Whittington and looked very fine indeed), and was altogether quite a success.

'Zoe looks lovely,' said Larry.

'Yes – but why do the principal boys parts *always* have to be taken by girls,' said Daisy, in the interval of a change of scenery. 'Do you remember in Aladdin, it was a girl who took Aladdin's part – and in Cinderella, a girl took the part of the Prince.'

'Shh!' said Bets. 'The curtain is going up again. Oh, there's the cat! And, oh, look – his skin is splitting down by his tail!'

So it was. The cat seemed to realise this and kept feeling the hole with his front paw. 'Meeow,' he said, 'meeow!' Almost as if he was a real cat, dismayed at the splitting of his coat!

'I hope he doesn't split it all the way down,' said

Bets. 'I bet he'd get into a row with that awful manager, if he did. Oh, isn't he funny! He's pretending to go after a mouse. *Is* it a mouse?'

'Only a clockwork one,' said Daisy. 'Well, Boysie may be peculiar in his head and all that – but I think he's really clever in his acting. I do really.'

Fatty thought so too. He was wondering if anyone quite so good at acting could be as silly as people said. Well – he would see if he could talk to Boysie afterwards – then he could make up his own mind about him.

The show came to an end. The curtain came down, went up once, and came down again. It stayed down. Everyone clapped and then got up to go home. It was past five o'clock.

'Now let's rush round to the stage door,' said Fatty. 'Come on!'

So, autograph books in hand, the five of them tore round to the stage door, anxious to catch all the actors and actresses before they left.

They waited for five minutes. Then Zoe came to the door, still with some of the greasepaint on her pretty face. But she had changed into a suit now, and looked quite different.

'Come along in and meet the others inside,' she said. 'They won't be out for a few minutes and it's cold standing at that door.'

So, feeling a little nervous, the five children trooped in at the stage door and followed Zoe to a big room, where one or two of the actors were gulping down cups of tea.

Peter Watting and William Orr were there, one elderly and rather sour-looking, one young and rather miserable-looking. They didn't look nearly so fine as they had done on the stage, when Peter had been Dick's master and William had been a very dashing captain, singing a loud, jolly song of the sea, the blue, blue sea!

They nodded at the children. 'Hello, kids! Autograph hunting? Well, we're flattered, I'm sure! Hand over your books.'

The two men scribbled in each book. Then Zoe introduced them to Lucy White, a tall, gentle-looking girl who had been Dick Whittington's sweetheart in the play. She had looked really beautiful on the stage, with a great mass of flowing golden curls, which the children had admired very much. But the mass of curls now stood on a side table – a grand wig – and Lucy was seen to be a quiet, brown-haired girl with a rather worried face.

She signed the books too. Then John James came in, burly, dour, and heavy-footed, a big man, just right for the king in the play. 'Hello!' he said. 'You don't mean to say that somebody wants our autographs! Well, well! Here's fame for you!'

He signed the books too. Fatty began to get into conversation with William and Peter. Larry tried to talk to John James. Pip looked round. Surely there should be somebody else to ask to sign their books?

There was – and he came in at that moment, a small, dapper little man, who had played the part of Dick's mother on the stage. He had been very good as the mother – neat and nimble, using an amusing high voice, and even singing two or three songs in a woman's voice very cleverly indeed.

'Could we have your autograph please?' said Fatty, going up to him. 'I did like your performance. I could have sworn you were a woman! Even your voice!'

'Yes – Alec was in great form with his singing today,' said Zoe. 'Got his high notes beautifully! You should see him imitate me and Lucy – imitates us really well, so that you'd hardly know it wasn't us! We tell him he's lost in this little company. He ought to be in the West End!'

'He thinks that himself, don't you Alec?' said John James, in a slightly mocking voice. 'But the manager doesn't agree with him.'

'Don't talk to me about *him*,' said Alec. 'We all detest the fellow. Here you are, kids – catch! And I hope you can read my signature!'

He threw them their books. Fatty opened his and saw a most illegible scrawl that he could just make out to be 'Alec Grant' – but only just.

Zoe laughed. 'He always writes like that. Nobody can ever read his writing. I tell him he might just as well write "Hot Potatoes" or "Peppermint Creams" and nobody would know the difference. I wonder your mother can ever read your letters, Alec.'

'She can't,' said Alec. 'She waits till I get home and then she gets me to read them to her. And I can't!'

Everyone laughed. 'Well, so long,' said Alec, winding a yellow scarf round his neck. 'See you tomorrow. And mind none of you knock the manager on the head tonight!'

16. THE PANTOMIME CAT HAS A TEA PARTY

The children thought they ought to go too. Fatty felt as if they had stayed too long already. Then he remembered something.

'Oh – what about the pantomime cat? We haven't got *his* autograph. Where is he?'

'Clearing up the stage, I expect,' said Zoe. 'That's one of his jobs. But he won't sign your albums for you – poor old Boysie can't write.'

'Can't he, *really*?' said Bets, in amazement. 'But I thought he was grown-up – isn't he?'

'Yes – he's twenty-four,' said Zoe. 'But he's like a kid of six. He can hardly read either. But he's a dear, he really is. I'll go and get him for you.'

But before she could go, the pantomime cat came in. He walked on his hind legs, and had thrown back the furry cat-skin head, so that it looked like a grotesque hood.

He had a big head, small eyes, set too close together, teeth that stuck out in front like a rabbit's, and a very scared expression on his face.

He came up to Zoe and put his hand in hers like a child. 'Zoe,' he said. 'Zoe must help Boysie.'

'What is it, Boysie?' said Zoe, speaking as if Boysie was a child. 'Tell Zoe.'

'Look,' said Boysie, and turned himself round dolefully. Everyone looked – and saw a big split in poor Boysie's cat-skin, near the tail. It had got much bigger since Bets had noticed it.

'And look,' said Boysie, pointing to a split down his tummy. 'Zoe can mend it for Boysie?'

'Yes Boysie, of course,' said Zoe kindly, and the cat slipped his hand in hers again, smiling up at her. He only reached to her shoulder. 'You're getting fat, Boysie,' said Zoe. 'Eating too much, and splitting your skin!'

Boysie now saw the children for the first time and smiled at them with real pleasure. 'Children,' he said, pointing at them. 'Why are they here?'

'They came to talk to us, Boysie,' said Zoe. ('He wouldn't understand what I meant if I said you wanted autographs,' she whispered to Fatty.)

Peter Watting and William Orr, tall and thin, now said good-bye and went. Lucy White followed, leaving her wig of golden curls behind. Boysie put it on and ran round the room grinning, looking perfectly dreadful.

'See? He's just like a six-year-old, isn't he?' said Zoe. 'But he's so simple and kind – does anything he can for any of us. He's very clever with his fingers – he can carve wood beautifully. Look – here are some of the things Boysie has made for me.'

She took down a row of small wooden animals, most beautifully carved. Boysie, still in his golden wig, came and stood by them, smiling with pleasure.

'Boysie! I think they're *beautiful*,' said Bets, overcome with admiration. 'How *do* you do such lovely carving? Oh, *look* at this little lamb – it's perfect.'

Boysie suddenly ran out of the room. He came back with another little lamb, rather like the one Bets admired. He pressed it into her hand, smiling foolishly, his small eyes full of tears.

'You have this,' he said. 'I like you.'

Bets turned and looked at him. She did not see the ugly face, the too-close eyes, the big-toothed mouth. She only saw the half-scared kindness that lay behind them all. She gave him a sudden hug, thinking of him as if he were a child much younger and smaller than herself.

'There! See how pleased the little girl is,' said Zoe. 'That's nice of you, Boysie.'

She turned to the others. 'He's always like that,' she said. 'He'd give away the shirt off his back if he could. You can't help liking him, can you?'

'No,' said everyone, and it was true. Boysie was funny in the head and silly, he was ugly to look at – but he was kind and sincere and humble, he had a sense of fun – and you simply *couldn't* help liking him.

'I can't bear it when people are unkind to Boysie,' said Zoe. 'Sometimes the manager is, and I just see red then. I did last Friday, didn't I Boysie?'

Boysie's face clouded over and he nodded. 'You mustn't go away,' he said to Zoe, and put his hand in hers. 'You mustn't leave Boysie.'

'He says that because the manager gave me notice on Friday,' said Zoe. 'He's afraid I'll go. But I won't. The manager doesn't want to lose me really – though I'd like a bit of a rest. But he said this afternoon he didn't mean what he said last Friday. He's a funny one. Nobody likes him.'

'I say – I suppose we really ought to go,' said Fatty. 'Are you coming, Zoe – may we call you Zoe?'

'Of course,' said Zoe. 'Well, no, I won't go yet. I must mend Boysie's cat-skin. I'll stay and have tea with him, I think. I say, Boysie – shall we ask all these nice children to stay to tea too?'

Boysie was thrilled. He stroked Zoe's arm, and then took Bets' hand. 'Boysie will make tea,' he said. 'You sit down.'

'Boysie, aren't you going to take off your cat-skin?' asked Zoe. 'You'll be so hot – and you might split it even more.'

Boysie paid no attention. He went off into a small cupboard-like place, and they heard him filling a kettle.

'We'd *love* to stay,' said Fatty, who thought Zoe was just about the nicest person he had ever seen. 'If we're no bother. Shall I pop out and buy some buns?'

'Yes. That would be a lovely idea,' said Zoe. 'Where's my purse? I'll give you the money.'

'I've plenty, thank you,' said Fatty hastily. 'I

won't be long! Coming Larry?'

He and Larry disappeared. Boysie watched for the kettle to boil, which it soon did. Just as he turned it off, Fatty and Larry came back with a collection of jammy buns, chocolate cakes and ginger biscuits.

'There's a plate in the cupboard where Boysie is,' said Zoe. 'My word – what a feast!'

Fatty went into the little cupboard. He watched Boysie with interest. The little fellow, still in his cat-skin, had warmed the brown teapot. He now tipped out the water from the pot and put in some tea.

'How many spoons of tea, Zoe?' he called.

'Oh, four will do,' said Zoe. 'Count them for him, will you? – he can't count very well.'

'I can count four,' said Boysie indignantly, but proceeded to put five in instead. Then he poured boiling water into the pot and put the lid on.

'Do you make tea every evening?' asked Fatty, and Boysie nodded.

'Yes. He's good at making tea,' said Zoe, as Boysie carried the teapot in and set it down on the table. 'He usually makes it for us as soon as the show is over – and then he makes some for the manager much later. Don't you Boysie?'

To the children's alarm, Boysie suddenly burst into tears. 'I didn't take him his tea. I didn't,' he wept.

'He's remembering about last Friday,' said Zoe, patting Boysie comfortingly. 'That policeman keeps on and on at him, trying to make him say he took a cup of tea to the manager and Boysie keeps saying he didn't. Though the manager says he *did*. I expect Boysie has got muddled and has forgotten.'

'Tell us about it, Boysie,' said Fatty, rather thrilled at getting so much first-hand information. 'You don't need to worry about talking to *us*. We're your friends. We know you didn't have anything to do with what happened on Friday night.'

'I didn't, did I?' said Boysie, looking at Zoe. 'You all went, Zoe. You didn't stay with Boysie like today. I was in my cat-skin because it's hard to take off by myself. You know it is. And I went into the back room where there's a fire!'

'He means the room behind the verandah,' explained Zoe. 'There's an electric fire there that Boysie likes to sit by.'

'And I saw you – and you – and you,' said Boysie surprisingly, poking his paw at Fatty, Larry, and

Pip. 'Not you,' he added, poking Bets and Daisy.

'You never said that before,' said Zoe in surprise. 'That's naughty, Boysie. You *didn't* see these children.'

'I did. They looked in the window,' said Boysie. 'I looked at them too. I frightened them! They looked again and I waved to them to tell them not to be frightened, because they are nice children.'

The five children looked at one another. *They* knew that Boysie was telling the truth. He *had* seen them that Friday night – he *had* waved to them.

'Did you tell the policeman this?' asked Fatty suddenly.

Boysie shook his head. 'No. Boysie didn't remember then. Remembers now.'

'What did you do after the children had gone?' asked Fatty gently.

'I made some tea,' said Boysie, screwing up his face to remember. 'Some for me and some for the manager.'

'Did you drink yours first?' asked Fatty. 'Or did you take *his* up first?'

'Mine was hot,' said Boysie. 'Very hot. Too hot. I played till it was cool, then I drank it.'

'*Then* did you pour out the manager's tea and take it to him?' asked Fatty. Boysie blinked his eyes and a hunted look came over his face.

'No,' he said. 'No, no, no! I didn't take it, I didn't, I didn't! I was tired. I lay down on the rug and I went to sleep. But I didn't take the tea upstairs. Don't make me say I did. I didn't, I didn't.'

There was a long pause. Everyone was wondering what to say. Fatty spoke first.

'Have a jammy bun everyone. Here, Boysie, there's an extra-jammy one for you – and don't you bother any more about that tea. Forget it!'

17. CHECKING UP THE ALIBIS

No more was said about Friday evening after that.
It was quite clear that talking about it upset Boysie
terribly. Fatty was very puzzled indeed. Boysie
had taken up the tea – the manager said so quite
definitely because, as now, he was still in his cat-
skin and was quite unmistakable. Then what was
the point of Boysie denying it? Was he trying to
shield somebody in his foolish way, by denying
everything to do with the doped cup of tea?

If so – who was he trying to shield? Zoe? No!
Nobody could possibly suspect Zoe of drugging
anyone's tea, or robbing a safe. Nobody – except
Mr Goon!

It was imperative to check up on all the other
alibis. If there was a single chink in any of them,
that was probably the person Boysie was trying to
shield. Fatty made up his mind that every other

alibi must be gone into the next day without fail. If he couldn't find something definite, it looked as if the poor old pantomime cat would be arrested, and Zoe too! Because Mr Goon would be sure that Zoe, whom Boysie obviously adored, was the person he was shielding.

It was a curious tea party, but the children enjoyed it. Towards the end, a loud voice came down the stairs outside the room.

'What's all the row down there? Who's there? I can hear *your* voice, Zoe!'

Zoe went to the door. 'Yes, I'm here. I'm stopping behind to mend Boysie's cat-skin. It's all split. And there are a few children here too, who came for our autographs. They're having a cup of tea with me and Boysie.'

'You tell them to be careful Boysie doesn't put something in their tea then!' shouted the manager, and went back to his room, banging the door loudly.

'Pleasant fellow, isn't he?' said Larry. 'We met him this morning. A very nasty bit of work.'

'I couldn't agree more,' said Zoe. 'Well dears, you'd better go. Get out of your skin, Boysie, if you want me to mend it.'

The children said good-bye, shaking hands with both Zoe and Boysie. Boysie looked intensely pleased at all this ceremony. He bowed each time he shook hands.

'A pleasure,' he said to each of them. 'A pleasure!'

They all went to get their bikes, which they had left in the stand inside the shed. 'Well! Fancy getting asked inside, meeting everyone, and having tea with Zoe and Boysie!' said Fatty, pleased.

'Yes. And hearing his own story,' said Larry, pushing his bike out into the yard. 'Do you believe him, Fatty?'

'Well, I know it's quite impossible that he shouldn't have taken in that cup of tea, but yet I feel Boysie's speaking the truth,' said Fatty. 'I've never been so puzzled in my life. One minute I think one thing and the next I think another.'

'Well, *Zoe* didn't do it,' said Bets loyally. 'She's much, much, much too nice.'

'I agree with you,' said Fatty. 'She couldn't have done that robbery any more than *you* could, Bets. Well, we must look elsewhere, that's all. We must check all the rest of the alibis tomorrow without fail.'

So, the next morning, the Find-Outers started off with their checking. Larry and Daisy set off to Mary Adams' flat, to find out about the gentle Lucy White. Fatty and Pip went off by the river, to find 'The Turret' and discover if William Orr and Peter Watting *had* been there on Friday night, as they said.

'Then we'll check up on John James and the cinema if we can this afternoon,' said Fatty, 'And on Alec Grant as well, if we've time. We'll have to look lively now, because it seems to me that Mr Goon will move soon. If he sees that poor Boysie any more he'll send him *right* off his head!'

Daisy found a half-embroidered cushion cover which she had never finished. She took the silks that went with it and wrapped the whole lot up in a parcel. 'Come along,' she said to Larry. 'We'll soon find out about Lucy White – though, honestly, I think it's a waste of time checking *her* alibi. She doesn't look as if she could say boo to a goose!'

They arrived at Mary Adams' flat and went upstairs to her front door. They rang, and the old lady opened the door.

'Well, well, well – *what* a surprise,' she said, pleased. 'Daisy *and* Larry. It's a long time since I've seen you – what enormous children you've grown into. You come along in.'

She led the way into her tiny sitting-room. She took down a tin of chocolate biscuits from the mantelpiece and offered them one. She was a small, white-haired old lady, almost crippled with rheumatism now, but still able to sew and knit.

Daisy opened her parcel. 'Mary, do you think you could possibly finish this cushion cover for me before Easter? I want to give it to Mummy, and I know I shan't have time to finish it myself, because I'm embroidering her some hankies too. How much would you charge for doing it for me?'

'Not a penny, Daisy,' said Mary Adams, beaming. 'It would be a pleasure to do something for you, and especially something that's going to be given to your dear mother. Bless your dear heart, I'd love to finish it just for love and nothing else.'

'Thank you so much Mary,' said Daisy. 'It's very kind of you – and I'll bring you some of our daffodils as soon as they're properly out. They're very behind this year.'

'Have another biscuit?' said Mary, taking down the tin again. 'Well, it *is* nice to see you both. I've been ill, you know, and haven't been out much. So it's a real change to see a visitor or two.'

'Do you know Lucy White?' said Larry. 'We got her autograph this afternoon. She's a friend of yours, isn't she?'

'Yes – dear Lucy! She came to see me every night last week, when I was bad,' said Mary. 'I had a lot of knitting to finish and that kind girl came in and helped me till it was all done.'

'Did she come on Friday too?' asked Daisy.

'Ah – you're like that Mr Goon – he's been round here three times asking questions about Friday evening,' said Mary. 'Yes, Lucy came along about quarter to six, and we sat and knitted till half past nine, when she went home. We heard the nine o'clock news, and she made us some cocoa, with some biscuits, and we had *such* a nice time together.'

Well, that seemed pretty definite.

'Didn't Lucy leave you at all, till half past nine?' said Daisy.

'Not once. She didn't so much as go out of the

178

room,' said Mary. 'There we sat in our chairs, knitting away for dear life – and the next day, Lucy took all the knitting we'd done that week and delivered it for me. She's a good kind girl.'

There came a ring at the door. 'I'll go for you,' said Daisy and got up. She opened the door – and there was Mr Goon, red in the face from climbing the steps to Mary's flat! He glared suspiciously at Daisy.

'What are *you* doing here?' he demanded. 'Poking your noses in?'

'We came to ask Mary to do some sewing,' said Daisy, in a dignified voice.

'Oh yes!' said Mr Goon, disbelievingly. 'Mary Adams in?'

'Yes I am,' called Mary Adams' voice, sounding rather cross. 'Is that you again, Mr Goon? I've nothing more to say to you. Please go away. Wasting my time like this!'

'I just want to ask you a few more questions,' said Mr Goon, walking into the little sitting-room.

'Theophilus Goon, since you were a nasty little boy *so* high, you've always been a one for asking snoopy questions,' said Mary Adams, and the two children heard Mr Goon snort angrily. They called good-bye and fled away, laughing.

'I bet he *was* a nasty little boy too!' said Larry, as they went down the stairs. 'Well, that was easy, Daisy.'

'Very,' said Daisy. 'And quite definite too. It rules out Lucy White. I do wonder how the others are getting on.'

Bets was waiting at home with Buster. She had wanted to go with Pip and Fatty, but Fatty had said no, she had better stay with Buster. He and Pip had gone off down by the river, taking the road along which William Orr and Peter Watting had said they went.

They came to a tall and narrow house, with a little turret. On the gate was its name. 'The Turret. Coffee, sandwiches, snacks.'

'Well, here we are,' said Fatty. 'We'll try the coffee, sandwiches, snacks. I feel very hungry.'

So in they went and found a nice table looking out on a primrose garden. A small girl came to serve them. She didn't look more than about twelve, though she must have been a good deal older.

'Coffee for two, please,' said Fatty. 'And

sandwiches. And something snacky.'

The girl laughed. 'I'll bring you a tray of snacks,' she said. 'Then you can help yourselves.'

She brought them two cups of hot, steaming coffee, a plate of egg, potted meat, and cress sandwiches, and a tray of delicious-looking snacks.

'Ha! *We've* chosen the right place to come and check up on alibis,' said Fatty, eyeing the tray with delight. 'Look at all this!'

The boys ate the sandwiches, and then chose a snack. It was delicious. 'Come on – let's carry on with the snacks,' said Fatty. 'We've had a long walk and I'm hungry. I don't care if I *do* spoil my dinner – it's a really good way to spoil it – most enjoyable.'

'But have you got enough money to pay, Fatty?' asked Larry anxiously. 'I haven't got much on me.'

'Plenty,' said the wealthy Fatty, and rattled his pockets. 'We'll start on checking the alibi as soon as we've finished our meal. Hello – LOOK who's here!'

It was Mr Goon! He walked in as if he owned the place, and then he saw Fatty!

18. MORE CHECKING - AND A FEW SNACKS

Mr Goon advanced on Fatty's table. 'Everywhere I go,' boomed Mr Goon, 'I see some of you kids. Now, what are you doing *here*?'

'Eating,' said Fatty politely. 'Did you come in for a snack too, Mr Goon? Not much left, unfortunately.'

'You hold your tongue,' said Mr Goon.

'But you asked me a question,' objected Fatty. 'You said . . .'

'I know what I said,' said Mr Goon. 'I'm fed up with you kids! I go to Mary Adams and I see some of you there. I come here and here you are again. And I bet when I go somewhere else, you'll be there as well! Lot of pests you are.'

'It's funny how often we see *you* too, Mr Goon,' said Fatty, in the pleasant, polite voice that always infuriated Mr Goon. 'Quite a treat.'

Mr Goon swelled up and his face went purple. Then the little girl came into the room, and he turned to her pompously. 'Is your mother in? I want a word with her.'

'No, she's not, sir,' said the little girl. 'I'm the only one here. Mother will be back soon, if you would like to wait.'

'I can't wait,' said Mr Goon, annoyed. 'Too much to do. I'll come tomorrow.'

He was just going when he turned to look at Fatty. He had suddenly remembered his fat cheeks. They didn't seem nearly so fat now.

'What you done to make your cheeks thin?' he said suspiciously.

'Well – I *might* have had all my back teeth out,' said Fatty. 'Let me see – did I Larry? Do you remember?'

'Gah!' said Mr Goon, and went. The little girl laughed uproariously.

'Oh, you are funny!' she said. 'You really are. Isn't he horrid? He came and asked Mummy and me ever so many questions about two men that came here last Friday night.'

'Oh yes,' said Fatty, at once. 'I know the men

– actors, aren't they? I've got their autographs in my autograph album. Were they here on Friday then? I bet they liked your snacks.'

'Yes, they came on Friday,' said the little girl. 'I know, because it was my birthday, and Peter Watting brought me a book. I'd just been listening to Radio Fun at half past six, when they came in.'

'Half past six,' said Fatty. 'Well, what did they do then? Eat all your snacks?'

'No! They only had coffee and sandwiches,' said the little girl. 'They gave me the book – it's a beauty, I'll show you – and then we listened to Radio Theatre at seven o'clock. And then something went wrong with the radio and it stopped.'

'Oh,' said Fatty disappointed, because he had been counting on the radio for checking up on the time. 'What happened then?'

'Well, Peter Watting's very good with radios,' said the little girl. 'So he said he'd try and mend it. Mummy said, "Mend it in time for eight o'clock then, because I want to hear a concert then".'

'And was it mended by then?' asked Fatty.

'No. Not till twenty past eight,' said the little girl. 'Mummy was very disappointed. But we got it going by then, quite all right – twenty past eight, I mean – and then Peter and William had to go. They caught the ferry and went across the river.'

This was all very interesting. It certainly proved beyond a doubt that William Orr and Peter Watting could not possibly have had anything to do with the robbery at the Little Theatre. That was certain. The little girl was quite obviously telling the truth.

'Well, thanks for a really good tea,' said Fatty. 'How much do we owe you?'

The little girl gave a squeal. 'Oh, I never counted your snacks. Do you know how many you had? I shan't half be in trouble with Mummy if she knows I didn't count.'

'Well, you ought to count,' said Fatty. 'It's too much like hard work for us to count when we're eating. Larry, I make it six snacks each, the sandwiches and the coffee. Is that correct?'

It was. Fatty paid up, gave the little girl a coin to buy herself something for the birthday she had had on Friday, and went off with Larry, feeling decidedly full.

'We've just got time to go to the cinema to see if we can pick up anything about John James' visit,' said Fatty. 'Oh dear – I wish I hadn't snacked quite so much. I don't feel very brainy at the moment.'

They went into the little lobby. There was a girl at a table, marking off piles of tickets.

'Good morning,' said Fatty. 'Er – could you tell us anything about last week's programme?'

'Why? Are you thinking of going to it?' said the girl, with a giggle. 'You're a bit late.'

'My friend and I have been having a bit of an argument about it,' said Fatty, making this up on the spur of the moment, while Larry looked at him in surprise. 'You see, my friend thinks the programme was *The Yearling* and I said it was – er – er – *Henry V*.'

'No, no,' said the girl graciously. 'It was *The Weakling*, not *The Yearling*, and *Henry the Fifteenth*, not *Henry V*.'

Fatty turned crossly and went out. He bumped into somebody coming up the steps.

He nearly fell, and clutched hold of the person he had collided with. A familiar voice grated in his ear.

'Take your hands off me! Wherever I go, I find one of you kids! What you doing *here*, I'd like to know?'

'They wanted to buy tickets for last week's programme,' called the girl from inside, and screamed with laughter. 'Cheek! I told them off all right.'

'That's right,' said Mr Goon. 'They want telling off. Coming and bothering you with silly questions.' Then it suddenly struck him that Fatty was coming about the same thing as he was – to check up on an alibi. He swung in a rage. 'Poking your n . . .' he began.

But Fatty had gone, and so had Larry. They were not going to stay and argue with Mr Goon and that girl.

'Cheek,' said Fatty, who was not easily outdone in any conversation. 'I'm afraid Mr Goon will get a lot more out of her than we shall.'

'Yes. We've rather fallen down on this alibi,' said Larry – and then he stopped and gave Fatty a sudden punch. 'I say – I know! We can ask Kitty, Pip's cook. She goes to the pictures every single Friday. She told Bets so one day and I heard her. She said she hadn't missed going for nine years.'

'Well, I bet she missed last Friday for the first time then,' said Fatty, gloomily. The cinema girl's cheek was still rankling. 'Anyway, we'll ask and see.'

'Well, thank goodness we're not likely to run into Mr Goon in Pip's kitchen,' said Larry.

They arrived at Pip's, and went into the kitchen. Kitty beamed at them, especially at Fatty, whom she thought was very clever indeed.

'Kitty, could we possibly have a drink of water?' began Fatty.

'You shall have some homemade lemonade,' said Kitty. 'And would you like a snack to go with it?'

The very idea of a snack made Fatty turn pale. 'No thanks,' he said. 'I've just had a snack, Kitty.'

'Well, do have another,' said Kitty, and brought out some small but very tempting-looking sausage-rolls. Fatty groaned and turned away.

'Sorry, Kitty – they look marvellous – but I'm too full of snacks to risk another.'

There was a pause while Kitty filled lemonade glasses.

'Did you go to the pictures last week?' said Larry. 'You always do, don't you?'

'Never missed for nine years,' said Kitty proudly. 'Yes, I went on Friday, same as usual. Oooh, it was a _lovely_ film.'

'What was it?' asked Fatty.

'Well, I went in at six and the news was on,' said Kitty. 'Then a cartoon, you know. Made me laugh like anything. Then at half past six till the end of the programme there was _He Loved Her So_. Oooh, it was _lovely_. Made me cry ever so.'

'A really happy evening,' said Fatty. 'See anyone you know?'

Kitty considered. 'No, I don't know as I did. I always get kind of wrapped up in the film, you know. It was a pity it broke down.'

Fatty pricked up his ears. 'What do you mean – broke down?'

'Well, you know what I mean, Frederick,' said Kitty. 'The picture sort of snaps – and stops – and there's only the screen, and no picture. I suppose the film breaks or something.'

'Did it do that a lot?' asked Fatty.

'Yes – four times,' said Kitty. 'All the way through, it seemed. Just at the wrong bits too – you know, the really exciting bits! Everyone was grumbling about it.'

'Pity,' said Fatty, getting up. 'Well, Kitty, thanks very much for the lemonade – and I hope you enjoy your film *this* Friday.'

'Oooh I shall,' said Kitty. 'It's called *Three Broken Hearts*.'

'You'll weep like anything,' said Fatty. 'You *will* enjoy that, Kitty. It's a pity I'll be too busy to come and lend you my hanky.'

'Oh, you are a rascal,' said Kitty, delighted.

'Come on, Larry,' said Fatty, and he pulled him out of Kitty's kitchen. 'We've learnt something there! Now, if we can only get hold of John James and find out it *he* noticed the breaks in the film – which he must have done if he was there – we shall be able to check *his* alibi all right!'

'So we shall,' said Larry. 'Jolly good work. But how can we get hold of John James? We can't just walk up to him and say, "Did you notice the breaks in the film, Mr James, when you were at the cinema on Friday?" '

'Of course we can't,' said Fatty. 'Gosh, it's almost time for dinner. We'll have to do that afterwards, Larry. Can you possibly eat any dinner? I can't.'

'No, I can't – and it's hot roast pork and apple sauce today,' said Larry with a groan. 'What a waste.'

'Don't even *mention* roast pork,' said Fatty with a shudder. 'Why did we eat so many snacks? Now my mother's going to worry because I can't eat a thing at dinner today – take my temperature or something!'

'What about John James?' said Larry. 'How are we going to tackle him? We don't even know where to find him. He won't be at the theatre because there's no show this afternoon.'

'I'll ring Zoe when I get home and see if she knows where we can get hold of him,' said Fatty. 'We'd better take Bets too. She'll be feeling left out if we don't.'

'Right,' said Larry. 'See you this afternoon sometime.'

19. JOHN JAMES AND THE CINEMA

Very fortunately for Fatty his mother was not in for lunch, so he was able to eat as little as he liked without anyone noticing. He was only at the table about five minutes and then he went to ring Zoe, hoping she was at her sister's as usual.

She was. 'Oh – hello, Zoe,' said Fatty. 'Can you tell me something? I want to have a talk with John James, if I can. Do you know if he'll be anywhere about this afternoon?'

'Well – let me see,' said Zoe's clear voice over the telephone. 'I did hear him say something about going across the river in the ferry, and taking a picnic tea up on the hill beyond. There's a marvellous view up there, you know.'

'Yes. I know,' said Fatty. 'Oh good – I'll slip across and see if I can spot him there. Do you know what time he is going?'

Zoe didn't know. Then she told Fatty that Mr Goon was going to see poor Boysie again that evening. 'And I heard him say that he's not going to stand any nonsense this time – Boysie's got to "come clean," the horrid fellow,' said Zoe, indignantly. 'As if he can make Boysie confess to something he doesn't know anything about!'

Fatty frowned as he hung up the receiver. He was afraid that Boysie *might* confess to the robbery, out of sheer terror and desperation. What a dreadful thing that would be – to have him confess to something he hadn't done – and have the real culprit go scot-free.

Fatty rang Larry, and then Pip, telling them of John James's plans for the afternoon. 'We've got to go and check up on his alibi,' he said. 'And we can only do that by questioning *him* – to see if he really was at the cinema on Friday night. And as it's a lovely day, let's all take our tea and go for a picnic up on the hill across the river, and kill two birds with one stone – enjoy ourselves, and do a spot of detecting as well!'

The others thought this was a splendid idea. 'Fatty always thinks of such nice things,' said Bets, happily. 'It will be lovely up there on the hills.'

Fatty had told Pip to go and ask Kitty once more about the breaks in the film on Friday night, just to make sure he had got it quite right. 'Ask if she remembers *exactly* how many breaks there were, when they came – and, if possible, the *time*,' said Fatty. 'Write it down, Pip, in case you forget the details. This may be important. It looks as if John James is our only hope now – I feel that we must count Alec Grant out, with his alibi of over a hundred people.'

The children met at the ferry at a quarter to three, laden with picnic-bags. Pip carried a mackintosh-rug. 'Mummy made me,' he said crossly. 'She said the grass is still damp. You're lucky to have a mother that doesn't fuss about things like that.'

'Mine fusses about other things,' said Fatty. 'And Larry's fusses about certain things too. Never mind, it's not much bother to sit down on a rug!'

'As a matter-of-fact,' said Bets, seriously, 'I've met one or two mothers who never fussed about their children – but, you know, I'm sure it was because they didn't care about them. I think I'd rather have a fussy mother really.'

'Here's the boat,' said Fatty, as the ferryman came rowing across. 'I'll pay for everyone. It's not much.'

They got into the boat. 'Rowed anyone across yet this afternoon?' asked Fatty. The boatman shook his head. 'No, not yet. Bit early.'

'Then John James hasn't gone across yet,' said Fatty to the others. 'Hey, Buster – don't take a header into the water, will you?'

They got across and made their way over a field and up a steep hill to the top. Fatty chose a place from where they could see the ferry.

'We'll watch and see when the ferryman goes out,' he said. 'I don't know if we could make out John James from here, but I expect we could. He's so burly.'

The spring sun was hot. The cowslips around nodded their yellow heads in the breeze. It was very pleasant up there on the hill. Larry yawned and lay down.

'You watch for J.J., you others,' he said. 'I'm going to have a nap!'

But he hadn't been asleep for more than ten

minutes when Fatty prodded him in the middle. 'Wake up, Larry. Can you see if that's John James standing on the opposite side of the river, waiting for the ferry?'

Larry sat up. He had very keen eyes. He screwed them up and looked hard. 'Yes, I think it is,' he said. 'Let's hope he comes this way. I don't feel like walking miles after him.'

Fortunately it *was* John James, and he *did* come that way. The children watched him get into the boat, land on their side of the river, and follow the same path as they had taken themselves.

'Now,' said Fatty, getting up, 'we'd better start wandering about till we see where he's going to sit. Then we'll settle somewhere near.'

'How are we going to start the checking up?' asked Pip.

'I'll start it,' said Fatty. 'And then you can all follow my lead, and ask innocent questions. Roll up your rug, Pip.'

The five children and Buster wandered about and picked cowslips, keeping a sharp eye on John James, who was coming very slowly up the hill. He found a sheltered place with a bush behind him, and lay down at full length, his arms behind his head so that he could look down the hill towards the river.

Fatty wandered near him. 'Here's a good place,' he called to the others. 'We'll have the rug here.' Then he turned politely to the man nearby.

'I hope we shan't disturb you if we sit just here,' he said.

'Not if you don't yell and screech,' said John James. 'But I don't suppose you will. You look as if you've all been well brought up.'

'I hope we have,' said Fatty, and beckoned to the others. Pip put down the rug. By this time the man was sitting up, and had put a cigarette in his mouth. He patted himself all over and frowned.

'I suppose,' he said to Fatty, 'I suppose you haven't got matches on you, by any chance? I've left mine at home.'

Fatty always had every conceivable thing on him, on the principle that you simply never knew what you might want at any time. He presented John James with a full box of matches at once.

'Keep the whole box,' said Fatty. 'I'm not going to be a smoker at all.'

'Good boy,' said John James. 'Very sensible. Thanks, old chap. I say – haven't I seen you before?'

'Yes,' said Fatty. 'We came into the back of the theatre yesterday – and you were good enough to sign our autograph albums.'

'Oh yes – now I remember you all,' said John James. 'Have you come up here for a picnic?'

'Yes. We're just about to begin,' said Fatty, though it was really much too early. But the effect of the snacks was beginning to wear off, and the lack of a midday meal was making itself felt! Fatty was more than ready for a picnic. 'Er – I suppose you wouldn't like to join us – we've got plenty.'

'Yes. I will,' said John James. 'I've got some stuff here too. We'll pool it.'

It was a very nice picnic, with plenty to eat, and some of Kitty's homemade lemonade to drink. For a short while, Fatty and the others talked about whatever came into their heads.

Then Fatty began his 'checking'. 'What's on at the cinema this week, Larry?' he asked.

Larry told him. 'Oh no,' said Fatty, 'that was last week!'

'You're wrong,' said John James at once. 'It was

Here Goes, the first part of the week, and *He Loved Her So*, the second. Both absolutely dreadful.'

'Really?' said Fatty. 'I heard that *He Loved Her So* was good. But I didn't see it. I suppose you did?'

'Yes. Saw it on Friday,' said John James. 'At least – I *would* have seen it, but it was so boring that I fell asleep nearly all the time!'

This remark disappointed all the Find-Outers very much indeed. If John James slept all the time, he wouldn't have noticed the breaks in the film – and so they wouldn't be able to check his alibi.

'Hope you didn't snore!' said Fatty. 'But I suppose people would wake you up if you did.'

'I did keep waking up,' said John James. 'I kept on waking because of people talking and sounding annoyed. I don't quite know what happened – I think the film must have broken unexpectedly – like they do sometimes, you know – and that made the audience fidgety and cross. But I soon went to sleep again.'

'Bad luck, to be woken up like that!' laughed Fatty. 'I hope you didn't get disturbed from your nap *too* many times!'

John James considered. 'Well, I should think that

199

wretched film must have gone wrong at least four times,' he said. 'I remember looking at the clock once or twice – once I got woken up at quarter to seven, and another time at ten past. I remember wondering where on earth I was when I woke up then. Thought I was in bed at home!'

'Bit of a boring evening for you,' said Fatty, watching Pip take out his notebook and do a bit of checking up on times. He nodded reassuringly to Fatty. Yes, John James's alibi was safe all right. There was no doubt at all that he had been in the cinema that evening, and had been awakened each time the film broke, by the noise of the impatient people around him.

'Yes. It was boring,' said John James. 'But it was something to do. Help yourself to my cherry cake. There's plenty.'

The talk turned to the robbery at the theatre.

'Who do *you* think did it?' asked Fatty.

'I haven't a notion,' said John James. 'Not a notion. Boysie didn't. I'm sure of that. He hasn't the brains or the pluck for a thing of that sort. He's a harmless sort of fellow. He just adores Zoe – and I'm not surprised. She's sweet to him.'

They talked for a little while longer and then Fatty got up and shook the crumbs off himself. 'Well, thanks for letting us picnic with you, Mr James,' he said. 'We'll have to be going now. Are you coming too?'

'No. I'll sit here a bit longer,' said John James. 'There's going to be a grand sunset later on.'

The Find-Outers went down the hill, with Buster capering along on his short legs. 'Well,' said Fatty, when they were out of hearing, 'John James is out of our list of suspects. His alibi is first rate. He was in the cinema all right on Friday evening. Gosh, this mystery is getting deeper and deeper. I'm stumped!'

'Oh *no*, Fatty,' said Bets, quite shocked to hear Fatty say this. 'You *can't* be stumped! Not with your wonderful brains!'

20. DEFEAT - AND A BRAINWAVE

Fatty racked his brains that night, but to no effect. However much he thought and thought, he could see no solution to the mystery at all. He was certain Boysie hadn't done the job. He was also quite certain that Zoe, whose alibi was a little shaky, had had nothing to do with it either. Everyone else had unshakeable alibis. It was true they hadn't checked Alec Grant's, but Fatty had looked up a local paper and had seen a report of the one-man concert that Alec had given on the Friday evening at Sheepridge.

'The report in the paper is a good enough alibi,' he said to the others. 'We needn't bother any more about Alec. But WHO is the culprit? Who did the job?'

In desperation, he went down that evening to talk to PC Pippin. He was there, walking up and down Mr Goon's little back garden, smoking a pipe.

He was pleased to see Fatty.

'Any news?' said Fatty. 'I suppose Mr Goon's out?'

'Yes, thank goodness,' said Pippin, feelingly. 'He's been at me all day long about something or other. Pops in and out on that bike of his, and doesn't give me any peace at all. He's gone down to see Boysie again now. I'm very much afraid he'll scare him into a false confession.'

'Yes, I'm afraid of that too,' said Fatty. 'What about Zoe? Does Mr Goon think she had anything to do with it?'

'I'm afraid he does,' said Pippin. 'He's got that handkerchief of hers with Z on, you know – that's one of his main pieces of evidence.'

'But that's nonsense!' said Fatty. 'The handkerchief might have been on that verandah for days! It doesn't prove she was there that night.'

'Goon thinks it does,' said Pippin. 'You see, he has found out that the cleaner swept that verandah clean on Friday afternoon at four o'clock! So the hanky must have been dropped after that.'

Fatty bit his lip and frowned. That was very bad indeed. He hadn't known that. Of *course* Mr Goon thought Zoe had crept to that verandah that evening and been let in by Boysie, if he found a hanky there with a Z on it – a hanky which must have been dropped after four o'clock! That was a very nasty bit of evidence indeed.

'What annoys Mr Goon is that Zoe keeps on denying it's her hanky,' said Pippin. 'Says she's never seen it before. It's a pity it's got Z on it – such an unusual initial.'

'I know,' groaned poor Fatty, feeling very much inclined to make a clean breast of how he had planted the handkerchief and all the other 'clues' on the verandah himself. Well – if Mr Goon did arrest Zoe and Boysie, he would certainly *have* to own up. He turned to Pippin.

'Telephone me Mr Pippin, if you hear any serious news – such as Mr Goon getting a false confession from Boysie – or making an arrest,' he said.

Pippin nodded. 'I certainly will. What have *you* been doing about the mystery? I bet you haven't been idle!'

Fatty told him how he had checked up all the alibis and found them unshakeable – except for Zoe's. He was feeling very worried indeed. It would be awful if Mr Goon solved the mystery the wrong way – and got the wrong people! If only Fatty could see a bit of daylight. But he couldn't.

He went back home, quite depressed, which was very unusual for Fatty. Larry telephoned him that evening to find out if he had heard anything fresh from PC Pippin.

Fatty told him all he knew. Larry listened in silence.

For once, Fatty was completely at a loss. There didn't seem anything to do at all. 'I don't see *what* we can do,' he said miserably. 'I'm absolutely stuck. Fat lot of good we are at detecting! We'll have to break up the Find-Outers if we can't do better than this.'

'Come up at ten tomorrow and have a meeting,' said Larry. 'We'll all think hard and talk and go over absolutely *every*thing. There's something we've missed, I'm sure – some idea we haven't thought of. There's no mystery without a solution, Fatty. Cheer up. We'll find it!'

But before ten o'clock the next day, the telephone rang, and PC Pippin relayed some very bad news to Fatty.

'Are you there? I've only got a minute. Mr Goon has got a confession from Boysie! And Zoe's in it too! Apparently Boysie said he and Zoe worked the thing together. He let Zoe in at the verandah door, they made the tea, Boysie took the cup up with the dope in to the manager – then when he fell asleep, Zoe went up and robbed the safe. She apparently knew where the key was and everything.'

Fatty listened in horror. 'But, Mr Pippin! *Mr Pippin*! Boysie couldn't have done it – nor could Zoe. Mr Goon's *forced* that confession out of a poor fellow who's so confused in his head he doesn't really know what he's saying.'

There was a pause. 'Well, I'm inclined to agree with you,' said Pippin. 'In fact – well, I shouldn't tell you this, but I must – I think from what Mr Goon has let slip, he *did* force that false confession from Boysie, poor wretch. Now, see here, I'm helpless. I can't go against Goon. You're the only one that can do anything. Isn't Inspector Jenks a *great* friend of yours? Won't he believe what you say, if you tell him you think there's been a mistake?'

'But I haven't any *proof*,' wailed Fatty. 'Now, if I *knew* who the robber was, and could produce him, with real evidence, the Inspector would listen to me like a shot. I'll go and see the others, and see what they think. If we can't think of anything better, I'll cycle over to the next town and see the Inspector myself.'

'Well, you'd better make . . .' began PC Pippin, and then Fatty heard the receiver being put back with a click. He guessed that Mr Goon had come in. He sat by the telephone and thought hard. This was frightful! Poor Zoe. Poor Boysie. What in the world could he do to help them?

He tore off to Pip's on his bicycle. The others were there already. They looked gloomy – and they looked gloomier still when Fatty told them what PC Pippin had said.

'It's serious,' said Larry. 'More serious than any other mystery we've tackled. What can we do, Fatty?'

'We'll go through all the suspects and the alibis, and run through all we know,' said Fatty, getting out his notebook. 'I've got everything down here. Listen while I read it – and think, think, think *hard* all the time. As Larry says – we've missed something – some clue, or some evidence, that will help us. There's something very wrong, and probably the explanation is sticking out a mile – if we could only *see* it!'

He began to read through his notes – the list of suspects. The alibi they had each given. The checking of all the alibis. Boysie's account of the evening of the crime. The manager's own account. The dislike that each member of the show felt for the manager, which would give each one of them a motive for paying him back. Everything in his notebook Fatty read out, clearly and slowly, and the Find-Outers listened intently, even Buster sitting still with ears cocked.

He finished. There was a long pause. Fatty looked up. 'Any suggestions?' he asked, not very hopefully.

The others shook their heads. Fatty shut his notebook with a snap. 'Defeated!' he said bitterly. 'Beaten! All we know is that out of the seven people who are suspects, the two who *could* have done it, didn't – Boysie and Zoe – we *know* they didn't. They're incapable of doing such a thing. And the others, who *might* have done it, all have first class alibis. How *can* the pantomime cat have done the deed when it isn't in his nature to do it?'

'It almost makes you think it must have been somebody else in Boysie's skin,' said Bets.

The others laughed scornfully. 'Silly!' said Pip, and Bets went red.

And then Fatty went suddenly and inexplicably mad. He stared at Bets with fixed and glassy eyes. Then he smacked her on the shoulder. Then he got up and did a solemn and ridiculous dance round the room, looking as if he was in the seventh heaven of delight.

'Bets!' he said, stopping at last. '*Bets*! Good, clever, brainy old Bets. She's got it! She's solved it! Bets, you deserve to be head of the Find-Outers! Oh my word, Bets, why, why, why didn't I think of it before?'

The others all stared at him as if he was out of his mind. 'Fatty, don't be an idiot. Tell us what you mean,' said Pip, crossly. 'What's Bets been so clever about? For the life of me I don't know!'

'Nor do I,' said Larry. 'Sit down Fatty, and explain.'

Fatty sat down, beaming all over his face. He put his arm round the astonished Bets and squeezed her. 'Dear old Bets – she's saved Boysie and Zoe. What brains!'

'*Fatty*! Shut up and tell us what you mean!' almost yelled Pip in exasperation.

'Right,' said Fatty. 'You heard what young Bets said, didn't you? She said, "It almost makes you think it must have been somebody else in Boysie's skin". Well? Well, I ask you? Can't you see that's the solution? Turnip-heads, you don't see it yet!'

'I'm beginning to see,' said Larry slowly. 'But you see it *all*, Fatty, obviously. Tell us.'

'Now, look here,' said Fatty. 'Boysie says he did *not* take the tea in to the manager, doesn't he? But the manager swears he *did*. And why does he swear that? Because Boysie, he says, was wearing his cat-skin. All right. Whoever brought the tea was certainly the pantomime cat – but as the manager never saw who was *inside* the skin, how does he know it was Boysie?'

The others listened in amazement.

'And as it happens, it *wasn't* Boysie!' said Fatty, triumphantly. 'Let me tell you what *I* think happened that night, now that Bets has opened my eyes.'

'Yes, go on, tell us,' said Pip, getting excited as he too began to see what Fatty was getting at.

'Well – the theatre cast all departed, as we know, at half past five, because we saw them go,' said Fatty. 'Only Boysie was left, because he lives there, and the manager was upstairs in his office.

'Now, there was a member of the cast who had a grudge against the manager, and wanted to pay him back. So that night, after *we* had gone home from our planting of false clues, this person came silently back – let himself in secretly, because Boysie didn't see him or he would have said so – and hid till he saw Boysie making the tea. He knew that Boysie always made tea and took a cup to the manager.

'Very well. Boysie made the tea, and poured himself out a cup. But he didn't drink it because it was too hot. He waited till it was cooler. And the hidden person slipped out, and put a sleeping-draught into Boysie's cup.

'Boysie drank it, felt terribly sleepy, went into the verandah room and snored by the fire. The hidden person then made sure that Boysie was doped and wouldn't wake up – and he *stripped the skin off Boysie . . .'*

'And put it on himself!' cried all the others together. 'Oh, *Fatty*!'

'Yes – he put it on himself. And made a cup of tea for the manager, putting into it a sleeping-draught, of course – and up the stairs he went! Well, how could the manager guess it was anyone but Boysie in his pantomime cat-skin! Wouldn't *anyone* think that?'

'Of course,' said Daisy. 'And then he waited till the manager had drunk his tea and fallen asleep – and did the robbery!'

'Exactly,' said Fatty. 'Took down the mirror, found the key in the manager's wallet, worked out the combination that would open the safe – and stole everything in it. Then he went down to the sleeping Boysie and pulled him into the skin again – and departed as secretly as he came, with the money!

'He knew that when the cup of tea was examined and traces of a sleeping-draught were found, the first question asked would be, "*Who* brought up the cup of tea to the manager?"' said Fatty. 'And the answer to that – quite untruly as it happens – was, of course, Boysie.'

'Oh, Fatty – it's wonderful,' said Bets, her face shining. 'We've solved the mystery!'

'We haven't,' said Larry and Pip together.

'We *have*,' said Bets indignantly.

'Ah, wait a minute, Bets,' said Fatty. 'We know how the thing was done – but the *real* mystery now is – *who was inside the skin of the pantomime cat?*'

21. THE LAST ALIBI IS CHECKED

Everyone felt tremendously excited. Larry smacked Bets proudly on the back. 'You just hit the nail on the head, Bets, when you made that brainy remark of yours,' he said.

'Well – I didn't know it was brainy,' said Bets. 'I just said it without thinking really.'

'I *told* you there was something sticking out a mile, right under our very noses,' said Fatty. 'And that was it. Come on now – we've got to find out who was in the skin.'

They all thought. 'But what's the good of thinking it's this person or that person?' said Pip at last. 'If we say "John James", for instance, it can't be, because we've checked his alibi and it's perfect.'

'Let's not worry about alibis,' said Fatty. 'Once we decide who the person was inside the cat-skin, we'll recheck the alibi – and, what's more, we'll then find it's false! It must be. Come on now – who was inside that cat-skin?'

'Not John James,' said Daisy. 'He was much too big – too fat.'

'Yes – it would have to be a small person,' said Fatty. 'Boysie is small, and only a person about his size could wear that skin.'

They all ran their minds over the members of the cast. Larry thumped on the floor.

'Alec Grant! He's the smallest of the lot – very neat and dapper and slim – don't you remember?'

'Yes! The others are *all* too big – even the two girls, who are too tall to fit the skin,' said Fatty. 'Alec Grant is the only member who could possibly get into the skin.'

'*And* he split it!' said Daisy suddenly. 'Oh, don't you remember, Fatty, how Boysie came and asked Zoe to mend it for him – and she looked at the splitting seams and said he must be getting bigger? Well, he wasn't! Somebody bigger than he was had used his skin and split it!'

'Gosh, yes,' said Fatty. 'Would you believe it – a clue as big as that staring us in the face and we never noticed it! But I say – *Alec Grant*? He's got the best alibi of the whole lot.'

'He certainly has,' said Larry. 'It's going to be a hard alibi to break too. Impossible, it seems to me.'

'No. Not impossible,' said Fatty. 'He couldn't be in two places at once. And so, if he was in the pantomime cat's skin at the Little Theatre on Friday evening, he was *not* giving a concert at Sheepridge! That's certain.'

'Fancy! The only alibi we didn't check,' said Larry.

'Yes – and I *said* that a good detective always checks everything, whether he thinks it is necessary or not,' groaned Fatty. 'I must be going downhill rapidly. I consider I've done very badly over this!'

'You haven't, Fatty,' said Bets. 'Why, it was you who saw that my remark, which was really only a joke, was the real clue to the mystery! I didn't see that, and nor did the others.'

'How are we going to shake this alibi of Alec Grant's?' said Larry. 'Let's keep to the subject. We haven't much time, it seems to me, if Mr Goon has got a false confession from poor Boysie. He'll be getting in touch with the Inspector any time now and making an arrest – two arrests, I suppose, if Zoe has to be in it too.'

'Anyone got friends in Sheepridge?' asked Fatty suddenly.

'I've got a cousin there – you know him, Freddie Wilson,' said Larry. 'Why?'

'Well, I suppose there's a chance he might have gone to Alec's concert,' said Fatty. 'Telephone him and see, Larry. We've got to find out something about this concert now.'

'*Freddie* won't have gone to a concert like that – to see a man impersonating women,' said Larry, scornfully.

'Go and phone him,' said Fatty. 'Ask him if he knows anything about it.'

Larry went, rather reluctantly. He was afraid that Freddie would jeer at his inquiry.

But Freddie was out and it was his eighteen-year-old sister, Julia, who answered. And she provided an enormous bit of luck!

'No, Larry, Freddie didn't go,' she said. 'Can you see him going to *any* kind of concert? I can't. But I went with Mother. Alec Grant was awfully good – honestly, you couldn't have told he was a man. I waited afterwards and got his autograph.'

'Hold on a minute,' said Larry, and went to report to Fatty. Fatty leapt up as if he had been shot. 'Got his *autograph*! Gosh – this is super. Don't you remember, idiot, *we've* all got his autograph too! I'd like to see the autograph *Julia* got! I'll eat my hat if it isn't quite different from the one *we've* got!'

'But Fatty – Alec Grant was there, giving the concert,' began Larry. 'Julia says so.'

Fatty took absolutely no notice of him but rushed to the telephone, with Buster excitedly at his heels, feeling that there really must be something up!

'Julia! Frederick Trotteville here. *Could* I come over and see you by the next bus? Most important. Will you be in?'

Julia laughed at Fatty's urgent voice. 'Oh, Frederick – you sound as if you're in the middle of a mystery or something. Yes, of course. Come over. I'll be most interested to know what you want!'

Fatty put down the receiver and rushed back to the others. 'I'm off to Sheepridge,' he said. 'Coming, anyone?'

'Of *course*,' said everyone at once. What! Be left out just when things were getting so thrilling! No, everyone was determined to be in at the death.

They arrived at Sheepridge an hour later, and went to find Julia. She was waiting for them, and was amused to see all five march in.

'Listen, Julia,' began Fatty. 'I can't explain everything to you now – it would take too long – but we are very curious about Alec Grant. You say he really was there, performing at the concert? You actually recognized him, and have seen him before?'

'Yes. Of course I recognised him,' said Julia.

Fatty felt a little taken aback. He had hoped Julia would say she didn't recognise him, and then he might be able to prove that somebody else had taken Alec's place.

'Have you your autograph album with his signature in?' he asked. Julia went to get it. All the Find-Outers had brought theirs with them, and Fatty silently compared the five signatures in their books with the one in Julia's.

Julia's was utterly and entirely different!

'Look,' said Fatty, pointing. 'The autographs he did for us are illegible squiggles – the one he did for Julia is perfectly clear and readable. It *wasn't* Alec

Grant who did that!'

'You'll be saying it was his twin-sister next,' said Julia with a laugh.

Fatty stared as if he couldn't believe his ears. 'What did you say?' he almost shouted. '*Twin-sister*, Julia? – you don't really mean to say he's got a twin-sister?'

'Of course he has,' said Julia. 'What *is* all this mystery about? I've seen his sister – exactly like him, small and neat. She doesn't live here, she lives at Marlow.'

Fatty let out an enormous sigh. 'Why didn't I think of a twin?' he said. 'Of course! The *only* solution! He got his twin to come and do his show for him. Is she good too, Julia?'

'Well, they're both in shows,' said Julia. 'As a matter-of-fact, Alec is supposed to be much better than Nora, his sister. I thought he wasn't so good last Friday really – he had such a terrible cold, for one thing, and kept stopping to cough.'

The others immediately looked at one another. Oh! A cough and a cold! Certainly Alec hadn't had one on Monday afternoon when they had all heard him sing. Nobody had seen any sign of a cold or cough then. Very, very suspicious!

'May we take this album away for a little while?' asked Fatty. 'I'll send it back. Thanks so much for seeing us. You've been a great help.'

'I don't know how,' said Julia. 'It seems very mysterious to me.'

'It *has* been very mysterious,' said Fatty, preparing to go. 'Very, very mysterious. But I see daylight now, though I very – nearly – didn't!'

The Five Find-Outers went off with Buster, excited and talkative. 'We've got it all straightened out now,' said Fatty happily. 'Thanks to Bets. Honestly Bets, we'd have been absolutely stumped if you hadn't made that sudden remark. It was a brainwave.'

They got back to Peterswood, having decided what to do. They would go and see PC Pippin first, and tell him all they knew. Fatty said they owed it to him to do that, and if he wanted to arrest Alec Grant, he could. What a shock for Mr Goon!

But when they got to Mr Goon's house, they had a shock. PC Pippin was there alone, looking very gloomy.

'Ah, Frederick,' he said, when he saw Fatty, 'I've

been trying to telephone you for the last hour. Mr Goon's arrested Boysie and Zoe, and they're both in an awful state! I'm afraid Boysie will go right off his head now.'

'Where are they?' asked Fatty, desperately.

'Goon's taken them over to the Inspector,' said PC Pippin. 'What's the matter with *you*? You look all of a dither.'

'I am,' said Fatty, sitting down suddenly. 'Mr Pippin, listen hard to what I'm going to tell you. And then tell us what to do. Prepare for some shocks. Now – listen!'

22. A SURPRISE FOR THE INSPECTOR

Pippin listened, his eyes almost falling out of his head. He heard about the false clues and frowned. He heard about the way the children had interviewed the suspects by means of asking for autographs – he heard about the tea party – the checking up of the alibis – and then he heard about Bets' bright remark that had suddenly set Fatty on the right track.

The autograph albums were produced and compared. The visit to Sheepridge related. The twin-sister came into the story, and PC Pippin rubbed his forehead in bewilderment as Fatty produced the many, many pieces of the jigsaw puzzle that, all fitted together, made a clear solution to the mystery.

'Well! I don't know what to think,' said poor PC Pippin. 'This beats me! Mr Goon's got the wrong ones, no doubt about that. And I think there's no doubt that Alec Grant is the culprit.'

'Can you arrest him then and take him to the Inspector?' cried Fatty.

'No. Of course not,' said Pippin. 'Not just on what you've told me. But I'll tell you what we *can* do – I can go and detain him for questioning. I can take him over to the Inspector and face him with all you've said.'

'Oh *yes* – that's a fine idea,' said Fatty. 'Can we come too?'

'You'll have to,' said PC Pippin. 'My word, I shan't like to look at the Inspector's face when he hears about those false clues of yours. Good thing you've solved the mystery, that's all I can say. Let's hope that will cancel out the mischief you got into first.'

Pippin's voice was stern, but his eyes twinkled. 'Can't be really cross with you myself,' he said. 'Your clues put me where I could see the crime when it was just done – and now it looks as if I'll be able to show Mr Goon up. He deserves it, brow-beating that poor, simple-headed fellow into a false confession!'

223

The morning went on being more and more exciting. Alec Grant was collected from the theatre, where he was rehearsing with the others, who were most alarmed at Zoe's arrest. He put on a very bold face and pretended that he hadn't the least idea why Pippin wanted to question him.

He was very surprised to see all the children also crammed into the big car that Pippin had hired to take them over to see the Inspector. But nobody explained anything to him. The children looked away from him. Horrid, beastly thief – and how *could* he let Zoe and Boysie take the blame for something he himself had done?

Pippin telephoned the Inspector before they left. 'Sir? Pippin here. About that Little Theatre job. I believe Mr Goon's brought his two arrests over to you. Well, sir, can you hold things up for a bit? I've got some fresh evidence here, sir. Very important. I'm bringing someone over to question – man named Alec Grant. Also, sir, I'm bringing – er – five children.'

'What?' said Inspector Jenks, thinking he must have misheard. 'Five *what*?'

'CHILDREN, sir,' said Pippin. 'You know, sir, you

told me about them before I came here. One's a boy called Frederick Trotteville.'

'Oh, *really*?' said the Inspector. 'That's most interesting. So he's been working on this too, has he? Do you know what conclusions he has come to Pippin?'

'Yes, sir, I know all about it,' said Pippin. 'Er – Mr Goon didn't want me to work with him on this case, sir, so – er – well . . .'

'So you worked with Frederick, I suppose,' said the Inspector. 'Very wise of you. Well – I'll hold things up till you come.'

He called Mr Goon into his room. 'Er, Goon,' he said, 'we must wait for about twenty minutes before proceeding with anything. Pippin has just phoned through. He's got fresh evidence.'

Goon bristled like a hedgehog. 'Pippin, sir? He doesn't know a thing about this case. Not a thing. I wouldn't let him work with me on it, he's such a turnip-head. Course, he's only been with me a little while, but it's easy to see he's not going to be much good. Not enough brains. And a bit too cocky, sir, if you'll excuse the slang.'

'Certainly,' said the Inspector. 'Well, we will

wait. Pippin is bringing a man for questioning.'

Goon's mouth fell open. 'A man – for questioning? But we've *got* the people who did the job. What's he want to bring a man for? Who is it?'

'And he's also bringing five children, he says,' went on the Inspector, enjoying himself very much, for he did not like the domineering, conceited Mr Goon. 'One of them is, I believe, that clever boy – the one who has helped us with so many mysteries – Frederick Trotteville!'

Goon opened and shut his mouth like a goldfish and for two minutes couldn't say a single word. He went slowly purple and the Inspector looked at him in alarm.

'You'll have a heart attack one of these days, Goon, if you get so angry,' he said. 'Surely you don't mind Frederick coming over? You are quite sure you have solved the case yourself, and arrested the right people – so what is there to worry about?'

'I'm not worrying,' said Goon, fiercely. 'That boy – always interfering with the law – always . . .'

'Now Goon, he *helps* the law, he doesn't interfere with it,' said the Inspector.

Goon muttered something about turnip-heads,

and then subsided into deep gloom. Pippin coming – and all those dratted children! What was up?

Pippin duly arrived with Alec Grant, the five children, and, of course, Buster. Goon's face grew even blacker when he saw Buster, who greeted him with frantic joy, as if he was an old friend, tearing round his feet in a most exasperating way.

'Ah, Frederick – so you're on the job again,' said the Inspector. 'Pleased to see you. Hello, Larry – Pip – Daisy – and here's little Bets too. Have they turned you out of the Find-Outers yet, Bets?'

'Turned her out! I should think not,' said Fatty. 'If it hadn't been for Bets, we'd never have hit on the right solution.'

There was a growl from Goon at this. The Inspector turned to him. 'Ah, Goon – you also think you have hit on the right solution, don't you?' he said. 'Your two arrests are in the other room. Now – what makes you think you have solved the case correctly, Goon? You were just about to tell me when I got Pippin's telephone call.'

'Sir, there's a confession here from Boysie Summers, the pantomime cat,' said Goon. 'Says as clear as a pikestaff that he did the job, with Zoe

Markham to help him. This here's her handker-chief, found on the verandah on the night of the crime – Z for Zoe, in the corner, sir.'

'Oh!' said Daisy. 'That's *my* old hanky, Inspector! And I put the Z in the corner, just for a joke. Didn't I, you others?'

The other four nodded at once. 'It's certainly not Zoe's,' said Daisy. 'She'd never have a dirty, torn old hanky like this. I should have thought Mr Goon would have guessed that.'

Mr Goon began to breathe heavily. 'Now look here!' he began.

'Wait, Goon,' said the Inspector, picking up the 'confession'. 'So this is what Boysie said, is it? Bring him in, please Pippin. He and Zoe are in the next room. They can both come in.'

Pippin went to fetch Zoe and Boysie. Zoe was in tears, and so upset that she didn't even seem to see the five children. She went straight up to the Inspector and tapped the 'confession' he held in his hand.

'Not one word of that is true!' she said. 'Not one word! *He* forced Boysie to say things that weren't true. Look at Boysie – can you imagine him doing a crime like that even with my help? He's nothing but a child, even though he's twenty-four. That policeman badgered him and terrified him and threatened him till poor Boysie was so frightened he said anything. Anything! It's wicked, really *wicked*!'

Boysie stood beside her. The children hardly knew him, out of his cat-skin. He did seem only a child – a child that trembled and shook and clutched at Zoe's dress. Bets felt the tears coming into her eyes.

'Well, Miss Markham,' said Inspector Jenks, 'we have here someone else for questioning. I think you know him.'

Zoe turned and saw Alec. 'Alec Grant!' she said. 'Did *you* do it, Alec? Alec, if you did, say so. Would you let poor Boysie be sent *right* off his head with this, if you could help it? You hated the manager. You always said so. Did *you* do it?'

Alec said nothing. The Inspector turned to Pippin. 'Pippin – will you say why you have brought this man here, please?'

Pippin began his tale. He told it extremely well and lucidly. It was plain to see that PC Pippin would one day make a very good policeman indeed!

The Inspector interrupted occasionally to ask a question, and sometimes Fatty had to put a few words in too. Goon sat with his mouth open, his eyes almost bulging out of his head.

Alec Grant looked more and more uncomfortable as time went on. When Pippin and Fatty between them related how the children had gone to Sheepridge and seen the different autograph in Julia's album – which Pippin placed before the Inspector as evidence – he turned very pale.

'So you think this man here got his twin-sister to impersonate him, while he slipped back to the theatre, doped Boysie, got into the cat-skin, took up a doped cup of tea to the manager, robbed the safe, and then pulled the skin on the sleeping Boysie again?' said Inspector Jenks. 'A most ingenious crime. We must get on to the man's twin-sister. We must bring her in too.'

'Here!' said Goon, in a strangled sort of voice. 'I can't have this. I tell you that man's not the culprit – he *didn't* do it. Haven't I got that confession there for you to see?'

And then poor Goon got a terrible shock. 'I *did*

do it!' said Alec Grant. 'Exactly as PC Pippin described it. But leave my sister out of it, *please*! She knows nothing about it at all! I telephoned her and begged her to take my place at the concert, and she did. She's done that before when I've felt ill, and nobody has known. We're as alike as peas. I impersonate women, as you know – and who's to know the difference if my sister impersonates *me*? No one! Only these kids – they're too clever by half!'

Inspector Jenks took the 'confession' and tore it in half. 'There's a fire behind you, Goon,' he said, in a cold voice. 'Put this in, will you?'

And Goon had to put the wonderful 'confession' into the fire and watch it burn. He wished he could sink through the floor. He wished he was at the other end of the world. If ever cruelty and stupidity and conceit were punished well and truly, then they were punished now, in the person of Goon.

'I've got all the money,' said Alec. 'I meant to give it back really. It was just to give the manager a nasty shock – he's a mean old beast. If I'd known Boysie and Zoe had been arrested I'd have owned up.'

'You *did* know,' said Pippin quietly. 'No good

saying that now.'

'Well,' said the Inspector, leaning back and looking at the children. 'Well! Once more you appear to have come to our rescue, children. I'm much obliged to you, Pippin, my congratulations – you handled this case well, in spite of being forbidden to work with Goon. Frederick, you are incorrigible and irrepressible – and if you place any more false clues, I shall probably be forced to arrest you! You are also a very great help, and most ingenious in your tackling of any problem. Thanks very much!'

The Inspector beamed round at the five children and Pippin, including Zoe and Boysie in his smile. Bets slipped her hand into his. 'You don't *really* mean you'd arrest Fatty?' she said anxiously. 'We were all as bad as he was with those clues and things, Inspector.'

'No. I was pulling his leg,' said the Inspector. 'Not that I approve of that sort of behaviour at all, you understand – very reprehensible indeed – but I can't help feeling that what you all did later has quite cancelled out what came before! And now, do you know what time it is? Two o'clock. Has anyone had any lunch?'

Nobody had, and the children suddenly became aware of a very hollow feeling in their middles.

'Well, I hope you will do me the honour of lunching with me at the Royal Hotel,' said the Inspector. 'I'll get someone to telephone your families, who will no doubt be searching the countryside for you now! And perhaps Miss Zoe would come too – and, er, – the pantomime cat?'

'Oh, thank you,' said Zoe, all smiles. 'Are we quite free now?'

'Quite,' said the Inspector. 'Goon, take this fellow Grant away. And wait here till I come back. I shall have a few words to say to you.'

Goon, looking like a pricked balloon, took Alec Grant away. Bets heaved a sigh of relief. 'Oh, Inspector Jenks, I was *so* afraid you'd ask Mr Goon to come out to lunch too!'

'Not on your life!' said the Inspector. 'Oh, you're there too, PC Pippin. Go and get yourself a good meal in the police station canteen, and then come back here and write out a full report of this case for me. And ring the children's parents, will you?'

Pippin saluted and grinned. He was very pleased

with himself. He winked at Fatty and Fatty winked back. Aha! There would be a spot of promotion for Pippin if he went on handling cases like this.

'I've really enjoyed this mystery,' said Bets, as she sat down at a hotel table and unfolded a snowy white napkin. 'It was very, very difficult – but it wasn't frightening at all.'

'Oh yes it was – to me and Boysie,' said Zoe. She filled a glass with lemonade and held it up to the children.

'Here's to you!' she cried. 'The Five Find-Outers – and Dog!'

The Inspector raised his glass too, and grinned. 'Here's to the great detectives – who solved the insoluble and most mysterious case in their career – the Mystery of the Pantomime Cat!'

The MYSTERY of the Invisible Thief

Contents

1. ONE HOT SUMMER'S DAY

'Do you know,' said Pip, 'this is the fourth week of the summer holidays – the fourth week, mind – and we haven't even *heard* of a mystery!'

'Haven't even smelt one,' agreed Fatty. 'Gosh, this sun is hot. Buster, don't pant so violently – you're making me feel even hotter!'

Buster crawled into a patch of shade, and lay down with a thump. His tongue hung out as he panted. Bets patted him.

'Poor old Buster! It must be terrible to have to wear a fur coat this weather – one you can't even unbutton and have hanging open!'

'Don't suggest such a thing to Buster,' said Fatty. 'He'd look awful.'

'Oh dear – it's too hot even to laugh,' said Daisy, picturing Buster trying to undo his coat to leave it open.

1

'Here we are – all the Five Find-Outers – and Dog,' said Larry, 'with nothing to find out, nothing to solve, and eight weeks to do it in! Fatty, it's a waste of the hols. Though even if we had a mystery, I think I'd be too hot to think about clues and suspects and what-nots.'

The five children lay on their backs on the grass. The sun poured down on them. They all wore as little as possible, but even so they were hot. Nobody could bear poor Buster being near them for more than two seconds, because he absolutely radiated heat.

'Whose turn is it to fetch the iced lemonade?' said Larry.

'You know full well it's yours,' said Daisy. 'You always ask that question when it's your turn, hoping somebody will get it out of turn. Go and get it, you lazy thing.'

Larry didn't move. Fatty pushed him with his foot. 'Go on,' he said. 'You've made us all feel thirsty now. Go and get it.'

A voice came up the garden. 'Bets! Have you got your sunhat on? And what about Pip?'

Bets answered hastily. 'Yes, Mother – it's quite

all right. I've got mine on.'

Pip was frowning at her to warn her to say nothing about him. He had, as usual, forgotten his hat. But his mother was not to be put off.

'What about Pip? Pip, come and get your sunhat. Do you want sunstroke *again*?'

'Blow!' said Pip, and got up. Larry immediately said what everybody knew he would say.

'Well, you might as well bring back the iced lemonade with you.'

'You're very good at getting out of your turn,' grumbled Pip, going off. 'If I'd been quick enough, I'd have told you to get my hat when you got the lemonade. All right, Mother. I'm COMING!'

The iced lemonade revived everyone at once. For one thing they all had to sit up, which made them feel much more lively. And for another thing, Pip brought them back a bit of news.

'Do you know what Mummy just told me?' he said. 'Inspector Jenks is coming to Peterswood this afternoon!'

'*Is* he?' said everyone, intensely interested. Inspector Jenks was a great friend of theirs. He admired the Five Find-Outers very much, because of the many curious mysteries they had solved. 'What's he coming for?' asked Fatty. 'There's not a mystery on, is there?'

'No, I'm afraid not,' said Pip. 'Apparently his little goddaughter is riding in the gymkhana in Petter's Field this afternoon, and he's promised to come and see her.'

'Oh – what a disappointment,' said Daisy. 'I thought he might be on the track of some exciting case or other.'

'I vote we go and say hello to him,' said Fatty. Everyone agreed at once. They all liked the burly, good-looking Inspector, with his shrewd twinkling eyes and teasing ways. Bets especially liked him. Next to Fatty, she thought he was the cleverest person she knew.

They began to talk of the mysteries they had solved and how Inspector Jenks had always helped them and encouraged them.

'Do you remember the missing necklace and how we found it?' said Larry. 'And that hidden house mystery – that was super!'

'The most exciting one was the mystery of the secret room, *I* think,' said Pip. 'Gosh, I shall never forget how I felt when I climbed that tree by the big empty house – looked into a room at the top and found it all furnished!'

'We've had some fun,' said Fatty. 'I only hope we'll have some more. We've never been so long in any holidays without a mystery to solve. The old brains will get rusty.'

'Yours could never get rusty, Fatty,' said Bets admiringly. 'The things you've thought of! And your disguises! You haven't done any disguising at all these hols. You aren't tired of it, are you?'

'Gosh, no,' said Fatty. 'But for one thing, it's been too hot – and for another, old Mr Goon's been away, and the other policeman in his place is such a stodge. He never looks surprised at anything. I'll be quite glad when Mr Goon comes back and we hear his familiar yell of "You clear orf!" Old Buster'll be pleased too – you miss your ankle hunt, don't you, Buster?'

Bets giggled. 'Oh dear – the times Buster has danced round Mr Goon's ankles and been yelled at. Buster really is wicked with him.'

'Quite right too,' said Fatty. 'I hope Mr Goon comes back soon, then Buster can have a bit of exercise, capering round him.'

Buster looked up at his name and wagged his tail. He was still panting. He moved near to Fatty.

'Keep off, Buster,' said Fatty. 'You scorch us when you come near. I never knew such a hot dog in my life. We ought to fix an electric fan round his neck or something.'

'Don't make jokes,' begged Daisy. 'It's honestly too hot to laugh. I don't even know how I'm going to walk to Petter's Field this afternoon to see the Inspector.'

'We could take our tea and ask the Inspector, plus goddaughter, to share it,' said Fatty.

'Brilliant idea!' said Daisy. 'We could really talk to him then. He might have a bit of news. You never know. After all, if there's any case on, or any mystery in the air, he's the one to know about it first.'

'We'll ask him,' said Fatty. 'Get *away*, Buster. Your tongue is dripping down my neck.'

'What we want, for a bit of excitement,' said Pip, 'is a nice juicy mystery, and Mr Goon to come back and make a mess of it as usual, while we do all the solving.'

'One of these days, Mr Goon will do all the solving and we'll make a mess of it,' said Daisy.

'Oh *no*,' said Bets. 'We couldn't possibly make a mess of it if Fatty's in charge.' The others looked at her in disgust – except Fatty, of course, who looked superior.

'Don't set Fatty off, for goodness sake,' said Pip. 'You're always hero-worshipping him. He'll be telling us of something wonderful he did last term now.'

'Well, as a matter-of-fact, I forgot to tell you, but something rather extraordinary *did* happen last term,' said Fatty. 'It was like this . . .'

'I don't know the beginning of this story but I'm sure I know the end,' said Larry gloomily.

Fatty was surprised. 'How can you know the end if you don't know the beginning?' he asked.

'Easily, if it's to do with you,' said Larry. 'I'm sure the end will be that you solved the extraordinary happening in two minutes, you caught the culprit, you were cheered and clapped to the echo and you had "As brilliant as ever" on your report. Easy!'

Fatty fell on Larry and soon they were rolling over and over on the grass with Buster joining

7

in excitedly.

'Oh shut up, you two,' said Pip, rolling out of the way. 'It's too hot for that. Let's decide about this afternoon. Are we going to take our tea or not? If we are, I'll have to go and ask my mother now. She doesn't like having it sprung on her at the last minute.'

Larry and Fatty stopped wrestling, and lay panting on their backs, trying to push Buster off.

'Yes, of course we're going to take our tea,' said Fatty. 'I thought we'd decided that. There'll be tea in the marquee in Petter's Field, of course, but it'll be stewing hot in there, and you know what marquee teas are like. We'll take ours and find the Inspector. He won't like marquee teas any more than we do, I'm sure.'

'There's a dog show as well as the gymkhana,' said Bets. 'Couldn't we enter Buster – or is it too late?'

'The only prize he'd win today is for the hottest dog,' said Fatty. 'He'd win that all right. Buster, keep *away* from me. You're like an electric fire.'

'We'd better go,' said Larry, getting up with a groan. 'It takes twice as long to get back home this hot weather – we simply crawl along! Come on,

Daisy, stir yourself!'

Daisy and Larry went down the drive and up the lane to their own home. Pip and Bets didn't have to move because they were already at home! Fatty found his bicycle and put his foot on the pedal.

'Buster!' he called. 'Come on. I'll put you in my bike basket. You'll be a grease-spot if you have to run all the way home.'

Buster came slowly up, his tongue out as usual. He saw the cook's cat in the hedge nearby, but he felt quite unable to chase it. It was just as well, because the cat felt quite unable to run away.

Fatty lifted Buster up and put him in his basket. Buster was quite used to this. He had travelled miles in this way with Fatty and the others.

'You'll have to take some of your fat off, Buster,' said Fatty, as he cycled down the drive. 'You're getting too heavy for words. Next time you see Mr Goon, you won't be able to dance round him, you'll only waddle!'

A call came from Pip's house. 'Lunch,' said Pip sitting up slowly. 'Come on – I hope it's salad and jelly – that's about all I want. Don't let's forget to ask Mummy about a picnic tea for this afternoon.

She'll probably be glad to get rid of us.'

She was! 'That's a good idea!' she said. 'Tell Cook what you want – and if you take drinks, *please* leave some ice in the fridge. You took it all last time. Yes – a picnic is certainly a very good idea – I shall have a lovely peaceful afternoon!'

2. AT THE GYMKHANA

The five children, and Buster of course, met in Petter's Field about three o'clock. The gymkhana had already begun, and horses were dashing about all over the place. Buster kept close to Fatty. He didn't mind passing the time of day with one or two horses in a field, but thirty or forty galloping about were too much.

'Anyone seen the Inspector?' asked Daisy, coming up with a big basket of food and drink.

'No, not yet,' said Fatty, getting out of the way of a colossal horse ridden by a very small boy. 'Is there any place in this field where there aren't horses tearing about? Buster will have a heart attack soon.'

'Look over there,' said Bets, with a giggle. 'See the woman who's in charge of that hoopla stall, or whatever it is? She might be Fatty dressed up!'

11

They all looked. They saw what Bets meant at once. The woman had on a big hat with all kinds of flowers round it, a voluminous skirt, very large feet, and a silk shawl pinned round her shoulders.

'Fatty could disguise himself like that beautifully!' said Daisy. 'Is she real – or somebody in disguise?'

'Inspector Jenks in disguise!' said Bets, with a giggle, and then jumped as somebody touched her on the shoulder.

'What's that you're saying about me?' said a familiar voice. All five of them swung round at once, their faces one big smile. They knew that voice!

'Inspector Jenks!' said Bets, and swung on his broad arm. 'We knew you were coming!'

'Good afternoon, sir,' said Fatty, beaming. 'I say, before anyone else gets hold of you – would you care to have a picnic tea with us – and bring your goddaughter too, of course? We've brought plenty of food.'

'So it seems,' said Inspector Jenks, looking at the three big baskets. 'Well, I wondered if I would see you here. Yes, I'd love to have tea with you – and so would Hilary – that's my small goddaughter. Well, Find-Outers – any more mysteries to report?

What exactly are you working on now?'

Fatty grinned. 'Nothing, sir. Not a mystery to be seen or heard in Peterswood just now. Four weeks of the hols gone and nothing to show. Awful waste of time.'

'And Goon is away, isn't he?' said the Inspector. 'So you can't bait him either – life must indeed be dull for you. You wait till he comes back though – he'll be full of beans. He's been taking some kind of refresher course, I believe.'

'What's a refresher course?' asked Bets.

'Oh – improving his police knowledge, refreshing his memory, learning a few new dodges,' said the Inspector. 'He'll be a smart fellow when he comes back – bursting to try out all he's learnt. You look out, Frederick!'

'It does sound funny when you call Fatty by his right name,' said Bets. 'Oooh, Fatty – let's hope we don't have a mystery after all, in case Mr Goon solves it instead of us.'

'Don't be silly,' said Pip. 'We can always get the better of Mr Goon. It's a pity something hasn't happened while he's been away – we could have solved it before he came back, without any interruptions from him.'

'Here's my small goddaughter,' said the Inspector, turning round to smile at a small girl in jodhpurs and riding jacket. 'Hello, Hilary. Won any prizes yet?'

Hilary sat on a fat little pony that didn't seem able to stand still. Buster kept well out of the way.

'Hello,' said Hilary. 'I'm going to ride now. I haven't won anything yet. Do you want to come and watch?'

'Of course,' said the Inspector. 'Let me introduce you to five friends of mine – who have helped me in many a difficult case. They want you and me to have a picnic tea with them. What about it?'

'Yes, I'd like to,' said Hilary, trying to stop her pony from backing on to an old gentleman nearby. 'Thank you.'

The pony narrowly missed walking on Buster. He yelped, and the restless little animal reared. Hilary controlled him and he tossed his head and knocked off the Inspector's trilby hat.

'Oh – sorry,' said Hilary, with a gasp. 'Bonny's a bit fresh, I'm afraid.'

'I quite agree,' said the Inspector, picking up

his hat before Bonny could tread on it. 'All right, Hilary – I'll come and watch you ride now – and we'll all have tea together when you've finished.'

Hilary cantered off, bumping up and down, her hair flying out under her jockey cap. Buster was most relieved to see her go. He ventured out from behind Fatty, saw a friend he knew and trotted over to pass the time of day; but what with horses of all sizes and colours rushing about he didn't feel at all safe.

It was a very pleasant afternoon. The policeman who had replaced Mr Goon while he was on holiday stood stolidly in a shady corner, and didn't even recognise the Inspector when he passed. It is true that Inspector Jenks was in plain clothes, but Bets felt that *she* would recognise him a mile off even if he was wearing a bathing costume.

'Afternoon, Tonks,' said the Inspector, as they passed the stolid policeman. He leapt to attention at once, and after that could be seen walking about very busily indeed. The Inspector there! Was there anything up? Were there pickpockets about – or some kind of hanky-panky anywhere? Tonks was on the look out at once, and forgot all about standing comfortably in the shade.

Hilary didn't win a prize. Bonny really didn't behave at all well. He took fright at something and backed heavily into the judges, which made them look at him with much dislike and disfavour. Hilary was very disappointed.

She met them in a shady corner for tea, bringing Bonny with her. Buster growled. What? – that awful horse again! Bonny nosed towards him and Buster hastily got under a tent nearby, squeezing beneath the canvas.

Hilary was very shy. She would hardly say a word. She kept Bonny's reins hooked round one arm, which was just as well, as Bonny was really a very nosey kind of horse. Daisy kept a sharp eye on the baskets of food.

The Inspector talked away cheerfully. The children were disappointed that he had no cases to offer them, and no mystery to suggest.

'It's just one of those times when nothing whatsoever happens,' said Inspector Jenks, munching an egg-and-lettuce sandwich hungrily. 'No robberies, no swindlings, no crimes of any sort. Very peaceful.'

He waved his sandwich in the air as he spoke and it was neatly taken out of his hand by Bonny. Everyone roared at the Inspector's surprised face.

'Robbery going on nearby after all!' said Daisy. Hilary scolded Bonny, who backed away into the next picnic party. Buster put his nose out from under the tent canvas, but decided not to come out and join the party yet.

It was while all this was going on that the next mystery loomed up in the very middle of the picnic tea! Nobody expected it. Nobody realised it at first.

Pip happened to be looking down the field, where Mr Tonks, the policeman, was standing beside the Red Cross tent, having attended to somebody who had fainted in the heat. He stood there, mopping his forehead, probably feeling that he would be the next one to faint, when a man came quickly up to him. He looked like a gardener or handyman.

He spoke to Mr Tonks, who at once took out his black notebook, licked his thumb and flicked over the pages till he came to an empty one. Then he began to write very earnestly.

Pip saw this, but he didn't think anything of

it. But then Mr Tonks walked over to where Inspector Jenks was sitting with the Five Find-Outers and Hilary.

'Excuse me for interrupting, sir,' he said. 'But there's been a daylight robbery in Peterswood. I'll have to go and investigate, sir. Seems pretty serious.'

'I'll come with you,' said the Inspector, much to the disappointment of the children. He glanced round. 'Sorry,' he said. 'Duty calls, and all that! I may not see you again if I have to go straight back to my office. Thanks for a very fine tea. Good-bye, Hilary. You rode very well.'

He stepped straight back on to Bonny, who also backed up and pulled Hilary right over with the reins. In the general muddle, Fatty spoke to Mr Tonks, the policeman.

'Where was the robbery?' he asked.

'At Norton House,' said Mr Tonks. 'Up on the hill.'

'Don't know it,' said Fatty, disappointed. He stood up and spoke persuasively to the Inspector. 'I'll come along with you, sir, shall I? I – er – might be of a little help.'

'Sorry, Frederick – can't have you along just

now,' said the Inspector. 'It'll be a plain enough job, I expect – rather beneath your powers! If it's not – well, you'll get going on it, no doubt!'

He went off with Tonks. Fatty stared after them gloomily. Now they would be first on the job – they would see everything, notice everything. And when Mr Goon came back and took over from Mr Tonks, he would settle it all up and put a feather in his cap!

He sat down again. If only he could have gone to Norton House and had a snoop round himself! Now he really couldn't – the Inspector would be annoyed to see him there after he had said he didn't want him – and certainly the householders wouldn't allow him to look round all by himself, if he went after the Inspector had left.

'Never mind, Fatty,' said Bets, seeing how disappointed he was. 'It's only a silly little robbery, I expect. Nothing to bother about – no real mystery!'

Then something surprising happened. Hilary burst into tears! She wailed aloud and tears ran down her podgy cheeks.

'What's the matter? Do you feel sick?' asked Daisy, alarmed.

'No. Oh dear – it's *my* home that's been burgled!' wept Hilary. '*I* live at Norton House. Uncle Jenks must have forgotten it's where I live. Oh, what shall I do?'

Fatty rose to the occasion at once. He put his arm round the weeping Hilary. 'Now, now,' he said, producing an extremely clean white handkerchief, and wiping Hilary's face with it. 'Don't you worry. I'll take you home myself. I'll look after you. I'll even look all round your house to make sure there isn't a single robber left!'

'Oh, thank you,' said Hilary, still sniffing. 'I should hate to go home by myself.'

'We'd better wait a bit till your godfather has had time to look round himself,' said Fatty, who wasn't going to bump into the Inspector if he could help it.

'Then we'll go – and I'll soon see that everything is quite safe for you, Hilary!'

3. FATTY TAKES HIS CHANCE

The others looked at Fatty in admiration. *Some*how he always got what he wanted. Things always went right for him. He badly wanted to examine that burgled house, and he had been left behind by the Inspector – and, lo and behold, he could now go there, taking charge of Hilary, and nobody could say a thing against it!

'I can't go just yet,' sniffed Hilary. 'I've got to ride once more. You won't leave, will you? You *will* take me right home? You see, my parents are away, and there's only Jinny there – she's our housekeeper.'

Better and better! With no parents even to deal with, Fatty felt sure he could snoop as much as he wanted to. Larry and Pip looked at him rather jealously.

'We'll take Hilary home too,' said Larry.

'Better not,' said Fatty. 'Too many cooks

etcetera, etcetera.'

Hilary looked at him, wondering what he meant. The others knew all right. Hilary's tears began to fall again. 'It's my riding prizes I'm thinking of,' she explained, between sobs. 'My cups, you know. I've won so many. The burglar might have taken them.'

This talk about prizes seemed rather surprising to the others, who had no opinion at all of either Hilary or Bonny as regards horsemanship. Fatty patted her on the shoulder and gave her his enormous handkerchief again.

'I'll come up to your room with you and see if your things are safe,' said Fatty, feeling very pleased to think of the first-hand examination he could make. 'Now don't cry any more, Hilary.'

Bets looked on a little jealously. That silly little Hilary! Why did Fatty make such a fuss of her? Surely he would be ashamed of her, Bets, if *she* fussed like that?

'I'll come too, Fatty,' she said. Fatty was about to say no, when he thought that probably it would be a good idea to let Bets come – Hilary could show her this, that, and the other – and he could slip away unseen and snoop round by himself.

'Right, Bets,' he said. 'You can come – you'll be company for Hilary.' Bets was pleased. Now that silly little Hilary wouldn't have Fatty all to herself – she would see to that!

An enormously loud voice began calling over the field. 'Class Twenty-Two, please take your places, Class Twenty-Two.'

'That's my class,' said Hilary, scrambling to her feet. She pulled her cap straight and rubbed her eyes again. She brushed the crumbs off her jacket. Bonny neighed. He wanted to be off, now that he could see various horses moving about again. He had eaten as much tea as the others! He seemed to be an expert at nosing into baskets.

Hilary went off with Bonny, a podgy little figure with a tear-stained face. Fatty looked round triumphantly, winking at the others.

'I shall be in at the start, after all,' he said. 'Sorry you can't come, Pip, Larry and Daisy – but we can't all descend on the house. They'd smell a rat. Bets might be useful though, she can take up Hilary's attention while I'm looking round.'

Bets nodded. She felt proud to be in at the start

with Fatty. 'Shall we go after Hilary's ridden in this show?' she asked. Fatty considered. Yes – Mr Tonks and the Inspector should surely be gone by then.'

So, after Class Twenty-Two had competed in jumping, and Hilary had most surprisingly won the little silver cup offered, Fatty, Bets, and the rest moved off, accompanied by a suddenly-cheerful Hilary.

She rode Bonny, who, now that he had won something, seemed a little more sensible. The others walked beside her, till they came to the lane where Larry and Daisy had to leave them. Then a little later, Pip left them to go down the lane to his home. Fatty and Bets went on up the hill with Hilary. Buster kept sedately at Fatty's heels. He kept an eye on Bonny's legs and thought privately to himself that horses had been supplied with far too many hooves.

They came to Norton House. The Inspector's car was still outside. Blow! Fortunately, Hilary didn't want to go in the front way. She wanted to take Bonny to the stables, which were round at the back.

Bonny was led into his stable. 'Don't you rub him down or anything before you leave him?' asked Fatty. 'I'd be pleased to do it for you, Hilary.

You've had a tiring afternoon.'

Hilary thought that Fatty was the nicest boy she had ever met in her life. Fancy thinking of things like that! She wouldn't have been so much impressed if she had known how desperately Fatty was trying to stay down in the stables till the Inspector had gone!

Fatty groomed the pony so thoroughly that even Hilary was amazed. Bets watched with Buster, rather bored. 'See if they've gone,' whispered Fatty to her, jerking his head towards the front garden. Bets disappeared. She soon came back. She nodded. Fatty straightened up, relieved. Now he could stop working on that restless pony!

'Now we'll go to the house and find out exactly what happened,' said Fatty to Hilary. 'I expect your housekeeper is there. She'll tell us everything. Then you must show Bets all the prizes you have won. She love to see them. Wouldn't you, Bets?'

'Yes,' said Bets, doubtfully.

'You must see them too, Fatty,' said Hilary. He nodded – also doubtfully.

'Come along,' said Hilary and they walked up a long garden path to the house. It was a nice house, square-built, with plenty of windows. Trees surrounded it, and it could not be seen from the road.

They went in at the back door. A woman there gave a little scream of fright. 'Oh, lawks! Oh, it's you, Hilary. I'm in such a state of nerves, I declare I'd scream if I saw my own reflection in a mirror!'

Fatty looked at her. She was a plump little woman, with bright eyes and a good-tempered, sensible mouth. He liked her. She sank down into a chair and fanned herself.

'I've heard about the robbery,' said Hilary. 'Jinny, this is a boy who's brought me home and this is a girl called Bets. They are friends of my godfather, Inspector Jenks.'

'Oh, *are* they?' said Jinny, and Fatty saw that they had gone up in her estimation at once. 'Ah, he's a fine man, that Inspector Jenks. So patient and kind. Went over everything, he did, time and time again. And the questions he asked me! Well there now, you'd never think anyone could pour them out like that!'

'It must have been a great shock for you, Jinny,' said Fatty, in his most courteous and sympathetic voice. He had a wonderful voice for that sort of thing. Bets looked at him in admiration. 'I was sorry for poor little Hilary too. I felt I really must see her home.'

'That was real gentlemanly of you,' said Jinny, thinking that Fatty was just about the nicest boy she had ever met. 'She's nervous, is Hilary. And I'll be nervous too, after this!'

'Oh, you don't need to be,' said Fatty. 'Burglars hardly ever come to the same place twice. Do tell us all about it – if it won't tire you too much.'

Jinny would not have been tired if she had told her story a hundred times. She began at once.

'Well, I was sitting here, half-asleep like, with my knitting on my knee – about four o'clock it must have been. And I was thinking to myself, "I must really get up and put the kettle on to boil," when I heard a noise.'

'Oooh,' said Hilary faintly.

'What sort of noise?' asked Fatty, wishing he could take out his notebook and put all this down. Still, if he forgot anything, Bets would remember it.

'A sort of thudding noise,' said Jinny. 'Out there

27

in the garden somewhere. Like as if somebody had thrown something out of the window and it had landed plonk in the garden.'

'Go on,' said Fatty, and Bets and Hilary listened, all eyes.

'Then I heard a cough upstairs somewhere,' said Jinny. 'A man's deep cough that was stifled quickly as if he didn't want to be heard. That made me sit up, I can tell you! "A man!" I ses to myself. "Upstairs and all! Can't be the master come back – anyway, that's not his cough." So up I gets, and I yells up the stairs, "If there's anybody up there that shouldn't be, I'm getting the police!" '

She paused and looked at the others, gratified to see their intense interest.

'Very very brave of you,' said Fatty. 'What happened next?'

'Well – I suddenly sees a ladder outside,' said Jinny, enjoying herself thoroughly. 'The gardener's ladder, it looked like – run up against the wall leading to the Mistress's bedroom. And I thinks to myself, "Aha! Mister Robber, whoever you are, I'll see you coming down that ladder! I'll take good notice of you too! If you've got a bunion on your toe, I'll notice it, and if you've got a squint in your eye, *I'll* know you again!" I know how important it is to notice what you can, you see.'

'Quite right,' said Fatty approvingly. 'And what *was* the robber like?'

'I don't know,' said Jinny, and she suddenly looked bewildered. 'He never came down that ladder after all!'

There was a pause. 'Well – how did he leave the house then?' asked Fatty. 'Did you hear him?'

'Never a sound,' said Jinny. 'I was standing in the hall, so I know he didn't come down the stairs – and there's only one set of stairs in this house. And there I stood, shivering and shaking I don't mind telling you – till I sees the telephone staring me in the face. And I grabs it and phones the police!'

'Go on,' said Fatty. 'What happened to the burglar? Was he still upstairs?'

'Well, just as I finished telephoning, who should come along but the baker and I yells to him, "Here you, come here and go upstairs with me. There's a burglar in the house." And the baker – he's a very very brave man for all he's so small – he came in and we went into every single room, and not a

29

person was there. Not one!'

'He must have got out of another window,' said Fatty at last.

'He couldn't!' said Jinny triumphantly. 'They were all either shut and fastened, or there's a steep drop to the ground, enough to kill anyone taking a jump. I tell you, he had to come down the stairs or get down the ladder – and he didn't do either! There's a puzzle for you!'

'Well, he must still be there then,' said Fatty and Hilary gave a scream.

'He's not,' said Jinny. 'The Inspector, he looked into every hole and corner, even in the chest in your Ma's room, Hilary. I tell you what *I* think – he made himself invisible! Oh, laugh if you like – but how else could he have got away without me seeing him?'

4. PLENTY OF CLUES

Fatty asked Jinny a great many questions, and she seemed very pleased to answer them. Hilary got bored. 'Come on upstairs and see my riding prizes,' she said. 'Jinny, *those* didn't get stolen, did they?'

'No, Hilary dear – not one of them!' said Jinny comfortingly. 'I went to look, knowing as how you set such store on them. It's things like your Ma's little silver clock and some of the jewellery she left behind, and your father's cigarette box that have gone. All things from the bedrooms – nothing from downstairs that I can see.'

'Come on, Bets,' said Hilary, pulling Bets out of the room. 'Let's go upstairs. You come too, Fatty.'

Fatty was only too pleased. Hilary ran on ahead up the stairs. Fatty had a chance to whisper to Bets.

'You must pretend to be awfully interested, Bets, OK? That will give me a chance to slip away

31

and have a snoop around.'

Bets nodded. She was bored with the horsey little Hilary, but she would do anything for Fatty. They all went upstairs. Hilary took them into her little room. Bets was quite astonished to see the array of cups and other prizes she had won. She began to ask all kinds of questions at once, so that Fatty might slip away.

'What did you win this cup for? What's this? Why are there two cups exactly the same? What's this printed on this cup?'

Hilary was only too anxious to tell her. Fatty grinned. He was soon able to slip away, with Buster trotting at his heels. He went into all the bedrooms. He noticed that in most of the rooms the windows were shut and fastened as Jinny had said. In Hilary's parents' room the window was open. Fatty went to it and looked out. A ladder led down from it to the ground.

That must be the ladder Jinny saw through the hall window, thought Fatty. I saw it myself as we went to the stairs. How did that thief get down from upstairs without being seen, if Jinny didn't see him come down the stairs or the ladder? He can't be here still, because the stolen goods are gone – and anyway, the place must have been thoroughly searched by the Inspector and Mr Tonks.

He went to see if there was any other window or balcony the thief could have dropped from unseen. But there wasn't.

Fatty concentrated his attention on the room from which the goods had been stolen. There were large dirty fingermarks on the wall by the window. Fatty studied them with interest.

The thief wore gloves – dirty gloves too, he thought. Well, he couldn't have been a very expert thief, to leave his prints like that! I'd better measure them.

He measured them. 'Big-handed fellow,' he said. 'Takes at least size eight-and-a-half in gloves, probably nines. Yes, must be nines, I should think. Hello, he's left his gloveprints here too – on the polished dressing-table.'

There were the same big prints again showing clearly. Fatty looked at them thoughtfully. It should be easy to pick out this thief – he really had very large hands.

He went to the window again. He leaned out

over the top of the ladder. 'He came up here by the ladder – didn't bother about the lower part of the house – he chucked the stuff out of the window – where did it land? Over there on that bed, I suppose. I'll go down and look. But yet, he didn't get *down* by the ladder? Why? Was he afraid of Jinny spotting him as he went down? He knew she was in the hall because he heard her shouting.'

Fatty pondered deeply. How in the world had the thief got away without being seen? It was true he could have slipped out of any of the other windows, but only by risking a broken leg, because there was such a steep drop to the ground – no ivy to cling to, no balcony to drop down to. Fatty went round the top part of the house again, feeling puzzled.

He came to a boxroom. It was very small and had a tiny window, which was fast-shut. Fatty opened it and looked down. There was a thick pipe outside, running right down to the ground.

Now – *if* the window had been open instead of shut – and *if* the thief had been even smaller than I am – so that he could have squeezed painfully out of this tiny window – he might have got down to the ground from here, thought Fatty. But the window's shut – and Jinny says all of them were, except the one with the ladder, and a few that nobody could leap from.

He went downstairs, hearing Hilary still talking soulfully about her cups. He couldn't hear a word from Bets. Poor Bets! She really was a great help.

'Who's that?' called Jinny sharply, as she heard Fatty come down the stairs.

'Only me,' said Fatty. 'Jinny, it's a puzzle how that thief got away without being seen, isn't it? Especially as he must have been rather a big fellow, judging from the size of his hands. I've been looking at all the windows. There's only one that has a pipe running by it down to the ground – the one in the boxroom – a tiny window. Was that shut?'

'Oh yes,' said Jinny. 'The Inspector asked me that same question. He said he found it shut too. And you're right – the thief couldn't possibly have squeezed out of that small window, he's too big. You should see his footprints out there on the bed – giant-size, I reckon!'

'I'll go and see, if you don't mind,' said Fatty.

Jinny didn't mind at all – she was only too pleased to let Fatty do anything – a nice, polite boy like that! You didn't come across them every day, more's the pity!

Fatty went out into the garden. He went to where the ladder was raised up against the house. He looked at the bed below. There were quite a lot of footprints there – certainly the thief had a large foot as well as large hands! Wears a shoe about size eleven or twelve, thought Fatty. Hm! Where's my measure?

Fatty measured a print and recorded it in his notebook. He also made a note of the pattern of the rubber heel that the thief wore on his boots – it showed clearly in the prints.

Then he went to where the thief had thrown the stolen goods. They had been thrown well away from the ladder, and had fallen in a bush, and on the ground around. Fatty poked about to see if he could find anything. He felt sure he wouldn't, because the Inspector had already been over the ground – and Fatty had a great respect for Inspector Jenks' ability to discover any clue left lying about!

He came across a curious print – large, roundish,

with criss-cross lines showing here and there. What could the thief have thrown out that made that mark? He went to ask Jinny.

'Ah, the Inspector, he asked me that too,' she said. 'And I couldn't tell him. There was nothing big taken as far as I know. I've seen the mark too – can't think what made it! It's a strange mark – roundish like that, and so big – big as my largest washing-up bowl!'

Fatty had measured the print and drawn it in his book, with the little criss-cross marks on it here and there. Funny. What could it be? It must have something to do with the robbery.

He shut his book. There was nothing more he could examine or find, he was sure of that. He was also sure that he hadn't discovered anything that the Inspector hadn't – probably he hadn't discovered so much! If the Inspector had found anything interesting, he would have taken it away. What a pity Fatty hadn't been on the spot with him when he came with Mr Tonks!

It won't be much of a mystery, I suppose, thought Fatty, going upstairs with Buster to fetch Bets. Surely a thief as large as this one will be easily found and caught. I shouldn't be surprised if the Inspector hasn't got him already!

This was rather a disappointing thought. Fatty went into Hilary's room and smiled when he saw poor Bets' bored face. She smiled back delightedly at him.

'Oh, Fatty – is it time to go? Hilary has been telling me all about her prizes.'

'Yes,' said Hilary, looking pleased with herself. 'Shall I tell *you* now, Fatty? See, this one was . . .'

'Oh, I've heard quite a lot, off and on,' said Fatty. 'You're wonderful, Hilary! To think you've won all those! You really must be proud.'

'Oh well . . .' said Hilary, trying to look modest. 'See, this one I . . .'

Fatty looked at his watch and gave such a loud exclamation that Bets jumped and Hilary stopped, startled.

'Good gracious! *Look* at the time! I shall have to see your prizes another time, Hilary. Bets, I must take you home – you'll get in an awful row if you're any later.'

Hilary looked disappointed. She had been quite prepared to go over the whole history of her riding prizes once again. Bets was overjoyed to think Fatty was at last going to leave.

'Thanks awfully, Hilary, for giving me such a lovely time,' said Bets politely but not very truthfully. Fatty patted Hilary on the shoulder and said it had been a real pleasure to meet her. Hilary beamed.

She went down to the front gate with them, and waved till they were out of sight. Bets heaved a sigh of relief when they at last turned a corner and the waving could no longer be seen.

'Oh, Fatty – did you find out anything? Is it a mystery?' she asked eagerly. 'Tell me!'

'I don't somehow think it is,' said Fatty. 'Just an ordinary little burglary, with one or two odd little touches – but I expect the Inspector and Mr Tonks have got more information than I have, actually, as they were there first. I'll go and see Mr Tonks, I think. He might let out something.'

'Why not ask the Inspector?' said Bets, as they turned down the lane to her home.

'Er – no – I think not,' said Fatty. 'I don't particularly want him to know I snooped round after all. Mr Tonks is the one to question. I'll see him tomorrow. Tell Pip I'll be round at eleven o'clock.'

He took Bets right up to the door of her house and said goodnight. 'And thanks for doing your bit for me,' he said. 'I know you were bored – but I couldn't have gone without you and snooped round – you were a real help.'

'Then I don't mind being bored,' said Bets. 'Oh dear – I never want to hear about riding prizes again!'

5. SOME INFORMATION FROM TONKS

Fatty went home and walked down to the shed at the bottom of the garden where he kept his most valuable possessions.

He cast an eye over the various chests and boxes in his closely-guarded shed. Here he kept his disguises – old clothes of various kinds; hats, boots, and ragged scarves. Here was a box containing many curious things that he didn't want his mother either to find or to throw away! False teeth to put over his own – false cheek pads to swell out his face – eyebrows of all colours – wigs that fitted him and wigs that didn't – big and little moustaches. Oh, Fatty had a most interesting collection in this shed of his at the bottom of the garden!

He gazed at the array of belongings. I'd like to do a spot of disguising, he thought. I will when Mr Goon comes back. It's not much fun doing it now unless there's a mystery on, or Mr Goon to deceive. Wonder when he's coming back. I'll ask Mr Tonks tomorrow.

He went to see Tonks the very next morning at about ten o'clock. Buster ran beside his bicycle. Fatty had decided he really was too fat for words – exercise would be good for him. So poor Buster panted beside the bicycle, his tongue lolling out first on one side of his mouth and then on the other.

Fatty knocked at the door. 'Come in!' cried a voice and in went Fatty. He found Mr Tonks poring over a sheaf of papers. The stolid policeman looked up and nodded.

'Ah – Frederick Trotteville, isn't it? Great friend of the Inspector's, aren't you? He was telling me yesterday some of the things you'd done.'

This seemed a very good beginning. Fatty sat down. 'I don't know if you're too busy to spare me a minute,' he said. 'I took Hilary home last night, she was so scared, poor little thing – you know, the Inspector's goddaughter.'

'Oh – so that's what he meant when he suddenly said, "My word – Norton House – that's Hilary's home,"' said the policeman. 'I didn't like to ask him.'

'I expect he didn't realise it was his goddaughter's house that had been burgled when he went off with you,' said Fatty. 'Anyway, she was frightened and I took her home. I had a look round, of course – and I wondered if I'd found anything of use to you.'

'Shouldn't think so,' said Tonks. 'Not that I'm much of a one for solving cases – never have been – but the Inspector was there, you see, and there's nothing much *he* misses. Still, it's very nice of you to come along and offer to help.'

'Not at all,' said Fatty, in his most courteous voice. 'Er – did *you* find anything interesting?'

'Oh – just fingerprints – or, rather, gloveprints – and footprints,' said Tonks. 'Same as you did, I expect. Pretty big fellow, the thief seems to have been. Made a good getaway too – nobody saw him go, nobody met him down the hill – might have been invisible!'

Fatty laughed. 'That's what Jinny said. You'd have thought a big fellow like that, carrying a sack or parcel of some kind, would have been noticed, wouldn't you? Pity the baker didn't spot him when he arrived with the bread.'

'Yes. He never saw a thing,' said Tonks. 'I must say, it was pretty brave of him to go upstairs with Jinny and look around – he's a tiny little fellow, and wouldn't be any match for a big man. I went along to see him last night. He reckons his coming disturbed the thief. He hadn't really stolen very much, as far as I can make out.'

'Did anyone else come that afternoon – to Norton House, I mean?' asked Fatty.

'The postman, a woman delivering election leaflets, and a man selling logs, according to Jinny,' said Tonks. 'We've seen them all – they didn't notice anything out of the ordinary, not even the ladder. Anyway, they came a good time before the thief.'

'Where was the gardener?' asked Fatty.

'He'd gone off to take some tackle down to the gymkhana for Hilary,' said Tonks. 'He came back just as all the excitement was over. The baker sent him off to tell me about the robbery, so down he went to Petter's Field again.'

Fatty fell silent. This was a strange kind of thief – big, clumsy, easy to see – and yet apparently invisible! Not a soul had noticed him.

'Did you find any other clues?' asked Fatty. Tonks looked at him doubtfully. He had already said rather a lot to this polite and quite helpful boy. But ought he to tell him everything?

'You needn't worry about what you tell me,' said Fatty, seeing at once that Tonks had something else to say and wasn't sure about it. 'I'm a friend of the Inspector's – you know that. All I do is help if I can.' 'Yes. I know that,' said Tonks. 'The Inspector said, "Well, well – if *we* can't find the thief, Tonks, Frederick certainly will!" '

'Well, there you are,' said Fatty, grinning. '*You* haven't found him yet – so give me a chance, Mr Tonks.'

The policeman produced two dirty bits of paper. He handed them to Fatty, who looked at them with much interest. One had scribbled on it,

2 Frinton

The other was even shorter. It simply said,

1 Rods

45

'What do they mean?' asked Fatty, studying the dirty little scraps of paper.

'Don't know any more than you do,' said Tonks, taking them back. 'Number two, Frinton. Number one, Rods. Looks like addresses of some sort. But I'm not going off to Frinton or Rods, wherever they are, to hunt for the thief! We found these bits of paper near the bush where the stolen goods had been thrown.'

'Funny,' said Fatty. 'Do you think they've really anything to do with this case? They look like scraps of paper torn up by someone and thrown away.'

'That's what I said,' agreed Tonks. 'Anyway, I'll have to keep them, in case they're important.'

Fatty could see there was nothing else to find out from Tonks. He got up. 'Well – I wish you luck in finding the thief,' he said. 'It seems to me the only way to spot him will be to snoop round everywhere till we see a man wearing size twelve shoes and size nine gloves!'

Tonks gave a sudden grin. 'Well – if Mr Goon likes to do that, he's welcome. He's taking over the case when he comes back. Nice for him to have something to do in this dead-and-alive hole. I'm used to a big town – I don't like these quiet country places where the only thing that happens is a dog that chases sheep, or a man that doesn't buy his TV licence.'

Fatty could have told Tonks how wrong he was. He could have told him of all the extraordinary and exciting mysteries that had happened in Peterswood – but he didn't because of Mr Tonks' unexpected piece of news about Mr Goon.

'Did you say Mr Goon was coming back?' he asked. 'When?'

'You sound pleased,' said Tonks. 'I did hear you didn't like one another! He's coming back this afternoon. I hand over then. I won't be having any more to do with this case. Anyway, Mr Goon ought to put his hands on the thief soon enough – he can't be far away.'

Fatty glanced at the clock on the mantelpiece. He must go, or he would keep the others waiting. He had found out all he wanted to know – though it wasn't much help really. And Mr Goon was coming back! Old Mr Goon. Clear-Orf, with his bombastic ways and his immense dislike of all the Five Find-Outers and their doings – to say nothing of Buster!

Fatty shook hands solemnly with Tonks, assured him that it had been a great pleasure to meet him, and went off on his bicycle, with Buster panting once again near the pedals.

The others were waiting for him in Pip's garden. It was very hot again, and they lay on their backs with iced lemonade in a patch of shade.

'Here's old Fatty,' said Pip, hearing his bicycle bell ringing as Fatty came at sixty miles an hour up the drive. 'How in the world can he ride at that pace when it's so hot?'

But Fatty was the bringer of news, and he didn't think once about the heat as he came riding up the garden path to the others. He flung his bicycle down and beamed round at them all.

'Mr Goon's coming back,' he said. 'This afternoon! *And* he'll take over the case of the invisible thief – so we shall have some fun.'

Everyone sat up at once. 'That's good news,' said Larry, who always enjoyed their tussle of wits with Mr Goon. 'Did you see Mr Tonks then? Had he anything to say?'

Fatty sat down. 'Not much,' he said. 'He and the Inspector didn't really find out any more than I did.

I'll tell you what I found out yesterday in a minute – unless Bets has already told you?'

No, Bets hadn't. She had thought that Fatty ought to tell everything – so he got out his notebook and went into all the details of the new case.

He told them of the setting-up of the ladder – the large footprints in the bed below – the equally large gloveprints in the bedroom above – the throwing out of the stolen goods – the apparently completely invisible getaway.

'Only two ways of escape – down the ladder or down the stairs,' said Fatty. 'And Jinny, the housekeeper, was standing in the hall, where she could see both – and she swears nobody came down either stairs or ladder.'

'Must have got out of another upstairs window then,' said Pip.

'All either fastened and shut, or too far from the ground,' said Fatty. 'There's only one that might have been used – and that is a tiny window in a boxroom – there was a fat pipe running by it to the ground. Anyone could have slithered down that – if he was tiny enough to get out of the window! But – the window was shut and fastened when

49

Jinny went round the upstairs part of the house.'

'Hmm – well, no thief could squeeze out of a window, hold on to a pipe, and then shut and fasten the window after him – from the inside!' said Pip. 'It's a bit of a puzzle, isn't it? Jinny's right – the man's invisible!'

'Well, if he is, he'll certainly perform again,' said Larry. 'I mean – an invisible thief has a great advantage, hasn't he!'

Fatty laughed. He showed them his notebook with the drawings of the footprints, the gloveprints – and the curious round-shaped print with the faint criss-cross marks.

'Can't imagine what made *that* mark,' he said. 'It was near the bush where the stolen goods were thrown. And look – can anyone make anything of this?'

He showed them the curious addresses – if they were addresses – that he had copied into his notebook too.

'"2 Frinton". "1 Rods",' he said. 'Those words and numbers were found on two separate dirty scraps of paper near the bush. What on earth do they mean?'

'Frinton,' said Bets, wrinkling her forehead in a frown. 'Wait a minute. That rings a bell, somehow. Frinton, Frinton. *Frinton!* Where have I heard that lately?'

'Oh – one of your friends sent you a postcard from Frinton-on-Sea, I expect, silly,' said Pip.

'No. Wait a minute – I'm remembering!' said Bets. 'It's that place down by the river – not very far from here, actually – the place where they take visitors – Frinton Lea!'

'Clever old Bets,' said Fatty, admiringly. 'There may be something in that. If we find a large-sized fellow slouching about there, we'll keep a watch on him.'

'What about "1 Rods",' said Larry.

Nobody could think up anything for that.

'We'll go round looking at the names of houses and find out if anyone has that name,' said Fatty. 'Rods. It's a peculiar name, anyhow. Well, Find-Outers – the mystery has begun!'

6. THE SECOND ROBBERY

Mr Goon arrived back that afternoon, bursting
with importance. His refresher course and the
things he had learnt at it had given him completely
new ideas about his job. Ah, he knew a lot more
about the ways of wrongdoers now! He knew a
good deal more about how to catch them. And he
also knew an enormous amount about the art of
disguising himself.

It was entirely because of Fatty that Mr Goon
had applied himself to the course given in the arts
of disguise. Fatty had bewildered, puzzled, angered
and humiliated poor Mr Goon so many times
because of his artful disguises. The times that boy
had turned up as a red-headed cheeky telegraph
boy – or an old man – or even a voluble and rude
old woman!

Mr Goon gritted his teeth whenever he thought

of them. Now – NOW – Mr Goon himself knew a bit about disguises, and he had brought back with him quite a remarkable collection of clothes and other gadgets.

He'd show that fat fellow he wasn't the only one to use disguises. Mr Goon patted his pocket as he travelled home by coach. Greasepaint – eyebrows – a beard – a wig – he was bringing them all back. He'd trick that toad properly. A real toad, that was what that boy was.

Mr Goon was most delighted to hear about the new robbery from Mr Tonks. Ah – here was something he could get his teeth into at once. With all the new things he had learnt, he could tackle this fresh case easily – finish with it long before Fatty had even begun it.

He was a little upset to find that Fatty had apparently already heard about it and was interested in it. 'That boy!' he growled to Tonks. 'Can't keep his nose out of anything!'

'Well, he couldn't very well help it this time,' said Tonks stolidly. 'He was there when I went and reported the robbery to the Inspector.'

'He would be,' said Goon, scowling. 'Look

here, Mr Tonks – I tell you this – if the Crown Jewels were stolen one dark night, that boy would somehow know all about it – he'd be there!'

'Rather far-fetched, that,' said Tonks, who thought Mr Goon was a bit of a turnip-head. 'Well, I'll be going. I've given you all the details – you've got those scraps of paper, haven't you? With those addresses on?'

'Yes. I'm going to do something about those at once,' said Goon pompously. 'I reckon if those places are watched, something'll come out – and watched they will be.'

'Right,' said Tonks. 'Well, good-bye Mr Goon. Good luck.'

He went off and Goon heaved a sigh of relief. He sat down to look through the papers that Tonks had left.

But he hadn't been studying them long before the telephone rang. Goon picked up the receiver and put it to his ear. 'Police here,' he said gruffly.

Someone spoke volubly and excitedly at the other end. Goon stiffened as he listened – ah – another robbery – things were getting interesting!

'I'll be along, madam. Leave everything as it

is. Don't touch a thing,' commanded Goon in his most official voice. He put on his helmet and went out to get his bicycle.

And this time those interfering children won't be there to pester me, he thought, as he cycled quickly along in the heat. I'll be in first on this.

He cycled through the village, turned up a side road, and came to a house. He got off his bicycle, wheeled it in at the gate, and went up to the front door.

It was opened by Fatty!

Mr Goon gaped. He scowled. He couldn't think of a word to say. Fatty grinned.

'Good afternoon, Mr Goon,' he said, in his politest voice, a voice that always infuriated Mr Goon. 'Come in. We've been expecting you.'

'What are *you* doing here?' said Mr Goon, finding his voice at last. 'Tricking me? Getting me here for nothing? I thought it all sounded a bit funny on the phone – silly sort of voice, and silly sort of tale. I might have guessed it was one of your tricks – just to welcome me home, I suppose! Well – you'll be sorry for this. I'll report you! You think because the Inspector is friendly to you, you can get away with anything! You think . . .'

'Woof!' said somebody – and Buster darted out in ecstasy, so pleased to hear the voice of his old enemy that he wagged his tail for joy! That was enough for Goon. He departed hurriedly, muttering as he went, his bicycle wobbling down the path.

'Well!' said Fatty, in surprise. 'What's up with him? He can't *really* think I'm hoaxing him! Larry, come here. Mr Goon's gone off his head!'

Larry and Daisy appeared. They looked after the departing Mr Goon, who was now sailing out of the gate.

'He's gone,' said Fatty. 'He came – he saw – and he didn't stay to conquer. What's up with him?'

'You'd have thought that with another robbery, he'd have stayed like a shot,' said Daisy.

'Well, Lucy reported it fully,' said Fatty. 'I heard her on the telephone.'

Somebody called out to them. 'Was that the police? Tell them to come in here.'

'It was Mr Goon,' said Fatty. 'He came – but he went at once. Funny.'

'Well, thank goodness you and Larry and Daisy are here,' said Mrs Williams. 'I don't know what I should have done without you.'

It had all happened very suddenly indeed. Fatty had gone to tea with Larry and Daisy that afternoon, as Pip and Bets had gone out with their mother. They had been having tea in the garden, when someone from the house next door began to call for help.

'Help! Robbers! Help! Help, I say!'

'Gosh – that's Mrs Williams yelling,' said Larry, getting up quickly. 'Our next door neighbour.'

'What's happened?' asked Daisy, half-frightened at the continual shouts.

'She's been robbed,' said Fatty. 'Come on – quick!'

All three climbed over the fence and appeared in the next door garden. Mrs Williams saw them from a window and beckoned. 'Come in, quickly! I'm scared!'

They rushed in at the back door. There was no one in the kitchen. A heap of groceries lay on the table, and four loaves sat neatly side by side. A parcel stood by the door.

Fatty's quick eyes noted everything as he ran through the kitchen into the hall. 'Kitchen door open – the thief went in there, probably. Wonder if it's the same one as yesterday.'

Mrs Williams was sitting on her sofa, looking rather white. She was a gentle, grey-haired old lady, and she was very frightened. 'Get me my smelling-salts out of my bag,' she said faintly to Daisy. Daisy got them and she held them to her nose.

'What happened, Mrs Williams?' said Fatty.

'Well, I was having my afternoon rest in here,' said Mrs Williams. 'And I suddenly heard the sound of heavy footsteps upstairs. Then I heard the sound of a deep, hollow sort of cough – rather like a sheep makes, really.'

'A hollow cough?' said Fatty at once, remembering that Jinny had also heard the same noise.

'Yes. I sat up, scared,' said Mrs Williams. 'I crept out of this room and went into the hall. And suddenly someone gave me a push into the cupboard there, and in I went. The door was locked on me, and I couldn't get out.'

Just as she was speaking, there came the sound of a key in the front door, and then the door was opened and shut. 'Who's that?' asked Fatty.

'Oh, that's Lucy, my companion – Miss Lucy,'

said Mrs Williams. 'Oh, I'm glad she's back. Lucy, Lucy, come here. A dreadful thing has happened!'

Miss Lucy came in. She was a little bird-like woman with very sharp eyes, and a funny bouncy way of walking. She went to Mrs Williams at once.

'What is it? You look pale!'

Mrs Williams repeated what she had told the children. They waited patiently till she came to where she had been locked in the cupboard.

'Well, there I was in the hall cupboard, and I could hear the thief walking about overhead again,' said Mrs Williams. 'Heavy-footed too, and clumsy by the way he knocked things over. Then he came downstairs – I heard him clearly because the stairs pass over the hall cupboard – and I heard that awful sheep-like cough again.'

She stopped and shuddered.

'Go on,' said Fatty gently. 'How did you get out of the cupboard? Did the thief unlock it?'

'He must have,' said Mrs Williams. 'I was so scared when I heard him coming downstairs that I must have fainted – and when I came round again, I found myself lying in a heap on all the boots and shoes and golf-clubs – and the door was unlocked!

59

I tried it – and it opened.'

'Hmmmm!' said Fatty. 'Miss Lucy, you'd better telephone the police, I think – and I'll take a little look round. This is very – very – interesting!'

7. MR GOON ON THE JOB

Miss Lucy ran to telephone the police at once and, as we know, got on to Mr Goon. Very excitedly and volubly she told him all that had happened, and then the household waited for Mr Goon to arrive.

Fatty took a hasty look round while they waited. He was sure the thief was the same as the one who had been to Norton House the day before. For one thing – that deep, hollow cough – and for another, the heavy-footed clumsiness sounded as if they belonged to the same burglar.

Fatty ran upstairs. The first thing he saw in one of the bedrooms was a print on the wall, just by the door – a large gloveprint! He flicked open his notebook and compared it with the measurements detailed there. Yes – pretty much exactly the same.

Now what about any footprints in the garden?

The ground was so dry now that, unless the thief obligingly walked on a flower-bed, he probably wouldn't leave any prints.

Fatty was just going out to see, when he caught sight of Mr Goon coming up the front drive, and went to the door. *What* a shock it would be for Mr Goon to see him! Fatty really enjoyed opening the door.

He was surprised when Mr Goon dashed off so soon. Surely he couldn't be idiotic enough to really think that Fatty had hoaxed him? Well, well – if so, then he, Fatty, might as well get on with his job of snooping round. Mr Goon wouldn't have let him do that if he had taken charge of the case, that was certain.

So Fatty made hay while the sun shone and slipped out into the garden, leaving Larry and Daisy to try and explain Mr Goon's sudden departure to Mrs Williams and Miss Lucy. They were most indignant.

Fatty went out through the kitchen door. He had decided that the thief had come in that way, as the front door had been shut. He went down the path that led from the kitchen. He saw a bed of flowers and walked over to it. The bed was underneath the sitting-room window, and it was in that room that Mrs Williams had been asleep.

Fatty gave an exclamation. On the bed were a couple of very large footprints. The same ones as yesterday – he was sure of it! He flicked open his notebook again.

The bed was drier than the one he had examined the day before for prints, and the rubber heel did not show this time – but the large prints were there, plain to see.

The thief came and looked in at the window, thought Fatty. And he saw Mrs Williams fast asleep. Hello – here are some more prints – on this bed. Why did he walk here?

There didn't seem any reason why the thief had walked on the second bed – but it was clear that the prints matched the others. In fact, everything matched – the gloveprints, the footprints, the hollow cough. Would there also be any mark like that big, roundish one that Fatty had seen at Norton House?

He hunted about for one; and he found it! It was very faint, certainly, and the criss-cross marks could hardly be seen. The roundish print was by the kitchen door, on the dusty path there. Something had been stood there – what was it?

Any scraps of paper this time?, wondered Fatty, rather struck by the way that everything seemed to be repeated in this second case of robbery. He hunted everywhere – but there were no scraps of paper this time.

He went indoors, and met Miss Lucy coming out to find him. 'Mr Goon has just telephoned,' she said. 'I can't make him out. He wanted to know if there had been a *real* robbery here! Well, why didn't he stay and ask us about it when he came? He must be mad.'

Fatty grinned. Mr Goon had evidently thought the whole thing over and decided that he had better find out for certain what the truth was – and, to his disgust, he had found that the robbery was real – it wasn't a trick of Fatty's after all!

'He's a bit of a turnip-head,' said Fatty cheerfully. 'Never mind. You tell him I'm on the job when he comes – he needn't worry about it at all. I've got it well in hand.'

Miss Lucy looked doubtfully at Fatty. She was

getting a little bewildered, what with thieves, and policemen who arrived and departed all in the same minute, and boys who seemed to be acting like policemen ought to, but didn't.

Fatty pointed to the groceries on the table. 'Who took these in?' he asked. 'Have you a cook?'

'Yes. But she's off for the day,' said Miss Lucy. 'I left the back door open for the grocer's girl to leave the groceries in the kitchen – she often does that for us. The baker's been too, I see – and the postman, because there's a parcel by the door. Mrs Williams has been in all afternoon, but she likes a nap, so the tradesmen never ring when Cook is out. They just leave everything, as you see.'

'Yes, I see,' said Fatty thoughtfully. He gazed at the groceries, the bread, and the parcel. Three people had come to the house in a short time. Had one of them noticed the thief hanging about anywhere? He must find out.

Mr Goon arrived again, a little shamefaced. Miss Lucy let him in, looking rather severe. She thought a policeman who behaved like Mr Goon was ridiculous.

'Er – sorry I didn't come in before,' said Mr

Goon. 'Hope I've not kept you waiting too long, er – urgent business, you know. By the way – that boy – has he gone?'

'If you mean young Trotteville, he is still here, examining everything,' said Miss Lucy coldly. 'He told me to tell you not to bother about the job. He's got it well in hand. I am sure he will recover the jewellery Mrs Williams has had stolen.'

Goon turned a curious purple colour, and Miss Lucy felt rather alarmed. She felt that she didn't want this peculiar policeman in the house at all. She tried to shut the front door – but Goon put his enormous foot in the crack at once.

Miss Lucy gave a faint shriek, and Mr Goon took his foot out again, trying to think of something reassuring to say to this aggravating, bird-like creature.

Miss Lucy promptly shut the door and even put up the chain. Goon stared at the door, and went purple again. He walked ponderously round to the back door, where he found Fatty examining the path for footprints.

'Gah!' said Mr Goon, in a tone of deep disgust. 'Can't get rid of you! First you're at the front door, now you're at the back door. You be off. This here case has got nothing to do with you. Nothing.'

'That's where you're wrong, Mr Goon,' said Fatty in the mild, courteous voice that made Goon see red. 'I was called in to help. I've found out a lot already.'

Larry and Daisy heard Goon's infuriated voice and came out through the kitchen to listen. They stood at the back door, grinning.

'You here too?' said Goon, in even greater disgust. 'Can't you keep your noses out of anything? Now, you clear orf, all of you, and let me get on with my work here. And just you call off that dog!'

Buster had now joined the trio, and was capering delightedly round Mr Goon's feet.

'He's missed his ankle-hunting,' Fatty explained. 'Don't grudge him a little fun, Mr Goon. And don't you kick him. If you do, I won't call him off.'

Mr Goon gave it up. He pushed past Larry and Daisy, went into the kitchen, still pursued by a delighted Buster, and through the door into the hall. By a clever bit of work, he managed to shut the door of the kitchen on Buster, who scraped at it, barking wildly.

'Well, he's gone to do a spot of interviewing,' said Fatty, sitting down on the kitchen doorstep. 'He won't find the two ladies very pleased with him, I fear. He's rather started off on the wrong foot with them.'

'Fatty, have you found out anything interesting?' asked Larry eagerly. 'I saw you with your measuring tape, out of the window. What have you discovered?'

'I've discovered exactly the same as I discovered yesterday,' said Fatty. 'Except that I haven't found any bits of paper with names and numbers on. Look at those prints over there.'

Larry and Daisy examined them with interest. 'I know only one person in this village with feet big enough to fit those prints,' said Daisy. Fatty looked up at once.

'Who? Perhaps you've hit on the very person! There can't be many people with such enormous feet.'

'Well – it's Mr Goon – old Clear-Orf!' said Daisy with a giggle. The others roared.

'You're right. His feet would certainly fit those

prints!' said Fatty. 'Unfortunately, he's about the only large-footed person who's absolutely ruled out.'

'We'll certainly have to go about with our eyes on people's feet,' said Larry. 'It's the one thing the thief can't hide! He can stick his great hands in his pockets and stop his hollow cough – but he can't hide his great feet!'

'No – you're right,' said Fatty. 'Well, let's not stop any more. Mr Goon's had about enough of us for one afternoon, I should think.'

They climbed over the fence into Larry's garden. Buster squeezed through a hole.

'Gosh – I'd forgotten we were in the middle of tea,' said Fatty, pleased to see the remains of sandwiches and cakes on the grass. 'What's happened to some of these potted-meat sandwiches? Your cat's been at them, Larry.'

'Buster – on guard!' said Larry at once, and Buster growled and looked round for the cat.

They finished their tea, talking about the two robberies. After a time, Buster growled again and went to the fence. 'Must be Mr Goon over the other side, doing a spot of detecting,' said Fatty with a grin. 'Let's go and see his turnip-brains at work.'

Goon was busy looking for prints and clues. He was most irritated to see three heads looking over the wall at him. They watched him solemnly as he measured and marked.

'Look! He's found a footprint!' said Larry, in an admiring voice. The back of Mr Goon's neck went scarlet but he said nothing.

'Now he's measuring it,' said Daisy. 'Oooh, isn't he *care*ful?'

'Brains, Daisy, brains,' said Fatty. 'What can we do against brains like that?'

Mr Goon felt as if he was going to burst. Those children! Toads! Pests! Always in his way, buzzing round like a lot of mosquitoes. He made a very dignified retreat into the kitchen, rather hurried at the end when he discovered that Buster had squeezed through the hole in the fence and was after him.

'Clear orf!' he shouted, slamming the door in Buster's face. 'You clear orf!'

8. FATTY MAKES SOME PLANS

Fatty called a meeting down in his shed the very next day. Larry and Daisy arrived punctually, and Pip and Bets soon after. Buster greeted them all exuberantly, as if he hadn't seen them for years.

'This is a proper meeting,' announced Fatty. 'An official one, I mean. We've got our mystery all right – and we've got just under four weeks to solve it. That ought to be plenty of time!'

'Yes, it ought – for old hands like us!' said Larry, grinning. 'Did you tell Pip and Bets all about yesterday's robbery next door to us? Do they know everything?'

'Yes. I went to tell them last night,' said Fatty. 'We've got to make plans this morning.'

'What? Lists of suspects and so on?' asked Bets eagerly.

'We haven't got a single suspect,' said Fatty. 'Not

one! It's about the only mystery we've ever had with two crimes and no suspects at all. Most extraordinary. It's going to be difficult to get on with the case till we find a few suspects to enquire about.'

'We've got plenty of clues,' said Daisy. 'Footprints – gloveprints – coughs – bits of paper . . .'

'What's your plan, Fatty?' asked Pip. 'I bet you've got one.'

'Well, I have, as a matter-of-fact,' said Fatty modestly. 'It's like this – all we've got to go on at the moment is what we think the thief looks like – big-footed, heavy-handed, clumsy, with a deep, hollow cough – and we've got two bits of paper possibly dropped by him – and if they are addresses or names, which they probably are, we must watch those addresses or people.'

'Yes,' said Larry. 'And what about asking the grocer, the baker, and the postman if they saw any sign of a big-footed fellow yesterday afternoon, when they delivered their goods in our road?'

'I was coming to that,' said Fatty. 'It seems to me we must split up a bit and each do a job, as we usually do.'

'Oh dear,' said Bets. 'I'm really not much good

by myself.'

'You're one of the best of us,' said Fatty warmly, and Bets blushed with pleasure. 'Who solved the mystery of the pantomime cat, I'd like to know? You did, Bets – oh yes you did – without your bright idea about it we'd never have solved it! So just you do your bit this time too.'

'Oh, I will, Fatty,' said Bets earnestly.

'Now you, Larry, go and interview the postman,' said Fatty. 'And you, Pip, go to the baker. If he's the same one that Jinny at Norton House called in to help her, the one who searched the upstairs rooms for her, all the better. He may have noticed something about the two cases that we haven't.'

'Right,' said Pip. 'I believe he is *our* baker too.'

'And you, Daisy and Bets, go and interview the grocer's girl,' said Fatty. 'Apparently it's a girl who delivers Harris's goods – that's the grocer. Go and get her to talk – listen to all she says – remember it, and we'll piece together everything when we meet again.'

There was a silence. Everyone wondered what little job Fatty had kept for himself.

'What are *you* going to do?' asked Bets.

'I'm going to disguise myself,' said Fatty, and Bets gave a squeal of joy. 'And I'm going to go and watch Frinton Lea, just to see if any big-footed fellow lives there! If I watch the house all day long, I may see something.'

'But, Fatty – you'll be noticed if you stand outside all day long,' said Daisy. 'Besides – what about meals?'

'I've thought of all that,' said Fatty. 'Leave it all to me! I won't tell you my disguise. When you've done your jobs, you can come along and see if you recognise me. I'll be within fifty yards of the house all day long – visible to everyone – but I bet you anything you like that nobody will pay a moment's attention to me!'

They all stared at him. He stared back, his eyes twinkling. 'We shall spot you at once,' said Daisy.

'All right. Spot me then,' said Fatty. 'Now, come on – let's get going. Clear orf, all of you – and let me disguise myself!'

They all went off, laughing, wondering what Fatty was going to do. They were absolutely certain that they would spot Fatty at once. So would everyone else notice him? How could anyone loiter outside a house all day long without being noticed? And what about meals? There was nowhere down by Frinton Lea where he could even have a snack. There were fields behind and the river ran just in front.

'I'm going back home to wait for the baker,' said Pip. 'He comes to us about twelve o'clock, I think.'

'Oh, that's an awfully good idea,' said Larry. 'I'll come with you, and wait for the parcel postman to come to your house too. Then we can keep each other company.'

'He may not come,' said Pip. 'We don't always have parcels.'

'I'll have to chance that,' said Larry. 'I don't feel like going to the post office and asking to interview the parcel postman there, in front of everyone! I half thought I'd have to do that at first!'

'What about the grocer's girl?' said Daisy. 'Do you have Harris for your grocer, Pip? If you do, Bets and I can be with you and Larry, and we can all be together.'

'No, we don't have Harris,' said Pip. 'Let me see now – what roads does the girl deliver to in the mornings? I've seen her somewhere. I know she only goes to your part of the town in the afternoon.'

'I know! She delivers down the other end of the town,' said Bets suddenly. 'I was at Mrs Kendal's once, with a message for Mummy – and the grocer's girl came then. We could go and wait about for her there, Daisy.'

'Right. Come on,' said Daisy. 'Good-bye, boys – don't start playing a game and forget all about your job!'

'Don't be silly, Daisy,' said Larry, quite annoyed. The boys went off to Pip's and the girls went off to the other end of the town.

They were lucky because they didn't have to wait very long. They sat in the small dairy near Mrs Kendal's, eating ice creams, keeping a watch for the grocer's van.

'There it is!' said Bets suddenly, and Daisy looked up to see Harris's yellow van coming round the corner. It came to a stop nearby.

Daisy and Bets paid quickly for their ice creams and hurried out. They were just in time to see the grocer's girl jump from the van, hurry to the back, undo the door, and drag out a big box piled with groceries.

'Let her go in with it first, and then we'll speak to her when she comes out,' said Daisy. They walked slowly to the back of the van. Then Bets saw that a little packet of soap powder had fallen out and was lying in the road.

'It must have fallen out of the girl's box,' she said to Daisy, and bent to pick it up just as the grocer's girl came out again, this time with her box empty.

'You dropped this,' said Bets, holding it out.

'Oh, thanks very much,' said the girl gratefully. 'I missed it when I took the things in just now. I'm in an awful hurry this morning – had an interview with the police, you know. About the robbery at Mrs Williams.'

This was just the opening the other two wanted. Daisy seized on it eagerly. 'Oh, did you really? Did you know that my brother and I live next door to Mrs Williams, and we rushed in to help her?'

'No! Well I never!' said the girl, astonished. 'Did you see anything of the thief? I hear he took quite a bit of Mrs Williams' jewellery.'

'Did he?' said Daisy, who hadn't heard yet what

exactly had been taken. '*You* went to the house yesterday afternoon too, didn't you? Did *you* see anything of the thief?'

'No, not a thing,' said the girl. 'I didn't see anyone at all. I think I must have come before he was there. I never saw or heard anything.'

'Did you see any loaves or any parcel in the kitchen when you went in?' asked Bets, wondering if the grocer's girl had gone to the house before the others.

'There were no loaves there when I went, and I didn't see any parcel,' said the girl, getting into her van. 'Mr Goon asked me a lot of questions this morning – and I couldn't tell him a thing. To think I was there and might have brushed against the robber! Well, it just shows, doesn't it?'

Bets and Daisy didn't know exactly what it showed, but they nodded their heads.

'Sorry I can't stop,' said the girl. 'I'd love to hear what you did too – but I'm so very late. To think I didn't hear or see a *thing*. Bad luck, wasn't it?'

She drove off. Daisy and Bets looked at one another. 'Well, that was unexpectedly easy,' said Bets. 'It took us hardly any time. We may as well go back and see how the boys are getting on.'

So they went off to the boys, who were patiently waiting for the postman and the baker. They were swinging on the gate so as not to miss them. They looked most surprised to see Daisy and Bets so soon.

'We had an easy job,' said Daisy. 'But nothing came of it. The grocer's girl delivered her goods before the others, and she didn't see or hear anything suspicious at all.'

'Nobody ever seems to see this thief,' said Larry. 'They hear him and see his footmarks and glovemarks, but they don't see him. I bet neither the postman nor the baker will have seen him either.'

'Here *is* the postman!' said Daisy. 'Look – coming up the road on his little cycle van. Let's hope he's got a parcel for your house, Pip.'

The postman delivered two parcels next door. He came out again, mounted his saddle, and pedalled slowly to Pip's house. He stopped. He rummaged in his little van and produced a parcel.

'Mrs Hilton,' he read out and looked at the children. 'Any of you a Hilton?'

'Yes, I am,' said Pip, going over to the van. 'I'll take it to my mother. It'll save you a long ride up the drive and back.'

'Thanks,' said the postman. 'Sign for it, will you?'

Pip signed. 'I hope you won't bump into a thief today,' he said, giving the postman back his stump of a pencil. 'I hear you almost ran into one yesterday!'

'Yes,' said the postman. 'Mr Goon the policeman has been trying to find out if I saw him. I didn't. I went to the back door, as the Cook had told me to, so as not to disturb Mrs Williams – and I saw all the groceries on the table, and I left my parcel by the door.'

'Were there any loaves on the table too?' asked Larry.

'Not as far as I remember,' said the postman. 'I just popped my hand in with the parcel and popped out again. I was in a hurry. I didn't see or hear anything at all. Off I went. I don't know whether the thief was there then or not – skulking round maybe – or hiding in a bush.'

He began to pedal slowly away. The children watched him go.

'Nobody's much help,' said Pip. 'I never knew such a thief for not being noticed by anyone. You'd think they'd see his big feet, anyhow, wouldn't you?'

'Now we'll wait for the baker,' said Larry. 'Then we'll scoot off down to Frinton Lea and spot Fatty. I *bet* we spot him. Even if he's disguised himself as a tree, we'll spot him.'

'Hurry up, baker!' said Bets, swinging on the gate. 'You're the last one left – and I guess you won't have noticed the thief either!'

9. THE PECULIAR FISHERMAN

The baker arrived at last. He was a cocky little bantam of a man, with a rather high voice, and a silly way of clearing his throat. He left his van at the bottom of the road and came along carrying his basket on his arm.

'Hello, kids,' he said, as he came up to the gate. 'Having a swing-swong, eh?'

'Shall we take the bread to our cook for you?' asked Pip.

'Well – there are thieves about, you know!' said the baker, pretending to look scared. 'My word – I nearly ran into one yesterday, up at Mrs Williams's. Did you hear about that?'

'What happened?' asked Larry, thinking it would be a good thing to let him talk.

'Well, nothing really as far as I'm concerned,' said the baker. 'I goes up there as usual, carrying my bread on my arm in my basket, like I always does. I knocks on the kitchen door before I remembers that Cookie is out. I sees the groceries on the table, and a parcel by the door, and I says, "Ah, the grocer girl's been and left her things, and so's the postman. Now it's your turn, baker!" '

He grinned at them as if he had said something rather clever.

'And so I looks at the note Cookie's left for me, and I sees as how she wants four loaves,' went on the cocky little baker. 'And I pops them down, and out I goes.'

'And you didn't see or hear anything of the thief at all then,' said Larry, disappointed.

'No. Nothing,' said the baker. 'All I see is some big footprints on a bed.'

'Ah – you saw those!' said Pip and Larry together. The baker looked surprised.

'What do *you* know about them?' he said. 'Yes, I see them – and I thinks – ah, somebody's been walking their big feet all over the beds. Maybe the window-cleaner or somebody. And off I goes.'

'That means that the thief must either have come and gone, or was still there, hiding somewhere while you were delivering your bread,' said Larry. 'Gosh – you might easily have seen him. What a pity you didn't.'

'I never seen him the other day either, at Norton House,' said the baker in his high, rather silly voice. 'I heard Jinny shouting and in I went – but we didn't see no thief at all.'

'Funny,' said Pip, puzzled. 'Well, baker – if you'd like to give me your basket, I'll take it up to our cook and let her see what bread she wants. It will save you a long walk up the drive.'

He held out his hand for the basket, but the baker backed away and shook his head.

'No thanks. I don't want boys messing about with my nice clean bread,' said the baker. 'I'm particular, I am. I'm the only baker in Peterswood that covers his bread up with a clean cloth.'

'Oh, all right,' said Pip. 'Take it yourself. I'm sure I don't want to lug it all the way to the back door. It looks pretty heavy to me.'

The baker went in at the gate and walked up the drive like a little strutting bantam. The children watched him and laughed. 'What a funny little fellow,' said Bets. 'So proud of his clean bread too.

You'd think he would keep his hands clean as well, if he's as clean as all that! They're filthy!'

They watched him disappear round the bend of the drive, looking spruce and smart in his little white coat, breeches, and small-sized, highly-polished boots with polished gaiters above.

'Most disappointing,' he said, as he came back again. 'No thief today anywhere. I don't mind telling you I'm on the lookout now. Anyone suspicious and I tell the police! I promised Mr Goon that. I go into nearly everyone's house, and I'm keeping my eyes open for him. He thinks there'll be more robberies soon!'

'Really?' said Larry politely. The little baker strutted back to his van whistling.

'Very pleased with himself, isn't he?' said Larry. 'I don't think I like him much.'

'Now, let's go down to Frinton Lea and see if we can find Fatty,' said Bets, jumping off the gate.

'Yes, let's,' said Daisy, pleased. 'We've done our bits now – not that we've found out anything.'

They walked down the lane to the river, then along the river-path that led to Frinton Lea. They soon came in sight of it. It was a big, rambling house, once built by rich people, and now owned by someone who ran it for paying guests.

Boats slid by on the water. Fishermen sat by the bank, stolid and patient, almost like bits of the scenery. Each had his little camp-stool, and each hunched himself over his rod, watching his float like a cat watching a mouse-hole.

'I've never seen any of these fishermen catch a fish yet,' said Bets, stopping by one.

'Sh!' said the fisherman angrily, and Bets went away, alarmed.

'You'll frighten away the fish he doesn't catch,' said Pip with a laugh. 'For goodness sake, don't go and disturb a fisherman again!'

They passed two labourers in a field, and then came to Frinton Lea. They looked about expectantly for a heavily-disguised Fatty. Was he anywhere about?

At first they could see nobody – and then, sitting in a little boat, not far from the bank, was a hunched-up figure, silently fishing. He had on the most extraordinary clothes.

His hat was a large cloth cap with a rather loud check pattern. His scarf was a curious sickly green. His coat was very tight blue alpaca, and he wore red braces that showed in front where the coat fell open.

The children stared at this peculiar figure. It took one look at them and then glanced away.

'There's *Fatty*!' said Pip. 'But what a get-up! It's not so much a disguise as fancy dress. What's he thinking of to dress like that!'

'He must have some reason for it,' said Daisy. 'Fatty never does anything without a reason. What braces!'

'Did you see his face when he looked round at us?' said Larry with a laugh. 'Fierce eyebrows and a fierce moustache, and he must have got his cheekpads in again, his face looks so fat.'

'I do wish he would look at us properly,' said Bets, who simply couldn't recognise Fatty at all.

'Don't be silly,' said Pip. 'He hopes we won't recognise him, the goof.'

Still the fisherman in the boat didn't look in their direction. He fished stolidly. Then he coughed.

'Very good cough,' said Pip in a loud voice. The fisherman took no notice.

'Pssssssst!' Larry said to him, and still he didn't

so much as turn his head. Any ordinary fisherman would certainly have lost his temper by now and ordered them away. It was most definitely Fatty.

'Don't be goofy!' called Pip in a low voice.

'We've spotted you!' said Daisy, also keeping her voice low. 'It was easy!'

The fisherman obstinately refused to look in their direction. After a little more 'Pssssssting' and attempts to make him turn round, the four gave up.

'We'll walk home and come back afterwards,' said Larry. 'It's getting late. Fatty's an idiot.'

They walked home, had their lunches, and came back again. Perhaps Fatty would be more amenable this afternoon.

'The boat's gone,' said Daisy. 'Oh no – look, it's there by the bank. And the fisherman is sitting on the grass, eating his lunch. *Now* we can get him to talk!'

They went up to him and sat down solemnly. He took a hurried look at them and then swallowed a mouthful so quickly that he choked.

'Bad luck,' said Larry, sympathetically. 'Caught many fish?'

'No,' said the fisherman in a strangled sort of

voice. He got up suddenly and went to his boat.

'Pssst!' said Larry. The fisherman clambered hurriedly into his boat, making it rock up and down. Larry was about to go to his help, meaning to whisper a few stinging remarks into Fatty's ear, when Bets caught hold of him and pulled him back. He looked down at her in surprise.

She looked up at him and shook her head, her eyes wide and frightened. She nodded towards the fisherman's boots. They were enormous – and so were his hairy hands!

Larry stopped with a jerk. Gosh – it wasn't Fatty after all! Of course it wasn't. Who was it then? And why had he behaved so strangely?

'Big feet – enormous hands!' whispered Bets. 'It's the thief! It is, Larry – it must be! That's why he's tried to shake us off. He's afraid we're on his track.'

The fisherman had pushed off into the river again. He sat now with his back to the children, hunched up as before. They gazed at him silently. How could they possibly have thought he was Fatty?

'What are we to do?' asked Daisy in a low voice. 'We ought to tell Fatty. But where is he? Is he somewhere near – in disguise? We can't let the thief go now we've found him! Where *is* Fatty? I simply can't see him anywhere!'

10. TELEPHONE CALL TO GOON

Larry thought hard. He was the head of the five when Fatty was not there. What was the best thing to do?

'If only we could spot Fatty!' he groaned. 'I'll tell you what we'd better do. Pip, you and Bets stay here and keep an eye on the thief. Daisy and I will wander about a bit and see if we can spot Fatty. He said he'd be within fifty yards of Frinton Lea, so he will be.'

'Right,' said Pip, and he and Bets settled down on the grassy bank. The other two walked off down the path. The fisherman heard their footsteps and turned round cautiously to see who it was.

'See him look round?' whispered Bets. 'He hoped we'd gone! Then I bet he was going to row to the shore and escape.'

It was rather dull sitting and watching the

fisherman. He didn't catch a single fish. He just sat there with his rod, seemingly asleep.

But he wasn't. He suddenly gave a nasty hollow cough. Bets clutched Pip.

'Did you hear that? I'm sure it's the thief now. He coughed just like a sheep barking – just like Mrs Williams said he did. I wish he'd do it again.'

He didn't. He slumped back in the boat and appeared to be asleep. But he wasn't, because whenever anyone came by, he turned and gave a quick look.

Not many people came by, however. The postman cycled by with some letters. The telegraph boy came once, whistling loudly as he turned in at Frinton Lea. The fisherman turned to give him a quick look, and the children eyed him well too, wondering if he could possibly be Fatty. But he wasn't. He was too thin. There was only one thing about himself that Fatty could not hide – his plumpness!

A nanny came by with a pram, and then the little baker appeared with his basket of bread. He had had to leave his van a good way away because there was no road right down to the river, only a path.

He recognised Pip and Bets, as he walked up with his cocky little stride. 'Hello, hello, *hello*!' he said in his high, sparrow-like voice. 'Here we are again! How many loaves today? Caught any thieves yet?'

Pip thought it was silly of the baker to talk to him as if he was about six-years-old. He merely jerked his head at him and turned away. But the baker was not to be put off.

He came up and gazed at the fisherman in the boat. 'There's a nice easy job!' he chattered on. 'Sitting in the sun with water lapping all round you, having a nap away from everyone else. Nobody to disturb you. No heavy basket to carry. My, why aren't I a fisherman?'

The fisherman had already turned his head once to glance at the baker. Now he took no notice. The baker called out to him.

'Hey there! Caught any fish?'

The fisherman did not turn round. 'Not yet!' he said in a curious deep voice.

The baker stood and talked away to Pip and Bets, but they took as little notice of him as the fisherman. They thought he was silly. He went at last, carrying his basket of bread through the gate of Frinton Lea.

'Silly little idiot,' said Pip. 'He's too big for his boots. He's got such a high opinion of himself that he just can't see he's a nuisance.'

'Well, let's move a little way off till he comes out again and goes,' said Bets, so they got up and walked in the opposite direction. The baker soon came out, gave them a wave, and strutted off on his spindly legs to his van.

'I wonder how Larry and Daisy are getting on,' said Bets. 'I hope they've found Fatty. It's maddening not to have him just at this important moment.'

Larry and Daisy had wandered all round Frinton Lea, but they hadn't seen Fatty. They had felt sure they had got him once – when they had seen a woman sitting on a stool, painting a picture of the river. She was rather big and had untidy hair and a hat that hid her face. Daisy nudged Larry.

'That's Fatty, surely! See – that woman painting. It would be a fine way of sitting and watching a house – to pretend to be an artist.'

'Yes. It might be Fatty,' said Larry. 'We'll stroll

over and see.'

The woman looked up at them as they came and stood beside her. At once Daisy and Larry knew she was not Fatty. Her nose was far too small. Fatty could make his nose bigger – but he certainly couldn't make it smaller!

'No go!' said Larry gloomily. 'Where on earth is he?'

'He might be one of those fishermen,' said Daisy. 'Look – sitting solemnly fishing on the bank. That one over there looks most like Fatty – the way he's sitting somehow. And he's got a position that gives him a very good view of Frinton Lea.'

'That's the one who said "Sh" to Bets,' said Larry. 'We'd better be careful, or he'll shush us too. Walk up very very quietly.'

So they walked up softly – so softly that the fisherman didn't hear them coming at all. They looked at his hands – hands were always a giveaway, because they couldn't very well be altered. But the fisherman wore gloves. They looked at his feet – he wore Wellingtons! He also wore a large shady hat that hid his face.

The fisherman had no idea at all that anyone

was just behind him. He suddenly opened his mouth and gave a bored yawn – and that gave the game away at once! It was Fatty's yawn! Fatty always yawned loud and long, and this was Fatty all right.

Larry sat down beside him with Daisy on the other side. 'Fatty!' said Larry in a low voice. 'We've found the thief.'

The fisherman immediately became Fatty, and gave a low whistle. He looked down at Larry and Larry felt quite startled. The eyes were Fatty's, but that was all! Fatty had his false teeth in, the ones that slid over his own, and he had also done something peculiar to his eyebrows. He wore a silly little moustache, and these things made him look a different person altogether. But his eyes were the same, direct and clear and shrewd.

'What did you say?' asked the fisherman, in Fatty's own voice. Larry repeated what he had said.

'See that fellow over there in the boat?' said Larry. 'Well, he's the thief! You should see his enormous feet and hands – and he's got a cough like a sheep too. He's the one, Fatty. I bet he lives at Frinton Lea. We've found him!'

Fatty was silent for a moment. 'Are you sure about it?' he said at last. 'Well, I'll sit here and keep an eye on him and you go and telephone Mr Goon.'

'Telephone Mr *Goon*?' said Larry, surprised. 'Why should we let *him* know? We're not working with *him*, are we?'

'Do as I say,' said Fatty. 'If he's not in, telephone again after a while. Tell him all about the awful fellow in the boat. He'll be thrilled. Tell him I'm keeping an eye on him till he comes down to arrest him.'

Larry and Daisy were puzzled. They looked at Fatty, but his face was so different, with its protruding teeth and moustache and eyebrows, that they could not tell what he was really thinking.

'All right,' said Larry, getting up, puzzled that Fatty did not show more excitement. He went off with Daisy to find Bets and Pip.

'I believe old Fatty's quite jealous because we found the thief before he did,' said Larry. 'Pretty tame ending to the mystery anyway – handing the thief over to Mr Goon like this!'

Daisy was disappointed too. It wasn't like Fatty

to be jealous. They went to Bets and Pip and sat down beside them. They told them in a whisper what they were to do.

'We'll *all* go and telephone,' said Daisy. 'I'm fed up with messing about here now. Fatty says he'll keep an eye on the thief out there. He can see him from where he is.'

They left the river and walked back up to the town. They decided to go to the post office to telephone – but, alas, Mr Goon was not in. His cleaning lady answered the phone. She didn't know where he was, but said he had left a note to say he would be back by half past four at the latest.

'Blow! It's only about a quarter *to* four now,' said Larry. 'Let's go and get some ice cream and lemonade, and wait for a bit.'

So they had ice creams – two each – and iced lemonade in the little sweetshop. That took them about half an hour. Then they strolled back to the telephone box to try their luck again.

This time, Mr Goon answered the telephone himself. Larry looked round at the others. 'He's in,' he said. 'Good!'

'Police here,' said Goon's voice sounding gruff

and sharp. 'What is it?'

'Mr Goon! It's Laurence speaking, Frederick Trotteville's friend,' said Larry. 'I've something to report – about that robbery case – the two cases, I mean.'

'Well – go on,' said Goon sharply.

'We've found the thief,' said Larry, unable to keep the excitement out of his voice. 'We saw him today.'

'Where?' asked Mr Goon.

'In a boat just opposite Frinton Lea,' said Larry. 'He's been there ages. Probably he lives at the boarding-house. You remember there was a scrap of paper with Frinton on it?'

There was a peculiar noise at the other end. 'What did you say?' said Larry, but Mr Goon was silent. Larry went on eagerly.

'He's a frightful-looking fellow, Mr Goon. We recognised him because of his colossal feet and huge hands. He's very ugly – puffy cheeks, rather protruding eyes – and he's got a cough like a sheep – just like Mrs Williams and Jinny said. If you go down to the river now, you'll catch him. Fatty's keeping his eye on him for you.'

Larry paused. Goon didn't seem to be taking this in. 'Mr Goon – are you going to arrest him?' asked Larry.

A loud snort came down the telephone – then a bang. Goon had put down his receiver so hard that surely he must have chipped it!

'He's rung off,' said Larry amazed. 'Whatever's the matter with him?'

11. A TEA PARTY - AND A BRAINWAVE

Larry and the others stepped out of the telephone box into which they had all crowded. Larry repeated the conversation. They were all very puzzled.

'Better go back and tell Fatty,' said Larry at last. 'It's quite obvious that Mr Goon doesn't believe us. So *we* shall have to do something about it now. I've a good mind to ring the Inspector.'

'No. Don't do that till we've asked Fatty,' said Bets. 'It seems to me there's something funny about all this. Let's go back to Fatty.'

'Why – there he is!' said Daisy suddenly, and sure enough, there *was* Fatty! He was himself now, very spruce and clean, with Buster trotting delightedly at his heels.

The others poured out of the post office and stared in astonishment at Fatty, who grinned back.

'Fatty! Have you left him? How did you get home and change so quickly? What's happened?' asked Larry.

'Oh, he went immediately after you left,' said Fatty. 'So I left too, of course.'

'Did you follow him? Where did he go?' asked Daisy.

'No. I didn't follow him,' said Fatty. 'There wasn't any point in doing so – I knew quite well where he was going. Did you telephone Mr Goon?'

'Yes. He was out the first time – but we got him the second time,' said Larry. 'I told him all about the frightful fellow in the boat – all the details, of course – and he just gave a snort and banged the receiver down. I suppose he didn't believe me.'

Fatty suddenly began to laugh. He laughed as if he had been keeping it in for some time. He exploded, held on to the railings, and laughed till the tears came into his eyes. Bets began to laugh too. He looked so funny, and his laughter was really infectious.

'What's the *matter*?' said Larry suspiciously. 'What's the joke? You're acting most peculiarly today, Fatty. So is Mr Goon.'

'Yes. You're right about *him*,' said Fatty, wiping his eyes. 'Oh dear – I'd have given anything to see Mr Goon's face when you rang him up and told him what a hideous fellow he was, with his big feet and hands and protruding eyes!'

The others stared, puzzled at first – and then a great light dawned on them. Larry sank down on to a wooden bench by the bus stop. He felt suddenly weak.

'Gosh! You don't mean to say – you don't *really* mean to say that that frightful fisherman in the boat was Mr *Goon* – Mr Goon himself!'

'Well – think back to him,' said Fatty. 'How you could all fall for that ridiculous disguise of his, I really don't know. You ought to be ashamed of yourselves. Why, Mr Goon himself stuck out a mile in that frightful get-up. And you actually go and think he's the thief!'

'Oh, Fatty – *I* put the idea into the others' heads,' said Bets, as if she was going to burst into tears. 'I saw his big feet – and hands – oh, Fatty!'

'You beast, Fatty – you told us to go and telephone Mr Goon – and we've gone and described him to himself!' said Daisy, full of horror.

'Oh, Fatty – you really are a beast.'

'Serves you right,' said Fatty unfeelingly, and began to laugh again. 'Fine lot of detectives you are, I must say – go and hunt for a thief and pick on the only policeman of the village, in disguise! As Mr Goon would say – Gah!'

'No wonder he snorted and banged the receiver down,' said Daisy, still more alarmed. 'I hope he won't go round and complain to our parents again.'

'He won't,' said Fatty. 'He doesn't know whether you really fell for his disguise or not. If he thinks you did, he'll be very happy to think he took you in. If he thinks you saw through his disguise and were pulling his leg when you phoned, he'll feel a bit of an idiot. He won't say a word either way. He'll only snort.'

'He won't be very fond of us now,' said Pip.

'He never was,' said Fatty. 'All the same, I was surprised to see him there this morning. I spotted him at once out in that boat.'

'You would!' said Larry, half-annoyed and half-admiring.

'When I saw him I knew he'd had the same idea as we had about Frinton Lea,' said Fatty.

'And what's more, he'll probably go and snoop outside Rods now, wherever that is.'

'Do you think it's much good snooping round either Frinton Lea or Rods, wherever that is?' asked Larry.

'No, I don't think I do,' said Fatty, considering the point. 'It's just that we can't afford to leave any clue unexplored. If we do, it's bound to be the only one that might lead us to the solution! Anyway, I had a bit of luck this afternoon, just before you came to talk to me, Larry and Daisy.'

'What?' asked Larry. 'You're a lucky beggar, Fatty – you always have any bit of luck that's going.'

'I was sitting fishing, when that artist woman came by,' said Fatty. 'I expect you saw her. My hat blew off at that very moment and she picked it up for me. I began to talk to her – and it turned out that she lives at Frinton Lea!'

'Golly!' said Larry. 'So you asked a few leading questions, I suppose?'

Fatty grinned. 'I did! And I found out that the only man staying at Frinton Lea has been very ill and is only just allowed to get up. So we can rule him out as the thief, who must be an agile fellow, to say the least of it!'

'Oh – well, that's good,' said Daisy. 'Your day hasn't been wasted, Fatty. You didn't see the thief, but you did find out he wasn't at Frinton Lea.'

'Your day wasn't wasted either,' said Fatty, beginning to laugh again. 'I hope I don't think of you telephoning old Mr Goon when I'm having dinner with my parents tonight. I shall choke if I do.'

'What about tea?' said Bets. 'I'm getting hungry.'

'You've just had two ice creams and a lemonade!' said Pip.

'Well, they don't make any difference,' said Bets. 'You don't eat those, you just swallow them. Anyway, we'd better go home quickly or we'll be too late for tea.'

'I'll treat you all,' said Fatty generously. 'I've got enough money on me.' He pulled out a handful of change and examined it. 'Yes, come on. We'll go to Oliver's and have meringues and chocolate slices – in celebration of finding the thief-who-wasn't.'

Everyone laughed. Bets took Fatty's arm. Dear, generous Fatty – he always seemed to have plenty of money, but he always shared it round. Bets squeezed his arm affectionately.

'The mystery's getting on, isn't it?' she said. 'We've ruled out Frinton Lea. Now we've got to find out what "1 Rods" is, and rule that out too.'

'Well, we won't be much further on with the mystery, silly, if we keep examining our clues and finding they're no good,' said Pip, exasperated with his small sister. 'Anyway, "1 Rods" sounds more like a note made by someone going fishing than anything else.'

'It's an idea,' said Fatty, taking them all into Oliver's. They sat down and ordered lemonade, egg sandwiches, meringues, chocolate éclairs and chocolate slices. Bets' mouth began to water.

'I never know whether to eat as quickly as possible so as to enjoy everything before I stop feeling hungry, or to eat slowly and taste every single bit,' said Bets, eyeing the pile of delicious-looking cakes.

'Idiot,' said Pip scornfully. 'You stop feeling hungry as soon as you've eaten a certain amount, whether you've eaten it quickly or not.'

'You eat how you like, Bets,' said Fatty, who always stuck up for Bets when her brother ticked her off. They all began on their tea, having a friendly argument as to whether the meringues were better than the éclairs. The dish was soon empty and Fatty, after examining his money again, called for a fresh supply.

'About this Rods place,' said Fatty. 'It's either the name of a house, shortened – or else it's the name of a family, either complete or shortened. I've never heard of anyone called Rods though.'

'How could we find out?' wondered Larry. 'We could look in the telephone book for names beginning with Rod or Rods.'

'Yes, that's a good idea,' said Daisy, taking her second éclair. 'And we've got a street directory at home, with everyone's house in it, and the name or number.'

'You're talking good sense,' said Fatty, sounding pleased. 'Anyone got an idea for finding a person with enormous feet? Apart from examining the feet of everyone we meet, I mean. I've rather ruled that out – it would be frightful to look at nothing but feet, feet, feet, all day long wherever we go.'

Bets giggled. 'And even if we find someone with

colossal feet, we can't very well stop them and say, "Excuse me, may I see the pattern of the rubber heels you're wearing?" '

'No, we can't,' said Pip. 'But I say – I tell you what we *could* do – I've just thought of it. It's a brainwave!'

'What?' asked everyone together.

Pip dropped his voice. One or two people in the shop seemed rather too interested in what they were all saying, he thought.

'Why can't we go to the cobbler's – there *is* only one in Peterswood now the other man's gone – and ask if he ever has any size twelve boots in for repair and, if so, whose are they?'

There was a little silence after this remarkable suggestion. Then Fatty solemnly reached out and shook hands with Pip.

'First class!' he said. 'Brilliant! Talk about a brainwave! Go up top, Pip. That really *may* lead us somewhere!'

12. FATTY, THE COBBLER - AND GOON

The next day, they set to work to follow up the suggestions made at the tea shop. Daisy and Larry said they would look up the streets directory and read down every single street to see if there was a house name beginning with Rod or Rods.

Pip and Bets were to look in the telephone directory for names. Fatty was to go to the cobbler's. Nobody particularly wanted to do that, because they couldn't think how to go about it without making the cobbler think they were either mad or silly.

'I'll manage it,' said Fatty. 'I'll think of a way. And, for goodness sake, don't get taken in again by any disguise of Mr Goon's – he's been studying hard, I can see, on his refresher course, and goodness knows what he'll produce next.'

'I shall just look at his feet,' said Bets, 'and if they're enormous, I'll know they belong to

Mr Goon!'

Fatty considered carefully how to approach the cobbler. He was known to be a hot-tempered man who would stand no nonsense at all. He would have to go to him with a sensible idea of some sort. But what?

Fatty remembered an old second-hand shop he had once seen in Sheepridge. He tried to remember if they sold boots. Yes, he had an idea that they did. In that case, it would be a good idea to catch the bus to Sheepridge, look in the second-hand shop and buy the biggest pair there – they would presumably want mending, and he could take them to the cobbler. Fatty felt certain that with that opening he could soon find out if the cobbler had any customers with really enormous feet.

Then I'll get their names, and see if any of them might be the thief, he thought. So off he went to catch the bus to Sheepridge. He found the second-hand shop and, feeling as if he wanted to hold his nose because of the musty, dusty smell, he went inside.

There was a special box of boots and shoes. Fatty

turned them all over, and at the bottom he found what he wanted – a pair of elevens, down at heel, and with a slit in one side.

He bought them very cheaply and went off with them, feeling pleased. He caught the bus back to Peterswood and went home. He debated whether or not to disguise himself, and then decided that he would, just for practice.

He went down to his shed and looked round at his things. An old tramp? He was rather good at that. Yes – that wouldn't be a bad idea at all – he could wear the frightful old boots too! They would make him limp but what did that matter? It would look all the more natural.

Fatty began to work deftly and quickly. He hoped his mother wouldn't come and look for him. She would be scared to see a dirty old tramp in the shed. After about half an hour the door opened, and the tramp came out and peered round cautiously.

He looked dreadful. Fatty had blacked out two of his front teeth, and had put in one cheekpad so that it looked as if he had toothache on the right side of his face. He had put on grey, untrimmed eyebrows, and had stuck on a bristly little grey moustache. His face was lined with dirty creases and wrinkles. Fatty was adept at creasing up his face! His wig was one of his best – grey straggling hair with a bald patch in the middle.

Fatty had laughed at himself when he looked in the long glass he kept in his shed. What a tramp! He wore holey old gloves on his hands, dirty corduroy trousers, an equally dirty shirt – and the boots!

Fatty could only hobble along in them, so he took an ash-stick he had cut from the hedge on one of his walks to help him along. He stuck an old clay pipe in the corner of his mouth and grinned at himself. He felt really proud, and for half-a-minute wondered if he should present himself at the back door and ask for a crust of bread from the cook.

He decided not to. The last time he had done that the cook had screamed the place down, and his mother had very nearly caught him. He went cautiously out of the shed to the gate at the bottom of the garden. He was not going to risk meeting any of his household.

The old tramp hobbled down the road, sucking at his empty pipe, and making funny little grunting noises. He made his way to the cobbler's and went inside the dark little shop.

The cobbler was at the back, working. He came into the shop when the bell rang. 'What do you want?' he said.

'Oooh – ah,' said Fatty, taking his pipe out of his mouth. 'It's my boots, Mister. They hurt me something crool. Too small they are, and they want mending too. You got any bigger ones to sell?'

The cobbler bent over his counter to look at Fatty's feet. 'What size are they – elevens or twelves?' he said. 'No, I haven't got that size to sell. It's a big size.'

The old tramp gave a peculiar wheezy laugh, 'Ah yes, it's big. I was a big man once, I was! I bet you haven't got anyone in this here neighbourhood that's got feet bigger than mine!'

'There's two people with big feet here,' said the cobbler, considering. 'There's Mr Goon the policeman and there's Colonel Cross – they're the biggest of all. I charge them more when I sole their boots – the leather I use for their repairs! Do you want me to mend your boots?'

'Ay, I do – if you can get me another pair to put on while you mend these,' said the old tramp, and he gave his wheezy laugh again. 'Or couldn't I borrow a pair of Colonel Cross's – have you got a pair in to mend?'

'No, I haven't – and you wouldn't get 'em if I had,' said the cobbler sharply. 'Get along with you! Do you want to get me into trouble?'

'No, no,' said the old tramp. 'Do his boots have rubber heels on?'

The cobbler lost his temper. 'What's that to do with you? Coming in here wasting my time! You'll be wanting to know if the butcher has brown or black laces next. Be off with you, and don't come back again.'

'That's all right, sir, that's all right,' wheezed the old man, shuffling to the door, where he stopped and had a most alarming coughing fit.

'You stop smoking a clay pipe and you'll get rid of that cough,' said the cobbler, bad-temperedly. Then he saw someone else trying to get past the coughing tramp. 'Get out of my shop and let the next person come in.'

The next person was a burly man with a little black moustache, a dark brown face, dark glasses, and big feet.

He pushed past the old tramp. 'Give me room,' he said in a sharp voice. Fatty pricked up his ears at once. He knew that familiar voice – yes, and he knew that unfamiliar figure too – it was Mr Goon!

Goon! In *another* disguise! thought Fatty in amazement and mirth. He's done better this time – with dark glasses to hide his frog-eyes, and some stuff on his red face to make it look tanned.

He looked at the burly Goon. He wore white flannel trousers and a shirt with no tie, and a red belt round his portly middle. On his feet were enormous white shoes.

'Why the disguise?' wondered Fatty. 'Just practising, like me? Or is he going to snoop round somewhere? Perhaps he has found out where or who Rods is. I'd better stand by and find out.'

He shuffled out and sat down on a wooden bench, just outside. He strained his ears to see if he could catch any words. What was Goon doing in the cobbler's? Surely he hadn't got the same bright idea as Pip had had – of asking about repairs to large-size boots!

Goon had! He was very pleased about it. He had made up a nice little story to help him along.

'Good morning,' he said to the cobbler. 'Did my brother leave his boots here to be mended? He asked me to come in and see. Very large size, twelves or thirteens.'

'What name?' asked the cobbler.

'He didn't give his name,' said Mr Goon. 'Just left the boots, he said.'

'Well, I haven't any boots as big as that here,' said the cobbler. 'I've only got two customers with feet that size.'

'Who are they?' asked Goon.

'What's that to you?' said the cobbler impatiently. 'Am I going to waste all my morning talking about big boots?'

'I know one of your customers is Mr Goon,' said Mr Goon. 'I know Mr Goon very well. He's a great friend of mine. Very nice fellow.'

'Oh, *is* he? Then you know him better than I do,' said the cobbler. 'I've got no time for that pompous old policeman.'

Mr Goon went purple under his tan. 'Who's your other customer?' he asked, in such an unexpectedly fierce voice that the cobbler stared. 'The one with big feet, I mean. You'd better answer my question. For all you know, I might have been sent here by Mr Goon himself!'

'Bah!' said the cobbler, and then thought better of it. 'The other fellow is Colonel Cross,' he said.

'Does he have rubber heels?' asked Mr Goon and was immediately amazed by the cobbler's fury.

'Rubber heels! How many more people want to know if he has rubber heels! What do I care? Go and ask him yourself!' raged the cobbler, going as purple as Mr Goon. 'You and that old tramp are a pair, you are!'

'What old tramp?' asked Goon in surprise.

'The one you pushed past at the door – with feet as big as yourself!' raged the cobbler. 'Clear out of my shop now. I've got work to do. Rubber heels!'

Goon went out with great dignity. He longed to tell the cobbler who he was – what a shock for him that would be. What was it he had called him? 'A pompous old policeman!' Goon put that away in his memory. One day he would make the cobbler sorry for that rude remark!

Now, what about this tramp with big feet? Where was he? He might be the thief! There didn't seem many people with enormous feet in

Peterswood as far as he could find out – only himself and Colonel Cross. He would have to enquire about Colonel Cross's boots – see if they had rubber heels – though it wasn't very likely that Colonel Cross went burgling other people's houses.

Goon blinked in the bright sunshine, quite glad of his dark glasses. Where was that tramp? Well – what a piece of luck – there he was, sitting on the bench nearby!

Goon sat down heavily beside him. Fatty took one look and longed to laugh. He saw Mr Goon looking at his big old boots. Ah – they had roused his suspicions. Well, Fatty was quite prepared to sit there as long as Goon – and to have a bit of fun too. He stuck his boots out well in front of him. Come on, Mr Goon – say something!

13. A LITTLE BIT OF FUN

Goon hadn't the slightest idea that he was sitting next to Fatty. He looked through his dark glasses at the old man. Could he be the thief? He tried to see his hands, but Fatty was still wearing the holey old gloves.

'Want some baccy?' said Mr Goon, seeing that Fatty's clay pipe was empty.

Fatty looked at him and then put his hand behind his ear.

'Want some baccy?' said Goon, a little more loudly.

Still Fatty held his hand behind his ear and looked enquiringly at Goon, sucking at his dirty old pipe, and squinting horribly.

'WANT SOME BACCY?' roared Goon.

'Oh, ah – yes – I've got a bad backache,' answered Fatty. 'Oooh, my backache. Something crool, it is.'

'I said, "WANT SOME BACCY?" ' yelled

Goon again.

'I heard you the first time,' said Fatty, with dignity. 'I'm having treatment for it at the hospital. And for me pore old feet too.'

He gave a long, wheezy cough and rubbed the back of his hand over his nose.

'You've got big feet!' said Goon loudly.

'Oh, ah – it's a nice sunny seat,' agreed the old tramp. 'I allus sits here of a mornin'.'

'I said – "you've got BIG FEET," ' shouted Goon.

'You're right. Not enough meat these days,' said the tramp and coughed again. ' 'Taint right. Meat's good for you.'

Goon gave it up. 'Silly old man,' he said in his ordinary voice, thinking that the tramp was absolutely stone deaf. Most surprisingly, the old fellow heard him.

'Here! Who are you calling a silly old man?' said the tramp fiercely. 'I heard you! Yes, I did! Think I was deaf, did you? But I heard you!'

'Now now – don't be silly,' said Goon, alarmed at the disturbance the tramp was making. 'Be calm.'

'Harm! Yes, I'll harm you!' said the tramp, and actually raised his stick. Goon retreated hurriedly to the other end of the bench and debated with himself. This old chap couldn't be the thief. He was deaf, his feet were bad, and he had backache. But where had he got those boots? It might be as well to follow him home and find out where he lived. It was no good asking him, that was plain. He'd only make some silly reply. So Goon took out his own pipe and proceeded to fill it, and to wait until the old tramp moved off.

Fatty was also waiting for Goon to move off, because he wanted to see if the policeman had discovered who or where Rods was. So there they both sat, one sucking an empty pipe, the other preparing and filling one.

And then he saw Larry, Daisy, Bets and Pip coming down the street! Thank goodness they hadn't got Buster, who would certainly have smelt Fatty at once and greeted him with joy. Buster was safely locked up in the shed, and was no doubt still scraping hopefully at the door.

Fatty sank his chin down on his chest, hoping that none of the four would recognise him. It would be maddening if they did, and came over to him and gave the game away to Goon.

They didn't recognise him. They gave him a mere glance, and then rested their eyes on Goon.

They walked by, giving backward glances at the disguised policeman, who pulled at his pipe desperately, praying that the four would go away. Thank goodness that big boy was not with them. He'd have spotted him at once, disguise or no disguise.

The four children stopped at the end of the street because Bets was pulling at Larry's sleeve so urgently. 'What is it, Bets?' asked Larry.

'See that big man sitting on the bench by the dirty old tramp?' said Bets. 'I'm sure it's Mr Goon! I'd know his big hairy hands anywhere. He's in disguise again – a better disguise this time, because his eyes are hidden. You just simply can't mistake those when you see them.'

'I believe Bets is right,' said Daisy, looking back. 'Yes – you can see it's Mr Goon – the way he sits, and everything. It *is* Mr Goon!'

'Let's have a bit of fun with him then,' said Pip. 'Come on, let's. He won't know if we've spotted him or not, and he'll be in an awful fix.'

Bets giggled. 'What shall we do?'

'Oh nothing much – just go up to him innocently and ask him questions,' said Larry. 'You know – what's the time, please? Have you got any change? Where does the bus start?'

Everyone laughed. 'I'll go first,' said Pip. He walked up to the bench. Fatty saw him coming, and felt alarmed. Surely Pip hadn't recognised him. It looked as if he was going to speak to him. No – Pip was talking to Mr Goon!

'Could you please tell me the time?' Pip asked innocently. Mr Goon scowled. He pulled out his big watch.

'Ten to twelve,' he said.

'Thanks very much,' said Pip. Fatty was astonished. Pip had his own watch. What was the point? Gosh! – could the others have recognised Mr Goon after all – and have made up their minds to have some fun with him?

Larry came next. 'Oh – could you possibly give me some change, sir?' he asked Goon politely. Fatty almost choked, but his choke was lost in Goon's snort.

'No. Clear orf,' said Mr Goon, unable to stop himself from using his favourite expression.

'Thanks very much,' said Larry politely and went off. Fatty got out his handkerchief, ready to bury his face in it if any of the others came along with a request. He hadn't bargained for this.

Up came Daisy. 'Could you tell me, please, if the bus stops here for Sheepridge?' she asked.

Goon nearly exploded. Those kids! Here he was, in a perfectly splendid disguise, one good enough to prevent anyone from knowing him, one that should be absolute protection against these pests of children – and here they all were, making a beeline for him. Did they do this sort of thing to everybody? He'd have to report them – complain to their parents!

'Go and look at the bus timetable,' he snapped at Daisy.

'Oh, thank you very much,' she said. Fatty chortled again into his handkerchief and Daisy looked at him in surprise. What a funny old man.

Bets was the last to come. 'Please, have you seen our little dog, Buster?' she asked.

'No,' roared Goon. 'And if I do, I'll chase him out of town.'

'Oh, thanks very much,' said Bets politely,

and departed. Fatty was nearly dying of laughter, trying to keep back his guffaws. He had another coughing fit in his handkerchief and Goon looked at him suspiciously.

'Nasty cough of yours,' he said. Poor Fatty was quite unable to answer. He prayed that the others wouldn't come back to ask any more questions.

Goon was debating with himself again. With those children about, pestering him like this, he'd never get anywhere. Had they seen through his disguise? Or was this kind of thing their usual behaviour? He saw Daisy bearing down on him and rose hurriedly. He strode off in the direction of the police station. He could bear no more.

Fatty collapsed. He buried his face in his handkerchief and laughed till he cried. Daisy looked at him in alarm. 'Are you all right?' she said timidly.

Fatty recovered and sat up. 'Yes thanks, Daisy,' he said in his normal voice, and Daisy stood and stared at him, her mouth open in amazement.

'Fatty!' she whispered. 'Oh, *Fatty*! We recognised Goon – but we didn't know the tramp was you! Oh, Fatty!'

'Listen,' said Fatty. 'I don't want to have to change out of this disguise – it takes ages to take off and put on – and I want to see if Mr Goon has found out anything about Rods. He's using his brains over all this, you know. Thought about going to see the cobbler and everything, just as we did. I don't want him to get ahead of us. I think I'd better trail him today.'

'All right,' said Daisy, sitting down near to him, and speaking in a low voice. 'You want us to get you some lunch, I suppose? There's a bus stop near Mr Goon's house. You could sit there and eat your lunch and read a paper – and watch for Mr Goon at the same time.'

'Yes – that's what I'll do,' said Fatty. 'I feel somehow as if Mr Goon's got going on this. If he's going to get ahead of us, I want to know about it.

'I couldn't find the streets directory this morning,' said Daisy, talking straight out in front of her, so that nobody would think she was talking to an old tramp. 'Larry's borrowing one this afternoon. Pip found two names in the telephone directory that might help – one is Rodney, the other is Roderick. The Rodneys live up on the hill, and the Rodericks live near you.'

'Oh yes – I remember now,' said Fatty. 'Well, we can rule the Rodericks out, I think. There's only an old lady, a Mrs Roderick, and a young one, a Miss. There's no one there who wears size twelve shoes. I don't know about the Rodneys though.'

'Shall I and the others go and see if we can find out anything at the Rodneys?' said Daisy. 'We could go this afternoon. Mummy knows them, so I could easily go on some excuse.'

'There's a jumble sale on in the town,' said Fatty. 'Couldn't you go and ask for jumble? *Especially* old boots – large size if possible as you know an old tramp who wears them!'

Daisy giggled. 'You do have bright ideas, Fatty,' she said. 'I suppose you're the old tramp who wears them! Yes, I'll go and ask for jumble. Bets can go with me. I'll go over to the others now. They're standing there wondering what on earth I'm doing, talking to myself!'

They were certainly very surprised to see Daisy sitting down after Goon had so hurriedly departed, apparently murmuring away to herself. They were just about to come over when she left the bench and went to them.

'What's up with you?' asked Larry. Daisy smiled delightedly. 'That was Fatty!' she whispered. 'Don't recognise him, for goodness sake. We've got to get some lunch for him somehow, because he thinks Mr Goon is on the track of something and he wants to trail him.'

The four marched solemnly past Fatty on the bench, and each got a wink from the old tramp.

'We're going off to get lunch,' said Daisy loudly, as if she was speaking to Larry. But the tramp knew quite well that she was speaking to *him*!

14. A VERY BUSY AFTERNOON

Fatty shuffled his way to the bus stop bench near Goon's house. He let himself down slowly as if he indeed had a bad back. He let out a grunt. An old lady on the bench looked at him sympathetically. Poor old man! She leaned across and pressed some money into his hand.

Fatty was so taken aback that he almost forgot he was a tramp. He remembered immediately though, and put his finger to his forehead in exactly the same way that his father's old chauffeur did when he came to see him.

'Thank you kindly,' he wheezed.

There was no sign of Mr Goon. He had gone hurriedly into the back door of his house, and was now engaged in stripping off his disguise. He was going out in his official clothes this afternoon – PC Goon – and woe betide any cobblers or others who were rude to him!

Soon Daisy came slipping back with a picnic lunch, done up in a piece of newspaper. Fatty approved of that touch! Just what he *would* have his lunch in if he really was an old tramp. Good for Daisy! His troop were coming along well, he considered.

Daisy sat down on the bench, bending over to do up her shoe. She spoke to Fatty out of the corner of her mouth. 'Here's your lunch. Best I could get. Larry's looked up the names of houses in the directory he borrowed. There's only one beginning with Rod, and that's one called Rodways, down by Pip's house.'

'Thanks. You go to the Rodneys about the jumble with Bets, and tell Larry and Pip to go to Rodways and snoop,' said Fatty. 'Find out if there's anyone there with large feet, who *might* be the thief. Rodways is only a little cottage, isn't it?'

'Yes,' said Daisy. 'All right. And you're going to trail Goon, aren't you, to see if he's up to something? We'll meet at your shed later.'

She laced up her shoe, sat up, and whispered goodbye. Then off she went – and behind her she left the newspaper of food. Very clever! thought Fatty, opening it. Good old Daisy.

He had a very nice lunch of egg sandwiches, tomato sandwiches and a large slice of fruit cake. Daisy had even slipped in a bottle of ginger beer! Fatty ate and drank everything, and then put his clay pipe back into his mouth again. He opened the newspaper, which was that day's, and began to read very comfortably.

Goon went into his little front room and sat down to go through some papers. He glanced out of the window, and saw the old tramp on the bench.

Turned up again like a bad penny! said Goon to himself. Well, I can certainly keep an eye on him if he sits there. Still, he can't be the thief – he's too doddery.

The tramp read his paper and then apparently fell asleep. Goon had his lunch, did a little telephoning, and then decided to get on with his next job. He looked at his notes.

Frinton Lea. He had crossed that out. What with watching it all day and enquiring about it, he had come to the conclusion that he could forget about that. Now for the other people or places – the

Rodericks – the Rodneys – and that house down the lane – what was it called? – Rodways. One of them must be the Rods on this scrap of paper. 'Rods. It's some sort of clue, that's certain. Good thing those children don't know about these bits of paper. Ha, I'm one up on them there.'

Poor Mr Goon didn't know that PC Tonks had shown them to Fatty, or he wouldn't have been nearly so pleased! He put his papers together, frowned, thought of his plan of campaign, and got up heavily, his great boots clomping loudly as he went out into the hall.

The old tramp was still on the bench. Lazy old thing! thought Mr Goon. He wheeled his bicycle quickly to the front, got on it and sailed away before Fatty could even have time to sit up!

'Blow!' said Fatty. 'He's out of disguise – and on his bike. I'm stuck! I never thought of his bike. I can't trail him on that.'

He wondered what to do. Well, the others were taking care of the Rodneys and the house called Rodways. He'd better go and find Colonel Cross's house. As he was apparently the only other person in Peterswood who wore size twelve or thirteen shoes, he certainly must be enquired into!

Goon had shot off to the Roderick's first. There he found out what Fatty already knew – that there was no man in the house at all. Right. He could cross that off.

He then went to see the Rodneys – and the very first thing he saw there were two bicycles outside the front fence – girls' bicycles, with Daisy and Bets just coming out of the gate towards them!

Those kids again! What were they doing *here*? And whatever were they carrying? Goon glared at them.

'Good afternoon, Mr Goon,' said Daisy, cheerfully. 'Want to come and buy a pair of shoes at the jumble sale?'

Goon eyed the four or five old pairs of boots and shoes wrathfully. 'Where did you get those?' he said.

'From Mrs Rodney,' answered Daisy. 'We're collecting for the jumble sale, Mr Goon. Have *you* got anything that would do for it? An old pair of big boots, perhaps?'

'Mrs Rodney let us look all through her cupboard of boots,' said Bets, 'and she gave us these.'

Goon had nothing to say. He simply stood and glared. The Rodneys! So these pests of kids had got on to that clue too – they were rounding up the Rods just as he was – but they were just one move in front of him.

He debated whether to go in or not now. Mrs Rodney might not welcome somebody else enquiring after shoes. He cast his eye again on the collection of old boots and shoes that Daisy and Bets were stuffing into their bicycle baskets.

Daisy saw his interest in them. 'No. None size twelve,' she said with a giggle. 'Size ten is the very largest the Rodneys have. That will save you a lot of trouble, won't it, Mr Goon?'

'Gah!' said Mr Goon, and leapt angrily on his bicycle. Interfering lot! And how did they know about the Rods anyway? Had Tonks shown those scraps of paper? He'd bite Tonks' head off, if he had!

He rode off to Rodways, the cottage down the lane that led to the river. He was just putting his bicycle against the little wall when he noticed two more there – boys' bicycles this time. Well, if it was any of those little pests' bikes, he'd have something to say!

Larry and Pip were there. They had stopped outside the cottage, apparently to have a game of ball – and one of them had thrown the ball into the cottage garden.

'Careless idiot!' Pip shouted loudly to Larry. 'Now we'll have to go and ask permission to get the ball!'

They went in and knocked at the door, which was wide open. An old woman, sitting in a rocking-chair, peered at them from a corner of the room inside.

'What do you want?' she asked, in a cracked old voice.

'We're so sorry,' said Larry politely. 'Our ball went into your garden. May we get it?'

'Yes,' said the old woman, beginning to rock herself. 'And just tell me if the milkman's been, will you? If he has, the milk bottle will be outside. And did you see the baker down the lane?'

'No, we didn't,' said Pip. 'There *is* a bottle out here on the step. Shall I bring it in?'

'Yes, thank you kindly,' said the old woman. 'Put it in the larder, there's a good lad. That baker!

He gets later every day! I hope I haven't missed him. I fall asleep, you know. I might not have heard him.'

Larry looked round the little cottage. He saw a big sou'wester hanging on a nail, and an enormous oilskin below it. Aha! Somebody big lived here, that was certain.

'What a big oilskin!' he said to the old woman. 'Giant-size!'

'Ah, that's my son's,' said the old woman, rocking away hard. 'He's a big man, he is – but kind and gentle – just like a big dog, I always say.'

Pip had pricked up his ears too, by this time. 'He must be enormous,' he said. 'Whatever size shoes does he wear? Sixteens!'

The old lady gave a cackle of laughter. 'Go on with you! Sixteens! Look over there, on that shelf – those are my son's boots – there's a surprise for you!'

It *was* a surprise – for the shoes were no more than size sevens, about Larry's own size! The boys looked at them in astonishment.

'Does he really only wear size seven?' said Larry. 'What small feet he has for such a big man.'

'Yes. Small feet and small hands – that's what my family always have,' said the old woman, showing her own misshapen but small feet and hands. Pip looked at Larry. Rodways was definitely ruled out. The thief didn't live here!

Someone came up the path and called in. 'Granma! Baker-boy here!'

'Gosh – it's that awful little peacock of a baker again!' said Pip, in disgust. 'We can't seem to get rid of him.'

'One loaf as usual, baker!' called the old lady. 'Put it in my pan for me.'

The baker put down his basket, took a loaf, and strutted in. He saw the two boys, and smiled amiably. 'Here we are again! Come to see old Granma?'

He flung the bread into the pan in the larder and strutted out again. He picked up his basket and went off, whistling, turning out his feet like a duck.

'Now you go and look for your ball,' said the old woman, settling herself comfortably! 'I can go to sleep now I know the milk and the bread have come.'

They went out, found their ball, and Larry threw

it out into the road. There was an angry shout.

'Now then, you there! What are you doing, throwing your ball at me?'

Mr Goon's angry red face appeared over the hedge. The boys gaped in surprise. 'Golly – did it hit you, Mr Goon?' said Pip, with much concern. 'We didn't know you were there.'

'Now look here – what are you *here* for?' demanded Mr Goon. 'Everywhere I go, you're there before me. What are you playing at?'

'Ball,' said Larry, picking up the ball and aiming it at Pip. It missed him, struck the wall, bounced back, and struck Mr Goon on the helmet. He turned a beetroot colour, and the boys fled.

'Toads!' muttered Mr Goon, mopping his hot neck. 'Toads! Anyone would think this was their case! Anyone would think they were running the whole show. Under my feet the whole time. Gah!'

He strode up the path to the front door. But the old lady had now gone to sleep, and did not waken even when Mr Goon spoke to her loudly. He saw the oilskin on the peg, and the same thought occurred to him, as had occurred to the two boys. Big oilskin – Big man – Big feet – The thief!

He crept in and began to look round. He fell over a shovel and the old woman awoke in a hurry. She saw Mr Goon and screamed.

'Help! Help! Robbers! Thieves! Help, I say!'

Mr Goon was scared. He stood up, and spoke pompously. 'Now, madam, it's only the police come to call. What size shoes does your son take?'

This was too much for the old woman. She thought the policeman must be mad. She began to rock herself so violently that Mr Goon was sure the chair would fall over.

He took one last look round and ran, followed by the old woman's yells. He leapt on his bicycle and was off up the lane in a twinkling. Poor Mr Goon – he was no match for an angry old woman!

15. MOSTLY ABOUT BOOTS

Fatty had gone off to find Colonel Cross's house. It was a pleasant little place not far from the river. Sitting out in the garden was a big man with a white moustache and a very red face.

Fatty studied him from the shelter of the hedge. He looked a bit fierce. In fact, very fierce. It was quite a good thing he was asleep, Fatty thought. Not only asleep, but snoring.

Fatty looked at his feet. Enormous! The cobbler was right – the Colonel certainly wore size twelve or thirteen boots. Fatty thought he could see a rubber heel on one of them too. Goodness – suppose he had at last hit on the right person! But Colonel Cross didn't look in the least like a thief or burglar. Anything but, thought Fatty.

Fatty wished he had a small telescope or long-sighted glasses so that he could look more closely at the rubber heel. He didn't dare to go crawling into the garden and look at the heels. The Colonel was certainly very fast asleep, one leg crossed over the other – but he might be one of those light sleepers that woke very suddenly!

The Colonel did wake suddenly. He gave an extra loud snore and woke himself up with a jump. He sat up, and wiped his face with a tablecloth of a handkerchief. He certainly was enormous. He suddenly caught sight of Fatty's face over the hedge and exploded.

'Did you wake me up? What are you doing there? Speak up, man!'

'I didn't wake you, sir,' said Fatty, in a humble voice. 'I was just looking at your feet.'

'Bless us all – my feet? What for?' demanded the Colonel.

'I was wishing you had an old pair of your boots to give me,' said Fatty, very humbly. 'I'm an old tramp, sir, and tramping's hard on the feet. Very hard, sir. And I've big feet, sir, and it's hard to get boots to fit me – cast-off boots, I mean.'

'Go round and ask my housekeeper,' said the Colonel gruffly. 'But see you do something in return if there's an old pair to give you! Hrrrrrumph!'

This was a wonderful noise – rather like what a horse makes. Fatty stored it away for future use. Hrrrrrump! Fine! He would startle the others with it one day.

'Thank you, sir. I'll chop up wood or do anything if I can have a pair of your boots!' he said.

He left the hedge and went round to the back door. A kindly-faced woman opened it.

'Good day, Mam, the Colonel says have you got a pair of his old boots for me?' asked Fatty, his hat in his hands, so that his straggly grey hair showed.

'Another old soldier!' sighed the housekeeper. 'There's not a pair of boots – but there may be an old pair of shoes. And even so, they're not really worn out yet! Dear me – the Colonel only came back yesterday and here he is giving his things away as usual!'

Fatty pricked up his ears. 'Where has he been?' he asked.

'Oh, India,' said the woman. 'And now he's home for the last time. Arrived by air yesterday.'

Ah, thought Fatty, then that rules out the Colonel. Not that I really thought it could be him

– he doesn't look in the least like a burglar! Still, all suspects have to be examined, all clues have to be followed.

The woman came back with a pair of old shoes. They had rubber heels on. Fatty's eyes gleamed when he saw them. The pattern of the heels looked extremely like the pattern he had drawn in his notebook! How interesting!

'Did you say you often give your master's shoes away?' he asked.

'Not only shoes – anything,' she said. 'He's fierce, you know, but he's kind too – always handing out things to his old soldiers. But since he's been away, I've sent his things to the jumble sales each year.'

'My – I hope you didn't send any of this size boots or shoes!' said Fatty jokingly. 'They would have done fine for me!'

'I sent a pair of boots last year,' said the woman, 'they would just have done for you. But who would buy such enormous ones, I *don't* know. I said to Miss Kay when she asked me for them, "Well there now, you can have them, but you won't sell them, I'll wager!" '

144

Fatty made a mental note to find Miss Kay and ask her if she remembered who bought the big boots belonging to the Colonel. It might have been the thief!

'The Colonel said I was to do a job for you,' said Fatty remembering.

'Well now, you go and weed that bed out in the garden,' said the housekeeper. 'I can't seem to get down to it. He's asleep again. I can hear him snoring, so you won't disturb him.'

'I'll be pleased to do it,' said the old tramp and shuffled off. The housekeeper stared after him. He seemed so feeble that she felt rather guilty at having asked him to weed that bed!

Fatty knelt down and began to weed. He spent a pleasant ten minutes pulling out groundsel and chickweed, and in sorting out the thoughts in his head. He was beginning to think that the clues of '2 Frinton' and '1 Rods' were not clues at all – simply bits of paper blown by chance into the Norton House garden. The real clues were the big footprints and gloveprints – and perhaps the strange print with the criss-cross marks on it.

Still, if the Colonel's boots led him to the thief

who had bought them, the scraps of paper would have come in useful after all, Fatty thought swiftly as he weeded.

He heard the sound of bicycle tyres on the lane outside. The sound stopped as someone got off the bicycle. A head looked cautiously over the hedge. Fatty looked up at the same moment.

Goon was peering over the hedge! He saw Fatty at the same moment as Fatty saw him, and gave a startled grunt. That tramp! He'd left him asleep on the bench outside his house – and now here he was weeding in the Colonel's garden. Goon couldn't believe his eyes.

Fatty nodded and smiled amiably. Goon's eyes nearly dropped out of his head. He felt very angry. Everywhere he went there was somebody before him – first those girls, then those boys, now this deaf, old, dirty tramp. If Goon had been a dog he would have growled viciously.

'What are *you* doing here?' said Goon, in a low, hoarse voice.

'Weeding,' answered Fatty, forgetting to be deaf. 'Nice job, weeding.'

'Any cheek from you,' began Goon, forgetting

not to wake the Colonel. But it was too late. Colonel Cross awoke once more with a jump. He sat up and mopped his forehead. Then he caught sight of Goon's brilliant red face over the top of the hedge. Goon was still addressing Fatty.

'What you doing in this neighbourhood?' Goon was saying aggressively.

The Colonel exploded. 'What's that! What's that! Are you addressing me, my man? What are *you* doing, I should like to know! Hrrrrrumph!'

The last noise startled Goon very much. Fatty chortled as he weeded.

'It's all right, sir. I was speaking to that tramp,' said Goon, with dignity. 'I – er – I had occasion to speak sternly to him this morning, sir. Can't have loiterers and tramps around – what with robberies and things.'

'I don't know what you're talking about,' said Colonel Cross. 'Go away. Policemen should know better than to come and wake me up by shouting to tramps who have been given a job in my garden.'

'I came to have a word with you, actually, sir,' said Goon, desperately. 'Privately.'

'If you think I'm going to get up and go indoors and hear a lot of nonsense from you about robberies and tramps and loiterers, you're wrong,' said the old Colonel fiercely. 'If you've got something to say, say it here! That old tramp won't understand a word.'

Fatty chortled to himself again. Goon cleared his throat. 'Well – er – I – came, sir – just to ask you about your boots!'

'Mad,' said the Colonel, staring at Goon. 'Mad! Must be the hot weather! Wants to talk about my boots! Go away and lie down. You're mad!'

Goon was afraid to go on with the matter. He wheeled his bicycle down the lane, and waited a little while to see if the old tramp came out. He meant to have a word with him! Ho! He'd teach him to cheek him in the Colonel's garden!

Fatty finished the bed and tiptoed out, because the Colonel was once more asleep. He said good day to the housekeeper, and went off down the path with the old pair of shoes slung round his neck. He was longing for a moment to open his notebook and compare the pattern of those rubber heels!

He didn't see Mr Goon till he was almost on top

148

of him. Then the policeman advanced on him, with fire in his eye. He stopped short when he saw the enormous pair of shoes slung round Fatty's neck.

To think he'd come all the way down there to talk politely to the Colonel about his boots, and had been ordered off and told he was mad – and this dirty old tramp had actually begged a pair, and was wearing them round his neck! Shoes that might be great big clues!

'Give me those!' ordered Goon, and grabbed at the shoes. But the feeble, shuffling old tramp twisted cleverly out of the way, and raced off down the road as if he was a schoolboy running in a race.

As indeed he was! Fatty put on his fastest speed, and raced away before Mr Goon had recovered sufficiently from his surprise even to mount his bicycle.

Fatty turned a corner and hurled himself through a hedge into a field. He tore across it, knowing that Goon couldn't ride his bicycle there. He would have to go a long way round to cut him off!

Across the field, over the stile, across another

field, down a lane, round a corner – and here was the front gate of his own house! Into the gate and down the path to the shed. The cook caught a brief glimpse of a tramp-like figure from the kitchen window and then it was gone. She hardly knew if she had seen it or not.

Fatty sank down in the shed, panting, and then got up again to lock the door. Phew! What a run! Goon was well and truly left behind. Now to examine the rubber heels.

16. ON THE TRACK AT LAST

Fatty pulled out his notebook and turned over its pages eagerly till he came to the drawings he had made of the footprints. He glued his eyes to his sketch of the pattern of the rubber heel shown in one of the prints.

'Line going across there, two little lines under it, long one there, and three lines together,' he noted. Then he compared the drawn pattern with the rubber heel on one of the shoes.

'It's the same!' he said exultingly. 'The absolute same! That proves it – although it's not the Colonel, it's somebody who wears his old boots – somebody who bought a pair last year at Miss Kay's jumble sale. I'm on the track at last!'

He was thrilled. After all their goings and comings, their watchings and interviewings, which seemed to have come to nothing, at *last* they had something to work on. Something Mr Goon hadn't got!

Fatty did a solemn little jig round his shed. He looked very comical indeed, for he was still disguised as a tramp. He carried one of the big shoes in each hand and waved them about gracefully, as if he was doing a scarf or flower dance.

He heard a sound at the window, and stopped suddenly. Was it Mr Goon? Or his mother?

It was neither. It was Larry's grinning face, enjoying the spectacle of the old tramp's idiotic dance. Fatty rushed to the door and unlocked it. All the others were there, smiling to see Fatty's excitement.

'What is it, Fatty? You've got good news,' said Daisy, pleased.

'I must get these things off,' said Fatty, pulling off his grey wig and suddenly appearing forty years younger. 'Phew – a wig's very hot in this weather! Now, report to me, all of you, while I make myself decent.'

They all made their reports. First the girls, who giggled when they told him of the boots and shoes they had got from the Rodneys for the jumble sale. 'We've taken them already to give to Miss

Kay, the person who's running it,' said Daisy. 'Oh dear – if you could have seen Mr Goon's face when he saw us staggering out with loads of shoes and boots! Anyway, there's nobody at the Rodneys with big feet, so that's another clue finished with. I don't somehow think those scraps of paper meant anything.'

'Nor do I,' said Larry. '*We* got mixed up with old Clear-Orf too – he arrived at Rodways when we were there. He nearly had a heart attack when he saw us, he was so furious! We really thought we'd got something at that place though, when we saw a colossal sou'wester and oilskin hanging up. But no – the owner wears small-size shoes after all!'

'Now tell us what *you* did down at Colonel Cross's,' said Daisy expectantly. 'Go on, Fatty!'

Fatty related his tale with gusto, and when he came to the bit where he had looked up from his weeding and seen Mr Goon's face glowering over the hedge, with the sleeping Colonel between them, the others went off into fits of helpless laughter.

'Oh, Fatty – if only I'd been there!' said Daisy. 'What about the shoes? Tell us.'

Fatty told them everything, and proudly

displayed the shoes. 'And now the greatest news of all!' he said, turning up the shoes suddenly so that they displayed the rubber heels. 'See the rubbers? Well, look!'

He placed his notebook down beside one of the shoes, so that the drawing and the rubber heel were side-by-side. The children exclaimed at once.

'It's the same pattern! The very same! Golly, we're getting somewhere now. But surely – it can't be the Colonel who's got anything to do with the robbery?'

'No,' said Fatty, and explained about how a pair of his boots had been sent to last year's jumble sale. 'And *if* we can find out who bought them, I think we've got our hands on the thief!' said Fatty exultingly. 'We shall find that the person who bought them is somebody else with big feet – somebody the cobbler doesn't know about because probably the fellow mends his own boots. We're on the track at last!'

Everyone felt thrilled. They watched Fatty become his own self again, rubbing away the greasy lines on his face, removing his eyebrows carefully, sliding his aching feet out of the stiff old boots he wore. He grunted and groaned as he took off the boots and rubbed his sore feet.

'I had three pairs of socks on,' he said, 'because the boots are so big and stiff – but even so, I bet I'll limp for days!'

'You do everything so thoroughly, Fatty,' said Bets admiringly, watching him become the Fatty she knew.

'Secret of success, Bets,' said Fatty with a grin. 'Now then – what do we do next? I feel that our next move is very, very important – and it's got to be done quickly before old Mr Goon gets another move on.'

Daisy gave a little giggle when she remembered how they had seen through Mr Goon's disguise that morning, and pestered him. Poor old Clear-Orf! 'Please can you tell us the time?', 'Please can you give us change?' Oh dear – however dared they be such pests!

'Anyone know Miss Kay?' asked Fatty, putting on his shoes and lacing them up. 'She apparently ran the jumble sale last year. Is she running it this year?'

'Yes,' said Daisy. 'She's the one we took the Rodneys' shoes to. But, Fatty, we can't very well go barging up to her and ask her straight out who bought those boots of the Colonel's last year – she'd think it awfully strange.'

'I'm not thinking of doing any barging or blurting out of silly questions,' said Fatty with dignity. 'I've got a very fine idea already – no barging about it!'

'Of *course* Fatty's got a good idea,' said Bets, loyally. 'He always has. What is it, Fatty?'

'I'm simply going to present our very finest clue to Miss Kay for her jumble sale – the Colonel's big shoes – and mention casually that perhaps the person who bought them last year, whoever he was, might like to buy the same size again this year!' said Fatty. 'Same kind of rubber heels and all!'

Everyone gazed admiringly at him. That was about the best and most direct way of getting the vital information they wanted, without arousing any suspicion at all! Trust Fatty to produce an idea like that.

'Very good, Fatty,' said Pip, and the others agreed.

'Let's have tea now,' said Fatty, looking at the time. 'I'll go and see if I can get something out of our cook. You come with me, Bets, because she likes you – and we'll take it out under that tree over there and have a picnic, and relax a bit after all our hard work today.'

He and Bets went off together. They came back with an enormous tea on two trays, and an excited Buster. The cook had looked after him all day, and kept him from following Fatty; now he was wild with delight to be with his friends again.

'It's a marvel both the trays haven't crashed,' said Fatty, putting his down carefully. 'I never knew such a dog for getting under your feet when you're carrying anything heavy. Get away from that cake, Buster. Daisy, do stop him licking it all over. There'll be no icing left. Oh golly, now he's stepped on the buns.'

Bets caught Buster and held him down beside her. 'He can't help dancing about, he's so pleased we're back,' she said. 'See what lovely things we've brought you all! I feel we've earned a good tea!'

They talked over their day as they ate, giggling whenever they thought of poor Mr Goon and his despair at finding them just in front of him, wherever he went.

'I'm going down to Miss Kay's this evening,' said Fatty. 'Taking the shoes! Oh, wonderful, magnificent shoes that will solve the mystery for us! And before seven o'clock comes, I'll be back with the name of the thief! A little telephoning to the Inspector – and a little explaining – and we shall be able to let Mr Goon know tomorrow that the case is closed – the mystery is solved – as usual, by the Five Find-Outers – and Dog!'

'Hip, hip, hurrah!' said Pip. 'I say, Bets – *don't* give Buster any more of those potted-meat sandwiches – I want some too! Fatty, stop her. Buster's fat enough as it is. If he gets much fatter he won't be able to help in any more mysteries. Not that he's *really* helped in this one much!'

'Now you've made him put his tail down,' said Bets, and gave him another sandwich. 'Oh, Fatty, do let me come with you to Miss Kay's. You know who she is, don't you? She's the cousin of that horrid little baker – the one who always tries to be funny.'

'She's just as silly as he is,' said Daisy. 'I told you that we took the Rodneys' boots and shoes to her this afternoon. She's got a dreadful collection of things there. Honestly, I think jumble is awful. She was very pleased with the boots and shoes. She says they go like hot cakes at a sale.'

'Well, I think I'll go now,' said Fatty, getting up and brushing the crumbs from his front. 'Coming, Bets? Yes, you can come too, Buster.'

Bets, Buster and Fatty went out. Fatty carried the Colonel's shoes wrapped in a bit of brown paper.

'Well, so long!' said Fatty cheerfully. 'Get out the flags for when we come back – we'll bring you the name of the thief!'

17. A BITTER DISAPPOINTMENT

Fatty and Bets walked off to Miss Kay's with Buster trotting at their heels. They kept a sharp lookout for Mr Goon. Fatty felt sure that he had guessed who the old tramp was that afternoon, and he didn't particularly want to meet him just then.

Miss Kay lived in a tiny cottage next to her cousin and his wife. Bets hoped they wouldn't see the little baker. 'I get so tired of trying to smile at his silly jokes,' she said to Fatty. 'Look – here we are – don't you think it looks like a place where jumble is taken? Daisy and I thought so, anyway.'

Bets was right. The cottage and its little garden looked untidy and 'jumbly', as Bets put it. A broken-down seat was in the little front garden, and a little, much-chipped statue stood in the centre. The gate was half off its hinges, and one of its bars had gone. The curtains at the window looked dirty and didn't match.

'I should think Miss Kay buys most of the jumble for herself!' whispered Bets, nodding at the broken seat and chipped statue.

Miss Kay looked a bit of a jumble herself when she opened the door to them. She was as small and sprightly as her baker-cousin, but not nearly so neat and spruce. 'She's all bits and pieces,' thought Bets, looking at her. 'Hung about with all the jumble nobody else buys – bead necklaces, a torn scarf, a belt with its embroidery spoilt, and that awful red comb in her hair!'

Miss Kay seemed delighted to see them. '*Do* come in!' she said, in a kind of cooing voice. 'It isn't often I get a nice young gentleman to see me. And this dear little girl again too – you came this afternoon, didn't you, dearie?'

'Yes,' said Bets, who didn't like being called 'dearie' by Miss Kay.

'And what have you brought me *this* time, love?' asked Miss Kay, leading the way into a little room so crowded with furniture that Fatty had great difficulty in finding where to step. He knocked over a small table, and looked down in alarm.

'I'm so sorry,' he said, and bent to pick up the things that had fallen. Miss Kay bent down at the same time and their heads bumped together.

'Oh, sorry,' said Fatty again. Miss Kay gave a little giggle, and rubbed her head.

'Oh, it's nothing! My cousin says I've got a wooden head, so a bump never matters to me!' She gave another silly little giggle, and Bets smiled feebly.

'This kind little girl brought me *such* a lot of nice things for the jumble sale this afternoon,' chattered Miss Kay. 'And I'm hoping *you've* brought something too. *What's* in that parcel?'

She put her head on one side, and her comb fell out. She gave a little squeal and picked it up. 'Oh dear – I seem to be falling to bits! You know, that cheeky cousin of mine says one day I'll be a bit of jumble myself, and be sold for a penny. He, he he!'

Fatty felt rather sick. He didn't like the baker, her cousin, but he liked Miss Kay even less. He opened his parcel and took out the shoes. All he wanted to do now was to get the information he needed, and go!

Miss Kay gave another squeal. 'Oh! *What* an

enormous pair of shoes! Are they *yours*? That's just a joke of course, I didn't mean it. I'm such a tease, aren't I? My, it's quite a good pair though.'

'It's a pair of Colonel Cross's,' said Fatty. 'He sent a pair of boots last year too. I thought perhaps the same person who had feet big enough to fit last year's boots would probably like to buy these. Do you know who it was?'

Bets' heart began to beat fast. She looked breathlessly at Miss Kay. She and Fatty waited for the name. What would it be?

'Oh, they weren't sold last year,' said Miss Kay. 'There was *quite* a little mystery about them! Really it gave me *quite* a shock. You see . . .'

'What do you mean – they weren't sold?' asked Fatty, determined to keep her to the point.

'Well, love – they just *disappeared*!' said Miss Kay, speaking with bated breath as if she hardly wanted anyone to hear. 'Disappeared! One night they were here, ready for the sale – and the next morning they were gone!'

'Were they stolen?' asked Fatty, bitterly disappointed.

'Oh yes – no doubt about it,' said Miss Kay. 'Funny thing is, nothing else was taken at all – just those big boots. They were under that table over there – where I've put all the boots and shoes this year – and the thief went there, picked out the big boots and went off with them. I'd marked them with a price and everything. As a matter-of-fact, I hoped to sell them to that nice policeman of ours – Mr Goon. But they just went one night.'

'Who stole them – do you know?' asked Fatty. 'Is there anyone you know who has big feet, who might think of stealing them? It must surely be someone in the village – how else would they know you had a pair of enormous boots here that would fit them? They knew where to find them too – under that table in your cottage!'

Miss Kay gave another little squeal. 'How very clever you are, love! As clever as that nice Mr Goon. No, I don't know who took the boots – and I don't know anyone with enormous feet either, who could wear them.'

'Did Mr Goon know about it?' asked Fatty.

'Oh no. My cousin said that as I'd only marked the boots cheaply, it wasn't worth taking up the time of the police over a pair of jumble boots,' said Miss Kay. 'He's very good like that, my cousin is.

He gave me some money towards the stolen boots and I gave some myself, and we put the money into the jumble box, so the sale didn't lose by it. I do hope you think I was right.'

'Quite right,' said Fatty, bored with all this niggling over jumble boots, and wild to think that their wonderful idea was no good. The boots had been stolen – and nobody knew who had taken them. Nobody even seemed to know anyone with outsize feet. There seemed to be a dearth of large feet in Peterswood. It was really most annoying. He seemed to run into a blank wall, no matter what clue he followed. Fatty felt very down in the dumps.

'I think, on the whole, I won't leave these big shoes here,' said Fatty, wrapping them up again. 'I mean – if there are thieves about here who have an urge for enormous boots and shoes, these might disappear as well. I'll bring them down to you on the day of the jumble sale, Miss Kay.'

Fatty wasn't going to leave his precious shoes, with their rubber heels, at Miss Kay's now that he hadn't got the information he wanted! It would be a waste of his clue. He was quite determined about that.

Miss Kay looked as if she was going to burst into tears. Fatty hurriedly went to the door with Bets before this disaster happened. He saw someone in the next garden – the little baker, Miss Kay's cousin. He groaned. Now there would be another volley of silly talk.

'Hello, hello, *hello*!' said the baker genially. 'If it isn't Frederick Trotteville, the great detective. Solved the mystery of the robbery yet, young man?'

Fatty always hated being called 'young man' and he especially disliked it from the little baker. He scowled.

Bets spoke up for him. 'He's nearly solved it. He soon will. We just want to find the name of the man with big feet, that's all. We almost got it tonight.'

'Shut up, Bets,' said Fatty in a low and most unexpectedly cross voice. Bets flushed and fell silent. But the little baker made up for her sudden silence.

'Well, well, well – we shall expect to hear great things soon! I suppose the same man did both the robberies? I saw his prints all right! Me and Mr Goon, we had a good old chinwag over it – ah, Mr Goon will get the thief all right – before you do, young man! He's on the track, yes, he's on the track. Told me so when I left his bread today. Those were his very words. "I'm on the track, Twit," he said, just like that.'

'Interesting,' said Fatty in a bored voice, and opened the gate for Bets to go through. The little baker didn't like Fatty's tone of voice. He strutted up to his own gate and stood there, going up and down on his heels in rather an insolent manner, leering at Bets and Fatty.

' "Interesting!" you says – just like that! Pride goes before a fall, young man. You watch your step. I've heard a lot about you from Mr Goon.'

'That's enough, Twit,' said Fatty in such a stern, grown-up voice that Bets jumped. So did Twit. He altered his tone at once.

'I didn't mean no harm. Just my joke, like. Me and my cousin, Miss Kay, we do like a joke, don't we, Coz?'

Coz was apparently Miss Kay, who was standing by her front gate, smiling and listening, bobbing up and down on her heels just like her cousin.

'Guard your tongue, Twit,' said Fatty, still in his grown-up voice. 'You'll get yourself into trouble if you don't.'

He walked off with Bets, angry, disappointed, and rather crestfallen. Twit and Miss Kay watched them go. Twit was red in the face and angry.

'Insolence!' he said to his cousin. 'Young upstart! Talking to me like that! I'll learn him. Thinks himself very clever, does he? Ah, Mr Goon's right – he's a toad, that boy.'

'Oh, don't talk like that!' said Miss Kay fearfully. 'You'll lose your customers!'

Bets slipped her hand through Fatty's arm as they went home. 'Fatty,' she said, 'I'm awfully sorry for what I said to Twit. I didn't think it mattered.'

'Well, I suppose it doesn't,' said Fatty, patting Bets' hand. 'But never talk when we're solving a mystery, Bets. You just might give something away – though it seems to me that Twit must know pretty well everything from Mr Goon – they sound like bosom friends!'

'Are you very disappointed, Fatty?' asked Bets, very sad to see Fatty so down in the dumps. It wasn't like him.

'Yes, I am,' said Fatty. 'We've come to a dead end, little Bets. There's no further clue to follow, nothing more to do. We'll have to give it up – the first mystery we've ever been beaten by!'

And, in a mournful silence, the two went dolefully down to the shed to tell the miserable news.

18. THE THIRD ROBBERY

For a day or two, the Five Find-Outers were very much subdued. It was horrid to have to give up – just when they had thought the whole thing was going to be solved so quickly and successfully too!

Fatty was quite upset by it. He worried a lot, going over and over all the clues and the details of the two robberies, trying to find another trail to follow. But he couldn't. As he had said to Bets, they had come to a dead end, a blank wall.

The weather broke and the rain came down. What with that and Fatty looking so solemn, the other four were quite at a loose end. They got into mischief, irritated their parents, and simply didn't know what to do with themselves.

Fatty cheered up after a bit. 'It's just that I *hate* being beaten, you know,' he said to the others. 'I never am, as a matter-of-fact. This is the first time

– and if anybody feels inclined to say, "Well, I suppose it's good for you, Fatty," I warn them, don't say it. It *isn't* good for me. It's bad.'

'Well, do cheer up now, Fatty,' said Daisy. 'It's really awful having you go about looking like a hen out in the rain! As for poor old Buster, I hardly know if he's got a tail these days, it's tucked between his legs so tightly. It hasn't wagged for days!'

'Hey, Buster! Good dog, Buster! I'm all right now!' said Fatty suddenly, to the little Scottie. He spoke in his old cheerful voice, and Buster leapt up as if he had been shot. His tail wagged nineteen to the dozen, he barked, flung himself on Fatty and then went completely mad.

He tore round and round Pip's playroom as if he was running a race, and finally hurled himself out of the door, slid all the way down the landing, and fell down the stairs.

The children screamed with delight. Buster was always funny when he went mad. Mrs Hilton's voice came up the stairs.

'Pip! Fatty! Come and catch Buster. He seems to have gone off his head. Oh – here he comes again. What *is* the matter with him?'

Buster tore up the stairs at sixty miles an hour, slid along the landing again and came to rest under a chair. He lay there, panting, quite tired out, his tail thumping against the floor.

Everyone felt better after that. Fatty looked at his watch. 'Let's go to Oliver's again and have a splash – I could do with three or four meringues.'

'Ooooh, yes – *I've* got some money today,' said Larry, pulling out some money. 'My Uncle Ted gave me it weeks ago and I couldn't think where I'd put it for safety. I found it today in my tie-box.'

'We'll all go shares,' said Pip. 'I've got two pounds, and Bets has got one.'

'Right,' said Fatty. 'The more the merrier. Come on. I'll just telephone my mother to tell her we're going to Oliver's.'

They went off, feeling happier than they had done for days. Buster's tail had appeared again and was wagging merrily as he ran along with them. His master was all right again – life was bright once more!

They stayed a long time over their tea, talking hard, and eating equally hard. Nobody said a word about the mystery. They weren't going to remember defeat when éclairs and meringues and chocolate cake were spread in front of them! That would be silly.

Feeling rather full, they walked back to Fatty's and went down the garden to the shed. Buster trotted on ahead. He surprised them all by suddenly barking urgently and loudly.

'What's up, Buster?' shouted Fatty, beginning to run. Larry raced down the path with him. Whatever could Buster be barking about like that?

Pip and Larry came to the shed. The door was wide open, though Fatty always left it shut and locked. Fatty ran in, amazed. He looked round.

His things were all in a muddle! Clothes had been dragged down from the pegs, drawers in a chest had been emptied, and everywhere was mess and muddle. Someone had been there and turned everything upside down.

'My money's gone, of course,' said Fatty in exasperation. 'I'd got two pounds I was saving for Mummy's birthday – why did I leave it here! I never do leave money in the ordinary way. Blow!'

'Anything else gone?' asked Larry. Pip, Daisy

and Bets crowded into the untidy shed. Bets burst into tears, but nobody took any notice of her, not even Fatty.

'My knife's gone – that silver one,' said Fatty. 'And that little silver case I kept odds and ends in. And yes – my cigarette case is gone, the one I use when I'm disguised. Well, the thief is welcome to that! I suppose he thought it was silver, but it isn't!'

'Oh, Fatty!' wailed Bets. 'What's happened? Has a robber been here? Oh, what shall we do?'

'Shut up, Bets,' said Pip. 'Behaving like a baby as usual. Go home if you can't be of any help.'

Bets stopped wailing at once. She looked at Fatty but he was completely engrossed in checking up his belongings.

She went outside to swallow her tears and be sensible – and then she suddenly saw something that made her stare. She yelled loudly.

'Fatty! FATTY! Come here, quick!'

Fatty appeared at top speed, the others behind him. Bets pointed to the muddy path near the shed. On it were clear footprints – enormous ones!

'Gosh!' said Fatty. 'It's our robber again. The very same one – look at the marks his rubber heels made – the same pattern as before.'

'Will there be gloveprints too?' asked Daisy excitedly, and she went back into the shed.

'Shouldn't think so,' said Fatty following. 'There's no wallpaper or distemper to show them up.'

'Well, look – there they are!' said Daisy, pointing triumphantly. And sure enough, there were two large gloveprints showing clearly on the looking-glass that Fatty had in his shed!

'He likes to leave his mark, doesn't he?' said Larry. 'You'd almost think he was saying, "This is the robber, his mark!" '

'Yes,' said Fatty thoughtfully. 'Well, it's the same fellow all right. He hasn't got away with a great deal, thank goodness – but what a mess!'

'We'll soon clear it up,' said Bets, eager to do something for poor old Fatty.

'Let's take a very, very careful snoop round before we move *any*thing,' said Fatty. 'The mystery has come right to our very door – it's all-alive-oh again. We may perhaps be able to solve it this time.'

'I suppose you're not going to inform the police!' said Larry with a laugh.

'No. I'm not,' said Fatty very firmly. 'First thing I'm going to do is to measure the footprints to make absolutely certain they're the same ones that we saw before – at Norton House and at Mrs Williams's.'

They were, of course, exactly the same. No doubt about it at all. The gloveprints were the same too.

'We can't find out whether there was a hollow cough this time,' said Pip, 'because there was nobody here to hear it. I suppose there aren't any scraps of paper, are there, Fatty?'

'None,' said Fatty. 'But there weren't at Mrs Williams's either, you know. I'm beginning to think that they really had nothing to do with the robberies. They don't really link up with anything.'

Daisy went wandering off down the path a little. She came to another print by the side of the path, almost under a shrub. She called Fatty.

'Look!' she said. 'Isn't this strange print like the ones you found in both the other robberies?'

Fatty knelt to see. On the wet ground under the shrub the mark was quite plain – a big roundish print with criss-cross lines here and there.

'Yes,' said Fatty puzzled, turning over the pages of his notebook to compare his drawing with the print. 'It's the same. I cannot *imagine* what makes it – or why it appears in all the robberies. It's extraordinary.'

They all gazed down at the strange mark. Pip wrinkled his forehead. 'You know – somehow I feel as if I've seen it somewhere else besides the robberies. Where could it have been?'

'Think, Pip,' said Fatty. 'It might help.'

But Pip couldn't think. All he could say was that he thought he had seen it somewhere on the day when they all went interviewing.

'That's not much help,' said Fatty with a sigh. 'We were all over the place that day. Now we'd better put everything back. I can't see that we can find any more clues. As a matter-of-fact, it seems as if this robbery is almost an exact repetition of the others – large footprints, gloveprints, strange unknown print, and small goods stolen.'

They hung up the clothes, and put back everything into the chest of drawers. They kept a sharp lookout for any possible clue, but as far as they could see there was none at all.

'How did the thief get down to the shed?' asked Larry. 'Did he get in through the back gate leading into the lane, do you think? It's not far from the shed. Or did he come down the path from the house?'

'Well – if he made that mark under the shrub, it rather looks as if he came from the house,' said Fatty. 'On the other hand, the large footprints are only round and about the shed – I didn't find any on the path up to the house, did you?'

'No,' said Larry. 'Well, it's more likely he would have come quietly in through the back gate down by the shed – he wouldn't be seen then. It's very secluded down here at the bottom of the garden – can't be seen from the house at all.'

'All the same, I think we'd better ask the cook and the maid if they saw anyone,' said Fatty. 'They just might have. And we'll ask who has been to the house this afternoon too. Any tradesman or visitor who might have seen somebody.'

'Yes. Good idea,' said Larry. 'Come on – let's go and find out.'

19. THE WARNING

The maid was out, and had been out all afternoon. The cook was in, however, and was rather surprised to see all five children and Buster trooping in at her kitchen door.

'Now don't you say you want tea,' she began. 'It's a quarter to six, and . . .'

'No, we don't want tea,' said Fatty. 'I just came to ask you a few things. Someone's been disturbing my belongings in the shed at the bottom of the garden. I wondered if you had seen anyone going down the path to the shed this afternoon.'

'Goodness,' said the cook alarmed. 'Don't tell me there's tramps about again. I thought I saw a very nasty-looking fellow slipping down that path the other day.'

Fatty knew who *that* was all right. So did the others. They turned away to hide their grins.

'No – it's today I want to know about,' said Fatty. 'Did you see anyone at all?'

'Not a soul today,' said the cook. 'And I've been sitting here at this window all the time!'

'You didn't have forty winks, I suppose?' asked Fatty, with a smile. 'You do sometimes.'

'Well, maybe I did for a few minutes,' said the cook with a laugh. 'I get really sleepy in the afternoons, when it's hot like this. Still, I was awake all right when the tradespeople came.'

'Who came?' asked Larry.

'Oh, the usual ones,' said the cook. 'The girl with the groceries, the milkman, the baker – and let me see, did the gasman come? No, that was this morning.'

'Anyone else?' asked Fatty.

'Well, Mr Goon called,' said the cook, 'and he asked for your mother, but she wasn't in. So he went away again. He came at the same time as the baker did. They had a good old talk together too, out in the front garden. I heard them. Mr Goon bumped into the baker just as he was leaving.'

'I bet they had a good talk about Bets and me,' said Fatty to the others. 'Anyone else call, Cook?'

'Not that I know of,' she said. 'I didn't have any talk with the baker – he's too much of a saucy one for me – I just left a note on the table to tell him how many loaves to leave. And I didn't see the milkman either – he knows how much to leave. I saw the grocer's girl and she was in a hurry as usual.'

'I wonder what Mr Goon wanted,' said Fatty as they left the kitchen to walk down to the shed again. 'I bet he wants to know if I was the old tramp the other day. As if Mummy would know!'

They were just walking out of the door when Daisy stopped suddenly and looked down at the ground.

'Look!' she said, and pointed.

They all looked – and there, just by the kitchen door, in a wet patch of ground, was the same roundish mark that they had seen under the shrub! The same as they had seen at the two other robberies as well.

'Gosh!' said Fatty staring down. 'The thief did actually come to the kitchen door then! He must have made that mark – but why?'

'Your cook said nobody else came except the

people she mentioned,' said Larry. 'It seems to me as if the thief came here, peeped in and saw the cook asleep, and went down to the shed to do his dirty work.'

'Then why didn't he leave large footprints here?' said Daisy. 'There's only small ones going to and from the bottom of the garden. I looked. There's no large ones at all – no larger than size seven, anyway.'

'It beats me!' said Pip.

It beat them all. Now there had been three separate robberies, all obviously done by the same man, who left exactly the same marks each time – and yet he had never once been seen, though he must really be a very big fellow indeed.

'He's invisible – that's how he can do all these things!' said Daisy. 'I mean – surely *some*body would have seen him *one* of the times. But all he does is come and go, and leave behind foot and gloveprints, and do just what he likes! He must be laughing up his sleeve at all of us.'

'It *can't* be old Mr Goon, can it?' said Bets hopefully. 'He has large feet and hands, and he *has* got a hollow, sheep-like cough, and he really does hate you, Fatty. He came here today too – why couldn't he have slipped down and been spiteful, turning all your things upside down and making a mess?'

'I daresay he'd *like* to,' said Fatty, 'but remember, he was away at the time of the first robbery – and honestly, I don't think he's mad enough to do such idiotic things – I mean, it's sheer dishonesty, robbing people like this, and Mr Goon wouldn't risk his job and his pension. No, rule that right out, Bets.'

'Are you going to ask the milkman and the others if they saw anyone?' asked Bets. Fatty shook his head.

'No. I'm pretty certain now that if the milkman, the baker, or grocer's girl had seen anyone here this afternoon, wandering about in large-size boots they would have told Cook. Anyway, I'm not interviewing that cocky little baker again – wouldn't he be pleased if he knew I'd been robbed! He'd rub his little hands like anything, and rock to and fro on his toes and heels with glee.'

'Yes, he would,' said Bets, rocking to and fro as she remembered how he had gone up and down on his heels. 'Nasty little man. I hope he doesn't hear about this.'

'No one is to,' said Fatty firmly. 'I'm not going to have Mr Goon strolling down the garden and fingering everything in my shed. How he'd love to look through my make-up box, and pick up all my moustaches and eyebrows and wigs!'

'Well, none of us will say a word about this afternoon's do,' said Larry. 'We'll keep the thief guessing! He'll wonder why there's no news of his last robbery.'

'The thief burst the lock on your door, Fatty,' said Bets. 'How will you lock it tonight?'

'I'll slip out and buy a padlock,' said Fatty. 'That will be the easiest thing to do tonight – put a padlock on the door. I'll come with you when you go home. I can get one at the garage – it stays open till seven.'

So, at ten to seven, Fatty and the others strolled up the lane to the garage in the village. They bought a strong little padlock, and came out examining it.

A voice behind them made them jump. It was Mr Goon, starting on his first night-round.

'Ho! A padlock! Maybe you'll need that, Frederick! You'd better be careful.'

Everyone swung round in astonishment. 'What do you mean, Mr Goon?' said Fatty.

'I've had notice that you'll be the next on the robbery list,' said Goon importantly. 'I came to warn your mother this afternoon. Just make sure that everything is well locked up tonight, windows fastened and everything. And have that there pesky little dog of yours in the front hall.'

'What *is* all this about?' said Fatty, hoping that nobody would blurt out anything about the robbery that had already happened that afternoon. 'What nonsense, Mr Goon!'

Mr Goon swelled up a little, and Bets was sure one of his uniform buttons was about to spring off. He fumbled in his breast-pocket and brought out his little notebook. He undid the elastic strap and ran through the pages. Everyone watched in silence.

He took out a scrap of dirty paper, and handed it to Fatty. 'There you are. If that isn't a plain warning I don't know what is. Course, you don't need to take no notice of it at all – and anyway, I'll be sure to be round two or three times tonight to see as everything is all right round at yours.'

Fatty took the scrap of paper. On it, printed in uneven lettering, were three words,

TROTVILLS NEXT. – Bigfeet

Fatty silently passed it round to the others. They knew what Goon didn't know – that the warning was too late. Bigfeet, the robber, had already been to the Trottevilles!

'There you are!' said Mr Goon, enjoying the interest he was causing. 'The impertinence of it! Good as saying "Fat lot of good you are – I'll tell you where I'm going to strike next." Signing himself Bigfeet too. He's got some sauce!'

'Mr Goon, have you got the other scraps of paper on you?' asked Fatty. 'The ones found at Norton House, with "2 Frinton" and "1 Rods" on? It would be useful to compare them.'

Goon gave a scornful little snort. 'Think I didn't compare them, Mr Smarty? 'Course I did. But this here note's in printed capitals and the others aren't. Can't see any likeness at all.'

'I think you're wrong, Mr Goon,' said Fatty, suddenly speaking like a grown-up again. 'And if you like, I'll show you the likeness.'

'Gah,' said Goon in disgust. 'Think you know everything, don't you? Well, I tell you I've compared the three scraps of paper, and this one's different.'

'I don't believe it,' said Fatty.

That stung Mr Goon and he glared. He felt in the little pocket of his notebook and produced the other two notes. He showed them to Fatty, together with the third one. 'See? No likeness at all!' he said triumphantly.

'I'm not thinking of the words written on the papers,' said Fatty. 'I'm thinking of the *paper* they're written *on*. It's exactly the same. Whoever wrote the first notes, wrote this one too. So those first scraps of paper *were* clues after all – though they led to nothing.'

Mr Goon stared at the scraps of paper. Fatty was right. They had obviously been torn from the same notebook or sheets of paper – they were all rather yellowed and the surface was a little fluffy.

Mr Goon cleared his throat. He felt a little awkward. That boy! Always putting him in the wrong. He put the scraps back into his pocketbook.

He cleared his throat again. 'Think I didn't

notice that?' he said. 'Why, it hits you in the eye!'

'It didn't seem to have given you a very hard blow then,' said Fatty. 'Well, I'm not heeding that warning, Mr Goon – so you can sleep in peace tonight! There will be no robbery at the Trottevilles, I can tell you that!'

20. MOSTLY ABOUT GOON

The five children, with Buster, went on their way, Fatty thinking deeply. The others respected his thoughts and said nothing. They came to the corner where they had to part with Larry and Daisy.

'Any orders, Fatty?' said Larry respectfully.

'Er – what? Oh, orders. No, none,' said Fatty, coming out of his trance. 'Sorry to be so goofy all of a sudden. But it's funny, isn't it? – that warning, I mean. Why did the thief send it? He must be really sure of himself – though, of course, he might have sent it to Mr Goon *after* he'd done the job. I just don't understand it.'

'When did Mr Goon get it?' said Daisy. 'I didn't hear him say. Did you ask him?'

'No. I was so surprised to find that the third scrap of paper was the same as the first two, which meant they really did have something to do with

189

the thief, that I didn't ask any of the questions I should,' said Fatty, vexed. 'That means I'll have to go back and get a little more information. Mr Goon will be pleased!'

'Is the mystery on again?' asked Bets.

'Very much on, Bets,' said Fatty. 'Oh very much! Blow Bigfeet! I shall dream about him tonight. It really is a puzzle how that fellow can get about without being noticed – I mean, there's all of us on the watch, and Mr Goon, and the baker, and the grocer's girl, and goodness knows how many other people too, looking for a large-footed man – and yet the fellow has the nerve to walk up the road to my house, go in at one of the front gates, walk up to the kitchen door, and all the way down to the shed, and then out again with his stolen goods – and not a single soul sees him.'

'He *must* be invisible!' said Bets, quite convinced.

'The case of the invisible thief – or the mystery of Bigfeet the robber!' said Fatty. 'It's a funny case this – lots of clues all leading nowhere.'

They said good-bye and parted. Fatty went back to Mr Goon's house. He must find out where that paper had been put when it was delivered, and what time it was sent.

He came to Mr Goon's house. Goon was back again, and was spending an interesting ten minutes trying on a supply of new moustaches that had arrived by post that day.

He was sitting in front of the mirror, twirling a particularly fine moustache when he heard the knock at the front door. He peered out of the window. Ah – that boy. Goon grinned to himself.

He crammed a hat down on his head, frowned, twisted his new moustache up, and leaned out of the window.

'What do you want?' he asked in a deep, rather sinister voice. Fatty looked up and was extremely startled to see the scowling, moustached face above him. In a trice he recognised Goon – there was no mistaking those frog-like eyes. However, if Goon wanted to think he could make himself unrecognisable by adding a moustache and a scowl, Fatty was quite willing to let him.

'Er – good evening,' said Fatty politely. 'Could I speak to Mr Goon? Or is he busy?'

'He's busy,' said the face, in a hollow voice and the moustache twitched up and down.

'Oh, what a pity. It's rather important,' said Fatty.

'I'll see if he'll see you,' said the face, and disappeared. Fatty chuckled. The door opened half a minute later, and Mr Goon appeared, minus scowl and moustache. Actually he felt quite amiable for once. His disguise had deceived that boy – ha, Fatty wasn't as clever as he thought he was!

'Good evening, Mr Goon,' said Fatty. 'Did your friend tell you I wanted to see you?'

'He did,' said Goon. 'What do you want?'

'I forgot to ask you how you got that third note and when,' said Fatty. 'It might be important.'

'I don't know how *or* when it came,' said Mr Goon annoyingly.

'Well – when did you find it?' asked Fatty.

'I was going through some papers in the office,' said Goon, 'and I was lost in them – very important papers they were, see. Well, the milkman and the baker came and left the bread and the milk as usual – and when I came into the kitchen to get myself a cup of tea, I picked up the bottle of milk – and there was the note on top of it!'

'Thank you,' said Fatty. 'So you don't really

know what time it came, except that it must have come after the milkman and baker. Did you hear *them* come?'

As Mr Goon had been fast asleep all afternoon he had heard no one at all, but he wasn't going to tell Fatty that.

'I expect I heard them come,' he said. 'But when I read through official papers – very important ones too – I get lost in them. I daresay the tradesmen came about the usual time – three o'clock or so.'

'Thanks,' said Fatty. 'That's all I wanted to know. You came along to my house then to give us the warning? Our cook told me you came.'

'Yes. I came along at once,' said Goon. 'As was my bounden duty. Pity you won't take no notice of that warning. Still, I'll be along tonight all right.'

'As is your bounden duty!' said Fatty. 'Well, I'll be off. I'm sorry to have disturbed that friend of yours, Mr Goon.'

'Oh, he won't mind,' said Goon, most gratified to find that Fatty apparently hadn't recognised who the 'friend' was.

'Good-looking fellow, isn't he?' said Fatty, innocently. Goon agreed instantly.

'Yes, quite. Fine moustache,' he said.

'Very, very fine,' said Fatty. 'Actually they are what made him good-looking. Without those, he'd have been very plain indeed, in fact, quite ugly. Don't you agree?'

And before poor Mr Goon could find his tongue, Fatty had gone. That boy! Slippery as an eel in all he said and did. Now, exactly what did he mean by those last remarks?

Fatty walked home, deep in thought again. He had his supper by himself because his parents were out, and didn't even notice what a delicious meal the cook had prepared for him, much to her disappointment. He was thinking so very hard.

He went up to his own room after his meal and tried to read a very thrilling mystery story; but his own mystery was much more interesting to him, and after a bit he pushed the book aside and fell into thought again.

What I can't understand is that all the different clues we have *ought* to fit together like a jigsaw puzzle and make a definite picture of the thief, said Fatty to himself. And they don't. They just don't. And yet, if I could find out how to fit them together, I could solve the mystery at once – who the thief is – how he gets about unseen – why he doesn't care whether his prints are all over the place or not – how he gets away with his goods without fear of being detected with them – and, above all, why he sent that warning. That's so boastful, somehow – he must be very, very certain of himself and his powers.

He fell asleep immediately as soon as he got into bed, and then woke up worrying again. Half-asleep and half-awake, he lay there with his mind milling round and round all the clues and details. Things got mixed up in his half-sleeping mind – the milkman's cart and the warning note on the milk bottle – the baker's basket and pairs of large boots – hollow coughs and large moustaches – there was no end to the pictures that came and went in his mind.

Then Buster began to bark! Fatty awoke properly and sat up. Gosh! Did that warning mean the thief was coming to the *house*? thought Fatty, dragging on his dressing-gown. He had imagined that it meant the robbery in the shed. He shot downstairs and opened the front door to let Buster out. The dog had run straight to the door and scraped at it.

'Well, if the thief's outside, you'll give him a shock, Buster,' said Fatty. Buster shot out and disappeared into the front garden. There came an agonised yell.

'Get out! Clear orf! Clear orf, I say!'

Fatty collapsed into laughter. It was poor old Mr Goon out there, solemnly 'doing his bounden duty' in the middle of the night. He had come to see that the Trotteville's house was not already burgled.

'Buster! Come here!' yelled Fatty, and the yell woke his parents, the cook and the maid at once. Everyone crowded on to the landing.

'Frederick! What *is* all this disturbance?' called his father, coming downstairs. Buster was now in Fatty's arms, struggling to go again. Oh, the joy of being let out in the middle of the night and finding Goon's ankles at his mercy! What a wonderful surprise it had been to Buster.

Mr Goon loomed up in the doorway, very angry. 'You set that there dog on me,' he began. 'And me doing my duty, and guarding your property.'

Mrs Trotteville had no time for Mr Goon. 'What

does he want?' she called down to Fatty.

'I don't really know,' said Fatty. 'What exactly did you say you wanted, Mr Goon?'

'I don't want anything, as you very well know,' said Mr Goon, in a real temper. 'I was just doing my duty, what with that warning and all . . .'

'What's he talking about?' said Mr Trotteville coming up to the front door.

'About a warning,' said Fatty.

'What warning?' asked Mr Trotteville, quite at sea.

'Why, that warning from Bigfeet,' said Mr Goon in surprise, not realising that Fatty had said nothing to his parents.

'Bigfeet! Is he mad?' said Mr Trotteville. 'Look here, Goon, you come along in the morning and talk about big feet all you like – but not in the middle of the night. You go home to bed.'

Goon snorted, and was about to say something very cutting when Mr Trotteville firmly shut the door. 'Is he mad?' he asked Fatty.

'Not any more than usual,' said Fatty. 'Well, if he comes again, I'll let Buster out – he won't come very often after that!'

But Goon didn't come again. He walked off wrathfully, thinking of all the things he would like to do to that young toad – yes, and to that pest of a dog too.

And me doing my bounden duty, he said to himself. Well, let'em be robbed good and proper – good and proper, is what I say!

21. PIP PLAYS A TRICK

The next morning, Fatty felt very gloomy again. He ate his breakfast in complete silence, much to his mother's surprise.

'Do you feel quite well, Frederick?' she asked him.

'What, Mummy? Oh yes – I'm all right,' said Fatty. 'Just thinking, that's all.'

'I hope you haven't got mixed up in one of those awful mystery affairs again,' said Mrs Trotteville.

Fatty said nothing. He *was* mixed up in one – and he was completely at a loss about it! Three different robberies – one in his own shed – heaps of clues – and no solution at all, unless he made up his mind that the thief was invisible, which was obviously impossible.

The worst of it is, he's laughing up his sleeve at us the whole time, thought Fatty, in exasperation. I feel that it's someone who knows us. Do we know *him*? And he's so jolly certain of himself and his ability to get away unseen that he even has the cheek to warn us where he's going to commit the next robbery.

He thought of his visit to Miss Kay, and his high hopes when he went there. If only those boots hadn't been stolen, everything would have been so easy.

'Frederick, you really must go and get your hair cut this morning,' said Mrs Trotteville. 'It's far too long.'

'All right, Mummy!' said Fatty, who had been expecting this suggestion for the last two weeks. He knew his hair was rather long, but it made disguises a bit easier if his hair was long and he wasn't going to wear a wig. He could pull it about a bit, and make it go different ways under a hat.

'Ring up and make an appointment,' said Mrs Trotteville, 'then you won't have to wait for ages.'

When the others came at ten o'clock to meet in Fatty's shed, and see if anything further had happened, they were met by a gloomy Fatty.

'Got to go and get my hair cut,' he said. 'I'll be

back in about half an hour. You can either wait for me here or go and have your first ice cream of the day while I'm at the hairdresser's.'

'All right,' said Larry. 'Anything further happened?'

'Nothing much – except that Mr Goon came in the middle of the night to see if we'd been burgled or not – and I really thought it might be the thief and let old Buster out. Gosh, he was thrilled to find Mr Goon's ankles out there!'

Everyone laughed, and Fatty cheered up a bit. 'Well, what are you going to do? Wait here?' asked Fatty.

'Yes. I think we will,' said Larry. 'We're all a bit short of cash today. We'll laze here under the trees till you come back. Don't be long.'

Fatty went off, still looking gloomy. The others looked at one another. It was not very nice when Fatty was in low spirits. It didn't often happen but when it did, it cast a definite gloom over the party.

'I wish we could do something to cheer Fatty up,' said Bets.

'Well – let's play a trick on him or something,'

said Pip.

'Too hot,' said Larry. 'Not enough time either. He'll be back so soon.'

Pip wandered into Fatty's shed. He looked round. He wondered what he could do – dress up and disguise himself so that Fatty wouldn't know him? No, there wasn't time to do that properly.

His eyes fell on the enormous pair of shoes that Fatty had got from Colonel Cross's housekeeper, and had refused to leave with Miss Kay. There they were, hanging on a peg by their laces. Pip looked at them – and an idea came into his head!

He grinned. Gosh, he certainly *had* got an idea – one that would make Fatty and the others sit up properly. He would enjoy himself over this idea. Talk about a little bamboozling!

He took off his rubber shoes and slipped them into his pocket. He took down the big shoes and pulled them on. They slip-slopped about on his feet, but he could just walk in them. Pip went cautiously out of the shed unseen by the others, who were on the other side of a bush.

He knew Fatty would come back through the

garden gate not far from the back of the shed. He also knew that there was a bed there that had just been dug over and prepared by the gardener for lettuces.

Pip walked painfully over to the nice smooth bed. He took a few steps this way on the earth, and a few steps that way. Then he stopped to see his footwork – marvellous! It looked for all the world as if Bigfeet the thief had visited them once again, and left his giant-size footprints plainly to be seen!

Pip grinned again. He took a few more steps, treading as hard as he could. Then he walked quietly back to the shed, took off the shoes, and put on his own once more. He'd like to see old Fatty's face when he came back and saw those footprints!

He walked out to the others. 'Shall we go and meet Fatty?' he said. 'Come on. He'd be pleased. It's only a little way.'

'All right,' said Larry, and Bets and Daisy agreed at once.

'I can see Mrs Trotteville in the front garden,' said Pip, peering through the trees. 'We'd better go and say hello to her.'

He didn't want to take the others past his beautifully-prepared footprints. He wanted the full glory of them to burst on everyone at once. He hugged himself gleefully.

They said a few polite words to Mrs Trotteville and then escaped. They walked almost to the hairdresser's before they met Fatty. He came towards them looking very smooth-headed indeed. Buster trotted as usual at his heels.

'Hello – come to meet me?' said Fatty, pleased. 'Right. ice creams for everyone in return!'

'Oh no, Fatty,' said Daisy. 'You're always spending your money on us.'

'Come on,' said Fatty, and they went to have ice creams. Pip sat as patiently as he could with his. He hoped everyone would hurry up. Suppose the gardener went down to that bed and raked over the footprints! His trick would be ruined.

They finished their ice cream at last, and walked back to Fatty's. Pip wished they would hurry, but they wouldn't, of course!

'We'll go in the garden gate way,' said Fatty, as Pip had hoped he would say. 'It's nearer.'

They all went in. The bed with the footprints was not very far from the gate. Bets was running ahead with Buster when she suddenly saw them. She stopped at once, amazed.

Then Fatty saw them. He stopped dead and stared as if he couldn't believe his eyes. Larry and Daisy looked down in astonishment.

'Gosh!' said Fatty. 'What do you make of *that*! Fresh made too!'

Pip grinned, and tried to hide it – but nobody was looking at him at all. Their eyes were glued to the enormous footprints.

'I *say*! The thief's been here – while we were gone!' said Daisy. 'Just those few minutes!'

'There's the gardener over there – we'll ask him who's been here,' said Fatty. But the gardener shook his head.

'Nobody came down the garden while I've been working here,' he said. 'And I've been here for an hour or more. Never saw a soul!'

'Invisible as usual!' groaned Fatty. 'I just can't make it out. He comes and goes as he likes, does what he likes – and nobody ever sees him.'

He took out a magnifying glass and bent to

look closely at the prints. He frowned a little, and then got out his notebook. He opened it at the drawings there. Then he straightened up.

'This is odd,' he said. 'I don't understand it. These prints are the same size – and the rubber heel pattern is the same – but the print isn't *quite* the same. The thief didn't wear the same boots.'

Clever old Fatty! thought Pip. He even spotted that the prints were made by those big shoes, and not by big boots worn by the real thief. He really is a marvel!

The five children walked to the trees and sat down. Pip kept his head turned away because he simply couldn't help grinning all over his face. What a joke! How marvellous to see the others taken in like this – all serious and solemn and earnest!

'It beats me,' said Fatty. 'It absolutely beats me. Running all over the bed like that for apparently no reason at all. He must be mad as well as a thief. I mean – what's the point? Just to show off, I suppose.'

Pip gave a little snort of laughter and tried to turn it into a cough. Bets looked at him in surprise. 'What are you grinning for?' she asked. 'What's the joke?'

'No joke,' said Pip, trying to straighten his face. But a moment later his mouth twisted into broad smiles again and he was afraid he was going to laugh out loud.

'At any moment I shall expect to see footprints suddenly walking in front of me now,' said Fatty gloomily. 'I've really got the things on my mind.'

Pip gave a squeal and burst into laughter. He rolled over on the ground. He laughed till he almost burst his sides. The others looked at him in amazement.

'Pip! What's the joke?' demanded Fatty.

'It's – er – oh dear – I can't tell you,' stuttered Pip, and rolled over again.

'He's gone potty,' said Larry, in disgust. Fatty looked at Pip hard. He poked him with his foot.

'Shut up now, Pip – and tell us what the joke is,' he said. 'Go on – you've been up to something. What is it?'

'Oh my – it's those footprints,' gasped Pip. 'I took you all in beautifully, didn't I!'

'What do you mean?' cried everyone, and Fatty

reached out and shook Pip.

'I made them!' said Pip, helpless with laughter. 'I put on those big shoes and made those prints myself!'

22. MEETING AT HALF PAST TWO

Larry, Daisy and Bets fell on Pip and pummelled him till he cried for mercy. Buster joined in and barked madly. Only Fatty did nothing. He just sat as if he was turned to stone.

The others realised at last that Fatty was not joining in Pip's punishment. They sat up and looked at him. Pip wiped his streaked, dirty face.

Fatty sat there as if a thunderbolt had struck him. He gazed out through the trees with such a tense concentration that it really impressed the others. They fell silent.

'Fatty! What are you thinking about?' asked Bets timidly at last. He turned and looked at them all.

'It's Pip's joke,' he said. 'Gosh – to think I never guessed how the thief did it! Pip's solved the mystery!'

The others gaped in surprise.

'How do you mean?' asked Larry at last.

'Can't you see even *now*?' said Fatty impatiently. 'What did Pip do to make us think he was a large-footed thief? He took off his small shoes and put on big ones – and simply danced about over that bed in them. But he's no more got big feet than Bets here! Yet we all fell for his trick.'

'I'm beginning to see,' said Pip.

'And we fell for the thief's trick, which was exactly the same!' said Fatty. He smacked himself hard on the knee. 'We're idiots! We're too feeble for words! We've been looking for a big-footed fellow, and the real thief has been laughing at us all the time – a fellow with small feet – and small hands too!'

'Oh – do you mean he wore big gloves over his hands?' asked Bets. 'To make people think he had both big hands *and* big feet?'

'Of course. He probably wore somebody's big old gardening gloves,' said Fatty. 'And no wonder he left so many clear marks – he *meant* to! He didn't *want* to be careful! The more prints the merrier, as far as he was concerned.'

Light was beginning to dawn very clearly

in everyone's mind now. All that hunting for large-footed, burly, big-handed men! They should have looked for just the opposite.

But who *was* the thief? They knew now he wasn't big – but that didn't tell them the name of the robber.

'I suppose that deep cough was put on too,' said Larry. 'What about those scraps of paper, Fatty? Do they really belong to the mystery?'

'I think so,' said Fatty frowning. 'I'm beginning to piece things together now. I'm . . . *gosh*!'

'What?' said everybody together.

'I think I know who it is!' said Fatty, going scarlet with excitement.

'Who?' yelled everyone.

'Well – I won't say yet in case I'm wrong,' said Fatty. 'I'll have to think a bit more – work things out. But I think I've got it! I think so!'

It was most exasperating that Fatty wouldn't say any more. The others stared at him, trying to read his thoughts.

'If I'm right,' said Fatty, 'all our clues, including the scraps of paper, belong to the mystery – yes, even that roundish print with the criss-cross marks.

And I believe I know how it was that the thief was able to take those big boots about without anyone ever seeing them – and remove the stolen goods too, without anyone ever guessing. Golly, he's clever.'

'Who *is* it?' asked Bets, banging Fatty on the shoulder in excitement.

'Look – I want to go and think this out properly,' said Fatty getting up. 'It's important I should be sure of every detail – very important. I'll tell you for certain this afternoon. Meet here at half past two.'

And with that, Fatty disappeared into the shed with Buster and shut the door! The rest of the company looked at each other in irritation. Blow Fatty! Now they would have to puzzle and wonder for hours!

Fatty opened the door and stuck out his head for one moment. 'If I can think of everything, so can you. You know just as much as I do! Use your brains too, and see what you can make of it all!'

'I can't make *any*thing,' said Pip kicking at the grass. 'The only thing I'm pleased about is that my trick set old Fatty on the right track. I think he's right, don't you? About the thief wearing boots too big for him?'

'Yes. I think he is,' said Daisy, and everyone agreed. She got up. 'Well, come on – Fatty doesn't want us mooning round if he's really going to solve everything and have it all cut and dried. My word – I do hope he thinks it all out before Mr Goon does.'

They all thought hard during the hours that followed. Fatty thought the hardest of all. Bit by bit, he pieced it all together. Bit by bit, things became clear. Of course! All those odd clues did fit together, did make a picture of the thief – and it could only be one thief, nobody else.

Fatty did a spot of telephoning early that afternoon. He telephoned Inspector Jenks and asked him if he could possibly come along at half past two that afternoon. The Inspector was interested.

'Does this by any chance mean that you have solved the latest mystery – the mystery of the big-footed thief?' he asked.

'I hope so, sir,' said Fatty modestly. 'May I ask Mr Goon to come along too, sir? He'll be – er – quite interested too.'

The Inspector laughed. 'Yes, of course. Right,

half past two, and I'll be there at your house.'

Mr Goon was also invited. He was astonished and not at all pleased. But when he heard that the Inspector was going to be present, there was nothing for it but to say yes, he'd be there too. Poor Goon – how he worried and puzzled all the rest of the morning. Did it mean that that big boy had got ahead of him again?

At half past two, the Inspector arrived. Mrs Trotteville was out, as Fatty very well knew. Then Mr Goon arrived. Then the rest of the Find-Outers came, amazed to see Inspector Jenks and Mr Goon sitting in the little study with Fatty.

'Why this room?' asked Bets. 'You never use it for visitors. Is it something to do with the mystery, Fatty?'

'Not really,' said Fatty, who was looking excited and calm all at once. Mr Goon fidgeted, and the Inspector looked at Fatty with interest. That boy! What wouldn't he give to have him as a right-hand man when he was grown-up! But that wouldn't be for years.

'We're all here,' said Fatty, who had got Buster under his chair so that he wouldn't caper round

Mr Goon. 'So I'll begin. I may as well say at once that I've found out who the thief is.'

Mr Goon said something under his breath that sounded like 'Gah!' Nobody took any notice. Fatty went on.

'We had a few clues to work on – very large footprints that were always remarkably well-displayed – and very large gloveprints, also well-displayed so that nobody could possibly miss them. We also had two scraps of paper with "2 Frinton" on one and "1 Rods" on the other. We also had a curious roundish mark on the ground, and that was about all.

'Now – the thing was – nobody ever saw this thief coming or going, apparently, and yet he must have been about for everyone to see – and he apparently had the biggest feet in Peterswood, with the exception of Mr Goon here and Colonel Cross.'

Poor Mr Goon tried to hide his feet under his chair, but couldn't quite manage it.

'Well, we examined every single clue,' said Fatty. 'We followed up the hints on the scraps of paper and went to Frinton Lea. We went to houses and families whose names began with Rod. We visited the cobbler for information about big shoes and he told us about Colonel Cross. Both Mr Goon and I went to see the Colonel – not together, of course – I was doing a spot of weeding, I think, Mr Goon, when you arrived, wasn't I?'

Goon glared but said nothing.

'Well, it was Colonel Cross who put us on the track of where the thief might have got his big boots,' went on Fatty. 'He gives his old ones to jumble sales! And we learnt that he had given a pair to Miss Kay last year for the jumble sale. We guessed that if we could find out who bought them, we'd know the thief!'

Goon made a curious noise and turned it into a throat-clearing.

'We had a shock then, though,' said Fatty. 'The boots hadn't been sold to anyone, they had been stolen! By the thief, of course, for future use! But that brought us to a dead-end. No boots, no thief. We gave up!'

'And then Pip played a trick and showed you how the thief did it!' called out Bets, unable to contain herself. Fatty smiled at her.

'Yes. Pip's trick made me realise that the thief was playing *us* a trick too – the same as Pip's trick! He was wearing very large boots over his small shoes in order to make enormous prints that would make us think he was a big fellow – and the same with his gloves.'

'Ha!' said the Inspector. 'Smart work, Frederick. Very smart!'

'So then I had to change my ideas and begin thinking of a *small* fellow instead of a very big one!' said Fatty. 'One who came unquestioned to our houses, whom nobody would suspect or bother about.'

Mr Goon leaned forward, breathing heavily. The others fixed their eyes on Fatty in excitement. *Now* he was going to tell them the name of the thief!

But he didn't. He paused, as if he were listening for something. They all listened too. They heard the click of a gate and footsteps coming along the path that led along the study wall to the kitchen.

'If you don't mind, sir, I'll introduce you to the thief himself,' said Fatty, and he got up. He went to the door that led from the study into the garden and opened it as a small figure came by.

'Good afternoon,' he said. 'Will you come in here for a minute? You're wanted.'

And in came a small, strutting figure with a basket on his arm – little Twit the baker!

23. WELL DONE, FATTY!

'Twit!' said Mr Goon, and half rose from his chair in amazement. The Inspector looked on, unmoving. All the children gaped, except Fatty, of course. Buster flew out at Twit barking.

'Down, Buster. Back under my chair,' ordered Fatty, and Buster subsided.

Twit looked round in surprise and alarm. 'Here! What's all this?' he said. 'I got my work to do.'

'Sit down,' said the Inspector. 'We want you here for a few minutes.'

'What for?' blustered Twit. 'Here, Mr Goon, what's all this about?'

But Goon didn't know. He sat stolidly and said nothing. He wasn't going to get himself into any trouble by appearing to be friendly with Twit!

'Twit,' said Fatty, 'I've got you in here for reasons of my own. Put your basket down – that's right. Take off the cloth.'

Twit sullenly took off the cloth. Loaves of bread were piled in the basket. Another cloth lay beneath them.

'Take out the loaves and put them on the table,' said Fatty. 'And the cloth under them too.'

'Now what's all this?' said Twit again, looking scared. 'I got my work to do, I tell you. I'm not messing about with my loaves.'

'Do as you're told, Twit,' said the Inspector.

Twit immediately took out his loaves and laid them on the table. Then he took out the cloth beneath them. Fatty looked into the bottom of the basket. He silently took out four things that lay closely packed there – two large boots and two large gloves!

He set them on the table. Twit collapsed on a chair and began to tremble.

'This is how he managed to go about, carrying the boots and gloves, ready for any chance he might have for a little robbery!' said Fatty. 'He never knew what afternoon he might find an easy chance – perhaps nobody in the house except a sleepy maid or mistress – which, as we know, he did find.'

Fatty picked up one of the boots and turned it over. He showed the Inspector the rubber heel. 'I expect, sir, you took a drawing of the footprint on the beds at Norton House,' he said, 'or Mr Tonks did – and so you will see that the rubber heels on these boots and in your drawing are the same. That's proof that the thief wore these boots that Twit has in his basket.'

Fatty turned to the trembling Twit. 'Will you give me your notebook – the one you put down any orders or telephone calls in?' he said. Twit scowled, but put his hand into his pocket and brought out a little pad of cheap paper.

Fatty took it. Then he spoke to Goon. 'Have you got those two scraps of paper on you, Mr Goon?'

Mr Goon had. He produced them. Fatty compared them, and the warning note too, with the paper on the pad. The paper was exactly the same – cheap, thin, and with a fluffy surface.

'Those two scraps of paper you found at Norton House, sir, were bits that Twit had made notes on to remind him of the amount of bread to leave

– two loaves for Frinton Lea, and one loaf for Rodways. He apparently makes notes of his orders, and slips them into his basket to remind him. The wind must have blown them out in the garden at Norton House.'

'Gah!' breathed Goon again, staring at the pad of paper and the notes. 'I never thought of that – orders for loaves!'

'Nor did I,' confessed Fatty. 'Not until I began to piece all the clues together properly and found that they added up to the same person – Twit here!'

'Wait a minute,' said Larry. 'How do you explain the thing that puzzled us so tremendously in the Norton House robbery – how did the thief – Twit, that is – come downstairs without being seen by Jinny.'

'That was easy,' said Fatty. 'He simply squeezed himself out of that little window in the boxroom, and slid down the pipe to the ground. He's small enough to do that without much difficulty.'

'Yes – but wait, Fatty – that window was *shut* when I and Tonks went round the house,' said the Inspector. 'He couldn't have escaped through there, and shut it and fastened it from the outside –

balanced on the pipe!'

'He didn't shut it *then*,' said Fatty with a grin. 'He simply slid down the pipe, ran to where he had thrown the stolen goods, stuffed them in his basket under the cloth, slipped off the big boots that he had put on over his own small ones – and then went as bold as brass to the back door – appearing there as Twit the baker!'

'And when he went upstairs to look for the thief with Jinny, he carefully shut and fastened the little window he had escaped from!' said Larry, suddenly seeing it all. 'Gosh, that was smart. *He* was the thief – and he came indoors after the robbery and pretended to hunt all round for the robber – and we all thought he was so brave!'

'Gah!' said Goon, looking balefully at Twit. 'Think yourself clever, don't you? Stuffing everybody up with lies – making yourself out a hero too – looking for a thief who was standing in your own shoes!'

'He certainly pulled the wool over everyone's eyes,' said Fatty. 'It was a pretty little trick, and needed quite a lot of boldness and quick thinking. It's a pity he doesn't put his brains to better use.'

'Fatty – what about that funny, roundish mark – the one with criss-cross lines?' asked Bets. 'Was that a clue too?'

'Yes,' said Fatty, with a grin. 'Come out for a minute and I'll show you what made that mark. I could have kicked myself for not thinking of it before!'

They all crowded to the door except Twit who sat nervously picking at his fingernails. Fatty carried the basket to the door. He set it down in a damp part of the path. Then he lifted it up again.

'Look! It's left a mark of its round shape – and little criss-cross basket lines!' cried Daisy. 'Oh, Fatty – how clever you are!'

'Golly – *I* saw that mark outside Rodways Cottage,' suddenly said Pip. 'Larry, don't you remember – when we were in that cottage with the old woman? The baker came, and left his basket outside to go and put the loaves in the pan. And after he had gone, I noticed the mark his basket had left, and it reminded me of something – of course, it was the drawing in Fatty's book!'

'That's it,' said Fatty. 'That mark was always left where a robbery was committed – because Twit had to stand his basket somewhere, and if he stood it on a dusty path or a damp place, the heavy basket always left a mark. That's why we found those roundish marks at each robbery! If we'd guessed what they were, we would soon have been on the track!'

They were now back in the room. Fatty replaced the loaves in the basket, wrapped up in their cloths.

'No wonder Twit was always so particular about putting cloths over his loaves to keep them clean,' he said. 'They were very convenient for hiding whatever else he had there – not only the boots and gloves, but also anything he stole!'

'Quite smart,' said the Inspector. 'Carried the things he needed for his robbery, as well as his loaves, and also had room for stolen goods too – all under an innocent white cloth. Where did you get all these bright ideas from, Twit?'

Twit said nothing, but gazed sullenly at his smartly-polished little boots, with their highly-polished gaiters.

'Where did you get the big boots from, Twit?' asked Fatty. 'Oh, you don't need to bother to answer. Your cousin, Miss Kay, runs the jumble sale, doesn't she? – and she had the boots given to her for it last year – and you saw them and took them. Goodness knows how many times you've carried those boots round in your basket, hoping to find a chance to wear them and play your big-footed trick!'

'I never stole them,' said Twit. 'I paid for them.'

'Yes – you paid a few coins!' said Fatty. 'Just so that everyone would think you were a kind, generous fellow, paying for jumble sale boots that had been stolen! I heard all about it, and it made me wonder. It didn't seem quite in keeping with what I knew of you.'

Mr Goon cleared his throat. 'I take it you are certain this here fellow is the thief, sir?' he said to the Inspector.

'Well, what do *you* think of the evidence, Goon?' said the Inspector gravely. 'You've been on the job too, haven't you? You must have formed opinions of your own. No doubt you also suspected Twit.'

Mr Goon swallowed once or twice, wondering whether he dared to say yes, he *had* suspected Twit. But he caught Fatty's eye on him, and decided he wouldn't. He was afraid of Fatty and his sharp wits.

'Well, no, sir – I can't say as I suspected the baker,' he said, 'though I was coming to it. Frederick Trotteville was just one move ahead of me, sir. Bad luck on me! I've tried out all the dodges I learnt at the refresher course, sir – the disguises and all that . . . and . . .'

'Mr Goon! Have you really disguised yourself?' said Fatty, pretending to be amazed. 'I say – you weren't that dirty old tramp, were you? Well, if you were, you took me in properly!'

Goon glared at Fatty. That old tramp! Why, surely it was Fatty himself who had gone shuffling round in tramp's clothes – yes, and eaten his lunch under Mr Goon's very windows. Gah!

'Take Twit away, Goon,' said Inspector Jenks, getting up. 'Arrange with him to find someone to take the bread round, or nobody will have tea this afternoon. Twit, I shall be seeing you later.'

Twit was marched out by Mr Goon, looking very small beside Goon's burly figure. All his strut and cockiness were gone. He was no longer a little bantam of a man, peacocking about jauntily – he looked more like a small, woebegone sparrow.

Inspector Jenks beamed round, and Buster

leapt up at him. 'Very nice work, Find-Outers,' he said. 'Very nice indeed. In fact, as my niece Hilary would say – smashing! Now, what about a spot of ice cream somewhere? I'm melting.'

'Oooh yes,' said Bets, hanging on to his arm. 'I knew you'd say that, Inspector! I felt it coming!'

'My word – you'll be as good as Fatty some day, guessing what people think and do!' said the Inspector. 'Well, Frederick, I'm pleased with you – pleased with all of you. And I want to hear the whole story, if you don't mind, from beginning to end.'

So, over double-size ice creams, he heard it with interest and delight.

'It's a curious story, isn't it?' said Fatty, when they had finished. 'The story of a cocky little man who thought the world of himself – and was much too big for his boots!'

Bets gave a laugh and had the last word. 'Yes! So he had to get size twelve and wear those, Fatty – but they gave him away in the end.'

'They did,' said Fatty. 'Well, that's another mystery solved – and here's to the next one! May it be the most difficult of all!'

Contents

1. WHAT A WASTE OF HOLIDAYS!

'I haven't liked these holidays one bit,' said Bets dolefully to Pip. 'No Larry, no Daisy, no Fatty – a real waste of summer holidays!'

'Well, you've had *me*,' said Pip. 'Haven't I taken you for bike rides and picnics and things?'

'Yes – but only because Mother said you had to,' said Bets, still gloomy. 'I mean – you had to do it because Mother kept saying I'd be lonely. It was nice of you – but I did know you were doing it because it was your duty, or something like that.'

'I think you're very ungrateful,' said Pip, in a huff.

Bets sighed. 'There you are – in a huff again already, Pip! I do wish the others were here. It's the first hols that everyone but us have been away.'

'Well, the other three will be back in a few days' time,' said Pip. 'We will still have two or three weeks left of these hols.'

'But will there be enough time for a mystery?' asked Bets, rolling over to find a shadier place on the grass. 'We nearly *always* have a mystery to solve in the hols. I haven't always liked our mysteries – but somehow I miss it when we don't have one.'

'Well, find one then,' said Pip. 'What *I* miss most is old Buster.'

'Oh *yes*,' said Bets, thinking of Fatty's joyful, mad little Scottie dog. 'I miss him too. The only person I *keep* seeing that I don't want to see is Mr Goon.'

Mr Goon was the village policeman, a pompous and ponderous fellow, always at war with the five children. Bets seemed to meet him three or four times a day, cycling heavily here and there, ringing his bell violently round every corner.

'Look – there's the postman,' said Pip. 'Go and see if he's got anything for us, Bets. There might be a card from old Fatty.'

Bets got up. It was very hot and although she

wore only a sundress of frilly cotton, she still felt as if she was going to melt. She went to meet the postman, who was cycling up the drive.

'Hello postman!' she called. 'I'll take the letters.'

'Right, Missy. Two cards – one for you and one for your brother,' said the postman. 'That's all.'

Bets took them. 'Oh, good!' she said. 'One's from Fatty – and it's for me!'

She ran back to Pip. 'A card for you from Larry and Daisy,' she said, 'and one for me from Fatty. Let's see what they say . . .'

Pip read his card out loud at once. 'Coming back the day after tomorrow, thank goodness. Any mystery turned up? We shan't have much time for one these hols unless we can dig one up quickly! We're very suntanned. You won't know us! Good disguise, of course! See you soon. Love to Bets – Larry and Daisy.'

'Oh *good*, *good*, *good*!' said Bets, in delight. 'They'll be round here tomorrow, sure as anything. Now listen to *my* card, Pip.'

She read it out. 'How's things, Bets? I hope you've got a first class mystery for me to set my brains to work on when I return the day after tomorrow. When do Larry and Daisy come back? It's time the Five Find-Outers (and Dog) got their teeth into something. Be nice to see you again, and old Pip too. Fatty.'

Bets rubbed her hands together in glee. Her face shone. '*All* the Find-Outers will be together tomorrow,' she said. 'And though there's not even the smell of a mystery about, I guess Fatty will run straight into one as soon as he comes.'

'Hope you're right,' said Pip, lying back on the grass again. 'I must say these hols have been pretty boring. I'd like a good thrilling, juicy mystery to end up with.'

'What do you mean – a *juicy* mystery?' said Bets, puzzled.

Pip couldn't be bothered to explain. He lay and thought of all the mysteries he and Bets, Larry and Daisy, Fatty (and Buster, of course) had solved. There was the burning cottage – and the disappearing cat – and the hidden house – gosh, there were a lot!

He suddenly felt hungry for another mystery. He sat up and looked at Bets. 'Let's get the morning paper and see if there's anything thrilling in it,' he said. 'Anything that has happened near us. We could tell Fatty as soon as he comes then, and he might get us all on to it.'

Bets was thrilled. She went to get the paper. She brought it out to Pip and they both studied it carefully. But there didn't seem to be anything happening at all.

'It's nothing but pictures of frightful women and their clothes, and horses racing, and what hot weather it is, and –'

'Cricket scores, and . . .' went on Bets, in a voice as disgusted as Pip's.

'Oh well – cricket scores are *interesting*,' said Pip, at once. 'Look here – see this bowling analysis here?'

Bets wasn't in the least interested in cricket. She turned the page.

'Just like a girl,' said Pip, in an even more disgusted voice. 'The only thing of real importance in the paper is the cricket – and you don't even look at it!'

'Here's something – look, it's something about Peterswood, our village,' said Bets, reading a small paragraph down in a corner. 'And it mentions

Marlow too – that's quite near.'

'What is it?' asked Pip, interested. He read the paragraph and snorted. 'Huh – that's not a mystery, or even anything interesting.'

Bets read it out. 'The weather has been very kind to the school camps on the hills between Peterswood and Marlow. This week two or three interesting visitors have joined the camps. One is little Prince Bongawah of Tetarua State who amused everyone by bringing a state umbrella with him. Needless to say he only used it once!'

'Well, if you think that even Fatty can make any mystery or even be *interested* in a silly thing like that, you'd better think again,' said Pip. 'Who cares about Prince Bongabangabing, or whatever his name is?'

'Bongawah,' said Bets. 'Where's Tetarua State, Pip?'

Pip didn't know and didn't care. He rolled over on his front. 'I'm going to sleep,' he said. 'I'm too hot for words. We've had five weeks of hot sun and I'm tired of it. The worst of our weather is that it never stops when it makes up its mind to do something.'

'I don't care about the weather or anything,' said Bets, happily. 'It can do what it likes now that Fatty and the others are coming back!'

Larry and Daisy came back first. They arrived home the next morning, helped their mother to unpack, and then went straight round to Pip and Bets.

'Larry! Daisy!' shouted Bets joyfully, as they came into the garden. 'I didn't think you'd be back so early. Gosh, how brown you are!'

'Well, you're not so bad either,' said Daisy, giving little Bets a hug. 'It's been ages since we saw each other! Such a waste of hols when we can't go mystery-hunting together!'

'Hello Bets, hello Pip,' said Larry. 'Any news? I must say you're a bad correspondent. I sent you four postcards and you never wrote once!'

'*You* sent them! I like *that*!' said Daisy, indignantly. 'I wrote every single one of them! You never even addressed them.'

'Well, I *bought* them,' said Larry. 'Hey – any news of old Fatty? Is he back yet?'

'Coming today,' said Bets joyfully. 'I keep listening for his bicycle bell, or old Buster's bark.

Won't it be lovely for all five of us – and Buster, of course – to be together again!'

Everyone agreed. Bets looked round at the little group, glad to have Larry and Daisy there – but nothing was ever the same without Fatty. Fatty, with his sly humour and enormous cheek and brilliant brains. Bet's heart swelled with joy to think he would soon be there too.

'There's the telephone,' said Pip, as a loud, shrilling ring rang out from the house. 'Hope it's not for me. I feel I simply cannot get up. I think I'm stuck to the grass.'

Mrs Hilton, Pip's mother, appeared at a window. 'That was Frederick on the telephone,' she called. 'He's back home, and will be round to see you very soon. He says, will you please watch out for him, as he's so brown you may not know him. He probably won't know any of *you* either, you're so tanned!'

Everyone sat up straight at this news. 'Oh, I *wish* I'd answered the phone,' said Bets. 'Fatty has such a nice *grinny* voice on the phone.'

Everyone knew what she meant. 'Yes – sort of chortly,' said Larry. 'Gosh, I wish I was always as sure of myself as Fatty is. He never turns a hair.'

'And he *always* knows what to do, whatever happens,' said Bets. 'I say – do you think he'll come in disguise, just for a joke?'

'Yes, of course he will,' said Larry. 'I bet he's got a whole lot of new tricks and disguises and things – and he'll want to practise them on us at once. I know Fatty!'

'Then we'd better look out for someone peculiar,' said Daisy, excited. 'We simply *can't* let him take us in the very first minute he comes back!'

Fatty was, of course, simply marvellous at disguising himself. He could make his plump cheeks even bigger by inserting cheek pads between his gums and his cheek inside his mouth. He had a wonderful array of false teeth that could be fitted neatly over his own. He had shaggy eyebrows to stick over his own modest ones, and any amount of excellent wigs.

In fact, most of his considerable pocket money went on such things, and he was a never-ending source of joy and amusement to the others when he donned one of his many disguises to deceive them or someone else.

'Now we'll watch out,' said Pip. 'Everyone who comes in at the gate is suspect – man, woman, or child! It *might* be old Fatty!'

They hadn't long to wait. Footsteps could be heard dragging up the drive, and then a large, feathered hat appeared bobbing above the hedge that ran along the pathway to the kitchen entrance. A very brown, plump face looked over the hedge at them, with long gold earrings dangling from the ears, and ringlets of black curls bobbing beneath the dreadful hat.

The children stared. The face smiled and spoke. 'Buy some nice white 'eather? Bring you luck!'

Round the hedge came a large gypsy woman, in a long black skirt, a dirty pink blouse, and a red shawl. Her feathered hat nodded and bounced on her black curls.

'Fatty!' screamed Bets at once, and ran over at top speed. 'Oh, you're Fatty, you are, you are! I recognised your voice – you didn't disguise it enough!'

2. FATTY ARRIVES

The other three children did not call out or run over. This woman seemed much too tall to be Fatty – though he *was* tall now. The gypsy woman drew back a little as Bets came running over, shouting joyfully.

''Ere! 'Oo are you a-calling Fatty?' she said, in a husky voice. 'What you talking about?'

Bets stopped suddenly. She stared at the woman, who stared back insolently, with half-closed eyes. Then the gypsy thrust a bunch of bedraggled heather at Bets, almost into her face. 'Lucky white 'eather,' she whined. 'Buy some, little Missy. I tell you, I ain't sold a spray since yesterday.'

Bets backed away. She looked round at the others. They still sat there, grinning now, because of Bets' sudden fright. She went very red and walked back to the other three children.

11

The woman followed, shaking her heather in quite a threatening manner. 'If you don't want my 'eather, you let me read your 'and,' she said. 'It's bad luck to cross a gypsy, you know.'

'Rubbish,' said Larry. 'Go away, please.'

'What do she want to call me Fatty for?' said the woman angrily, pointing at poor Bets. 'I don't reckon on insults from the likes of you, see?'

The cook suddenly appeared, carrying a tray of lemonade for the children. She saw the gypsy woman at once.

'Now you clear off,' she called. 'We've had enough strangers lately at the back door.'

'Buy a spray of 'eather,' whined the woman again and thrust her spray into the cook's angry face.

'Bets – run and fetch your father,' said the cook, and Bets ran. So did the gypsy woman! She disappeared at top speed down the drive and the children saw her big, feathered hat bobbing quickly along the top of the hedge again.

They laughed. 'Gosh,' said Pip, 'just like old Bets to make an idiotic mistake like that. As if anyone could think that awful old creature was Fatty! Though, of course, she did have rather a husky voice for a woman. That's what took Bets in.'

'It nearly took me in too,' said Daisy. 'Hello, here's someone else!'

'Butcher boy,' said Pip, as a boy on a bicycle came whistling up the drive, a joint of meat in his basket on the front.

'It *might* be Fatty,' said Bets, joining them again, looking rather subdued. 'Better have a very good look. He's got a fine butcher boy disguise.'

They all got up and stared hard at the boy who was now standing at the back door. He whistled loudly, and the cook called out to him.

'I'd know it was you anywhere, Tom Lane, with that whistling that goes through my head. Put the meat on the table, will you?'

The four children gazed at the boy's back. He certainly *might* be Fatty with a curly brown wig. Bets craned forward to try and make out if his hair *was* a wig or not. Pip gazed at his feet to see if they were the same size as Fatty's.

The boy swung round, feeling their stares. He screwed up his face at them cheekily. 'Never seen anyone like me before, I suppose?' he said. He turned himself round and round, posing like a model. 'Well, take a good look. Fine specimen of a butcher's boy, I am! Seen enough?'

The others stared helplessly. It *could* be Fatty – it was more or less his figure. The teeth were very rabbitty though. Were they real or part of a disguise?

Pip took a step forward, trying to see. The boy backed away, feeling suddenly half-scared at the earnest gaze of the four children.

'Here! Anything wrong with me?' he said, looking down at himself.

'Is your hair real?' said Bets suddenly, feeling sure it was a wig – and if it was, then the boy must be old Fatty!

The butcher's boy didn't answer. He looked very puzzled, and put up his hand to feel his hair. Then, quite alarmed by the serious faces of the others, he leapt on his bicycle and pedalled fast away down the drive, completely forgetting to whistle.

The four stared after him. 'Well – if it *was* Fatty, it was one up to him,' said Larry, at last. 'I just don't know.'

'Let's have a look at the meat he left on the table,' said Pip. 'Surely even Fatty wouldn't go bicycling about with joints of meat, even if he *was* pretending to be a butcher's boy. Sausages would be much cheaper to get.'

They went into the scullery and examined the meat on the table. The cook came in, astonished to see them bending over the joint.

'Don't tell me you're as hungry as all that,' she said, shooing them away. 'Now don't you start putting your teeth into raw meat, Pip!'

It did look as if Pip was about to bite the meat; he was bending over it carefully to make quite sure it was a real joint, and not one of the many 'properties' that Fatty kept to go with his various disguises. But it was meat all right.

They all went out again, just as they heard a rat-a-tat-tat at the front door. 'That's Fatty!' squealed Bets and rushed round the drive to the front door. A telegram boy stood there with a telegram.

'Fatty!' squealed Bets. Fatty had often used a telegram boy's disguise, and it had been a very useful one. Bets flung her arms round his plump figure.

But, oh dear, when the boy swung round, it certainly was not Fatty. This boy had a small, wizened face, and tiny eyes! Clever as Fatty was at disguises, he could never make himself like this! Bets went scarlet.

'I'm so sorry,' she said, backing away. 'I – I thought you were a friend of mine.'

Her mother was now standing at the open door, astonished. What was Bets doing, flinging her arms round the telegram boy? The boy was just as embarrassed as Bets. He handed in the telegram without a word.

'Behave yourself, Bets,' said Mrs Hilton, sharply. 'I'm surprised at you. Please don't play silly jokes like that.'

Bets crept away in shame. The telegram boy stared after her, amazed. Larry, Pip, and Daisy laughed till they ached.

'It's all very well to laugh,' said Bets, dolefully. 'I shall get into an awful row with Mother now. But honestly, it's exactly like one of Fatty's disguises.'

'Well, of course, if you're going to think every telegram boy is Fatty, just because Fatty's got a telegram boy's uniform, we're in for a funny time,' said Pip. 'Gosh, I wish old Fatty would come. It's ages since he telephoned. The very next person *must* be Fatty!'

It was! He came cycling up the drive, plump as ever, a broad grin on his good-humoured face, and Buster running valiantly beside the pedals!

'Fatty! FATTY!' shrieked everyone, and almost before he could fling his bicycle into the hedge, all four were on him. Buster capered round, mad with excitement, barking without stopping. Fatty was thumped on the shoulder by everyone, and hugged by Bets, and dragged off into the garden.

'Fatty – you've been ages coming!' said Bets. 'We thought you'd be in disguise, and we watched and watched.'

'And Bets made some simply frightful mistakes!' said Pip. 'She's just flung her arms round the telegram boy! He was really startled.'

'He still looked alarmed when I met him cycling out of the gate,' said Fatty, grinning at Bets. 'He kept looking round as if he expected Bets to be after him with a few more hugs.'

'Oh, Fatty, it's great to see you again,' said Bets, happily. 'I don't know *how* I could have thought any of those people here this morning were you – that gypsy woman, the butcher boy, and the telegram boy.'

'We honestly thought you'd be in disguise,' said Larry. 'Gosh, how brown you are. You haven't got any paint on, have you? I've never known you get burnt so brown.'

'No, I'm just myself,' said Fatty modestly. 'No powder, no paint, no false eyelashes, no nothing. I must say you're all pretty brown yourselves.'

'Woof,' said Buster, trying to get on to Bets' knee.

'He says he's sunburnt too,' said Bets, who could always explain what Buster's woofs meant. 'But it doesn't show on him. Darling Buster! We *have* missed you!'

They all settled down to the iced lemonade that was left. Fatty grinned round. Then he made a surprising statement. 'Well, Find-Outers – you're not as smart as I thought you were! You've lost your cunning. You didn't recognise me this morning when I came in disguise!'

They all set down their glasses and stared at him blankly. In disguise? What did he mean?

'What disguise? You're not in disguise,' said Larry. 'What's the joke?'

'No joke,' said Fatty, sipping his lemonade.

'I came here in disguise this morning to test out my faithful troop of detectives, and you didn't recognise your chief. Shame on you! I was a bit afraid of Bets though.'

Pip and Bets ran through the people who had appeared since breakfast that morning. 'Mrs Lacy – no, you weren't her, Fatty. The postman – no, impossible. The man to mend the roof – no, he hadn't a tooth in his head. That old gypsy woman – no, she really was too tall and, anyway, she ran like a hare when she thought I was going to fetch Daddy.'

'The butcher boy – no,' said Larry.

'And we know it wasn't the telegram boy, he had such a wizened face,' said Daisy. 'You're fooling us, Fatty. You haven't been here before this morning. Go on, own up!'

'I'm not fooling,' said Fatty, taking another drink. 'I say, this lemonade is super. I *was* here this morning and I tell you, Bets was the only one I thought was going to see through me.'

They all stared at him disbelievingly. 'Well, who were you then?' said Larry at last.

'The gypsy woman!' said Fatty, with a grin. 'I

took you in properly, didn't I?'

'You weren't,' said Daisy, disbelievingly. 'You're pulling our legs. If you'd seen her, you'd know you couldn't be her. Awful creature!'

Fatty put his hand in his pocket and pulled out a pair of long, dangling gilt earrings. He clipped one on each ear. He pulled out a wig of greasy black curls from another pocket and put it on his head. He produced a bedraggled spray of heather and thrust it into Daisy's face.

'Buy a bit of white 'eather!' he said, in a husky voice, and his face suddenly looked exactly like that of the gypsy. The others looked at him silently, really startled. Even without the big feathered hat, the shawl, the basket, and the long black skirt, Fatty was the gypsy woman!

'You're uncanny!' said Daisy, pushing the heather away. 'I feel quite scared of you. One minute you're Fatty, the next you're a gypsy woman. Take that awful wig off!'

Fatty took it off, grinning. 'Believe me now?' he asked. 'Gosh, I nearly twisted my ankle though, when I sprinted down the drive. I honestly thought young Bets here was going to get her father. I wore really high-heeled shoes, and I could hardly run.'

'So that's why you looked so tall,' said Pip. 'Of course, your long skirt hid your feet. Well, you took us in properly. Good old Fatty. Let's drink to his health, Find-Outers!'

They were all solemnly drinking his health in the last of the lemonade when Mrs Hilton appeared. She had heard Fatty's arrival and wanted to welcome him back. Fatty got up politely. He always had excellent manners.

Mrs Hilton put out her hand, and then stared in astonishment at Fatty. 'Well really, Frederick,' she said, 'I cannot approve of your jewellery!'

Bets gave a shriek of delight. 'Fatty! You haven't taken off the earrings!'

Poor Fatty. He dragged them off at once, trying to say something polite and shake hands all at the same time. Bets gazed at him in delight. Good old Fatty – it really was lovely to have him back. Things *always* happened when Fatty was around!

3. DISGUISES

Bets quite expected some adventure or mystery to turn up immediately, now that Fatty was back. She awoke the next morning with a nice, excited feeling, as if something was going to happen.

They were all to meet at Fatty's playroom that morning, which was in a shed at the bottom of his garden. Here he kept many of his disguises and his make-up, and here he also tried out some of his new ideas.

Many a time, the others had arrived at his shed to have the door opened by some frightful old tramp, or grinning errand boy, all teeth and cheeks, or even an old woman in layers and layers of skirts, her cheeks wrinkled, and with one or two teeth missing.

Yes, Fatty could even appear to have a few of his front teeth missing, by carefully blacking out one here and there, so that when he smiled, black gaps appeared, which seemed to be holes where teeth had once been. Bets had been horrified when she had first seen him with, apparently, three front teeth gone!

But this morning, it was Fatty himself who opened the door. The floor was spread with open books. The four children stepped over the madly-barking Buster and looked at them.

'Fingerprints! Questioning of witnesses! Disguises!' said Bets, reading the titles of some of the books. 'Oh, Fatty, is there another mystery on already?'

'No,' said Fatty, shutting the books and putting them neatly into his bookcase at the end of the shed. 'But I seem to have got a bit out of practice since I've been away – I was just testing my brains, you know. Anyone seen old Mr Goon lately?'

Everyone had. They had all bumped into him that morning as they rode round to Fatty's on their bicycles. As usual, the policeman had been ringing his bell so violently that he hadn't heard theirs, and he had ridden right into the middle of them.

'He fell off,' said Daisy. 'I can't imagine why,

23

because none of *us* did. He went an awful bump too, and he was so angry that nobody liked to stop and help him up. He just sat there shouting.'

'Well, he enjoys that,' said Fatty. 'Let's hope he is still sitting there, shouting, then he won't interfere with *us*!'

'Woof,' said Buster, agreeing.

'What are we going to do for the rest of these hols if a mystery doesn't turn up?' asked Pip. 'I mean, we must all have had picnics and outings and things till we're tired of them. And Peterswood is always half-asleep in the summer. Nothing happening at all.'

'We'll have to wind up old Mr Goon then,' said Fatty, and everyone brightened at once. 'Or what about my ringing Inspector Jenks and asking him if he wants a bit of help on anything?'

'Oh, you *couldn't* do that,' said Bets, knowing quite well that Fatty could do anything if he really wanted to. 'Though it would be really nice to see him again.'

Inspector Jenks was their very good friend. He had been pleased with their help in solving many mysteries. But Mr Goon had not been nearly so

24

pleased. The bad-tempered village policeman had wished many a time that the five children and their dog lived hundreds of miles away.

'Well, perhaps I won't bother the Inspector just yet – not till we've smelt out something,' said Fatty. 'But I was thinking we ought to put in a bit of practice at disguises or something like that – we haven't done a thing for weeks and weeks – and suppose something did turn up, we'd make a muddle of it through being out of practice.'

'Oh, *do* let's practise disguises!' said Bets. 'All of us, do you mean?'

'Oh yes,' said Fatty. 'I've got some fantastic new disguises here. I picked them up on my cruise.'

Fatty had been for a long cruise, and had called at many exciting places. He opened a trunk and showed the four children a mass of brilliant-looking clothes.

'I picked these up in Morocco,' he said. 'I went shopping by myself in the native bazaar – my word, things were cheap! I got suits for all of us. I thought they would do for fancy dress, though they will do for foreign disguises too!'

'Oh Fatty – let's try them on!' said Daisy,

thrilled. She picked out a bright red skirt of fine silk, patterned in stripes of white.

'There's a white blouse to go with that,' said Fatty, pulling it out. 'Look, it's got red roses embroidered all over it. It will suit you fine, Daisy.'

'What did you get for me, Fatty?' asked Bets, dragging more things out of the trunk. 'You are a most surprising person. You're always doing things nobody else ever thinks of. I'm sure Pip would never bring me home any clothes like this if he went to Morocco.'

'I certainly wouldn't,' said Pip grinning. 'But then, I'm not a millionaire like old Fatty here!'

Fatty certainly seemed to always have plenty of money. He was like a grown-up in that, Bets thought. He seemed to have dozens of rich relations who showered gifts on him. He was always generous with his money though, and ready to share with the rest of them.

Bets had a curious little robe-like dress that reached her ankles. It had to be swathed round and tied with a sash. The others looked at her, and marvelled.

'She looks like a little foreign princess!' said

Larry. 'Her face is so sunburnt that she looks like an Indian – she might *be* an Indian! What a wonderful disguise it would make for her!'

Bets paraded round the shed, enjoying herself. She glanced into the big clear mirror that Fatty kept there, and was startled. She looked like a real little princess! She drew the hood of the dress over her head, and looked round with half-shut eyes. Fatty clapped.

'Very good! An Indian princess! Here Larry – stick this on. And this is for you, Pip.'

The boys pulled on brilliant robes, and Fatty showed them how to wind cloths for bright turbans. All of them seemed to be transformed into a different nationality altogether. Nobody would have thought them English.

Fatty stared at the four parading round his shed. He grinned. His brain set to work to try and evolve a plan to use these bright disguises. A visiting princess? A descent on Mr Goon for some reason? He racked his brains for some bright idea.

'We might be the relations of the little Prince Bongawah of Tetarua State,' said Bets, suddenly. 'I'm sure we look exactly like them!'

27

'And who's Bongawhatever-it-is when he's at home?' asked Larry. Bets explained.

'He's a foreign prince who is staying at one of the school camps on the hills between Peterswood and Marlow,' she said. 'We read about him in the paper. He brought a state umbrella with him, but the paper said he only used it once!'

'I bet he did,' said Larry, grinning. 'Got a state umbrella, Fatty?'

'No,' said Fatty, regretfully. He looked at everyone admiringly. 'Honestly, you're wizard! Of course, your suntans make you look first class in those foreign clothes. *Any*one would think you belonged to a different nationality. I only wish you could parade through the village!'

'You dress up too, Fatty, and let's go parading!' said Bets. But Fatty had no time to answer because Buster began to bark loudly, and tore out of the open door at sixty miles an hour.

'Now what's up with *him*?' said Fatty, in surprise. 'I wonder if old Mr Goon's anywhere about?'

Bets peered out of the door and up the garden path. 'It's three boys,' she said. 'Goodness, I know who one is! It's ERN!'

'Ern!' echoed everyone, and ran to the door. Three boys were coming down the path towards the shed, and Buster was dancing excitedly round Ern's ankles, barking madly.

Fatty shut the door of the shed and faced the others. His eyes sparkled.

'It's Ern Goon!' he said. 'Old Mr Goon's nephew! Let's pretend you're foreign royalty visiting me. If you speak English, speak it badly, see? And if I speak to you in nonsense language, you speak the same. Let's see if we can take old Ern in properly!'

Ern was, as Fatty said, a nephew of Mr Goon the policeman. He had once been to stay with his uncle and had been involved in a mystery. Mr Goon had not been kind to Ern, but the Five Find-Outers had, and Ern thought the world of Fatty. Now here he was, coming to pay a visit with two friends. What a chance to try out the foreign 'disguises'!

Footsteps came right up to the door. Ern's voice could be heard speaking sternly to his two companions. 'Now you behave yourself, see? Both of you. And spit that toffee out, young Sid.'

Whether Sid spat the toffee out or not could not

be gathered by the five children in the shed. Bets giggled and Pip gave her a sharp nudge.

There was a knock on the shed door. Fatty opened it and stared solemnly at Ern. Then his face took on a surprised and pleased expression. He smiled broadly and held out his hand.

'Ern! Ern Goon! This *is* a pleasure! Do come in, Ern, and let me introduce you to my foreign visitors!'

4. ERN, SID AND PERCE

Ern was still the same old Ern. He was plump, red-faced, and his eyes bulged slightly, just as his uncle's did, though not quite so much. He grinned shyly at Fatty, and then gazed in awe at the four silent 'foreigners' dressed in such brilliant clothes.

'Pleased to see you, Fatty,' he said, and shook hands for a long time. Then he turned to the two boys behind him. They were not as old as he was, and very alike.

'These here boys are my twin brothers,' he explained. 'This one's Sid – and this one's Perce. Speak up, Sid and Perce. Remember your manners. Come on, say "how do you do" like I told you.'

'How do you do,' said Perce, and bobbed his tousled head, going a brilliant scarlet with his effort at manners.

'Ar,' said Sid, hardly opening his mouth at all.

Ern glared at him.

'You still sucking that toffee, Sid? Didn't I tell you to spit it out, see?'

Sid made an agonised face, pointed to his mouth, and shook his head.

''E means, his teeth's stuck fast again,' explained Perce. ''E can't say a word then. Couldn't speak all day yesterday, neither.'

'Dear me,' said Fatty, sympathetically. 'Does he live on toffee then?'

'Ar,' said Sid, with another effort at opening his mouth.

'Does "Ar" mean yes or no?' wondered Fatty. 'But I'm forgetting *my* manners now – Ern, let me introduce you to some very distinguished friends of mine.'

Ern, Sid, and Perce stared unblinkingly at Bets, Pip, Larry, and Daisy, not recognising them in the least as ordinary children. Bets turned her head away, afraid of giggling.

'You have no doubt heard of the little Prince Bongawah of Tetarua State,' went on Fatty. 'This is his sister, Princess Bongawee.' He waved his hand towards the startled Bets.

'Lovaduck!' exclaimed Ern, staring. 'So this is the Prince's sister, is it? We've seen Prince Bongawah, Fatty – we're camping out in the field next to his. He's a funny little fellow with a cocky little face.' He turned to Sid and Perce.

'You can see they're sister and brother, can't you?' he said, to Bets' indignation. 'Like as two peas!'

'You're right, Ern,' said Perce.

'Ar,' said Sid, working the toffee round a bit to produce his usual remark.

Bets inclined her head majestically and looked at the three awed boys through half-closed lids.

'Popple, dippy, doppy,' she said in a high and mighty voice.

'What's she say?' asked Ern.

'She says, "Your hair is very untidy,"' said Fatty, enjoying himself.

'Coo,' said Ern, and swept his hand over his standing-up hair. 'Well, I didn't know as we were going to see royalty, like, else I'd have done me hair. Who are the others, Fatty?'

'This is Pua-Tua,' said Fatty, waving his hand towards Daisy. 'She is a cousin of the Princess's, and waits on her – a very nice girl indeed.'

Ern bowed, because Daisy did. Perce bowed too, but Sid didn't. His toffee had got stuck again, and he was concerned with that. His jaws moved unceasingly.

'And the others are Kim-Pippy-Tok, and Kim-Larriana-Tik,' said Fatty, making Bets long to burst into giggles.

Pip moved forward, put his face close to Ern's, and rapidly rubbed noses. Ern started back in surprise.

'It's all right,' said Fatty, soothingly. 'That is their way of greeting a friend.' Sid and Perce backed away, afraid of the same kind of greeting.

'Pleased to meet you,' said Ern, with a gasp. Then he gazed at Fatty in awe. 'You haven't half got some posh friends,' he said. 'What about those other friends of yours – Larry and Daisy and Pip and little Bets?'

'They're not very far away,' said Fatty truthfully. 'Did you say you were camping out somewhere, Ern?'

'Yes,' said Ern. 'We got a chance of a campout, me and Sid and Perce together – got the loan of a tent, see, and Ma said she'd be glad to see the last of us for a bit. So off we skipped, and put up our tent in the field next to one of the school camp fields. We aren't half having a good time.'

'Sright,' said Perce.

'Ar,' said Sid. He suddenly put his hand into his pocket and brought out a round tin. He took off the lid and offered the tin to Fatty. Fatty peered in. It was almost full of dark brown, revolting-looking toffee in great thick pieces.

'Er, no thanks, Sid,' said Fatty. 'I don't want to spoil my dinner. And don't offer it to my visitors, because they will probably have to make speeches this afternoon, and I don't want them to be struck dumb by your toffee.'

'Ar,' said Sid, understandingly, and replaced the lid carefully.

'Where does he get that toffee from?' asked Fatty. 'I've never seen anything like it!'

''E gets it from the 'oopla stall at the Fair near the camp,' explained Perce. ''E's a nib at throwing rings round things, is our Sid. Gets himself a tin of toffee that way each day.'

'Ar,' said Sid, beaming proudly.

'Tickly-pickly-odgery, podgery, pooh,' announced

Larry suddenly. Ern, Sid, and Perce stared at him.

'What's 'e say?' asked Perce.

'He says that Sid looks rather like a bit of toffee himself,' said Fatty, at once. 'Chewed-up toffee, he says.'

There was a pause, in which at least five of the children longed to burst into laughter.

'Bit rude that,' said Ern at last. 'Well, I suppose we'd better be off. Been nice to see you, Fatty. Sorry we couldn't see the others too.'

'Have you seen your uncle, Mr Goon?' asked Fatty.

'Coo, no,' said Ern. 'I'd run a mile if I saw him. Don't you remember how he treated me when I stayed with him last year? Sid and Perce don't like him neither. I say, Fatty – any more mysteries going?'

'Not yet,' said Fatty. 'But you never know when one might spring up, do you?'

'Tooky-oola-rickity-wimmy-woo,' said Pip, solemnly. 'We-go-get-icy-cream.'

'Why, he can speak English!' said Ern, in amazement. 'Hear that? I say, why don't we all go and get ice creams? There's a man down by the river we could go to. I don't want to go into the village in case I meet my uncle.'

Fatty grinned. He looked at the other four, who gazed back expectantly. Their 'disguises' had gone down so well with Ern, Sid, and Perce that they were longing to go out in them. Fatty didn't see why they shouldn't! If they took the river road, they wouldn't meet a great many people or attract a crowd, but it would be fun to see the faces of the few they met!

'Iccky, piccky, tominy, wipply-wop, Kim-Pippy-Tok,' he said, politely bowing to Pip, and waving him to the door. 'We'll all go and get ice creams by the river. The Princess must go first, Ern.'

'Course,' said Ern, hurriedly getting out of the way. 'Now *she* would look fine with a state umbrella like her brother had. It'd suit her all right and, what's more, I wouldn't mind carrying it either, she's such a little duck.'

Bets drew her hood over her face to hide her laughter. Fatty looked at Ern as if suddenly struck with a good idea. The others waited expectantly.

'Ah, yes – of course. I'd forgotten that the Princess Bongawee must not go out without her state umbrella,' he said. 'What a good thing you reminded me, Ern.'

'Lovaduck! Has she got one too?' asked Ern.

Fatty disappeared and the others waited. Whatever sort of 'state umbrella' was Fatty going to fetch?

He came back, with an enormous, brightly-coloured umbrella over his head. Actually, it was his mother's golf umbrella, but as Sid, Pearce, and Ern had never seen a golf umbrella in their lives, they honestly thought it was a very grand 'state umbrella'.

'Here, Ern – you can do as you said, if you like, and carry it over the Princess's head,' said Fatty, and Ern nearly had a fit.

'Would she let me?' he asked.

'Dimminy-dooly-tibbly-tok,' said Bets, and gave him a sudden smile. He blushed and looked at Fatty.

'What's she say?' he asked.

'She says, she likes you, and she wants you to carry it for her,' said Fatty promptly.

'The way you understand their language beats me!' said Ern, admiringly. 'But then you always were a one, weren't you, Fatty? Well, I'll be proud to hold the umbrella over Her Highness, or whatever she's called. Sid and Perce, get behind.'

The Five Find-Outers were by now quite unable to contain their laughter. Pip was purple in the face with his efforts to stop exploding. Fatty looked at him.

'Tickly-kickly-koo, jinny-peranha-hook!' he said, and then burst into laughter as if he had made a joke. The others immediately took the opportunity of joining in and Larry, Daisy, Pip, and Bets rocked from side to side, roaring with laughter, holding on to one another, much to the astonishment of Ern and his two brothers.

'What's the joke?' asked Ern, suspiciously.

'It's too difficult to translate it for you,' said Fatty. 'Come on now, the Princess in front, with Ern carrying her umbrella – her cousin, Pua-Tua, just behind – and us following.'

The little procession went down the garden path, passing the kitchen door on the way. The maid stood there, shaking a mat, and she stared open-mouthed as they passed. Ern felt terribly important.

It was very disappointing not to meet more people on the way down to the river. They met old

Mrs Winstanton, who was so short-sighted that all she saw was the big umbrella, which made her think it must be raining. She hurried home before she got caught in a shower!

They met the grocer's boy, who stared in amazed and mystified silence. Bets giggled. Ern gave the boy a dignified bow which mystified him still further. What was all this going on? He followed them a little way, and then went to deliver his goods and a tale of 'dressed-up visitors under a HUGE umbrella' to a fascinated housekeeper.

They met nobody else at all. They came to the river path and walked solemnly along it.

'There's the ice cream man!' said Ern, thankfully. 'Pore Sid, he won't be able to have one, what with his toffee and all!'

5. MR GOON GETS A SURPRISE

The ice cream man was lying on the river bank, fast asleep, his tricycle-van pulled back into the shade. Fatty woke him.

He sat up, amazed at the brilliant group around him, topped by the huge umbrella held by Ern, who was now getting a little tired of its weight.

'What's all this?' said the ice cream man. 'Charades or something?'

Ern opened his mouth to introduce the Princess Bongawee, but Fatty frowned at him. He didn't want the joke to go too far – and he had an uneasy feeling that the ice cream man wouldn't be taken in quite as easily as some people. It wouldn't do to spoil the joke for Ern. Ern, Sid, and Perce were in the seventh heaven of delight to think they had gone walking with a princess and her followers.

'Nine ice creams, please,' said Fatty. Ern

corrected him.

'Eight, you mean,' he said.

'You've forgotten Buster,' said Fatty.

'Coo, yes,' said Ern, suddenly remembering that Buster also loved ice cream. Buster had been as good as gold, following the procession solemnly, and hadn't even been to say hello to any dogs he met.

The ice cream man handed out the ice creams, making a few more remarks as he did so.

'Pouring with rain, isn't it?' he said to Ern, who was still valiantly holding the umbrella over Bets. 'Just as well not to get wet.'

'Funny, aren't you?' said Ern.

'Not so funny as you look,' said the ice cream man. 'Where'd you get that umbrella? Out of a cracker?'

'Ha, that's where *you* came from, I spose,' said Ern, at once. 'BANG – and out of a cracker you fell!'

'That's enough, Ern,' said Fatty hastily, seeing a storm about to blow up between the ice cream man and Ern. 'Come on, let's take our ice creams a bit further down the path, where it's cooler.'

The ice cream man remarked that he knew where he could get Ern a clown's hat to go with his umbrella, but Ern was not allowed to reply. Fatty hustled him away, and his umbrella caught in the low-swinging branches of a tree. Bets had to stand still while poor Ern struggled to release it, his ears burning at a few more remarks from the witty ice cream man.

They went on at last again, holding the freezing ice cream cartons in their hands. Sid had one too, and everyone was curious to see how he could manage to eat an ice cream with his mouth still full of toffee. His toffee slab seemed unending. So far as anyone knew, he still had the same piece in his mouth.

And then someone came cycling round the corner of the path – someone burly and red-faced, with a dark blue uniform and helmet!

'It's Uncle!' gasped Ern, in a panic.

'Mr Goon!' said Fatty. 'Old Clear-Orf! Well, well, this is going to be funny!'

Buster recognised Mr Goon with delight. He tore up to his bicycle and jumped at his feet. Goon got off at once and kicked out at the excited little Scottie.

'Clear orf!' he said angrily. 'Here, you, call this dog orf, or I'll push him into the river. Proper little pest, he is.'

'Hello, Mr Goon,' said Fatty, politely. 'I haven't seen you for a very long time. Come here, Buster. Heel, boy, heel!'

Buster ran to Fatty reluctantly, and Mr Goon had time to take in the whole group. He gaped. What a lot of foreigners – and Ern with them. *Ern*! He didn't even know Ern was in the district. He advanced on Ern, who almost dropped the huge umbrella he was still holding.

'ERN! What you doing here?' thundered Mr Goon. 'And bless me, if it isn't Sid and Perce too! What's all this about? And what's the umbrella for?'

'Uncle! Don't shout like that,' begged Ern. 'This is a princess here, and that's why I'm holding an umbrella over her. It's a state umbrella. Don't you know one when you see one?'

Mr Goon didn't even know a golf umbrella when he saw one, much less a state one. He stared at Ern disbelievingly. Ern went on in an urgent voice.

'Uncle, you've heard of Prince Bongawah, who's staying in one of the camps, up on the hills over there, haven't you? Well, this is his sister, Princess

Bongawee – and that's her cousin – and . . .'

Goon was amazed. He looked at Bets, wrapped closely and gracefully in her robes, the hood partly drawn across her sunburnt face. Her face seemed faintly familiar to him, but he didn't for one moment think of Bets Hilton. She stood there rather haughtily, a little scared, without saying a single word.

Goon cleared his throat. He looked at Fatty, who said nothing. 'They were visiting Fatty,' explained Ern. 'And, of course, I told them about Prince Bongawah, who's camping in the field next to us, Uncle – and I'd have known this princess was his sister, they're as alike as two peas.'

'But how did *you* come to be mixed up with them?' asked Goon, suspiciously.

'Your nephew, Ern, came to pay a visit to us, that's all, Mr Goon,' said Fatty, delighted that Ern should be telling Mr Goon such a marvellous tale. 'And the Princess Bongawee liked Ern, and requested him to hold her – er – her state umbrella over her. And Ern's good manners are well-known – so here he is.'

Mr Goon had never had any opinion of Ern's

manners at all. He considered that Ern had none. He stared first at Ern, then at the haughty little princess, and then at Fatty. Fatty stared back unwinkingly.

'She a real princess?' asked Mr Goon, in a confidential aside to Fatty. Before Fatty could answer, Bets spoke in a high little insolent voice that amused Fatty immensely.

'Ikky-oola-potty-wickle-tok,' she said.

'What's she say?' asked Goon with interest.

'She wants to know if you're a real policeman,' said Fatty, promptly. 'What shall I tell her?'

Mr Goon glared at him. Bets interrupted again. 'Ribbly-rookatee, paddly-pool,' she said.

'What does *that* mean?' asked Mr Goon. Fatty put on an embarrassed look.

'I don't like to tell you, Mr Goon,' he said.

'Why? What's it matter?' said the policeman, curiously.

'Well, it's rather a personal remark,' said Fatty. 'No, I don't really think I can tell you, Mr Goon.'

'Go on – you tell me,' said Goon, getting angry.

'Yes, you tell him,' said Ern, delighted at the idea of the princess saying something rude about his uncle.

'Ar,' put in Sid, unexpectedly. Goon turned on him at once.

'What you interfering for? And what do you mean by standing there with your mouth full in front of royalty? Go and empty your mouth!'

'Ar,' said Sid, in panic.

'It's toffee, Uncle,' said Ern. 'Stick-me-tight toffee. It can't be spat out.'

Bets went off into a peal of laughter. Then she hurriedly spoke a few more words. 'Wonge-bonga-smelly-fiddly-tok.'

'There she goes again,' said poor Goon. 'You tell me what she said then, Frederick.'

'I couldn't possibly,' persisted Fatty, making Goon feel so curious that he could hardly contain himself. His face began to go purple, and his eyes bulged a little. He stared at the little princess, who giggled again.

'I only say, why he got FROG face!' said Bets, in a very foreign voice. Everyone immediately exploded, with the exception of poor Sid who couldn't get his mouth open.

Mr Goon exploded too, but in a different way. He was very angry. He took a step forward and Ern

47

instinctively lowered the umbrella and put its vast circle just in front of Mr Goon's nose.

'Don't you hurt the princess, Uncle,' came Ern's quavering voice from behind the huge umbrella. Then Buster joined in the fun again, and flew at Mr Goon's ankles, snapping very deftly at the bicycle clips that held his trousers tightly round his legs.

Mr Goon roared in anger. 'I'll report that dog! I'll report you too, Ern – trying to stick that umbrella into me!'

'Mr Goon, I hope you won't upset the relations of the British with the Tetaruans,' said Fatty, solemnly. 'We don't want the Prince of Tetarua complaining that you have frightened his sister. After all, Tetarua is a friendly state. If the Prime Minister had an incident like this reported to him by an angry prince, there might be . . .'

Mr Goon didn't stay to listen to any more. He knew when he was defeated. He didn't know anything about the Tetaruans, but he did know that little states were very touchy nowadays, and he was rather horrified to hear what Fatty said. He got on his bicycle and sailed away in purple dignity.

'I'll have something more to say to you, young

Ern,' he shouted, as he pedalled past, with Buster at his back wheel, making him wobble almost into the river. 'I'll come up to your camp, you see if I don't!'

He left Ern petrified by his threat, but still valiantly holding the umbrella. Everyone collapsed weakly on the grass, and even Sid managed to open his mouth wide enough to let out a sudden guffaw.

'Our poor ice creams,' said Bets, suddenly relapsing into English, and looking at the ice cream in her carton. It was like custard. Nobody noticed she was speaking English except Fatty, who gave her a little frown.

They licked up their ice creams with difficulty. Sid managed to pour his somehow into his mouth, between his stuck teeth. Fatty grinned round.

'A most creditable performance!' he said. 'Princess, my congratulations!'

'Binga-bonga-banga,' said Bets, graciously.

'What about fresh ice creams?' said Fatty. But Ern, Perce, and Sid couldn't stay. Ern had heard the church clock striking twelve, and as he had been promised a camp dinner by the caravanners next to his tent if he got back at half past twelve, he felt impelled to go.

He bowed most politely to Bets, and handed the state umbrella to Fatty. 'Pleased to have met you,' said Ern. 'I'll tell your brother about you when next I see him over the hedge. Like as peas in a pod, you are!'

Sid and Perce nodded a good-bye, and then they all went off to get the ferry across the river to the hills on the other side.

'Thank goodness we can talk properly again,' said Larry. 'My word, Fatty – what a morning! I don't know when I've enjoyed myself so much!'

6. DISAPPEARANCE

Two days later, Fatty, Larry, and Pip all had tremendous shocks. Fatty got down to breakfast before his mother and father, and poured himself some coffee. He took the two papers they had each morning to his own place, and prepared to enjoy them in peace.

The headlines flared at him, big and black. 'Disappearance of a Prince from Camp. Vanishes in the night. Prince Bongawah gone.'

And in Larry's house, Larry too was reading the same headlines out to Daisy, having found the papers on the front doorstep and brought them in.

In Pip's house, Pip was, as usual, trying to read his father's newspaper back to front. The back page was never very interesting to Pip, because it was all about horse-racing, golf, and tennis – none of which he took any interest. Cricket scores were

51

usually in too small print for him to see. So he waited patiently for his father to study the cricket scores himself on the back page, when Pip would be able to read the front page.

And there, staring at him, were some very interesting headlines. 'Prince vanishes. Tetarua informed. Boys in camp questioned.'

Pip nudged Bets and nodded his head towards the paper. She read the headlines too. Good gracious! That must be the Prince Bongawah whose sister she had pretended to be. How very extraordinary! Bets thought hard about it. Would it matter her having pretended? No, it couldn't. They had only done it to play a trick on Ern.

Yet another person was most interested in the disappearance of the young prince. That was Mr Goon, of course. He also read it in his morning newspaper, and a few minutes later, his telephone rang and he had the news from headquarters. He thought rapidly.

My word – I've met the prince's sister, he thought. If we get hold of her, we might get some news! I'd better get on to the Inspector straightaway.

He corrected himself. 'I should say the *Chief*

Inspector! He's had a promotion again. I've never had any. Got enemies, I have, no doubt of that. Keeping a good man down, that's what they are. Wait till I get them!'

He brooded for a few minutes on enemies that prevented promotion, and then rang up headquarters again and asked for the Chief Inspector.

'He's busy,' said the voice at the other end. 'What do you want him for, Goon?'

'Something to do with the Prince Bongawah disappearance,' said Goon, pompously. 'Very interesting.'

'Right. Hold on a minute,' said the voice. Then Goon heard the Chief Inspector's voice – sharp, confident, and a little annoyed.

'What is it, Goon? I'm busy.'

'Sir, it's about that Prince Bongawah, or whatever his name is,' said Goon. 'I've met his sister, sir, the little Princess Bongawee. I wondered if anyone had thought of questioning her. She might know something about her brother's disappearance.'

There was a moment's silence. Then the Chief Inspector's voice came again, sounding astonished.

'Sister? What sister? This is the first time I've heard of her.'

Goon swelled with importance. 'Yes, sir. I met her two days ago, sir, with her cousin, who looks after her. And two of her train, sir, all very posh and high and mighty.'

There was another astonished pause. 'Is that really you speaking, Goon?' said the Chief Inspector's voice at last. 'This really is so astonishing.'

'Course it's me speaking, sir,' said Goon, surprised and hurt. 'Why shouldn't it be? I'm just reporting something to you, as is my duty. Would you care for me to interview the princess, sir?'

'Wait a minute, wait a minute,' said the Chief Inspector. 'I must ask a few questions of somebody here. We've had no reports of any sister or princess or cousin! I must find out why.'

Goon waited, feeling pleased to have caused such a commotion. Ha – let Chief Inspector Jenks ask all the questions he liked, he'd have to let him, Goon, handle this in the end! That was a bit of luck meeting Fatty with those Tetaruans and their umbrella. A thought struck him. How was it that *Fatty* knew them?

Drat that boy! thought poor Goon. Here I've got a fine bit of investigation in my hand – and I've got to say it's that big boy who introduced me to the princess! Then the Chief Inspector will get on to that toad of a boy, and he'll take the whole matter out of my hands!

He sat and brooded about this, the telephone receiver stuck to his left ear. Then he brightened. He could say that his nephew, Ern, had introduced him. After all, it *was* Ern who had given him all the details. That was quite true. He needn't bring Fatty into it at all.

The Chief Inspector's voice came down the telephone again, making Goon jump.

'Are you there, Goon? Well, I've made a few enquiries this end, and nobody seems to know anything about a sister who's called Princess Bongawee. But seeing that you appear to have met her, I suppose we must enquire into it. How did you meet her?'

'Well, sir – my nephew Ern was with her, and he told me about her and who she was,' said Goon.

'*Ern* – your nephew *Ern*!' said the Chief Inspector, astounded. He remembered the plump, rather spotty, extremely plain nephew of Mr Goon quite clearly. Hadn't he been mixed up in another mystery? Oh yes – and had come quite well out of it too, in the end. But *Ern*! In the company of a Tetaruan princess! The Chief Inspector wondered again if this telephone call was a hoax. But, no, it couldn't be. He knew that harsh voice of Mr Goon's only too well!

'What was Ern doing with the princess?' asked the Chief Inspector, at last.

'Well – he was holding a – a state umbrella over her,' said Mr Goon, beginning to feel that this tale of his didn't really sound very credible.

There was another pause. The Chief Inspector swallowed once or twice. Was Goon all right? Had he got a touch of the sun? This tale of a princess – and Ern – and a state umbrella sounded nonsense to him. The Chief Inspector simply didn't know what to make of it at all.

'Look here, Goon,' he said, 'this is all very extraordinary, but I suppose there may be something in it if you think it's important enough to telephone me about it. I think I will leave you to contact this – er – princess, and ask her a few questions. Why she's here, when she came, what she's doing, who she's with, and so on. Go and do that now. I'll send a man over to check what you find.'

'Right sir, thank you, sir,' said Goon, pleased that he was going to handle the matter first. He clicked down the receiver, and went to get his helmet. It was a great pity he had to go and see that toad of a boy, Fatty. Frederick Trotteville. Huh! He'd soon show him he'd got to answer his questions though. He'd stand no nonsense from that pest.

He cycled round to Fatty's house. He knocked sharply at the front door. The maid opened it, and he asked for Fatty.

'He's gone out, sir,' said the maid.

'Where's he gone?' demanded Mr Goon.

Mrs Trotteville, Fatty's mother, heard Mr Goon's rather loud voice, and came into the hall.

'Oh, it's you, Mr Goon,' she said politely. 'Did you want Frederick? He's out, I'm afraid. Was there something you wanted to ask him?'

'Well, madam, I did want to ask him a few questions about the Princess Bongawee,' said Mr Goon. 'But perhaps you can tell me. Was she staying here?'

Mrs Trotteville looked amazed. '*What* princess?' she asked. 'I've never even heard of her.'

'She's the sister of that Prince Bongawah that's vanished,' explained Mr Goon.

This didn't convey anything to Mrs Trotteville at all. She hadn't taken any interest in the morning's report of the prince's disappearance. She had merely thought he hadn't liked cold baths or something, and had run away. And anyway, what was it to do with Frederick?

'I'm afraid I can't help you, Mr Goon,' she said. 'Frederick has only been back home for two or three days and, as far as I know, he hasn't been about with any princesses at all. I feel sure he would have introduced them to me if he knew any. Good morning.'

'But – do you mean to say you didn't ask her in to tea or anything?' said Mr Goon desperately.

'Why should I, if I have never even met her?' said Mrs Trotteville, thinking that Mr Goon must be out of his mind. 'Good morning.'

She shut the door and left a perspiring Mr Goon outside. Now he had got to go and find that boy.

Where would he be? He might be round at those precious friends of his – the Hilton's – or those other's – Larry and Daisy somebody-or-other.

Mr Goon cycled first to Larry's house. But again he drew a blank. Larry and Daisy were both out.

'Probably round at Frederick Trotteville's,' said their maid. But Mr Goon knew better. Nobody was going to send him trapesing back there again!

He cycled, very red in the face now, down the road, and all the way to Pip's. He cycled up to the front door, and hammered angrily on the knocker.

The five children were out in the garden with Buster. Buster growled at the knocking and Fatty put a restraining hand on him.

Bets went peeping round the hedge to see who it was at the front door. She ran back, looking scared.

'It's Mr Goon. Old Clear-Orf. He looks very red and cross,' she said. 'Oh dear – do you think he's come to ask us about the princess I pretended to be? He's really so very silly, I'm sure he thinks I was real!'

Fatty got up. 'Come along,' he said. 'Out of the gate at the bottom of the garden we go, top speed. If anyone calls us, we're not here. If Goon is hunting for the Princess Bongawee, let him hunt! Do him good. Shut up, Buster – if you bark, you'll give the game away!'

They all fled silently down the garden to the little gate that opened onto the lane at the bottom. Buster ran too, without even half a growl. Something was up, was it? Well, he could play his part too, then!

When Mrs Hilton took Mr Goon out into the garden to find the children, there was no one there. No one in the summer-house either! How peculiar!

'I am *sure* I heard them out here a minute ago,' she said. 'Pip! Bets! Where are you?'

No answer at all. Mrs Hilton called once more and then turned to the purple Mr Goon. 'I expect you will find them either at Frederick Trotteville's, or at Larry's,' she said. 'Perhaps you would like to go there.'

Mr Goon had a vision of himself chasing from one house to another, endlessly in search of an elusive Fatty. He scowled, and sailed away morosely on his bicycle.

'Really,' thought Mrs Hilton, 'that policeman's manners get worse and worse every day!'

7. ERN AND MR GOON

Somebody else was also very excited that morning, besides the Find-Outers and Mr Goon. Ern was most astonished when he heard the news of Prince Bongawah's disappearance. He learnt it in rather a peculiar fashion.

Ever since he had met the Princess Bongawee at Fatty's house, he had kept a lookout for the little prince over the hedge. He was longing to tell him that he had met his sister.

But, somehow, he hadn't caught sight of him. Still, Ern didn't give up, and that very morning he had squirmed right through the hedge, hoping to find the prince himself.

He was most astonished to find two policemen nearby. They pounced on Ern at once. 'What are you doing in this field?' demanded one, his hand on Ern's neck.

'I only just came over to look for someone,' said Ern wriggling. 'Lemme go. You're hurting.'

'You'll get hurt a lot more if you come interfering here now,' said the policeman grimly. 'You might even disappear – like the little prince!'

This was the first Ern had heard of any disappearance. He stared at the two policemen. 'Has he disappeared?' he said, astonished. 'Coo, think of that! When did he go?'

'Sometime in the night,' said the policeman, watching Ern closely. 'Hear anything? You're camping in that tent, I suppose?'

'Yes. I didn't hear nothing at all,' said Ern at once. 'Coo – to think I met his sister, the princess, a few days ago!'

'Oh yes?' said one of the policemen, mockingly. 'And did you have tea with his mother, the Queen, and dinner with his old man?'

'No. But I had an ice cream with his sister,' protested Ern.

'Oh yes?' said both policemen at once. One of them gave him such a violent shake that Ern almost fell over. 'Now you get along,' he said. 'And just remember, it's always best to keep your nose out of trouble. You and your tales!'

Ern squeezed back through the hole in the hedge, hurt to think that his tale had been disbelieved. He was determined to go and tell Fatty about the prince's disappearance. It didn't occur to him that it was already in all the papers.

He set off by himself, without Sid or Perce. Perce was in a bad temper that morning, and Sid as usual had his mouth full of stick-me-tight toffee, so there was no conversation to be got out of him at all. Ern felt that he wanted a little intelligent company. Neither Sid nor Perce could be called really interesting companions.

He decided to borrow a bicycle from one of the nearby caravanners. There was one there, leaning against the caravan. Ern snooped round, looking for the owner.

He found him at last, a boy a bit older than himself. 'Lend me your bike?' called Ern.

'Cost you,' called back the thrifty owner. Ern parted reluctantly with some money and rode off down the field path to the gate, wobbling over the ruts.

Meanwhile, Mr Goon was cycling grumpily

back home again. Just as he turned a corner, he caught sight of a plump boy cycling towards him. It was Ern. Ern, however, was not particularly anxious to meet his uncle, so he turned his bike round hurriedly and made off in the opposite direction.

For some reason, Mr Goon took it into his head to think that the boy in the distance was Fatty in one of his errand boy disguises.

He began to pedal furiously. Oho! So that toad of a boy was up to his tricks again, was he? He was disguising himself so as to keep away from Mr Goon and his questions, was he? Well, he, Mr Goon, would soon put an end to that! He would cycle after him till he caught him.

So Mr Goon cycled. The pedals went up and down furiously, he rang his bell furiously as he rounded the corner, and he looked furious too. Anyone looking at Mr Goon at that moment would have thought that he was on very important business indeed.

Ern took a look over his shoulder when he heard the furious ringing of Mr Goon's bell coming round the corner. He was horrified to find his uncle racing after him down the street. Ern began to pedal very quickly indeed.

'Hey you!' came a loud voice from halfway down the street. Ern's heart almost failed him. His uncle sounded so very stern. But what had he, Ern, done now? Was his uncle going to scold him for protecting the princess with the state umbrella?

Ern pedalled away and shot round a corner. So did Mr Goon. Both got hotter and hotter, and Ern became more and more panic-stricken. Mr Goon began to get very angry indeed. He was absolutely certain it was Fatty leading him this dance. Wait till he got him! He'd pull off his wig, and show him he couldn't deceive him!

Ern turned another corner, and found himself cycling up a path into a barn. He couldn't stop. Hens and ducks fled out of his way. Ern ended up on the floor of a dark barn, panting, and almost in tears.

Mr Goon came up the path at top speed too. He also landed in the dark barn, but not on the floor. He came to a stop just by Ern.

'Now, you just take off that wig,' commanded

Mr Goon, in an awful voice. 'And let me tell you what I think of boys who lead me a dance like this, just when they know I want evidence regarding the Princess Bongawee!'

Ern stared up at his uncle in amazement. What was he talking about? Did he think Ern was wearing a wig? It was dark in the barn, and at first Mr Goon did not see that it was Ern. Then, as his eyes grew used to the shadows, he saw who it was. His eyes bulged almost out of his head.

'ERN! What are you doing here?' he almost yelled.

'Well, Uncle – you chased me, didn't you?' said Ern, in alarm. 'I was frightened. Didn't you know it was me? You pedalled after me all right.'

Mr Goon collected himself with an effort. He stared down at Ern, who was still on the floor. 'What did you run away from me for?' he asked sternly.

'I told you. You chased me,' said Ern.

'I chased you because you were running away,' said Mr Goon, majestically.

'Well, Uncle – I ran away because you were chasing me,' said poor Ern again.

'You being cheeky?' asked Mr Goon, in an awful voice.

'No, Uncle,' said Ern, thinking it was time he got up. He was too much at Mr Goon's mercy on the floor. Anything might happen to him with his uncle so furious! Ern didn't know what was the matter at all. All he had done was to try to get away from his uncle.

'Have you seen that big boy today?' asked Mr Goon, watching Ern slowly and cautiously get up.

'No, Uncle,' said Ern.

'You seen that there princess again?' asked his uncle.

'No, Uncle,' said Ern, in alarm. 'I say – you're not after *her*, are you?'

'Do you know where she lives?' said Mr Goon, thinking that perhaps he might get something out of Ern, if he couldn't find the elusive Fatty.

'Why don't you ask Fatty?' said Ern, innocently. 'He knows her very well. I expect she sees him every day. Coo – she might know something about her brother's disappearance. I never thought of that!'

'Now you listen here, Ern,' said Mr Goon, solemnly. 'You remember Chief Inspector Jenks?

Well, I've been talking to him on the phone today, see, about this same disappearance. And he's put me in charge of the case. I'm trying to find that princess to question her. But do you think I can find that pest of a boy to ask him about her? He's nowhere to be found! Makes me think *he's* disappearing too – on purpose!'

Ern picked up his bike, listening hard. He thought it very likely indeed that Fatty was avoiding Mr Goon. Ern considered it was a very sensible thing to do. Perhaps Fatty was on to this case too? Perhaps – oh joy – perhaps a mystery had suddenly turned up right under his very nose? Maybe Fatty was avoiding Mr Goon so that he wouldn't have to give away what he knew about the princess.

Ern grinned suddenly, much to his uncle's astonishment. 'What you grinning at all of a sudden?' he asked suspiciously.

Ern didn't answer. His grin faded. 'Now you look here, young Ern,' boomed Mr Goon, 'if I catch you hanging round Peterswood, hobnobbing with that pest of a boy, I'll have you and Sid and Perce cleared out of that camp in double-quick time – do you hear me? You don't know nothing about this case at all, and you aren't going to know anything, either. I know you and your ways – telling tales of this and that and the other! All you can tell that boy this time is that I'm in charge of this, and if he doesn't tell me all he knows about that princess before teatime, so's I can report to the Chief Inspector, he'll get into serious trouble. Very serious trouble.'

Mr Goon was quite out of breath after this long speech. Ern edged out of the barn. The hens peeping round the door scattered at once, clucking. Ern leapt on his bicycle and rode out at top speed.

'You go and tell that boy I want him!' yelled Mr Goon, as a parting shot. 'I'm not going all over the place after him again!'

Ern cycled quickly to Fatty's, relieved to have got away from his uncle without too much trouble. He hoped to goodness he would find Fatty at home. He was lucky! Fatty was in his shed with the others, keeping a watch for Goon.

Ern poured out his tale, and was disappointed to find that the others already knew about the prince's disappearance from the papers. 'What about that princess, Fatty?' said Ern. 'Don't she know nothing about her brother?'

'Ern – she wasn't a real princess,' said Fatty, thinking it was time to own up to their joke. 'That was only young Bets here dressed up in some things I brought from Morocco. And her cousin was Daisy, and the others were Larry and Pip!'

'Kim-*Larri*ana-Tik, at your service,' said Larry, with a bow.

'Kim-*Pip*py-Tok,' said Pip, with another bow. Ern stared, bewildered. He rubbed his hand over his eyes. He stared again.

'Lovaduck!' he said at last. 'No, I can't believe it! Just you dressed up, little Bets! And you looked a real princess too. Coo! No wonder my uncle's wanting to see you, Fatty, and ask about the princess – and no wonder you don't want to see *him*! Took him in properly, we did! Me with the state umbrella and all!'

Bets began to laugh. 'You were fine, Ern,' she said. 'Oh dear – didn't we talk a foreign language beautifully! Onna-matta-tickly-pop!'

'Beats me how you can talk like that,' said

Ern, wonderingly. 'But I say – what's the Chief Inspector going to say about all this? My uncle says he told him all about the princess this morning, and he's been put in charge of the case! He says I'm to tell you to keep off! *He's* met the princess too, he says, and you've got to tell him where she lives so that he can interview her.

Fatty groaned. 'I knew this would happen! Why did I do such a fool thing! It was just because you turned up when you did, Ern. Well – I suppose I'd better ring up the Chief Inspector and tell him everything. All I hope is that he'll laugh.'

'Better go and do it now,' said Pip, nervously. 'We don't want old Mr Goon round complaining about us again. If you get the Chief Inspector on your side, we'll be all right.'

'Right,' said Fatty, getting up. 'I'll go now. So long! If I'm not back in five minutes, you'll know the Chief Inspector has gobbled me up!'

He went off down the garden path to the house. The others looked rather solemnly at one another. What in the world would the Chief Inspector say when he heard there was no princess?

And worse still – whatever would *Mr Goon* say? He must have told the Chief Inspector all about her. He wouldn't like it one little bit when he knew it was all a joke!

8. TWO UNPLEASANT TALKS

The Chief Inspector was not at all pleased with Fatty's tale. At first, he couldn't make head or tail of it, and his voice became quite sharp.

'First Goon telephones a cock-and-bull story of some princess who says she's Prince Bongawah's sister, and now you ring me and say there's no such person, it was only Bets dressed up,' said Chief Inspector Jenks. 'This won't do, Frederick. A joke's a joke, but it seems to me you've gone rather far this time. You've made Goon waste time on a lot of nonsense, when he might have been doing a bit of more useful investigation.'

'I quite see that, sir,' said poor Fatty. 'But actually it was all an accident – we'd no idea when we dressed up and called Bets the Princess Bongawee that Prince Bongawah was going to disappear. It was a most unfortunate coincidence. I mean, we couldn't possibly have guessed that was going to happen.'

'Quite,' said the Chief Inspector. 'You have a very curious knack of turning up in the middle of things, Frederick, haven't you? Accidental or otherwise. You'll certainly make Goon gnash his teeth over this! By the way, how on earth did that nephew of his – Ern, or some such name – come to be mixed up in this idiotic princess affair?'

'He just happened to barge in on us when we were dressing up,' explained Fatty. 'You know he and his twin brothers are camping in the field next to where the little prince was camping, don't you? It's a pity he's such an idiot or he might have noticed something.'

There was a pause. 'Yes,' came the Chief Inspector's voice, at last. 'I'd let Goon question them, but I don't think he'd get much out of Ern, somehow. You'd better see if you can find out something, Frederick – though you don't deserve to come in on this, you know, after your asinine behaviour.'

'No, sir,' said Fatty humbly, his face one huge grin at the thought of 'coming in on this'! That meant a little detective work again. Aha! So these hols were going to have something exciting, after all!

'All right,' said Chief Inspector Jenks. 'Make your peace with Goon if you can, and tell him to telephone me afterwards. He will *not* be pleased with you, Frederick. Neither am I. You'd better try and rub off this black mark quickly!'

Without saying good-bye, the Chief Inspector rang off, and Fatty heard the receiver click back into place. He put back his own, and stood by the wall, thinking hard. He felt thrilled, but rather uncomfortable. Quite by accident, he had got mixed up with the Prince Bongawah, simply because Bets had dressed up as a princess and Ern had seen her! How could he have known the prince was going to disappear, and that old Mr Goon would immediately spread the news about his mythical sister? Just like Goon! Always on to the wrong thing!

It was going to be most unpleasant breaking the news to Mr Goon that the Princess of Bongawah was just a joke. She didn't really exist. It was only Bets, dressed up, who had taken in old Mr Goon!

I play too many jokes, thought Fatty to himself. But it's going to be a pretty poor life for me and the others if I cut out all the tricks and jokes we like. We play them too well, I suppose. Gosh – there's Mr Goon coming in at the front gate! Now for it!

Fatty went to the front door before Mr Goon could hammer at the knocker. He wasn't particularly anxious for his mother to hear what he had to say to Goon.

Goon stared at Fatty as if he couldn't believe his eyes. 'Here I've been chasing you all day and you come and open the door to me before I've even knocked!' he said. 'Where have you been?'

'That doesn't matter,' said Fatty. 'Come into this room, Mr Goon. I've something to say to you.'

He took the burly policeman into the little study, and Goon sat down in a chair, feeling rather astonished. 'I've got plenty to ask *you*,' he began. 'Been after you all day to get some information.'

'Yes. Well, you're going to have quite a lot of information,' said Fatty. 'And I'm afraid it will be a bit of a shock to you, Mr Goon. There's been an unfortunate misunderstanding.'

'Huh!' said Mr Goon, annoyed at Fatty's way of speaking. 'I don't want to know about unfortunate misunderstandings, whatever they may be – I just want to ask you about this here Princess Bonga – er, Bonga-what's-her-name.'

'Bongawee,' said Fatty, politely. 'I was going to tell you about her. She doesn't exist.'

Goon didn't take this in at all. He stared at Fatty, bewildered. Then he poked a big fat finger into the boy's face.

'Now you look here – you can pretend all you like that she doesn't exist, but I saw her with my own eyes. She's important in this here case, see? You may want to pretend that you don't know her now, nor where she is, but I'm not having any of that. I'm in charge of this, and I'm going to demand answers to my questions. Where's this princess now?'

Fatty hesitated. 'Well, I've already told you she doesn't exist,' he said. 'There's no such princess. It was only Bets dressed up.'

Goon went a dull red, and his eyes bulged a little more. He pursed up his mouth and glared. *Now* what was this boy up to? The princess was Bets dressed up! What nonsense! Hadn't he heard her talk a foreign language with his own ears?

77

'You're making up a tale for some reason of your own, Frederick,' he burst out at last. 'I not only saw the princess, but I heard her. She talked all foreign. Nobody can talk foreign if they don't know the language.'

'Oh yes, they can,' said Fatty. 'I can "talk foreign" for half an hour if you want me to. Listen!'

He poured out a string of idiotic, completely unintelligible words that left Mr Goon in a whirl. He blinked. How did this boy do these things?

'There you are,' said Fatty, at last. 'Easy! You try, Mr Goon. All you have to do is to let your tongue go loose, if you know what I mean, and jabber at top speed. It doesn't *mean* anything. It's just complete nonsense. You try.'

Mr Goon didn't even begin to try. Let his tongue go loose? Not in front of Fatty, anyway! He might try it when he was by himself, perhaps. In fact, it might be a good idea. He, too, might be able to 'talk foreign' whenever he pleased. Mr Goon made a mental note to try it out sometime when he was quite by himself.

'See?' said Fatty, to the dumbstruck policeman. 'I only just let my tongue go loose, Mr Goon. Do try. Anyway, that's what Bets and the others did – we didn't really "talk foreign", as you call it.'

'Do you mean to say that that procession Ern was with was just Bets and your friends dressed up?' said poor Mr Goon, finding his tongue at last. 'What about the state umbrella?'

Fatty had the grace to blush. 'Oh that – well, actually it was a golf umbrella belonging to my mother,' he said. 'I tell you, it was all a joke, Mr Goon. Ern happened to come along when they were all dressed up, and you know what he is – he just fell for everything, and swallowed the whole tale of princess and lady-in-waiting and all! We went out for ice creams – and then we met *you*!'

Mr Goon suddenly saw it all now. He was full of dismay and horror. To think of all he had told the Chief Inspector too! How was he to get out of *that*? He buried his face in his hands and groaned, quite forgetting that Fatty was still there.

Fatty felt extremely uncomfortable. He didn't like Mr Goon at all, but he hadn't meant to get him into this humiliating fix. He spoke again.

'Mr Goon, it was a silly mistake and most unfortunate, of course, that the Prince Bongawah should go and disappear just after we'd pretended Bets was his sister. I've told the Chief Inspector all about it. He's just as annoyed with me as you are, but he does see that it was pure coincidence – just an unlucky chance. We're all very sorry.'

Mr Goon groaned again. 'That golf umbrella! I told him it was a state umbrella. He'll think I'm potty. Everyone will think I'm potty. Here I am, struggling for promotion, doing my very best, and every time you come along and upset the apple cart. You're a toad of a boy, that's what you are!'

'Mr Goon, I *am* sorry about this,' said Fatty. 'Look here – let's work together this time. I'll try and make up for this silly beginning. We'll solve this mystery together. Come on – be a sport!'

'I wouldn't work with you if the Chief Inspector himself told me to!' said Mr Goon, rising heavily to his feet. 'Once a toad, always a toad! And what would working with you mean? *I'll* tell you! False clues put under my nose! Me running about at night to find people that aren't there! Me arresting the wrong person while you've got the right one up your sleeve! Ho – *that's* what working with you would mean!'

'All right,' said Fatty, getting angry at being called a toad so often. 'Don't work with me then. But if I can put any information your way I will, all the same – just to make up for upsetting your apple cart.'

'Gah!' said Goon, stalking out. 'Think I'd listen to any information from you! You think again, Frederick Trotteville. And keep out of this. I'm in charge, see, and I'll solve this mystery, or my name's not Theophilus Goon!'

9. A LITTLE 'PORTRY'

Mr Goon went to telephone the Chief Inspector. He felt extremely gloomy and downhearted. Why did he always believe everything Fatty said and did? Why didn't he spot that the state umbrella was no more than a golf umbrella? What was there about that pest of a boy that always made him come to grief?

I'll never believe a word he says again, thought Mr Goon, picking up the telephone receiver. Never in this world! He's a snake in the grass! He's a – a toad-in-the-hole. No – that's a pudding. Talking about me working with him! What sauce! What cheek! What . . .

Letting your tongue go loose too, he went on thinking. What does he mean? Let's try it – abbledy, abbledy, abbledy . . .

'What's that you say?' asked a surprised voice at

the other end, and Mr Goon jumped. 'Er – can I speak to Chief Inspector Jenks, please?' he asked.

The conversation between the Inspector and Mr Goon was short, and much more satisfactory to Mr Goon than he had dared to hope. Apparently Inspector Jenks *was* annoyed with Fatty, and although a little sarcastic about people who believed in false princesses and particularly in state umbrellas, he said far less than Mr Goon had feared.

'All right, Goon,' he finished. 'Now, for pity's sake, put your best foot forward, and get something sensible done. It's in your district. Go and interview the boys up in the camp, use your brains, and PRODUCE RESULTS!'

'Yes, sir,' said Goon. 'And about that boy, Frederick Trotteville, sir – he's not to . . .'

But the Chief Inspector had rung off, and Goon stared at the silent receiver crossly. He had meant to put in a few well-chosen remarks about Fatty's shocking deception, and now it was too late.

Fatty told the others the result of his telephone call to the Chief Inspector, and of his interview with Mr Goon. Bets was sorry for Mr Goon. She didn't like him any more than the others did, but all the same she thought he hadn't had quite a fair deal this time – and it was really her fault because she had passed herself off so gleefully as the Princess Bongawee!

'We really will try to help him this time,' she said. 'We'll pass him on anything we find out.'

'He probably won't believe a word,' said Fatty. 'Still, we could pass anything on through Ern. He might believe Ern.'

Ern was still there. He looked alarmed. 'Here, don't you go telling me things to pass on to my uncle,' he protested. 'I don't want nothing to do with him. He don't like me, and I don't like him.'

'Well, Ern, it would only be to help him,' said Bets, earnestly. 'I feel rather awful about everything really – especially about the bit where I called him "frog face" in broken English!'

Fatty laughed. 'Gosh, I'd forgotten about that. Fancy *you* doing that, young Bets! He'll be calling you a toad, if you call him a frog!'

'It was awfully rude of me,' said Bets. 'I can't think what came over me. Ern, you *will* pass on anything we want you to, to your uncle, won't you?'

Ern couldn't resist Bets. He had a tremendous admiration for her. He rubbed his hand over his untidy hair, and stared helplessly at her.

'All right,' he said. 'I'll do what you say. But mind, I don't promise he'll believe me. And I'm not going too near him either. I'll tell him over a fence or something. You don't know what a temper my uncle's got.'

'Oh yes, we do,' said Fatty, remembering some very nasty spurts of temper that Mr Goon had shown in the past. 'We don't *really* want to help him, Ern, but we do want to make up for messing him about this time, that's all. We'll make amends, if we can't be friends.'

'I say! That last bit sounds like portry,' said Ern.

> We'll make amends,
> If we can't be friends.

'See? It's portry, isn't it?'

'No, it just happened to rhyme, that's all,' said Fatty. 'By the way, you used to write a lot of poetry, er, portry, I mean. Ern, do you still write it?'

'Not so much,' said Ern, regretfully. 'It don't

seem to come, like. I keep on starting pomes, but that's as far as I get. You know, just the first line or two, that's all. But I've got one here that's three lines almost.'

'Oh Ern, read it!' said Daisy, delighted. Ern's poems were always so very dismal and gloomy, and he was so very serious over them.

Ern fumbled in his pocket and brought out a dirty little notebook with a pencil hanging to it by a string. He licked his thumb and began to turn the pages.

'Here we are,' he said, and cleared his throat solemnly. He struck an attitude, and began to recite his 'pome' haltingly.

> *A pore old gardener said, "Ah me!*
> *My days is almost done,*
> *I've got rheumatics . . ."*

Ern stopped and looked at the others in despair. 'I got stuck there,' he said. 'That's what always happens to me. I just get stuck – in the very middle of a good pome too. Took me two hours and twenty-one minutes to get that far. I timed meself.

And now I can't finish it.'

'Yes, I can tell it would be a good pome,' said Fatty, solemnly. 'It goes like this, Ern.'

And Fatty also struck an attitude, legs apart, hands behind his back, face turned upwards – and recited glibly, without stopping.

> *A pore old gardener said, "Ah me!*
> *My days is almost done,*
> *I've got rheumatics in my knee,*
> *And now it's hard to run.*
> *I've got a measle in my foot,*
> *And chilblains on my nose,*
> *And bless me if I haven't got*
> *Pneumonia in my toes.*
> *All my hair has fallen out,*
> *My teeth have fallen in,*
> *I'm really getting rather stout,*
> *Although I'm much too thin.*
> *My nose is deaf, my ears are dumb,*
> *My tongue is tied in knots,*
> *And now my barrow and my spade*
> *Have all come out in spots.*
> *My watering can is . . ."*

Larry shouted with laughter and Pip thumped Fatty on the back, yelling. Bets collapsed with Daisy on the rug. 'Don't,' said Bets. 'Stop, Fatty! How do you do it!'

Fatty stopped, out of breath. 'Had enough?' he said. 'I was just coming to where the watering can was feeling washed out, and the spade was feeling on edge, and . . .'

'*Don't*, Fatty!' begged Bets again, giggling helplessly. 'Oh dear – HOW do you do it?'

Only Ern was silent, without a smile or a laugh. He sat on the edge of a chair, struck with absolute wonder. He gazed at Fatty, and swallowed hard. He couldn't make it out. How could Fatty stand there and recite all that without thinking about it?

'Struck dumb, all of a sudden?' asked Fatty, amused. 'How do you like the way your "pome" goes on, Ern? It's a pity you didn't finish it, you know. You could have read it out to us then, instead of my saying it to you.'

Ern was even more bewildered. He blinked at Fatty. 'Do you mean to say, if I had finished that pome that's what it would have been like?' he asked, in an awed voice.

'Well, it's your pome, isn't it?' said Fatty cheerfully. 'I mean, I only just went on with it. I think you work too hard at your pomes, Ern. You just want to throw them off, so to speak. Like this.'

> *The little Princess Bongawee*
> *Was very small and sweet,*
> *A princess from her pretty head*
> *Down to her tiny feet.*
> *She had a servant, Ern by name,*
> *A very stout young fella,*
> *Who simply loved to shield her with*
> *A dazzling . . .*

'STATE UMBRELLA!' yelled everyone, except Ern. There were more yells and laughs. Ern didn't join in. He simply couldn't understand how Fatty could be so clever. Fatty gave him a thump.

'Ern! Wake up! You look daft, sitting there without a smile on your face. What's up?'

'You're a genius, Fatty, that's what's up,' said Ern. 'The others don't know it, because they don't know how difficult it is to write portry. But I do. And you stand there and – and . . .'

'Spout it out,' said Fatty. 'It's easy, that kind of stuff. I'm not a genius, Ern. Anyone can do that kind of thing, if they think about it.'

'But that's just it,' said Ern. 'You don't even think about it. It's like turning on a tap. Out it comes. Coo, lovaduck! If I could do portry like that, I'd think meself cleverer than the King of England.'

'Then you'd be wrong,' said Fatty. 'Cheer up, Ern. One of these days, your portry will come gushing out and then you'll be miserable because you won't be able to write it down fast enough.'

'I'd get a shock if it did,' said Ern, putting away his dirty little notebook with a sigh. 'I'm proud to know you, Fatty. If the others don't know a genius when they see one, I do. I'm not a very clever fellow, but I know good brains when I come across them. I tell you, you're a genius.'

This was a very remarkable speech indeed from Ern. The others looked at him in surprise. Was there more in Ern than they suspected? Bets slipped her hand through Fatty's arm.

'You're right, Ern,' she said. '*I* think Fatty's a genius too. But not only in poetry. In everything!'

Fatty looked pleased but extremely embarrassed.

He squeezed Bets' hand. He coughed modestly, and then coughed again, trying to think of something to say. But Larry spoke first, amused at Fatty's modest coughs.

> *It was a coff,*
> *That carried him off,*
> *It was a coffin*
> *They carried him offin,*

he said in a solemn and lugubrious voice. Whereupon the meeting dissolved in squeals of laughter and yells and thumps. Ern was delighted. What a set of WONDERFUL friends he had!

10. UP AT THE CAMP

That afternoon, Fatty began to 'investigate' in earnest. He had studied the papers, but had learnt very little from them. Apparently, the little prince had joined in a camp singsong the night he had disappeared, and had then had some cocoa and gone off to his tent with the three other boys he shared it with.

These three boys could give no help at all. They had been tired and had fallen asleep immediately they had got into their sleeping-bags. When they awoke, it was morning, and the prince's sleeping-bag was empty.

That was all they could say.

There's not very much to go on, thought Fatty. I suppose someone has kidnapped the boy. I'll have to question Ern and Sid and Perce, though I don't expect any of them know a thing – and I'll have to snoop round the camp a bit too, and keep my ears open.

He cycled round to Pip's that afternoon and found Larry and Daisy there. 'Has anyone got a relation of some sort up at the camping ground?' asked Fatty. 'I haven't as many relations as you have. Larry, can't you produce a cousin or something who might be staying at the camp?'

'No,' said Larry. 'What about you, Pip?'

'What schools are up there?' said Pip. 'Where's the paper? I saw a list of them today.'

They scanned the list carefully. 'Ah, there are boys from Lillington-Peterhouse,' said Pip. 'I know a cousin of mine goes there. He might be at the camp.'

'What's his name?' asked Fatty.

'Ronald Hilton,' said Pip. 'He's older than I am.'

'We could go and find the Lillington-Peterhouse lot,' said Fatty, 'and ask for Ronald. If he's there, you can have a powwow and the rest of us will have a snoop round, and keep our ears open.'

'I don't much want to have a powwow with Ronald,' said Pip. 'He'll think it awful cheek. I tell you, he's older than I am.'

'Do you realise this may be a mystery?' said

Fatty severely. 'I know it doesn't seem like one at all, and we've begun all wrong, somehow – but it's a *possible* mystery, so it's your duty to do what you can, Pip.'

'Right,' said Pip, meekly. 'I'll powwow then. But if I get a clip on the ear, come and rescue me. I hope if it's a mystery, it livens up a bit. I can't get up much interest in a little foreign prince being kidnapped.'

'Nor can I,' admitted Daisy. 'But you never know. I bet we don't get much out of Ern, Sid, or Perce, Fatty. They wouldn't notice anything if it went on under their noses!'

'Got your bikes, Larry and Daisy?' asked Fatty. 'Come on then, let's go. We won't use the ferry, we'll go round by the bridge and up to the camp that way. It's not very far on bikes.'

They set off, with Buster as usual in Fatty's basket. He sat up there, perky and proud, looking down his nose at any other dog he met.

'If you get any bigger I won't be able to take you in my basket much longer, Buster,' panted Fatty, as he toiled up a hill.

'Woof,' agreed Buster, politely. He turned round

and tried to lick Fatty's nose, but Fatty dodged.

They got to the camp at last. It was in a very large field, sloping down to the river on one side. Clumps of trees stood here and there. Tents were everywhere, and smoke rose from where a meal was cooking. Boys hurried about, yelling and laughing.

The Find-Outers put their bicycles against a hedge. Fatty spoke to a boy coming along.

'Hey! Where's the Lillington-Peterhouse lot?'

The boy jerked his head towards the river. 'Last tents down there.'

The five children strolled down to the tents. Pip looked nervous. He really didn't like accosting a cousin two years older than himself, and very much bigger. He hoped he wouldn't see him.

But in a moment or two, he got a thump on the back and a cheerful-faced boy, three inches taller than Pip, shouted at him.

'Philip! What are *you* doing? Don't say you've come to look me up!'

Pip turned round. He grinned. 'Hello Ronald!' he said. 'Yes, I did come to look you up. Hope you don't mind.'

It was funny to hear Pip being called by his right

name, Philip. Pip introduced his cousin to the others. Ronald stared hard at Fatty.

'Hey! Aren't you the chap Philip is always gassing about – the one that works with the police or something?'

Fatty looked modest. 'Well, I do help the police sometimes,' he admitted.

'Are you on a job now?' asked Ronald eagerly. 'Come and tell us about it!'

'No – no, I can't,' said Fatty. 'We've just come up here to see you – and out of interest because of the disappearance of that young prince.'

'Oh, that fellow!' said Ronald, leading them all into a very spacious tent. 'Don't bother about *him*! Jolly good riddance, *I* say! He was the most awful little beast imaginable!'

There was a long wooden table in the tent and on it were spread plates of jam sandwiches, potted meat sandwiches, buns, and slices of fruit cake. Jugs of lemonade stood at intervals down the length of the table.

'You do well for yourselves!' said Larry.

'Help yourselves,' invited Ronald. 'I'm helping with the catering this week – head cook and bottlewasher, you know. It's a bit early for tea, but everything's ready and we might as well get what we want before the hungry hordes rush in.'

They each got plates, and piled them with food. It really was not more than an hour or so since they had finished their lunches, but that made no difference. All of them could eat, hungrily, at any time of the day or night, including Buster, who was now sniffing about under the table, snapping up all kinds of tasty bits and pieces.

Ronald led them out into the field again, complete with plates of food, and took them down to the river. 'Come on, we'll sit and eat in peace here,' he said. 'My word, Trotteville, I'm pleased to meet you. Philip's told me no end of tales about you at one time and another – and I've told them to my pals too.'

Fatty told him a few more, and enjoyed himself very much. Pip got bored. His cousin took no further notice of him, he was so wrapped up in Fatty. Pip finished his tea and got up. He beckoned to Larry.

'Come on, let's go for a wander round,' he said. 'We might pick up something.'

They strolled round the field. Nobody took much notice of them. Larry stopped a boy going by. 'Where's the tent Prince Bongawah slept in?' he asked.

'Over there, if it's any interest to you!' said the boy cheekily, and hurried off.

Pip and Larry walked over to the tent he had pointed out. Outside sat three boys, munching sandwiches. They were all about Pip's age.

'Good tent, yours,' said Larry to the boys. It certainly was a very fine one indeed, much better than any other tent nearby.

'Supplied by his Royal Highness, Prince Bongawah-wah-wah,' said one of the boys.

Pip laughed. 'Why do you call him that?' he asked. 'Didn't you like him?'

'No,' said the boys, all together. A red-haired one waved his sandwich at Larry.

'He was a frightful, cocky little fellow,' he said. 'And a real idiot. He yelled at everything, like a kid of seven!'

'That's why we called him Wah-wah,' said another boy. 'He was always wah-wahing about something.'

'Did he talk English?' asked Larry.

'Well, he was supposed to know hardly a word,' said Red-Hair. 'He just talked rubbish usually – but he could speak our language all right if he wanted to! Though goodness knows where he picked it up! Talk about Cockney!'

'What school did he go to?' asked Larry.

'None. He had a tutor,' said Red-Hair. 'He was a regular little urchin, for all he was a prince! All his clothes were of the very very best, even his pyjamas – but did he wash? Not he! And if you said you'd pop him into the river he'd run a mile, wah-wahing!'

'Lots of boys are like that,' said the third boy, munching away. 'We've got two at our school. One never cleans his teeth and the other howls if he gets a kick at football.'

'Do you think the prince got kidnapped?' asked Pip, feeling rather thrilled with all this first-hand information.

'I don't know and I don't care,' said Red-Hair. 'If he *is* kidnapped, I hope he stays kidnapped, that's all. Have a look at his sleeping-bag. Did you ever see one like it?'

Larry and Pip peeped inside the marvellous tent.

Red-Hair pointed to a sleeping-bag at one side. It certainly was most magnificent, padded and quilted and marvelously embroidered.

'Try it,' said Red-Hair. 'I tried it once. It's like being floated away on a magic carpet or something when you get inside – soft as feathers!'

Pip wriggled inside. It certainly was an extraordinarily luxurious bag, and Pip felt that if he closed his eyes he would be wafted away into sleep at once. He wriggled down a little further and felt something hard against his leg. He put his hand down to feel what it was.

It was a button! A very fine button too, blue with a gold edge. Pip sat up and looked at it. Red-Hair glanced at it.

'One of the buttons off his pyjamas,' he said. 'You should have seen them! Blue and gold with those buttons to match.'

'Do you think I might keep it as a souvenir?' said Pip. He really wondered if by any chance it might turn out to be a clue!

'Gosh, what do you want a souvenir for? Are you daft?' said the second boy. 'Keep it if you want to. I don't reckon Wah-wah will want it again! If he loses a button, he'll be provided with a new set of pyjamas!'

'Did he leave his pyjamas behind?' asked Larry, thinking it might be a good idea to look at them.

'No. He went off in them,' said Red-Hair. 'That's what makes everyone think he was kidnapped. He'd have dressed himself if he had run away.'

Larry and Pip wandered out into the open air again. A loud voice suddenly hailed them.

'Larry! Pip! What you doing up here?' And there was Ern's plump face grinning at them from over the nearby hedge. 'Come on over! We've got *our* tent here!'

11. A LITTLE INVESTIGATION

'Hello, Ern!' said Larry, surprised. He had forgotten that Ern had been camping so near the big camp field. The faces of Sid and Perce now appeared, Perce grinning, Sid very solemn as usual.

Larry and Pip said good-bye to Red-Hair and his friends and squeezed through the hedge to Ern. Pip had put the pyjama button safely into his pocket. He didn't know whether it might be useful or not.

Ern proudly showed the two boys his tent. It was a very small and humble affair, compared with the magnificent one they had just left – but Ern, Sid, and Perce were intensely proud of it. They had never been camping before, and were enjoying it immensely.

There were no sleeping bags in the tent, merely old, worn rugs spread over a groundsheet. Three mugs, three broken knives, three spoons, two forks

('Perce lost his when he was bathing,' was Ern's mystifying explanation), three macintosh capes, three enamel plates, and a few other things.

'Fine, isn't it?' said Ern. 'We get water from the tap over in the camp field. They let us use it if we just go straight there and back. But they won't let the caravanners use it. So we get it for them, and in return they sometimes cook us a meal.'

There were a good many caravans scattered about, and also one or two more small tents. The caravan standing next to Ern's tent was empty, and a litter of papers was blowing about.

'The people there have gone,' said Ern. 'There was a woman and two kids – the kids were babies. Twins like Perce and Sid.'

'Ar,' said Sid, who was following them about, chewing. 'Ar.'

'What's he mean, arr-ing like that?' asked Pip, annoyed. 'Can't he ever talk properly?'

'Not while he has toffee in his mouth,' said Ern. 'Ma don't allow him so much when he's at home, of course, so he talks a bit more there. But here, when he can eat toffee all day long, he never says much except "Ar". Do you, young Sid?'

'Ar,' said Sid, trying to swallow the rest of his toffee quickly, and almost choking.

'He seems to want to say something,' said Pip, interestedly. 'Do you, Sid?'

'Ar,' said Sid frantically, going purple in the face.

'Oh, it's only to tell you about the twin babies, I expect,' said Ern. 'He was cracked on them, was our Sid. He used to go over to that caravan and pore over the pram for hours on end. He's dippy on babies.'

Pip and Larry looked at Sid with surprise. He didn't seem at all the kind of boy to be 'dippy on babies'.

Sid pointed down to the ground, where there were four different sets of pram wheel marks.

'There you are, you see – I said he wanted to tell you about them twins,' said Ern. 'He used to stand by their pram and pick up all the rattles and things they dropped. I bet he's ready to howl now they're gone. He's a funny one, Sid is.'

'Ar,' said Sid, in a strangled voice, and almost choked again.

'You're disgusting,' said Ern. 'You and your toffee. You've et a whole tin since yesterday. I'll tell Ma on you. You go and spit it out.'

Sid wandered away, evidently giving up all hope of proper conversation. Pip heaved a sigh of relief. Sid and his toffee gave him a nightmare feeling.

'Sid was proper upset this morning, when the twins went,' said Perce, entering amicably into the conversation. 'He went over to joggle the pram like he does when their mother wants them to go to sleep – but she yelled at him and chased him away. That made the babies yell too, and there wasn't half a set-to.'

'What did she want to do that to our Sid for?' said Ern, quite annoyed at anyone yelling at his Sid. 'He's been good to those smelly kids, he's wheeled their big pram up and down the field for hours.'

Pip and Larry were getting tired of all this talk about Sid and the babies. Who cared anyway?

'Ern, did you hear anything at all last night when Prince Bongawah was supposed to be kidnapped?' asked Larry. 'Did Sid or Perce?'

'No. We none of us heard anything,' said Ern, firmly. 'We all sleep like tops. Sid don't even wake if there is a thunderstorm bang over his head. The whole camp could have been kidnapped, and we wouldn't have known a thing. Good sleepers, the Goons are.'

Well, that was that. There didn't seem to be anything at all to be got from Ern. How maddening to know someone living just across the hedge from the prince, and to get nothing out of him at all!

'You did *see* the prince though, didn't you?' said Larry.

'Yes. I told you,' said Ern. 'He was a funny little fellow with a cocky little face. He made faces.'

'Made faces?' said Larry, in astonishment. 'What do you mean?'

'Well, whenever Sid or Perce or me peeped through the hedge, he'd see us and make a face,' said Ern. 'He may have been a prince, but he hadn't been brought up proper. Brown as a berry, of course.'

'Browner than us?' asked Pip.

''Bout the same,' said Ern.

'Why did you say that he and Bets were as alike as peas in a pod?' asked Pip, suddenly remembering this extraordinary remark of Ern's.

Ern blushed. 'Oh well, seemed as if brother and

sister ought to look alike,' he muttered, and busily kicked a stone along. 'Coo, I wonder what happened to his state umbrella! You should have seen it, Pip. Somebody came to visit him, and one of them put up this enormous umbrella – all blue and gold it was – and carried it over him. He didn't half scowl.'

'Didn't he like it then?' asked Pip.

'Well, everyone laughed and yelled and shouted,' said Ern. 'It looked a bit strange, you know.'

'Hello there!' suddenly came Fatty's voice over the hedge. 'Why did you wander off like that? You left me to do all the talking, Pip.'

'That's why I went,' said Pip. 'You like talking, Fatty, don't you?'

'Can we come through the hedge?' called Daisy's voice. 'Is there a place where we won't tear our clothes?'

Ern gallantly held aside some prickly branches as the girls squeezed through the hedge. Fatty followed. 'Nice cousin of yours, that fellow Ronald,' Fatty said to Pip. 'We had quite a chat.'

'You must have done quite a lot of "questioning of witnesses" then,' said Pip slyly, remembering the books Fatty had been studying a day or two before. 'Did you get any interesting information about this case?'

'Well, no,' said Fatty, who had actually spent the whole time relating some of his own exploits to the open-mouthed Ronald. 'No. I didn't gather much.'

'What about you, Pip?' asked Bets. 'Have you been questioning Ern, Sid and Perce?'

'Yes,' said Pip. 'But Larry and I didn't get much out of them. They slept all night long and didn't hear a thing. They haven't the faintest idea what happened to Prince Bongawah.'

'Ar,' said Sid, joining them suddenly. His jaws chewed frantically. Pip looked at him in disgust.

'Go away,' he said. 'And don't come back till you can say something else. I shall start "arring" myself in a minute. ARRRRRRRR!'

He made such a fierce noise that Sid gave him an alarmed glance and fled.

Pip took out the blue and gold button from his pocket and showed it to the others.

'This is the solitary clue – if it can be called a clue – that we've found,' he said. 'I found it in the sleeping bag belonging to the prince. It came off his blue and gold pyjamas.'

'Well, what use do you think that is?' asked Fatty. 'Is it going to help us to find out who kidnapped the prince, or when or how, or where he's gone? Not much of a clue, Pip.'

'No,' said Pip, pocketing the button again. 'I thought it wasn't. But you always tell us to examine everything and keep everything just in case. So I did. By the way, he didn't dress, he disappeared in his pyjamas.'

That made Fatty stare. 'Are you sure, Pip? Who told you?'

'The boys who slept in his tent,' said Pip.

'Well, that's funny,' said Fatty.

'Why?' asked Daisy. 'There wouldn't be any time, would there, for him to dress? Besides, wouldn't he disturb the other boys if he did?'

'Not if he stole outside in the dark when they were asleep,' said Fatty. 'He could take his clothes with him and dress quickly. Anyone wandering about in pyjamas would be spotted.'

'But Fatty, surely there wouldn't be *time* for anyone to dress if he was being kidnapped,' said

Daisy again. 'They'd just grab the prince out of his tent and make off with him, in his pyjamas.'

'Oh no, Daisy,' said Fatty. 'You're not being very clever. Kidnappers would never creep through a crowded field, falling over tent ropes and pegs, finding their way to one special tent, opening the flap, dragging out one special boy in the darkness, who would surely yell the place down. After all, he was called Bongawah-wah-wah because he howled so much.'

'Oh,' said Daisy. 'Yes, that was very silly of me. Of course kidnappers wouldn't do it like that. What do you think they did?'

'I think somebody arranged for him to steal out after lights-out,' said Fatty. 'Perhaps they said they'd take him to that Fair in the next town – it goes on till all hours! Something like that. You can't tell. And if he was going to be kidnapped, the kidnappers would find it easy – there he would be, waiting at the gate for them, already dressed, thinking what a lad he was.'

'I see – and they'd just whisk him away in a car and that would be that,' said Pip.

'Oh, *now* I see why you're surprised he was in

pyjamas,' said Daisy. 'If the kidnapping was planned in that way, he certainly wouldn't be in pyjamas!'

'Correct,' said Fatty, with a grin.

'Maybe he couldn't spot his clothes in the darkness,' suggested Ern, helpfully.

'This isn't a mystery, it's a silly sort of puzzle,' said Bets. 'Nobody heard anything, nobody saw anything. Nobody knows anything. I'm beginning to feel it couldn't have happened!'

12. SID FINDS HIS VOICE

'Come on – it's time we went,' said Fatty, getting bored. 'We're absolutely at a dead end here. Wherever Prince Bongawah is, he's probably still in his blue and gold pyjamas. Good luck to him!'

They rode off, waving good-bye to Ern and Perce. Sid was nowhere to be seen, for which everyone was thankful.

'He chews his toffee like a cow chewing the cud,' said Pip. 'Have you noticed how spotty he is? I really do believe he lives on toffee and nothing else.'

'I never want to see him again,' said Bets. 'He makes me feel sick.'

'Well, there's no reason why we ever *should* see him again,' said Fatty. 'So long as Ern comes alone to see us. *I* don't intend to visit dear Sid and Perce.'

But he did see Sid again, and that very evening

too! Fatty was trying on one of his newest disguises down in his shed, when there came a knock at the door.

Fatty looked through a hole, pierced in the door for spying, to see who was outside. Gosh – it was Ern – with Sid! How aggravating, just as he was going to practise this disguise.

Fatty turned quickly and looked at himself in the big mirror. He grinned. He'd try the disguise out on Ern and see if it worked!

Fatty opened the door. Ern stood outside, ready with a smile. Sid beside him. The smile faded as Ern saw, not Fatty, but a bent old man with side-whiskers, a straggly beard, shaggy white eyebrows, and wispy white hair on a bald pate. He was dressed in a loose, ill-fitting old coat, with dragged-down pockets, and corduroy trousers, wrinkled and worn.

'Oh, er, good evening,' said Ern, startled. 'Is, er, is Mr Frederick Trotteville in?'

The old man put a trembling hand behind one ear and said, 'Speak up! Don't mumble. What's that you say?' His voice was as quavery as his hand.

Ern shouted, 'IS MR FREDERICK IN?'

'Now don't you shout,' said the old man, in a cross voice. 'I'm not deaf. Who's Mr Frederick?'

Ern stared. Then he remembered that Fatty was always called Fatty. Perhaps this old man only knew him by that name.

'Fatty,' he said, loudly. 'FATTY.'

'You're a very rude boy,' said the old man, his voice quavering higher. 'Calling me names.'

'I'm not,' said Ern, desperately. 'Look here – where's the boy who lives here?'

'Gone,' said the old fellow, shaking his head, sadly. 'Gone to live in London.'

Ern began to think he must be in a dream. Fatty gone to London! Why, he'd only seen him an hour or so ago. He glanced anxiously at the shed. Had he come to the right place?

'Why has he gone?' he asked at last. 'Did he leave a message? And what are you doing here?'

'I'm his caretaker,' said the old fellow, and took out a big red handkerchief. He proceeded to blow his nose with such a loud trumpeting noise that Ern fell back, alarmed. Little did he know that Fatty was hiding his gulps of laughter in that big red handkerchief!

Sid backed away too. He slid down the path but Ern caught him by the arm.

'Oh no, you don't, Sid! You've come here to say something important, and say it you're going to, if it takes us all night to find Fatty. If you go back to the camp, you'll fill your mouth with toffee again, and we won't none of us get a word out of you! You're the only one of us with a real clue, and Fatty's going to know it!'

'I *say*! Has he really got a clue?' said the old man, in Fatty's crisp, clear voice. Ern jumped violently and looked all round. Where was Fatty?

The old man dug him in the ribs and went off into a cackle of laughter that changed suddenly into Fatty's cheerful guffaw. Ern stared at him open-mouthed. So did Sid.

'Lovaduck! It's *Fatty*!' cried Ern, overjoyed and astounded. 'You took me in properly. Coo, you're an old man to the life. How do you make yourself bald?'

'Just a wig,' said Fatty, lifting it off his head and appearing in his own thatch of hair. He grinned. 'I was practising this disguise when you came. It's a new wig, and new eyebrows, side-whiskers, and beard to match. Good, aren't they?'

'You're a marvel, Fatty, honest you are,' said Ern, wonderstruck. 'But your voice – and your laugh! You can't buy *them*! You ought to be on the stage.'

'Can't,' said Fatty. 'I'm going to be a detective. It's a help to be a good actor, of course. Come in. What's all this about Sid and a clue?'

'Well,' said Ern solemnly, 'it's like this. Sid wanted to tell us all something this afternoon and he couldn't, because of his toffee. Well, he worked and he worked at his toffee till it all went.'

'Tiring work,' said Fatty, sympathetically. 'And then, I suppose, he found his voice again. Can he really say something besides "ar"?'

'Well, not much,' said Ern honestly. 'But he did tell us something very strange – very strange indeed, Fatty. So I've brought him down here to tell *you*. It may be very, very important. Go on, Sid – you tell him.'

Sid cleared his throat and opened his mouth. 'Ar,' he began. 'Ar – you see, I heard them yelling. Ar, I did.'

'Who was yelling?' enquired Fatty.

'Ar, well,' said Sid, and cleared his throat again.

116

'They were yelling, see.'

'Yes. We know that,' said Fatty. 'Ar.'

That put Sid off. He gazed beseechingly at Ern. Ern looked back forbiddingly.

'See what happens to you when you get toffee mad?' he said. 'You lose your voice and you lose your senses. Let this be a lesson to you, young Sid.'

'Has he really come just to tell me somebody was yelling?' asked Fatty. 'Isn't there anything else?'

'Oh, yes. But praps I'd better tell you,' said Ern, and Sid's face cleared at once.

'Ar,' he said.

'And don't you interrupt,' said Ern, threateningly. Sid had no intention of interrupting at all. He shook his head vigorously, not even venturing another 'ar'.

'Well, this is what Sid told us,' said Ern, beginning to enjoy himself. 'It's peculiar, Fatty, honest it is. You'll hardly believe it.'

'Oh, get on Ern,' said Fatty. 'This may be important. Begin at the beginning, please.'

'I told you – at least I told Larry and Pip – that our Sid here is mad on babies,' said Ern. 'He's always going about joggling their prams and

117

picking up their toys and saying "Goo" to them. Well, next to our tent there's a caravan – you saw it. It's empty now. The people went today.'

Fatty nodded. He was listening hard.

'The woman in the caravan had a couple of twin babies,' said Ern. 'And being twins, Sid got more interested in them than usual – him and Perce being twins, you see. So he played with them a lot. Didn't you, Sid?'

'Ar,' said Sid, nodding.

'Well, this morning, Sid heard those babies yelling like anything,' said Ern, warming up to his tale. 'And he went over to joggle the pram. The woman was in the caravan, packing up, and when she saw our Sid there, she flew out at him and smacked him on the head. A fair clip it was! She told him to clear off.'

'Why?' asked Fatty. 'Sid was only doing what he'd been in the habit of doing. Had the woman ever objected before?'

'No,' said Ern. 'She let him wheel them up and sometimes down, too. And a heavy job it was, because it's a big double pram, made to take twins. Well, she smacked his head and Sid went off, upset like.'

'I don't wonder,' said Fatty, wondering when the point of all this long tale was coming. 'What came next?'

'The woman dragged the pram round to the back of the caravan,' said Ern, 'where she could keep her eye on it. But those babies still went on yelling, and our Sid here, he couldn't bear it.'

'Ar,' said Sid, feelingly.

'So when the woman took some things and went off down to one of the other caravans, Sid popped over to the pram to see what was the matter with the babies,' said Ern. 'They sounded as if they was sitting on a safety pin or something. Anyway, Sid put his hand down under them and scrabbled about like – *and he felt somebody else down in that big pram*, Fatty!'

Fatty was really startled. He sat up straight. 'Somebody else!' he said, incredulously. 'What do you mean?'

'Well – just that,' said Ern. 'Sid felt somebody else, and he pulled the clothes back just a little bit, and saw the back of a dark head, and a bit of dark cheek. Then one of the babies grabbed at Sid, and rolled over and hid whoever it was in the pram.'

Fatty was astounded. He sat silent for a minute. Then he looked at Sid. 'Who did you think it was in the pram?' he asked.

'The prince,' said Sid, quite forgetting to say 'ar' in his excitement. 'He was hiding there. He didn't know I saw him. Ar.'

'*Well*!' said Fatty, taking all this in. 'So *that's* what happened. He simply crept out of his tent in his pyjamas, and hid in the caravan for the night – and in the early morning, the woman packed him into the bottom of that big pram, hidden under the babies! How uncomfortable! He must have been all screwed up – and awfully hot.'

'Ar,' said Sid, nodding.

'Then the woman must have got someone to fetch all her goods, and wheeled the pram away herself, with the little prince in it,' said Fatty. 'Nobody would guess. But why did it happen? What has *she* got to do with it? Why did the prince creep away to her? Gosh – it's a mystery all right!'

'I thought you'd be pleased, Fatty,' said Ern, happily. 'Good thing Sid got rid of his toffee, wasn't it? That's what he was trying to tell us this afternoon. Almost choked himself trying to get the news out.'

'It's a pity he didn't tell somebody as soon as he knew this,' said Fatty.

'He did try,' said Ern. 'But I just thought he wanted to go swimming or something when he kept pointing to the caravan. Sid's never very talkative, even in the ordinary way. His tongue never grew properly, Ma says.'

'I'll have to think what to do,' said Fatty. 'Ern, you must go and tell your uncle. I said we'd tell him everything we found out. You'd better go and tell him straight away.'

'Lovaduck! I can't do that!' said poor Ern. 'Why, he'd give me such a scolding that I wouldn't recover for a month of Sundays!'

13. MR GOON HEARS THE NEWS

All the same, Ern had to go. Fatty didn't want to ring up the Chief Inspector quite so soon after his ticking-off – and if Goon knew, he could report the matter himself. So poor Ern was sent off to Goon's with Sid trailing behind. Neither of them felt very happy about it.

Mr Goon was in his kitchen at the back of his house. He was alone – and he was practising. Not disguises, like Fatty. He was trying to 'let his tongue go loose', as Fatty had advised. *Could* he 'talk foreign' by merely letting his tongue go loose?

He stood there, trying to make his tongue work. 'Abbledy, abbledy, abbledy,' he gabbled, and then paused. For some reason, 'abbledy' seemed the only thing he could think of. He tried to remember the string of foreign-sounding words that Fatty had fired off the other afternoon, but he couldn't.

Surely it must be easy to say a string of rubbish?

But it wasn't. His tongue merely stopped when it was tired of saying 'abbledy', and his brain could think of nothing else at all.

Mr Goon tried reciting.

'The boy stood on the burning deck, abbledy, gabbledy, abbledy. No, it's no good.'

Meanwhile, Ern and Sid had arrived. Ern didn't like to knock in case his uncle was having a nap, as he so often did. He turned the handle of the front door. It wouldn't open, so he thought it must be locked from the inside.

'Come on round to the back, Sid,' said Ern. 'He might be in the garden.'

They tiptoed round to the back, and came to the kitchen window. It was wide open. A noise came from inside the room. 'He's there,' whispered Ern. 'He's talking. He must have a visitor.'

They listened. 'Abbledy, abbledy, abbledy,' they heard. 'Abbledy, abbledy, ABBLEDY.'

Ern looked at Sid, startled. That was his uncle's voice. What was he gabbling about? Ern cautiously poked his head a bit further forward and peeped in at the corner of the window. Yes – his uncle was there with his back to him, standing on the rug, looking at himself in the mirror and gabbling his curious rubbish on and on.

Ern didn't like it at all. Had his uncle got a stroke of the sun? Was he out of his mind?

'Abbledy, abbledy,' came again and again. And then, suddenly, 'The boy stood on the burning deck.'

That decided Ern. He wasn't going to interfere in anything like this, important clue or not. He stole down by the side of the house, and made his way to the front gate. But alas, Mr Goon had heard footsteps, and was at the front door at once. He was just in time to see Ern and Sid opening the gate.

'What you doing here this time of the evening?' he roared. 'What you doing going out before you've even come in? You been listening outside the window?'

Ern was terrified. He stood trembling at the gate with Sid.

'Uncle, we only came to tell you something,' quavered Ern. 'A clue. Most important.'

'Aha!' said Goon. 'So that's it. Come along in then. Why didn't you say so before?'

He just stopped himself saying, 'abbledy, abbledy.' He must be careful. He'd gone and got that on his mind now!

Ern and Sid came in, treading like cats on hot bricks. Mr Goon took them into his sitting-room. He sat down in his big armchair, crossed his legs, put his hands together and looked up at the two boys.

'So you've got a clue,' he said. 'What is it?'

Sid couldn't say a word, of course, not even 'ar'. Ern was almost as bad. However, it all came out with a rush at last.

'Uncle, Sid found the clue. You know that Prince Bongawah that was kidnapped? Well, he wasn't. He put himself in a pram with twin babies and he was wheeled away this morning.'

Mr Goon listened to this with the utmost disbelief. Put himself in a pram? With twins! And got himself wheeled away! What nonsense was this?

Mr Goon rose up, big and terrible. 'And why did you come and tell me this ridiculous nonsense?' he began. 'Why don't you go and tell it to that big boy? Let *him* believe you! I won't. Cock-and-bull story! Gah! How DARE you come

125

and tell me such a tale?'

'Fatty told us to,' blurted out poor Ern, almost crying with fright. 'We told him and *he* believed us. He said we were to tell *you*, Uncle, really he did. To help you.'

Mr Goon swelled up till Ern and Sid thought he must be going to burst all the buttons off his already-tight tunic. He towered above them.

'You go and tell that toad of a boy that I'm not such an idiot as he thinks I am,' he bellowed. 'You tell him to take his tales of prams and twin babies to the Chief Inspector. Sending you here to fill me up with nonsense like that! I'm ashamed of you, Ern. For two pins, I'd give you a hiding. How DARE you!'

Ern and Sid fled. They fled down the hall passage, through the front door, and out of the gate without waiting for another word. Sid was crying. Ern was white. Why had Fatty sent him on such an errand? He, Ern, had known quite well that his uncle wouldn't believe him. And he hadn't.

'Come on back to the camp,' panted Ern. 'We'll be safe there. Run, Sid, run!'

Poor Ern didn't even think of going back to

Fatty's to tell him what had happened. He and Sid fled for their lives, looking over their shoulders every now and again, fearful that Mr Goon might be after them.

Perce was thankful he hadn't gone with them when he heard their tale. He was just as much scared of his uncle as the others. Ern had often told him and Sid dreadful tales of the time when he had been to stay with Mr Goon – the punishments and shoutings-at that he had had.

'Still, it was worth it,' Ern would end cheerfully. 'I made friends with those five kids – specially with Fatty. He's a wonder, that boy!'

Meantime the 'wonder boy' was having a quiet little think to himself about Sid's surprising piece of news. It was all very, very extraordinary. Could Sid possibly be right? Could it really have been the young prince huddled down in that big double pram? Of course, such a trick *had* been played before, to get people away in secret.

Just have to take out the two seats, put the person in the well of the pram, and stick the babies on top of him, thought Fatty. Yes – it's easy enough. But why, why, why, did the prince creep through the hedge at night and get himself parked in the pram the following day?

It was a puzzle. Fatty thought he had better sleep on it, and then discuss it with the others in the morning. He wondered what Mr Goon had thought of Ern's appearance and news. Was he acting on it? Had he telephoned the Chief Inspector?

Fatty half-expected Mr Goon to telephone him for his opinion on Ern's news. But no, on second thoughts he wouldn't, decided Fatty. He would want to work out things on his own, so that he could say he had done everything himself.

Well, let him, thought Fatty. If he can unravel the puzzle more quickly than I can, good luck to him! I'm in a real muddle. Why – when – where – how – and, particularly, *why*, seem quite unanswerable!

Fatty telephoned Larry.

'Is that you, Larry? Meet in my shed tomorrow morning, half past nine, sharp. Most important and mysterious developments. Ern and Sid have just been down with amazing news.'

'Great!' came Larry's voice, tense with excitement. 'What is it? Tell me a bit, Fatty!'

'Can't say it over the phone,' said Fatty.

'Anyway, it's most important. Half past nine sharp.'

He rang off, leaving Larry in a state of such terrific excitement that he could hardly prevent himself from rushing down to Fatty's at once! Daisy and he spent the whole evening trying to think of what Fatty's mysterious news could be – without any success, of course.

Fatty telephoned Pip next. Mrs Hilton answered the phone. 'Pip's in the bath,' she said. 'Can I take a message?'

Fatty hesitated. Mrs Hilton was not at all encouraging where mysteries were concerned. In fact, she had several times said that Pip and Bets must keep out of them. Perhaps, on the whole, it would be best not to say much. Still, he could ask for Bets.

So Bets came to the telephone, in her dressing-gown, having a feeling that Fatty had some news.

'Hello Fatty,' came her voice. 'Anything up?'

'Yes,' said Fatty, in a solemn voice. 'Extraordinary news has just come through – from Ern and Sid. Can't tell you over the phone. Meet here at half past nine tomorrow morning, sharp.'

'*Fatty*!' squealed Bets, thrilled. 'You *must* tell me something about it. Quick! Nobody's about, it's quite safe.'

'I can't possibly tell you over the phone,' said Fatty, enjoying all this importance. 'All I can say is that it's very important, and will need a lot of discussion and planning. The real mystery is about to begin, Bets!'

'Ooooh,' said Bets. 'All right – half past nine tomorrow. I'll go straight away and tell Pip.'

'Now don't you go shouting all this through the bathroom door,' said Fatty, in alarm.

'No, I suppose I'd better not,' said Bets. 'I'll wait till he comes out. But I'll jolly well go and hurry him though!'

Pip was so thrilled at this sudden and unexpected telephone call that he, like Larry, almost felt inclined to dress and shoot off to Fatty. But as his mother would certainly be most annoyed to find him dressing again and going out after a hot bath, he reluctantly decided he must wait.

Fatty sat in his bedroom and thought. He thought hard, turning over in his mind all the things he knew about the young prince. He got the encyclopaedia and looked up Tetarua. He found a store catalogue of his mother's which, most fortunately, pictured not only a single pram but a double one as well, with measurements.

Fatty decided it would be the easiest thing in the world to hide someone at the bottom of a double pram. Probably the most uncomfortable thing in the world too, he thought. I wonder what old Goon is making of all this!

Goon wasn't making anything of it at all. He just simply didn't believe a word, so he had nothing to puzzle over. 'Gah!' he said, and dismissed the matter completely!

14. TALKING AND PLANNING

Before half past nine had struck, the Five Find-Outers (and Dog) were all gathered together in Fatty's shed. Buster was very pleased to welcome them. He pranced round in delight, and finally got on to Bets' knee.

'Now Fatty – don't keep us waiting – tell us exactly what's happened,' said Larry, firmly. 'Don't go all mysterious and solemn. Just tell us!'

So Fatty told them. They listened in astonishment.

'Hidden in the *pram*!' said Larry. 'Then the prince must have known that woman very well. She must have been camping nearby for a reason.'

'Do you think she could have been the prince's nurse, and knew perhaps he wasn't happy at camp, and arranged to smuggle him away?' said Bets.

'Bright idea, Bets,' said Fatty, approvingly. 'I thought of that myself. But the twin babies are rather a difficulty there. I don't feel the prince would have a nurse with twin babies somehow.'

'She might have been an *old* nurse of his, and got married, and had twins,' said Bets, using her imagination.

'It's not much good having theories and ideas about all this until we get a few more actual details,' said Fatty. 'I mean, we must find out who the woman is, if the caravan belongs to her, if she came there when the prince arrived, if those babies are really hers, or borrowed so that she could take that big double pram for hiding purposes – oh, there are a whole lot of things to find out!'

'And are we to snoop round and find all these details?' asked Daisy. 'I rather like doing that.'

'There's a great deal to find out,' said Fatty. 'We'll have to get busy. Anyone seen the papers this morning?'

'I just glanced at them,' said Larry, 'but I was really too excited to read anything. Why?'

'Only because there's a bit more about the prince and his country in today,' said Fatty. He spread a newspaper on the floor and pointed to a column.

Everyone read it.

'Well, as you will see,' said Fatty, 'Tetarua isn't a very big country, but it's quite important from the point of view of the British, because there's a fine airfield there we want to use. So we've been quite friendly with them.'

'And they've sent their young prince here to be educated,' said Larry. 'But, according to the paper, there's a row on in Tetarua between the present king and his cousin, who says *he* ought to be king.'

'Yes. And the possibilities are that the cousin has sent someone over here to capture Prince Bongawah, so that, if he doesn't ever appear again, he, the cousin, will be king,' said Fatty. 'There are no brothers or sisters apparently.'

'An old, old plot,' said Larry. 'Do you suppose they will demand a ransom for the prince?'

'No,' said Fatty. 'I think they want to put him out of the way for good.'

There was a silence after this. Nobody liked to think of the young prince being 'put away for good'. Bets shivered.

Daisy rubbed her forehead, puzzled. 'And yet – though that's what the papers say – *we* know differently,' she said. '*We* know he wasn't kidnapped in the way they think, just swept out of his tent and rushed off in a car somewhere. *We* know that, of his own free will, apparently, he crept out of his tent in his pyjamas, went through the hedge to that caravan, and allowed himself to be hidden and wheeled away in that pram! That couldn't be called kidnapping.'

'No. It couldn't,' said Fatty. 'There's something strange about this. I believe Sid, you know. For one thing, he would never, ever have the imagination to make up all that.'

'Did you ring the Chief Inspector?' said Pip. 'What did he say?'

'Well, as a matter-of-fact, I didn't telephone him,' said Fatty. 'I don't feel he's very pleased with me at the moment – with any of us, as a matter-of-fact – so I sent Ern and Sid round to Mr Goon, to tell *him*. He would naturally ring up the Chief Inspector himself, and get his own orders.'

'But wouldn't the Chief Inspector ring *you*, when he got Mr Goon's message?' asked Pip.

'I rather thought he might,' said Fatty, who was feeling a little hurt because there had been no word at all from the Chief Inspector. 'I expect he's still peeved with me. Well, I won't bother him till I've got something first rate to tell him. Let Mr Goon get on with his own ideas about this – we'll get on with ours! At least I've passed on Sid's information to him.'

There was another silence. 'It's rather a peculiar mystery really,' said Bets at last. 'There doesn't actually seem anywhere to *begin*. What do we do first?'

'Well, as *I* see it, we had better follow up the definite clues we have,' said Fatty. 'We must first of all find out about that woman – who she is. Get her address. Interview her. Try and frighten something out of her. If she is hiding the prince, we must find out where. And why.'

'Yes,' said Larry. 'We must do all that. Hadn't we better begin before Mr Goon gets going? He'll probably be working along the same lines as us.'

'Yes. I suppose he will,' said Fatty, getting up. 'This part is pretty obvious to anyone – even to Mr Goon! Well, let's hope we don't bump into him today. He'll be annoyed if we do!'

'Woof,' said Buster joyfully.

'He says he hopes we *do* bump into him,' said Bets, hugging the little Scottie. 'You love Mr Goon's ankles, don't you Buster? Nicest ankles in the world, aren't they? Biteable and snappable and nippable.'

Everyone laughed. 'You're an idiot, Bets,' said Pip. 'Are we going up to the camp, Fatty? We shall have to find out who lets out those caravans, and see if we can get the name and the address of the woman who was in the one with the twin babies.'

'Yes. That's the first thing to do,' said Fatty. 'Everyone got bikes?'

Everyone had. Buster was put into Fatty's basket, and off they all went, ringing their bells loudly at every corner, just in *case* Mr Goon was coming round in the opposite direction!

Ern, Sid, and Perce were most delighted to see them. Fatty looked at Sid, but when he saw his jaws working rhythmically as usual, he snorted.

'Not much good asking Sid anything,' he said. 'We'll only be able to get "ar" out of him. Sid, if you get many more spots, you'll be clapped into hospital and treated for measles!'

Sid looked alarmed. Ern spoke to him sternly. 'Go and spit it out. You're a disgrace to the Goon family.'

'Ar,' said Sid, looking really pathetic.

'He can't spit it out,' said Perce. 'It's not the kind of toffee for that. Try some, Ern, and see.'

'No thanks,' said Ern. 'Well, count Sid out of this, Fatty. He's hopeless.'

'Yes – but he's quite important,' said Fatty. 'Well, he'll just have to nod or shake his head, that's all, when I ask him questions. Sid, come here. Stop chewing and listen. I'm going to ask you some questions. Nod your head for "yes", and shake it for "no". Understand?'

'Ar,' said Sid, and nodded his head so violently that some of the toffee went down the wrong way and he choked.

Ern thumped him on his back till his eyes almost fell out of his head. At last, Sid was ready again, and listening.

'Sid, do you know the woman's name?' asked Fatty.

'Ar,' said Sid and shook his head.

'Did you ever see her speaking to the prince?'

asked Fatty.

'Ar,' said Sid and shook his head again.

'Don't keep saying "ar" like that,' said Fatty, aggravated. 'It's positively maddening. Just shake or nod, that's all. Did you see where the woman went when she wheeled away the pram?'

Sid shook his head dumbly.

'Do you know ANYTHING about her except that she had twins and lived in that caravan?' asked Fatty, despairing of ever getting anything out of Sid at all. Sid's head was well and truly shaken again.

'A man in a lorry came to get the things out of the caravan,' volunteered Perce, unexpectedly.

'What was the name on the lorry?' asked Fatty at once.

'Wasn't none,' said Perce.

'Well, a fat lot of help you and Sid are,' said Fatty in disgust. 'You don't know a thing – not even the name of the woman!'

'Oogleby-oogleby,' said Sid suddenly, looking excited. Everyone looked at him.

'Now what does *that* mean?' wondered Fatty. 'Say it again, Sid – if you can.'

'Ooogleby-oogleby-*oogle*by!' said Sid valiantly,

going red in the face.

'He's talking foreign, isn't he?' said Ern, with a laugh at his own wit. 'Here, Sid – write it down. And mind your spelling!'

Sid took Ern's pencil and wrote painfully on a page of his notebook. Everyone crowded round to see what he had written.

'MARGE and BURT', Sid had printed.

'Marge and Burt,' said Larry. 'Does he mean margarine and butter?'

Everyone looked at Sid. He shook his head at once, and then pretended to hold something in his arms and rock it.

'*Now* what's he doing?' wondered Bets. 'Rock-a-bye baby – Sid, you're dippy!'

'Oh, *I* know, he's pretending to be holding two babies – he must have written the names of the twins!' cried Daisy. Sid nodded, pleased.

'Ar,' he said. 'Oooogly-oogly.'

'Well, I don't know if it's going to help us to know the name of those twin babies,' said Fatty, looking extremely doubtful, 'but I suppose it might. Thanks for your help, Sid – such as it is. Ern, see he doesn't eat any more toffee. Honestly, it's disgraceful.'

'What are we going to do now?' asked Pip.

'We're going to find out who lets these caravans and see if they'll tell us the name and address of the woman who took that one,' said Fatty, waving towards the empty caravan nearby. 'Come on. We'll go now.'

'Can I come too?' asked Ern eagerly. But Fatty said no, he'd no bicycle. He didn't want Ern, Sid, and Perce trailing round them all morning. It would look rather conspicuous to go about in such a large company.

'All right,' said Ern, mournfully. 'Spitty.'

Bets looked at him in delight. 'Oh, *Ern*! I'd forgotten you used to say that, when you meant "It's a pity". Fatty – don't you remember how he used to run all his words together when we knew him before?'

'Yes,' said Fatty, getting on his bike. 'Swunderful! Smarvellous! Smazing!'

15. AN INTERESTING MORNING

And now began a morning of real investigation for the Find-Outers. They rode off down to Marlow, where the agent lived who let the caravans. Fatty had copied down the address from a big notice in the field.

'CARAVANS TO LET,' it said, 'APPLY CARAVANS LTD, TIP HILL, MARLOW.'

They found Tip Hill, which was a little road leading up a hill. Halfway up, in a small field, stood a caravan marked, 'CARAVANS LTD. Apply here for caravans to be let.'

'Here we are,' said Fatty. 'Who would like to do this part?'

'Oh you, Fatty,' said Bets. 'You always do this sort of thing so well. We'll come and listen.'

'No, you won't,' said Fatty. 'I'm not going to have a lot of giggling and nudging going on behind

142

me. If I do this, I do it alone.'

'All right – do it alone,' said Pip.

Fatty went in through the little gate and up to the door of the caravan. He knocked on it.

It opened, and a youth stood there with a cigarette hanging from the side of his mouth.

'Hello!' he said. 'What you want?'

'I'm anxious to find the person who rented one of the caravans next to the school camp field,' said Fatty. 'Could you tell me her name and address, please? I'd be most obliged. She left before I could ask her what I wanted to know.'

'My word – aren't we la-di-da!' said the youth. 'Think I've got time to hunt up names and addresses of your caravan friends, Mister?'

Fatty glanced at the side of the caravan. He saw the name of the owners there in small letters. 'Reg and Bert Williams.' He guessed the youth was just an employee.

'Oh well, if you haven't time, I'll go and ask Mr Reginald Williams,' said Fatty, at a venture. He turned away.

The youth almost fell down the caravan steps. 'Ere, you! Why didn't you tell me you knew Mr Reg?' he called. 'I'll get the address if you wait half a tick.'

Fatty grinned. It was nice to bring that lazy little monkey to heel! 'Very well. But make haste,' said Fatty.

The youth made haste. Fatty thought that Mr Reg, whoever he was, must be a pretty terrifying person if he could shake up a fellow like this merely at the mention of his name! The youth hunted through a large file and produced a list of the caravans up on the hill by the school camp field.

'Now which caravan is it?' he asked. Fatty had noted the name, of course.

'It was called "River View",' he said. 'Quite a small one.'

The youth ran his finger down a list. 'Ah – here we are – Mrs Storm, 24 Harris Road, Maidenbridge. That's not far from here – 'bout two miles.'

'Thanks,' said Fatty, and wrote it down.

'You going to see Mr Reg?' asked the youth, anxiously, as Fatty turned to go.

'No,' said Fatty, much to the youth's relief. He went out to where the others were waiting.

'Got it!' he said, and showed them the name

and address. 'Mrs Storm, 24 Harris Road, Maidenbridge. About two miles from here. Come on – let's get going.'

Feeling rather excited, the five rode off to Maidenbridge. Had Mrs Storm got the prince? Would she tell them anything at all?

They came into Maidenbridge, and asked for Harris Road. It turned out to be a narrow, rather dirty little street, set with houses in a terrace.

They arrived at number 24. It was even dirtier than the rest in the street. Ragged curtains hung at the windows, and the front door badly wanted a lick of paint.

'I'll tackle this too,' said Fatty. 'You ride to the end of the street and wait for me. It looks funny for so many of us to be standing at the front door.'

Obediently, the others rode off. Fatty stood his bicycle at the kerb and knocked. An untidy woman, her hair half down her back, opened it. She said nothing, but just looked at Fatty, waiting.

'Oh – er, excuse me,' said Fatty, 'are you Mrs Storm?'

'No. I'm not,' said the woman. 'You've come to the wrong house. She don't live here.'

This was a bit of a shock.

'Has she left then?' asked Fatty.

'She never did live here, far as I know,' said the woman. 'I've bin here seventeen years, with my husband and my old Ma – I don't know no Mrs Storm. Not even in this street, I don't.'

'How strange,' said Fatty. He looked at the paper with the name and address on. 'Look – it says Mrs Storm, 24 Harris Road, Maidenbridge.'

'Well, that's this house all right – but there's no Mrs Storm,' said the woman. 'There's no other Harris Road but this, either. Why don't you go to the post office? They'll tell you where she lives.'

'Oh thanks, I will,' said Fatty, 'sorry to have troubled you for nothing.' He departed on his bike, puzzled. He joined the others, told them of his failure, and then they all cycled to the post office.

'I want to find someone's address here please,' said Fatty, who was certainly in command that morning. 'I've been given the wrong address, I'm afraid. Could you tell me where a Mrs Storm lives?'

The clerk got out a directory and pushed it across to Fatty. 'There you are,' he said. 'You'll find all the Storms there, hail, thunder, and snow!'

'Ha, ha, joke,' said Fatty politely. He took the directory and looked for STORM. Ah – there were three Storms in Maidenbridge.

'Lady Louisa Storm,' he read out to the others. 'Old Manor Gate. No, that can't be her. She wouldn't rent a caravan. Here's another – Miss Emily Storm.'

'She wouldn't have twin babies, she's a Miss,' said Bets. 'We want a Mrs.'

'Mrs Rene Storm,' read out Fatty. 'Caldwell House. Well, that seems to be the only one that's likely.'

They left the post office. Fatty turned to Daisy. 'Now *you* can do this bit, Daisy,' he said. 'You must find out if Mrs Rene Storm has twin children.'

'Oh, I *can't*,' said Daisy, in a fright. 'I simply can't walk up and say, "Have you got twin babies?" She would think I was mad.'

'So you would be if you did it like that,' said Fatty. 'Now – you're a Find-Outer, and you haven't had much practice lately. You think of a good way of finding out what we want to know, and go and do it. We'll sit in some ice cream shop and wait for you.'

Poor Daisy! She racked her brains frantically

as they all rode along to find Caldwell House. It was a little house set in a pretty garden. Round the corner was a café, and here Fatty and the others sat down to have ice creams and wait for Daisy.

'A nice big double ice cream for you, Daisy, when you come back with your news,' said Fatty. 'In fact, a treble one if this Mrs Storm is the right one. Remember, we only want to know if she has twin babies.'

Daisy rode off. She rode round a block of houses two or three times, trying to think how she could find out what Fatty wanted to know. And then an idea came to her. How simple after all!

She rode to Caldwell House, and put her bicycle by the fence. She walked up to the front door and rang the bell. A little wizened maid opened the door. She looked about ninety, Daisy thought!

'Please excuse me if I've come to the wrong house,' said Daisy, with her nicest smile, 'but I'm looking for a Mrs Storm who has twin babies. Is this the right house?'

'Dear me, no,' said the little maid. 'My Mrs Storm is eighty-three, and she's a great-grandmother. She has never had twins, neither have her children, nor her grandchildren. No twins in the family at all. I'm sorry.'

'So am I,' said Daisy, not quite knowing what else to say. 'Er – well, thank you very much. I'm afraid she's not the Mrs Storm I'm looking for.'

She escaped thankfully and rode quickly to the ice cream shop. The others were pleased to see her come in beaming.

'Is it the right woman?' said Fatty.

'No, I'm afraid not,' said Daisy. 'I'm only beaming because I managed it all right. This Mrs Storm is eighty-three and a great-grandmother – and there aren't any twins in her family at all.'

'Gosh,' said Fatty dolefully. 'Now we're at a dead end then. That wretched caravan woman gave a false name and address. We might have guessed that! We can go hunting the country up and down all we like, but we'll never find a Mrs Storm with twins!'

'Where's my ice cream?' said Daisy.

'Oh, *sorry* Daisy!' said Fatty. 'What am I thinking of! Waitress, a double ice cream please – and another single one all round.'

As they ate their ice creams, they discussed what to do next. 'Could we possibly look about for twin babies?' asked Bets.

'It's *possible*,' said Fatty, 'but I feel it would take rather a time, looking for all the twin babies there are in this district!'

'How would you set about it, Bets?' asked Pip, eyeing her teasingly. 'Put up a notice – "Wanted, twin babies. Apply Bets Hilton".'

'Don't be silly,' said Bets. 'Anyway, have you got a better idea? What *can* we do next? We haven't a single clue now.'

'Only my button,' said Pip, and pulled out his blue and gold button. He put it down on the table. They all looked at it. It really was a beautiful button.

'Beautiful, but completely useless as a clue,' said Fatty. 'Still, keep it if it pleases you, Pip. If you happen to see a pair of blue and gold pyjamas on a washing line with one button missing, you'll be lucky!'

'Well, that's an idea,' said Pip. 'I shall look at all the lines of washing I see. You just never know!' He put the button back into his pocket.

'What about baby shows?' said Daisy, suddenly. 'We might see twin babies there, and find out where they live.'

'*Baby* shows!' said Pip, in disgust. 'Well, if anyone's going to snoop round baby shows, it won't be me. You and Bets can do that.'

Bets gave a little exclamation, and pointed dramatically to a notice on the wall of the shop. They all looked, and jumped in surprise.

'BABY SHOW,' said the notice. 'At Tiplington Fair, 4 September. Special prizes for TWINS.'

16. OFF TO TIPLINGTON FAIR

'Funny coincidence,' said Fatty, with a laugh. 'Now, let's see – where's Tiplington? Other side of Peterswood, isn't it?'

'You don't *really* think there's anything in Bets' idea, do you?' said Pip, in surprise.

'Well, there's just a chance, I suppose,' said Fatty. 'Bets has had good ideas before. Will you and Daisy go over, Bets?'

'Yes,' said Bets promptly and Daisy nodded. 'Why can't you boys come too? After all, it's a Fair. It should be quite fun. We could take Ern too – he might recognise the twins if they *did* happen to be there!'

'Right. We will take Ern,' said Fatty. 'But not Sid or Perce.'

'I don't mind Perce so much, but I can't bear Sid,' said Bets. 'He's so *chewy*.'

'I can think of a lot more things I don't like about Sid,' said Larry.

'So can we all. Let's change the subject,' said Fatty, feeling in his pocket for money. 'Now, how many ice creams did we have?'

'Oh, Fatty – don't pay for all of them,' said Daisy. 'Larry and I have got plenty of pocket money today.'

'My treat,' said Fatty. 'I'm your chief, don't forget, and I expect to pay some of the – er – expenses we run up.'

'Thank you, Fatty,' said Bets. 'You're a very, very *nice* chief.'

'The fourth of September is tomorrow,' said Daisy. 'I hope it's fine. Who'll tell Ern?'

'Pip,' said Fatty, promptly. 'He hasn't done much in the way of jobs today – you and Bets and I seem to have done most. Pip's turn to do something.'

'All right,' said Pip. 'But if Sid comes "arring" at me I shall throw him into the river.'

'Do,' said Fatty. 'It will probably make him swallow all his toffee at once and get rid of it!'

They decided to meet the next day at Larry's, and all go over to Tiplington together on their bicycles. Ern was to join them at Larry's too, and

Larry would borrow an old bicycle for him.

'Two o'clock,' said Fatty. 'And tell Ern to wash his face and brush his hair and clean his nails, and put on a clean shirt if he's got one. My orders.'

Ern took these orders in good part. Nothing that Fatty said could ever annoy him. 'He's the cat's whiskers,' he told Pip. 'A genius, he is. Right, I'll be there, all spruced up, like. What are we going over to the Fair for? Anything cooking?'

'Might be,' said Pip. 'Don't be late, Ern.'

'I won't,' said Ern. 'Slong!'

It took Pip a moment or two to realise what 'Slong' meant. Of course – 'So long!' Where did Ern learn to mix up his words like that? 'Slong!' What a word!

Ern set off joyfully to go to Larry's the next day. He had difficulty in stopping Sid and Perce from coming too. 'Well, you can't,' he said. 'Look at your hair – and your faces – and your nails – and your shirts! Disgraceful! You can't go out in company like that.'

'Well, it's the first time you've brushed your hair or cleaned your nails,' grumbled Perce.

Ern walked down to the river and took the little

ferry boat across. He then walked to Larry's. On the way, to his horror, he met his uncle. Mr Goon advanced on him, even redder in the face than usual, with the heat.

'Ha! Young Ern again!' he began. 'And where may *you* be off to, I'd like to know! You got any more fairy tales for me about princes in prams with twin babies?'

'No, Uncle. No,' said Ern. 'I'm afraid I can't wait. I mustn't be late.'

'Where you going?' asked Mr Goon, and a heavy hand descended on Ern's shoulder.

'To Larry's,' said Ern. Mr Goon looked him over carefully. 'You're all dressed up – hair brushed and all,' he said. 'What are you up to?'

'Nothing, I tell you, Uncle,' said poor Ern. 'We're all going over to Tiplington Fair, that's all.'

'What – that potty little Fair?' said Mr Goon in astonishment. 'What are you going there for? Has that big boy got something up his sleeve?'

'He might have,' said Ern, wriggling free with a sudden movement. 'He's brainy, he is. He believes the things I tell him, see? Not like you! We're investigating hard, we are! And for all you know, we're on to something!'

He ran down the road, leaving Mr Goon breathing hard. Now, did Ern mean what he said? Was there something going on at Tiplington that he, Mr Goon, ought to know about? Why was that toad of a boy taking all his lot over there?

Mr Goon went home, brooding over the matter. He suddenly made up his mind. He would go to Tiplington too! He ought to keep an eye on that boy anyway. You never knew when he would smell out something.

Mr Goon wheeled out his bicycle and mounted it with a sigh. He didn't like bicycling in hot weather. He was sure it wasn't good for him. But duty called, and off he went.

He started before the others, who had waited for Ern, and had had an ice cream each in the sweetshop in the village before they set off. Buster was in Fatty's bicycle basket as usual, his tongue hanging out contentedly. He was at his very happiest when he was with all the Find-Outers together.

Ern was happy too. He had forgotten about his uncle. He was proud to be with the Find-Outers, and proud that they wanted him. He beamed all over his plain, plump face.

'Slovely,' he kept saying. 'Streat.'

'What do you mean – Street?' asked Daisy, trying to work it out.

'He means, it's a treat,' said Bets laughing.

'SwatIsaid,' said Ern, puzzled.

'Swatesaid,' chorussed everyone in delight.

They rode off down the lanes to Tiplington. After about a mile, they caught sight of a familiar figure in dark blue, labouring at the pedals of his bicycle.

'It's Mr Goon!' said Pip, in surprise. 'Surely *he's* not going to Tiplington too! Don't say he's visiting the baby show as well! Ern! Did you tell him we were going to the Fair?'

Ern went red. 'Well, yes, I did,' he said. 'Didn't I ought to have? I didn't think it mattered?'

'You certainly ought not to have,' said Fatty, annoyed. 'Now we shall have him shadowing us all the time. Still, he probably won't want to do the important thing – look at the twins in the baby show! You'll have to take Ern into the baby show with you, Bets and Daisy – in case you want him to identify any twins.'

'Coo,' said Ern. 'Let me off the baby show! I'm not Sid. I'd run a mile from a baby show!'

'Well, you won't run a mile from this one,' said Daisy, firmly. 'If there are any likely twins, I shall fetch you in, Ern. So don't dare to disappear.'

'Sawful,' said poor Ern. 'Really, sawful this.'

'Sagonizing,' said Fatty. 'Sunendurable.'

'You talking foreign again?' asked Ern, with interest.

'Not more than you are,' said Fatty. 'Now – altogether – pass Mr Goon and ring your bells hard. Bark, Buster, bark. And everyone yell, "Good afternoon, how are you!" '

And so, to Mr Goon's alarm, annoyance and discomfort, six children rode noisily past him with bells ringing, Buster barking madly, and everyone shouting loudly.

'GOOD AFTERNOON, HOW ARE YOU!'

Mr Goon nearly went into the ditch. He scowled after the backs of the six speeding cyclists. He was almost exhausted already. Still, Tiplington wasn't really very far away now. He pedalled on manfully. If there was anything at Tiplington that he'd got to know about, he must certainly be there. There was no knowing what that pest of a boy was up to.

The Fair was certainly not much of a show. It was in a small field. In one big tent was a flower show, a fruit show, a jam show, and a baby show. There were the usual sideshows – a small roundabout, swings, and a hoopla stall. A fortune-teller sat in a very small tent, reading people's hands for them, telling them of great good fortune to come, voyages across the sea, and all the usual fairy tales.

Apparently the Fair was to last three days, but the local flower, fruit and baby shows only this one afternoon. 'Lucky we saw the notice yesterday,' said Bets, as they paid the entrance fee at the gate. Buster was let in for nothing, but Fatty put him on a lead.

'When does the baby show begin?' wondered Daisy. 'Look – there's a notice on that tent. And here are some babies arriving too. Goodness, they look hot, poor things!'

Prams of all types were wheeled in. The four boys wandered off, but Daisy and Bets stood watching the babies being wheeled into the tent.

Daisy clutched Bets' arm suddenly. 'Look, a double pram – and another. Twins!' she said.

'Where's Ern? We shall never know if the babies are the ones that were up in the caravan.'

Ern had completely disappeared. He had been having a lovely time on the roundabout, riding on an elephant, when he had caught sight of his uncle wheeling his bicycle in at the gate, red in the face, dripping with perspiration, and panting loudly. Ern didn't like the look of him.

So, when the roundabout stopped, he slipped quietly off the elephant and made his way to the tent of the fortune-teller. He hid behind it, watching Mr Goon's movements. Ern was not going to have any more to do with his uncle than he could help.

Daisy and Bets disappeared into the big tent, for the baby show was about to begin. How annoying of Ern to vanish! Still, perhaps he would come along soon.

'Four sets of twins!' said Bets. 'Oh, aren't these babies fat? I don't think I like them quite so fat. And they look so hot and miserable. I'm sure this tent is too hot for them.'

'Come and look at the twins,' said Daisy. 'I say, we don't really *need* Ern, you know, because we know the twins' names – Marge and Bert!'

'Oh *yes*,' said Bets, remembering. 'We can just ask the mothers their names. That's easy.'

The first twins, one big and one small, and quite unalike, were called Ron and Mike, their proud mother informed the two girls.

'No good,' whispered Bets. 'They're boys. We want a girl and a boy.'

The next two were both girls – Edie and Glad, so their mother said. The next pair were again boys, exactly alike, down to the same spot on their chins. Alf and Reg.

'Here's a girl *and* a boy,' said Bets. 'What are their names?'

'The girl's Margery, and the boy's Robert,' said the mother proudly. 'Big for their age, aren't they?'

Bets and Daisy thought they were far too big, far too fat, and far too hot. But their names were right – or almost right!

'Margery and Robert!' said Bets to Daisy in a low voice. 'Marge and Bert. Where's Ern? We'll have to ask him to come and look at them.'

They made their way out of the tent in great excitement and, at last, ran into Ern behind the fortune-teller's tent, where he was still hiding. They pulled him over to the tent.

'You simply *must* tell us if we've found the right babies!' said Bets, and got a sudden punch in the back from Daisy! She gave a squeal. 'Why did you . . .' she began.

And then she saw why! Mr Goon was standing just at the entrance to the tent. He was most interested in what Bets had just said to Ern! Oho! So they *had* got Ern over for something special, thought Mr Goon.

Ern went into the tent, followed by Mr Goon. 'Oh blow,' said Bets. 'Ern, it's the babies at the far end of the row. Just walk quietly by them and tell us if they're the ones we're looking for. Nod your head if it is. Shake it, if not. And look out for Mr Goon!'

Ern walked down the row of babies. Bets and Daisy watched anxiously. Would he shake or nod his head? But, most annoyingly, Ern did neither!

17. THE BABY SHOW

Mr Goon also walked down the row of babies.
The little things were terrified of his big, blue-clad
figure and his brilliant red face. They began to cry.

'Yow!' they wailed. 'Wow-yow-wow!' Mr Goon
scowled at them. He didn't like babies. Also, he was
worried. He was remembering Ern's extraordinary
tale of the prince being smuggled away in a pram
with twin babies. And, lo and behold – here was
a row of twin babies! Did Fatty really believe that
tale then? *Could* there be something in it?

Mr Goon decided to take quite a lot of notice
of the twins. He stood gazing at them. He prodded
one or two. He watched Ern walk by them all,
looking carefully. He watched him go out of the
back flap of the tent, and then he followed him.

The mothers were thankful to see him go.
'What's he want to come in here for, frightening

our babies?' said one mother. 'He's set them all off crying with his scowls and his prods!'

Ern had found Bets and Daisy.

'Ern, *why* didn't you either nod or shake your head?' asked Bets crossly. 'You said you would. We *must* know if they are the twins or not. Are they?'

'I don't know,' said Ern, helplessly. 'All those babies in there look alike to me. I couldn't tell t'other from which. Oh, Bets – I'm sorry. They're as like as peas.'

'How *annoying*,' said Daisy. 'Especially as those two are called Margery and Robert.'

'Of course, Bert might be short for Albert or Hubert, as well as Robert,' said Bets. 'We don't know that Bert, the twin Sid knew, was short for *Robert*.'

'*I* know!' said Daisy, suddenly. 'Let's look for the pram that Margery and Robert came in. Ern could surely recognise *that* if it was the one.'

'Oh yes,' said Ern, confidently. 'It was – let me see – was it dark blue, or dark green?'

The two girls stared at him, exasperated. 'You're perfectly hopeless!' said Daisy. 'What good are you to us, I'd like to know! You never notice a thing!'

Ern looked very woebegone indeed. Mr Goon

emerged from the tent at that moment and, to the girls' great annoyance, Ern at once made off at top speed! Now they would lose him all over again!

'Ern! Come back and look at the prams!' shouted Bets. Mr Goon pricked up his ears again. Prams! Prams! There *was* something up this afternoon. Those kids *were* investigating something, drat them!

Bets and Daisy gave up on Ern. They wandered over to where the prams were neatly set out in a row, empty of their babies. There were two enormous double prams, one fairly big one, altered to take two children, and any amount of ordinary single prams.

'Perhaps we'd better wait about here for Ern,' said Bets, bored. 'He'll come back sooner or later, I suppose. I wonder what the three boys are doing. Oh, do look at Mr Goon. He's interested in prams too!'

Mr Goon was now examining the prams. Could he find anything in them that would help him? He didn't think so. He considered each pram carefully, much to the amazement of a mother coming out to get something for her baby.

'Thinking of buying a pram?' she asked him.

Mr Goon didn't deign to reply. He wandered off in search of Ern.

Soon the mothers began to bring out their babies to their prams. They had all been judged, and 'Margery and Robert' had a big rosette each, with 'First Prize, Twins' on it.

'Oh!' said Bets, starting forward. 'Did they get first prize! How lovely! Let me carry one for you. I like babies.'

'Well, perhaps you'd just bring me my pram,' panted the mother, loaded down with her two heavy children. 'It's over there.'

'Which one?' asked Bets.

'That one,' said the mother, nodding at a rather shabby small pram. It was a single pram! Bets had been sure she would have had a double one – what a disappointment. Margery and Robert *couldn't* be the twins they were looking for, after all! Ern and Sid had been quite certain that the pram belonging to the twins in the caravan was a double one.

She brought the little single pram over. 'There now, Madge,' said the mother, settling the little girl at one end, and then putting the boy at the other. 'Now now, Robbie – don't you start yelling. Haven't you got first prize? Laugh then, laugh!'

Daisy looked at Bets. Madge and Robbie – not Marge and Bert! That settled it. They were not the twins and this was not the mother. All this way over to the Fair for nothing!

'Come along, Bets – let's have a bit of fun now,' said Daisy. 'We've done our investigation – and like all our investigations so far, it's just come to nothing. I don't believe we'll ever find anything out in this mystery!'

They went off to the swingboats. Then they had a try at the hoopla and Bets got a ring round a little red vase, much to her delight.

Then up came Fatty. 'Bets! Daisy! Any good? Were they the twins? What did Ern say?'

'Oh Fatty, such a disappointment! There were twins there whose names were Margery and Robert and we felt sure they were the ones!' said Daisy. 'But they weren't. They were called Madge and Robbie! Ern wasn't a bit of good. He had a look at all the twins, but he said they were as like as peas, and he wouldn't know if they were the caravan twins or not!'

'And, anyway, they have a single pram not a double one,' said Bets. 'We've come all this way for nothing.'

'Oh no, you haven't,' said Fatty, pulling her over to the roundabout. 'Come on, choose your animal and I'll pay the roundabout boy twice as much as usual to go on twice as long. You can have the longest ride you've ever had in your life!'

Bets chose a lion and the roundabout boy set the roundabout going at top speed, so that Bets and the others yelled in glee! He let them have such a long ride that everyone stared in surprise.

'That was fun,' said Bets, getting off her lion and feeling rather wobbly about the legs. 'Goodness, I still feel as if I'm going round and round.'

Fatty suddenly saw Mr Goon in the distance. He grinned. He went over to the roundabout boy, and had a long talk with him. The boy laughed and nodded. Fatty slid some money into his hand and walked away.

'What have you been up to, Fatty?' said Daisy. 'You've got a wicked look on your face.'

'I've just been arranging for Mr Goon to have a nice long ride,' said Fatty. 'Giving him a real treat,

I am! Just you watch!'

Mr Goon had given up searching for the elusive
Ern. In any case, he would never find him because
Ern was lying hidden under a caravan belonging to
one of the Fair people at the end of the field. So
now Mr Goon was wandering over to where he
saw Fatty, Bets, and Daisy. They were joined by
Larry and Pip, who had been unlucky at hoopla,
and had no money left.

'Watch,' said Fatty under his breath. They
all watched, though not quite certain what they
were supposed to watch. The roundabout boy and
another one got up on the roundabout as Mr Goon
drew near. They began to shout at one another.

Everyone turned to see what was happening.
'You give it to me, I say!' yelled one boy. 'Or I'll box
your ears!'

'Shan't!' shouted the other boy, and lunged out
at the first boy. Down he went on the platform of
the roundabout, and rolled about, yelling loudly.

'Don't worry, Bets. It's all pretence,' said Fatty,
grinning. 'Now watch what happens!'

Mr Goon heard all the rumpus, of course. He
pulled down his tunic, put his helmet quite straight,

and walked ponderously over to the roundabout.

'Hey, you boys! What's the matter there? Behave yourselves!'

'Help, help! He's on top of me!' yelled one of the boys. 'Help! Fetch the police!'

Mr Goon mounted the platform of the roundabout, watched by scores of people, looking very impressive indeed. 'Now what's all this?' he began, and then he suddenly clutched at a nearby tiger.

The roundabout boy had slid off the platform and had started the roundabout! Round it went and round, the music sounding very loud indeed in Mr Goon's startled ears. He nearly fell over. He clasped his arms round the neck of the tiger and yelled ferociously.

'Stop this thing! Stop it, I say!'

But nobody heard him through the din of the strident music! The roundabout went faster and faster, it simply WHIZZED round, till Mr Goon's figure could no longer be clearly seen. Fatty began to laugh. The others rolled about, squealing with joy. Everyone yelled. Mr Goon was not popular in Tiplington!

The roundabout slowed down at last. Mr Goon still clutched the neck of the tiger. He dared not let go. Poor Mr Goon – the world still went round for him, and the tiger seemed his only friend!

18. PIP'S DISCOVERY

'I have a sort of feeling we'd better go,' said Fatty. 'Where's Ern? Oh, there he is. Good thing he saw a bit of the fun!'

Ern came over to them, grinning. 'I say, look at Uncle on the roundabout. He's still got hold of the tiger. Was it an accident, Fatty?'

'Not quite,' said Fatty, with a rich chuckle. 'Do come on, everyone. Mr Goon won't be fit to follow us on his bike for quite a while. He'll probably want to go round in circles for ages.'

He winked at the roundabout boy, who winked back. Mr Goon straightened up, unwrapped one arm cautiously from the tiger, and took a step away from it. But the world immediately seemed to swim round him again, and he embraced the tiger more lovingly than ever.

'If I look any more, I shall die of laughing,' said

Larry. 'I've already got a frightful stitch in my side. I have never laughed so much in my life. Dear old Mr Goon – I feel quite fond of him for making me laugh so much. How he will ever get off that roundabout, I don't know!'

Fatty had to shove everyone along. They all so badly wanted to see Mr Goon get off the roundabout and walk unsteadily over the field. The roundabout boy was now shouting at him. 'Sorry, sir! Quite an accident. Won't charge you a penny, sir! Free ride for the police force!'

Mr Goon decided not to deal with that roundabout boy just yet. His words seemed to swim round in his head. He didn't want to argue with anyone just then. He held the tiger still more tightly, and shut his eyes to see if the world would steady itself again.

The Find-Outers and Ern found their bicycles and mounted them. 'Come down this path,' said Ern. 'It's a shorter way to the road. I saw it when I was hiding under the caravan.'

So they took Ern's path that led across the field, past the caravans, and out into a lane that went straight to the road.

And it was when they were cycling slowly past the caravans that Pip suddenly saw something that made him almost wobble off his bicycle!

Clothes lines stretched here and there, hung with the washing belonging to the Fair people. Pip glanced at it idly as he went by. He saw a blouse there, a blue blouse made of rather common material – but it wasn't the blouse that gave him such a surprise – it was the buttons on it!

'Gosh!' said Pip. 'Surely they're the same as the button I've got in my pocket – the button that came off Prince Bongawah's pyjamas!'

He took the button out of his pocket and went over to the clothes line. He compared it with the buttons on the blouse. They were exactly the same – blue and gold, very fine indeed.

Pip glanced at the nearby caravan. It was bright green with yellow wheels. He would remember that all right. He rode fast after Fatty, almost upsetting the others on the narrow path as he passed them.

'Stop it, Pip!' cried Bets angrily, as he almost brushed her pedal. 'What's the hurry?'

Pip caught Fatty up at last. 'Fatty! Quick. Stop a

minute, I've got something important to say!'

Fatty stopped in surprise. He got off his bicycle and waited by the little gate that led into the lane. 'Wheel your bike out under those trees, so that we can't be seen talking,' panted Pip.

Everyone was soon standing under the trees, surprised and puzzled. 'What is it, Pip?' said Fatty. 'What's up all of a sudden?'

'You know this button that came off Prince Bongawah's pyjamas?' said Pip, producing it. 'Well, Fatty, when we passed those clothes lines I saw a blouse hanging on one – and it had buttons *exactly* like these all down the front! And you must admit they're very fine and very unusual buttons!'

'Gosh!' said Fatty, startled by this remarkable statement of Pips'.

He took a quick look at the button and then walked back the way he had come, wheeling his bicycle. 'I must check up,' he said in a low voice as he went. 'Wait for me. I'll pretend to be looking for something I've dropped in the grass.'

He went along with bent head until he came to the clothes line. He spotted the blouse at once. He went right up to it, still pretending to look for something on the ground – and then took a good look at the blouse which was now almost touching his nose.

He came back quickly. 'Pip's right,' he said, his voice sounding excited. 'This is very important. We thought we'd wasted the afternoon, coming after twin babies – and so we had from that point of view – but we're on to something much better!'

'What?' asked Bets, thrilled.

'Well, obviously those buttons are off the prince's pyjamas,' said Fatty. 'And quite obviously, also, the pyjamas have been destroyed in case they might be recognised. But whoever destroyed them couldn't bear to part with the lovely buttons – and put them on that blouse, thinking they would never be noticed!'

'They wouldn't have been if Pip hadn't found that button, and noticed the washing!' said Bets. 'Oh Pip, you *are* clever!'

'Let's think,' said Fatty. 'Let's think quickly. What does it mean? It means that the prince is probably somewhere here – hiding – or being hidden. Probably in that caravan near the washing line. We'll have to try and find out.'

'We can't very well stop now,' said Pip. 'Mummy said Bets and I were to be back by six – and we won't be if we don't hurry.'

'*I'll* stop behind,' said Fatty, making up his mind quickly. 'No, I won't. I'll go back, change into some disguise, and come back here. I'll get into talk with the Fair people and see if I can pick something up. Yes, that's the best thing to do. One of us must certainly make enquiries quickly.'

'Let me stop too,' said Ern.

'Certainly not,' said Fatty. 'You go back with the others, Ern. Go on. Do as you're told. I'm chief here. Let's ride back quickly because it will take me a little time to put on a disguise.'

'What will you be, Fatty?' asked Bets, excited, as they all cycled quickly down the lane, Ern looking a little sulky.

'A pedlar,' said Fatty. 'Selling something. I can easily get into talk with the Fair people then. They'll think I'm one of them. I simply must find out if there has been a new boy added to their company just lately!'

'Good gracious! From being quite unsolvable, this mystery has jumped almost to an end!' said Bets.

'Don't you believe it,' said Fatty grimly. 'There's more in this than meets the eye. It's not as straightforward as it looks. There's something funny about it!'

This all sounded extremely exciting. The six of them rode along in silence, each thinking the same tumultuous thoughts. What would Fatty find out? Would he discover the prince that evening? What was the 'something funny' he meant?

They got home in good time. Fatty went straight down to his shed. He knew exactly what disguise he would wear. It was one he had worn before, and he felt it was just right.

It was an ordinary schoolboy who went into the little shed – but an ordinary schoolboy didn't come out! No, a pedlar crept out, a dirty-looking creature with long earrings in his ears, a cloth cap pulled down over his face, a brilliant red scarf round his neck, and protruding teeth. Fatty was in disguise!

Dirty flannel trousers clothed his legs and old gym shoes were on his feet. He wore a red belt and a dirty yellow jersey. On his back was a pack. It held bottles of all kinds marked 'Cold Cures',

'Cures for Warts', 'Lotion for Chilblains', and all kinds of weird concoctions that Fatty had invented himself for his pedlar's pack!

He grinned as he crept up the path. His protruding teeth showed, ugly and white. He had fixed a fine false set over his own, made of plastic. Fatty was going investigating – and nobody in the world would have guessed he was anything but a dirty little travelling tinker or pedlar!

He cycled off, back to Tiplington. That was clever of Pip to spot those buttons. Very clever. It put the mystery back on the map, so to speak. Fatty thought rapidly over his plan.

I'll go to the Fair field. I'll sit down and get into talk with the roundabout boy or someone. I'll find out who lives in that green and yellow caravan, and pretend I know the people there – and perhaps get the roundabout boy to take me over and introduce me. Then I'll see who's in the caravan and have as good a snoop round as I can. Well, I hope the plan will work!

He was soon back at the Fair. There were more people now because it was evening. The roundabout was swinging round bravely. The swingboats were flying high. There was a babble of talk and laughter everywhere.

Now then, thought Fatty, carefully hiding his bicycle in the middle of a thick bush. Now then! Once more into the breach, dear friend – and see what's what!

He sauntered in to the field. No one asked him for entrance money because he looked exactly like one of the Fair folk themselves. Fatty looked round. The roundabout boy was there at his place. Should he have a word with him? No, he was too busy. What about the hoopla boy? No, he was busy too. Fatty strolled along, keeping his eyes open.

He came to the swingboats. The man looking after them was standing holding his arm as if in pain. Fatty walked up. 'What's up, mate? Hurt yourself?'

'One of these swingboats came back and knocked my elbow,' said the man. 'Look after them for me for a few minutes, will you, while I go and get something for it?'

'Right,' said Fatty, and looked after the swingboats faithfully till the man came back, his arm neatly bandaged.

'Thanks,' he said. 'You with us, or have you just come along?'

'Just come along,' said Fatty. 'Heard that maybe someone I knew was here. Thought I'd give them a call-in.'

'Name of what?' said the man.

'I can't remember the name for the moment,' said Fatty, taking off his cap and scratching his head hard. He screwed up his face. 'Let me see now – Barlow, Harlow, no, that wasn't it.'

'What line were they in?' said the man.

'Ah wait – something's coming back to me!' said Fatty. 'They had a green caravan with yellow wheels. Anyone here in a caravan like that, mate?'

'Oh yes, the Tallerys,' said the man, taking some money for a ride in his swings. 'Those who you mean? They've got that green and yellow caravan over there!'

'That's right – the Tallerys!' exclaimed Fatty. 'How did I come to forget the name! Are they all still there, mate?'

'Well, there's old Mum, and there's Mrs Tallery, and there's a nephew, Rollo,' said the man. 'That's all. Old Man Tallery's not there. He's on a job.'

'Ah,' said Fatty, as if he knew quite well what the job was. 'Well, I feel uncomfortable at going along to them if Old Man Tallery's not there. The others might not remember me.'

'I'll take you along, chum,' said the obliging swingboat man. 'Say, what's your name?'

'Smith,' said Fatty quickly, remembering that many gypsies were called Smith. 'Just Jack Smith.'

'You wait till this lot's finished their swings and I'll take you over,' said the man. 'Maybe they aren't there though. I did see Old Mum and Mrs Tallery going off this afternoon.'

'Well, I'd be glad if you'd take me across,' said Fatty. 'You can tell them I knew Old Man Tallery!'

19. ROLLO TALKS A LOT

The swingboat man took Fatty across to the yellow and green caravan. An old woman was outside, sitting in a sagging wicker chair that creaked under her great weight.

She was calling loudly to someone, 'Rollo! Drat the boy, where is he? I'll give him such a hiding when I get hold of him!'

'Hello, Old Mum,' said the swingboat man, coming up. 'That scamp of a Rollo gone again? I'll give him a clip on the ear if I see him, and send him over to you. He's the laziest young 'un I ever did see in my life.'

'He is that,' grumbled Old Mum. 'His aunt's gone down to the town, and he was told to clean the windows of the caravan. They're that dirty I can't see to knit inside!'

She peered at Fatty. 'Who's this? I don't know

him. Do you want Old Man Tallery? He's not here. Won't be back for a few days.'

'Oh, I'm sorry,' said Fatty. 'I wanted to see him.'

'Friend of his,' the swingboat man explained to Old Mum. 'Name of Jack Smith.' He turned to Fatty. 'You sit and talk to the old lady a bit. She'll love that! What have you got in your pack? Anything to interest her? I'm going back to my swings.'

Fatty opened his pack and displayed his bottles and tins. Old Mum took one look at them and laughed a wheezy laugh.

'Ho ho! That's your line, is it? Coloured water and coloured powders! My dad was in the same line and very paying it was too. Shut your pack up, lad, I've no use for them things. I'm too old and too spry to be caught by such tricks!'

'I wasn't going to sell you any, Old Mum, or try to,' said Fatty, in a voice very like Ern's. 'When did you say Mrs Tallery would be back?'

'Oh, I never know how long she'll be,' said Old Mum crossly. 'Here, there, and everywhere she is. Here today, gone tomorrow – leaves me alone for days on end, she do. Off she went a few days ago, never said where – and back she comes without a word.'

Fatty pricked up his ears. Could Mrs Tallery be the woman in the caravan – the woman with the babies?

'Let me see now,' said Fatty, 'how many children has she got?'

'She and Old Man Tallery never did have children,' said Old Mum. 'Nary a one. That's why they took on Rollo, though gracious knows why they wanted to pick on him, the little pest. But his Ma's got eleven kids besides him, so she was glad to get rid of him.'

'Oh, of course,' said Fatty, quite as if he knew all about it! He was about to ask a few more questions when the swingboat man came up again, leading a boy by the ear.

'Here's Rollo, Old Mum,' he said. 'Shall I set him to work cleaning the windows, or shall I put him across my knee and give him a hiding first?'

'No!' yelled Rollo, squirming about. 'I'll do the windows, you big beast!'

The swingboat man shook him, laughed, and went off again. Fatty looked at the angry boy. He wasn't very big, about Pip's size, and the scowl on his face made him very ugly and unpleasant. Old Mum began to scold him soundly, the words pouring out of her mouth in an endless stream. The boy made a rude face at her.

He then went to get a pail of water and a cloth, presumably to clean the very dirty windows. Old Mum heaved herself up to go into the caravan.

'I'm chilly,' she said. 'Just keep an eye on that boy, will you? Give me a call if he stops his work!'

Fatty helped the old woman into the caravan. She seemed surprised at his help. 'Well, 'tisn't often my son, Old Man Tallery, has friends like you!' she said. 'First time I've known one of them help me up the steps!'

She disappeared into the smelly, dirty caravan. The boy sulkily sloshed water over the windows, and made them so wet and smeary that Fatty thought they were worse than ever!

He sat and waited till the boy had finished. Rollo emptied the water, threw the cloth under the caravan, and made a face at Fatty.

'Here,' said Fatty, taking some money out of his pocket. 'I'm hungry. Go and buy something with this, bring it back, and we'll share it. Skip along!'

'Right,' said the boy, looking less sulky. He took the money and went. Soon he was back with two meat pies, gingerbeer, and four enormous jam tarts. He sat down by Fatty.

'You a friend of Old Mum's?' he said. 'Misery guts she is. I like my aunt better. No nonsense about *her*.'

'You've got plenty of brothers and sisters, haven't you?' said Fatty, eating the pie. He didn't like it at all. It was dry and musty.

'Yes. Eleven,' said Rollo. 'The youngest are twins. Always yelling they are.'

'*Twins*?' said Fatty at once. 'How old are they?'

'Don't know,' said Rollo. 'Just babies. They came to stay with my aunt when my mum was ill.'

'What, here?' said Fatty, munching away. 'I shouldn't have thought there was room for all of you in the caravan.'

'They was only here for a day,' said Rollo. 'Then my aunt got a caravan up on the school camp field and had them there.'

Fatty went on munching solidly, but his eyes suddenly gleamed in his dirty face. Aha! He was

187

on the track now all right! So the aunt was the woman in the caravan – and Rollo's twin brother and sister were the twins in the pram!

'Let me see – Marge and Bert are the twins, aren't they?' said Fatty. Rollo nodded.

'That's right. You know the family all right, don't you! There's Alf, George, Reenie, Pam, Doris, Millie, Reg, Bob, Doreen – and Marge and Bert.'

'And you're the one they chucked out, are you?' said Fatty, gazing at the jam tarts and wondering if he dared to tackle one.

'Ere! Oo said I was chucked out!' said Rollo indignantly. 'What do you suppose Old Man Tallery picked *me* out of the lot for? *I'll* tell you. Because I can act, and because I've got brains, and because I'm jolly useful to him!'

'I bet you're nothing but a nuisance to him, a dirty little rascal like you!' said Fatty, trying to rouse Rollo into telling him a lot more things. Rollo rose to the bait at once. He scowled.

'I'm going to tell you something, Mister,' he said to Fatty. 'I can act anything, I can. I can be a boy leading a blind fellow – that's one way Old Man Tallery and me get money – and I can be a nice kid going shopping with my aunt, and slipping things up my sleeve when Aunt's talking to the shop girl – and I can even be a *prince*!'

Fatty jumped. A prince! Now what did he mean by that? Fatty turned and stared at the gypsy boy, who looked back impudently at him.

'Ah, that made you stare!' said Rollo, triumphantly. 'I bet you don't believe it, Mister.'

'No, I don't,' said Fatty, hoping to lead the boy on and on. His mind was in a whirl. A prince? What did it all mean?

'I thought you wouldn't believe me!' said Rollo. 'Well, I've said too much. I'd better not say any more.'

'That's because you've got nothing to say,' said Fatty promptly. 'You're making up a lot of tales and you know it. Prince, my foot! Dirty little rascal like you a prince! What do you take me for?'

The boy glared at him. Then he looked all round as if afraid that someone might overhear. 'Look here,' he said, 'do you remember the fuss in the papers about that prince being kidnapped. Prince Bonga-Bonga or something. Well, I was him!'

'Go and tell that fairy tale to the twins!' said

Fatty scornfully, but inwardly very excited. 'There's a *real* Prince Bongawah, who belongs to a real kingdom called Tetarua – I've seen photographs of him.'

'Well, I tell you, I was him!' persisted the boy, angry that Fatty wouldn't believe him.

'Really? Well maybe you'll tell me how you were kidnapped then, and how you got away, and were taken here,' said Fatty sarcastically.

'Easy,' said the boy. 'I wasn't kidnapped. I just had to stay a few days at the camp, see, and pretend to be the prince and just talk gibberish – and then on a certain night, I had to creep through the hedge, find my aunt's caravan, and hide there. You'll never guess how I got away though!'

Fatty thought he could make a very good guess indeed, but he pretended to be quite bewildered.

'My word – this is a tale and a half!' he said. 'Do you really mean to say you did all that? Well then – how *did* you get away?'

'My aunt took the bottom boards out of the twins' double pram, and I curled myself up in the space there,' said Rollo, grinning. 'And she sat the twins down on top of me. They didn't half yell!'

'And then she wheeled you back here,' said Fatty, as if overcome with admiration. 'Well, you are a one, Rollo! I didn't believe a word at first, but I do now. You're a marvel!'

Rollo beamed at once at this unexpected praise. He leaned over to Fatty and whispered, 'I could tell you something else if I wanted to!' he said. 'I could tell you where the *real* prince is! The coppers would give a lot to know what *I* know, I can tell you! Not half they wouldn't!'

20. FATTY RIDES HOME

Fatty was so astonished that he couldn't say a word! He gazed speechlessly at Rollo and Rollo grinned delightedly.

'You're a friend of my uncle's, Old Man Tallery, so it won't matter telling *you* all this,' he said, suddenly struck by the fact that he had been telling a lot of secrets! 'But don't you let on to him that I told you.'

'No, I won't,' said Fatty. 'He's not here, anyway. Where is he?'

'Well, he thinks I don't know, but I do,' said Rollo. 'He's down in Raylingham Marshes. I heard him and Joe talking when they didn't know I was near.'

'Is that where the prince is – the real prince?' asked Fatty.

Rollo grew suddenly cautious. 'Here, I'm telling

you too much. What's come over me! You just forget what I said about the prince, see? I don't know where he is.'

'You said you did just now,' said Fatty.

'Well, maybe I do and maybe I don't,' said Rollo. 'Anyway I'm not telling *you*.'

'Right,' said Fatty. 'Why should I want to know anyway? But what beats me is why you had to dress up as the prince and then run away and make people think you were kidnapped. It doesn't make sense to me.'

'Well, it ought to,' said Rollo rudely. 'But maybe your brains want a bit of polishing up.'

'Go on!' said Fatty. 'You and your cheek! I don't say I'm as bright as you are, by a long chalk. I could think a hundred years and not see why all this was done!'

'Well, you look here,' said Rollo, really enjoying himself. 'There's a prince that someone wants to get rid of, see – so that he won't have the throne. Got that?'

'Yes,' said Fatty, humbly.

'But it would be jolly difficult to kidnap him and get him out of the country before his disappearance was discovered, wouldn't it?' said Rollo. 'So all that happened was that when he was sent down to the school camps by car, the chauffeur stopped at an arranged place, the prince was whisked away in another car – and I popped into the first car, all dressed up posh like the prince!'

Fatty suddenly saw light. So *that* was the how and the why and the where! Someone wanted the prince out of the way, but didn't want the kidnapping to be discovered till he had had time to get the boy away somewhere – and with the chauffeur in the plot, it was easy! Exchange boys on the journey down, let the second boy stay a few days in the camp and behave as if he were the real prince – and then creep away to his convenient aunt, and disappear with the twins in the double pram! No one would ever think the woman had anything to do with the second 'kidnapping', which, to all intents and purposes, was the first and only kidnapping. Nobody guessed about the genuine kidnapping!

'What a plan!' said Fatty, in a tone of deepest admiration. 'Old Man Tallery is a whole lot cleverer than I thought he was. My word, next time I meet him, I'll ask him to let me come in on his next job. There must be a lot of money in these things.'

'There is,' said Rollo, boasting hard now. 'I reckon he'll clear hundreds of pounds. I'm going to have some myself, for my part in playing the prince.'

'My word – you'll be rich!' said Fatty. 'How did you like being a prince? Didn't you ever forget your part?'

'No. It was easy,' said Rollo. 'My colouring is as dark as the prince's, and we was both little fellows, and I didn't have to speak any English – only nonsense. But when one of the big fellows – the ones who arranged all this, you know – came down to see how I was getting on and insisted on having the state umbrella up, I didn't like that. I felt a fool. All the boys yelled at me.'

'Did you enjoy being a prince?' Fatty asked him.

'Not so bad,' said Rollo. 'I slept in pyjamas for the first time in my life – lovely silk they were, all blue and gold, with buttons to match. My aunt was told to burn the pyjamas as soon as I got here, and she did, in case anyone saw them. But she kept the buttons and sewed them on a blouse. She didn't like throwing those away, they were too good.'

Fatty couldn't help thinking what a good thing it was that Rollo's aunt had been thrifty over the buttons! If she hadn't sewn them on her blouse, if she hadn't washed it and hung it on the line, Pip would never have spotted the buttons and he, Fatty, would never have got on to the well-hidden trail!

'I suppose Old Man Tallery helped to arrange everything,' said Fatty. 'He's great, isn't he, your uncle?'

'No flies on *him*,' said Rollo proudly. 'He's a card, he is. I quite enjoyed being a prince, but when they wanted me to go swimming, I didn't half kick up a fuss. The way they talked about me not wanting to wash, too. Wash, wash, wash, clean your teeth! Many a time I wanted to talk back at those kids up at camp. I did say a few things in English – but I was a bit afraid of giving myself away if I lost my temper.'

'Of course,' said Fatty. 'Well, you seem to have done very well. I don't believe anyone suspected you weren't the real prince. Are you like him to look at?'

'Near enough,' said Rollo. 'He wasn't anything

special to look at and neither am I. I was a bit scared of someone who knew the prince coming down to see me, but nobody did.'

'And you say you know where they took the prince?' said Fatty. 'Haven't they got him away from there yet?'

Rollo became secretive again. 'I'm not telling that,' he said. 'I don't want to be skinned alive by my uncle, see? He doesn't even know I heard where he's gone to.'

Fatty decided that he couldn't find out anything else from Rollo. He knew the whole plot now – very simple, very slickly carried out – the real kidnapping cleverly masked by the false one so that the police were completely bamboozled, not looking for the prince until some days after he had *really* been kidnapped!

Had the real prince been spirited away yet? Would he ever be heard of again? There really was no time to be lost if he was still being kept in hiding. Anything might happen to him at any time!

Raylingham Marshes. If Rollo's uncle, Old Man Tallery, was there, possibly the whole gang were there, and the Prince too. Where were Raylingham Marshes? Fatty decided to look them up immediately he got home.

He got up to go. It was getting dark and only the Fair people were now left on the field. He had missed dinner – thank goodness his parents were out, and wouldn't know he wasn't there. 'Well, so long!' he said to Rollo. 'I must be going.'

'Aren't you going to wait and see my aunt?' said Rollo, who had taken quite a fancy to Fatty. 'What did you say your name was?'

'Jack Smith,' said Fatty. 'No, I can't wait. Give her all the best from me, and say I'll look in another time. She may not remember me, of course.'

She jolly well won't! thought Fatty to himself, as he went to find his bicycle and ride home. Blow! I haven't got a lamp. I forgot I might be home after dark. Hope I don't get caught by old Mr Goon!

Fatty rode off quickly. His mind was working at top speed. What a plot! No wonder it had seemed such a peculiar mystery – there had been two kidnappings, but only one – the false one – was made known!

Raylingham Marshes. Was there a house in the marshes? Was the prince hidden there? Had Rollo got the name right, or was he doing a little make-up on his own? He was talkative and boastful and conceited – some of what he said might quite well not be true. Fatty rode along so lost in thought that he was in Peterswood before he realised it.

He rode cautiously down the road. As he had no lights he was extra careful – but suddenly a dark figure stepped out from behind a tree, and said sharply, 'Here you! Stop! What you doing, riding without a light? Don't you know it's against the law?'

Mr Goon! thought Fatty. Just my luck! He got off his bicycle, debating what to say and do.

Goon flashed his lantern at him, and saw what appeared to be a dirty tramp with a pack. Mr Goon was suspicious at once.

'This your bike?' he asked sharply.

'Might be!' said the pedlar, insolently.

'Now you come-alonga me,' began Mr Goon, 'and give a proper account of yourself. Riding without a . . .'

'Here hold my bike for a minute while I do up

my shoe,' said the pedlar, and shoved the bicycle at Goon. He had to catch it to save it from falling on top of him – and while he stood there holding it, Fatty was off like a streak of lightning!

'Oho! So that's the way of things, is it?' said Goon. 'He's stolen this bike, that's what he's done.'

Goon mounted the bicycle and rode after the running figure. But it darted off down a path here cyclists were not allowed to ride, and Goon was beaten! He had no wish to ride a bicycle without lights down a path where cycling was forbidden! Ten to one, if he did, that big boy would appear from somewhere and see him! Goon got off and wheeled it carefully back to his house. The bicycle seemed somehow vaguely familiar to him. He took it into his hall and had a good look at it. Then he got out his notebook and wrote down a full description.

'Full-size. Make – Atlas. Colour – black with red line. Basket in front. No front lamp. In good condition.'

Then he wrote a full description of the man he had seen with it.

'Tramp. Cloth cap pulled down over face. Red

scarf. Dirty jersey. Dirty flannel trousers. Earrings. Rude and insolent. I had to force him to give up the bicycle, which I guessed was stolen. After a terrific struggle I got it, and the man ran off, scared.'

Just as he finished writing all this, the telephone rang and made him jump. He picked up the receiver.

'Police here,' he said.

'Oh, Mr Goon, is that you?' came Fatty's voice at the other end. '*So* sorry to bother you – but I have to report to you that my bike's been stolen. It's gone. Not in the shed. Vanished. I'm afraid you'll never find it or the thief, but I thought I'd better report it.'

'Details of your bike please,' said Goon, in a most official voice.

'Right,' said Fatty. 'Full-size, of course. It's an Atlas, a rather nice one in good condition. It's black with a red line, and there's a basket in front. And . . .'

Goon cleared his throat and spoke pompously. 'I have it here, Frederick. I stopped a tramp with it fifteen minutes ago. Very nasty fellow he was too. Most insolent. Didn't want to give up the bike at all when I challenged him.'

'How did you get it then?' asked Fatty in an awed voice.

'Well, I struggled with him,' said Goon letting his imagination go. 'It was a bit of a struggle, you know – but I got it from him. He was so scared that he ran for his life. I brought the bike here. You can come round for it, if you like.'

'My word, you've done some pretty quick work, Mr Goon!' said Fatty admiringly. Mr Goon stood up very straight. Aha – it wasn't often that boy said things like that to him.

'I don't let the grass grow under my feet,' said Mr Goon, with dignity. 'Well, you'll be along in a minute or two, Frederick, I suppose?'

'Give me ten minutes, and I'll be there!' said Fatty cheerfully, and rang off with a click.

21. MR GOON HAS A BAD TIME

Fatty arrived in ten minutes, looking spruce and clean. He had just had time to get out of his disguise and clean himself up. He had given himself one minute to laugh very loudly indeed at Goon's story of the tramp and the fight he had had.

Goon opened the door. He was still pompous. 'There's your bike,' he said, waving to where it stood in the hall. 'Can't beat the police, you know, Frederick.'

'Well, I must say it was pretty smart work, Mr Goon,' said Fatty so admiringly that Mr Goon told the story of the tramp all over again, adding a few more trimmings.

'Mr Goon, I'm much obliged to you,' said Fatty earnestly. 'And, in return, I must pass on a bit of news. We've discovered a bit more about the kidnapping – I know Ern told you about the prince hiding in a pram under the babies, didn't he? Well, we've found out now that that wasn't the real prince. It was a gypsy boy. The real prince is, we *think*, somewhere in Raylingham Marshes.'

Mr Goon's face slowly grew thunderous as Fatty reeled all this off. 'Now look here,' he said, 'why don't you think up some better tale? How many more princes are you going to tell me about?'

'I'm not fooling you, Mr Goon,' said Fatty. 'I said I'd help you this time, and I'm trying to. But you make it very difficult.'

'So do you,' said Mr Goon. 'What with your dressing up as foreigners, and talking foreign, and then telling Ern to tell me about princes in prams with babies, and now you say he was a gypsy, and you want me to go gallivanting off to Raylingham Marshes after another prince. Not me!'

'I don't want you to do any gallivanting at all,' said Fatty. 'All you've got to do is to ring up the Chief Inspector and tell him everything. He'll tell you what to do.'

'Look here,' said Mr Goon, beginning to turn his usual purple, 'didn't I ring up and tell the Chief all about Princess Bongawee, the Prince's sister – and it was all made up on your part to make me look small? Oh, you needn't shake your head, I know it was! Then you wanted me to tell him another idiotic story – and now this. Well, I shan't!'

'You'd better,' said Fatty. 'Or shall I? If I do, I'll get all the credit again, you know.'

'Don't you do any telephoning either,' snapped Mr Goon. 'Can't you keep out of this? I'm in charge of this case, I tell you. Interfering with the law! That's what you do all the time. You're a toad of a boy, a . . .'

'Shush shush, Mr Goon,' said Fatty, beginning to wheel his bicycle out of the hall. 'Naughty naughty! Mustn't lose temper.'

He wheeled his bicycle to the front gate and mounted it. Then he called back, 'Oh, I say, I forgot to ask you something, Mr Goon. Did that tramp you fought with do up his shoe after all?'

And, without waiting for an answer, Fatty rode chuckling down the road. Mr Goon stared after him in the darkness. He was puzzled. How did that boy know that the tramp had said he wanted to do up his shoe? Certainly Mr Goon had mentioned no such thing. Then *how* did Fatty know it?

Light suddenly dawned on Mr Goon. He staggered into his sitting-room and sat down heavily in his chair. He put his head in his hands and groaned. The tramp had been Fatty! He had taken his bike away – and patted himself on the back when Fatty had reported it gone – and given it back to him without so much as mentioning the missing front lamp!

Why, oh why, had he made up such a wonderful story? How Fatty must have laughed up his sleeve! Mr Goon spent half an hour thinking of all the horrid things he would like to do to Fatty but, alas, he knew he would never, ever get the chance to do them. Fatty could look after himself too well!

The telephone rang and Mr Goon jumped. He picked up the receiver fiercely. If it was that boy again, he'd tell him what he thought of him!

But it wasn't. It was a message from the Chief Inspector, delivered shortly by another constable.

'That PC Goon? Message from the Chief. A report has come through from one of our men to say it is now thought that the boy at the camp was not the real prince – but someone masquerading as him. Photographs shown to boys on the field have not been recognised as the boy who was with them as the prince. The Chief says, have you had any inkling of this – if so, please send in your report.'

Mr Goon gaped. He didn't know *what* to say. Why, it seemed as if the message Ern had delivered to him from Fatty might have been correct after all then – not a fairy tale. That story about the prince getting away in the pram – and now Fatty's tale about it being a gypsy boy after all! Was it all true?

'PC Goon? Are you still there?' said the voice at the other end impatiently. 'Did you hear me?'

'Yes – oh yes,' panted Goon, feeling suddenly as if he had been running a long way. 'Thanks. Interesting report. I'll – er – think about it – and send in mine shortly.'

'Right. Goodnight,' said the voice, and the telephone clicked off.

For the second time that night, Goon sank down into his chair and put his head in his hands, groaning. Why hadn't he told the Chief all that Ern had told him? Now someone else had got the information, and got in before him. Goon began seriously to wonder if he owned as good brains as he thought himself to have.

First I ring up and tell the Chief about that dressing-up and Princess Bongawee, which was nonsense, he thought. And then I *don't* tell him about the prince going off in the pram with those babies. That's why those kids were over at the Fair, no doubt about that – trying to trace the babies and their mother.

He sat and brooded for some time. Then he thought of the last thing Fatty had said to him – that he thought the *real* prince was in Raylingham Marshes.

Was that true? Did he really think so? Dare he ring up and tell the Chief that – or would it turn out that there wasn't such a place or something?

Mr Goon began to get into a state. He paced up and down. He clutched his head. He groaned. He'd lose his job over this if he didn't do something special now!

He got down a police map of the district. He looked up Raylingham Marshes. Yes, there was such a place. But was it just marshes and nothing else? Suppose there wasn't even a house there?

'There's only one thing to do,' said Mr Goon, making up his mind. 'I must go and see this place.

Let's see, what's the time? There seems to be a station within a mile or two of the place. Is there a train I can catch?'

He looked up the timetable. There was a train, the very last train, in three-quarters of an hour. Mr Goon began to do things in a great hurry.

He took off his uniform and put on ordinary clothes. It wouldn't do to go snooping round a hide out in police uniform. He dragged on a pair of enormous, grey flannel trousers, added a grey jersey with a bright yellow border at the neck and bottom, and a cap. He put on a tweed coat, rather baggy, and then looked at himself in the glass.

Nobody would guess I was a police officer! he thought. Talk about disguises! Well, I can do a bit of that too. I'm just a hiker now, that's all. I'll put a few things in a kit-bag to make meself seem real.

He caught the train by the skin of his teeth. It arrived on time at the station near to Raylingham Marshes – Raylingham Station – a sleepy little place with one man who was porter, ticket clerk and everything.

He seemed surprised to see Mr Goon on the last train. 'Did you want to get out here, mate?' he asked.

'I did,' said Mr Goon. 'Er, I'm a hiker, you see. I'm – er – seeing the countryside.'

'Well, don't you go hiking over them marshes in the dark,' said the porter, puzzled.

'Are there any houses in the marshes?' asked Goon.

'Not many,' said the porter. 'Two, that's all. One's a farm, on high ground, and the other's a big house. Belongs to foreigners, so people says.'

Aha! thought Goon. That's the house I want. I'll get there somehow, and snoop round. I might find the prince. I might even rescue him.

Wonderful pictures of himself carrying the prince on his back across dangerous marshes came into Mr Goon's mind. Even more wonderful pictures came after that – photographs of himself and the prince in the papers. Headlines – 'Brave Constable Rescues Kidnapped Prince'.

Mr Goon left the dimly-lit station and stepped out into the darkness. There was a lane outside the exit. He would follow that – very, very cautiously. It must lead somewhere!

The porter watched him go. 'Funny chap,' he said to himself. 'Mad as a hatter! Hiking over the marshes in the middle of the night. The police ought to be told about *him* – ought to keep an eye on him, they ought!'

But nobody kept an eye on the brave and valiant Mr Goon. He was quite, quite alone.

22. DISAPPEARANCE OF MR GOON

Fatty had done nothing that night except to look up the map to find Raylingham Marshes, if there *was* such a place. There was, as Goon had already found. Fatty examined the map closely.

I believe I could get into the marshes from this bit of high ground here, he thought. There's a path or something marked there. Two buildings marked as well – one at one end of the marsh, one in the middle. There's a station too. Well, I certainly won't go by train – much too conspicuous.

He decided to go to bed and sleep on the whole idea. He would tell the others about it in the morning. He was much too tired to do any more 'gallivanting' about that night and, anyway, he wasn't going to lose himself in unknown marshes in pitch darkness!

The telephone rang while he was eating

his breakfast next morning. The maid answered it and came into the room.

'Frederick, it's for you,' she said. 'Chief Inspector Jenks on the telephone.'

Fatty jumped. His father looked at him at once. 'You haven't been getting into any trouble, Frederick, I hope,' he said.

'I don't think so,' said Fatty and disappeared hurriedly into the hall, wondering what in the world the Chief wanted at this time of the morning.

'Frederick? Is that you?' came the Chief's crisp voice. 'Listen – Goon's disappeared. Do you know anything about it?'

'Gosh!' said Fatty, startled. 'No, I don't, sir. I saw him late last night. He – er – found my bicycle for me after I had – er – reported it gone. He certainly didn't make me think he was going to disappear.'

'Well, he has,' said the Chief Inspector, sounding annoyed. 'He didn't answer his telephone this morning and when I sent a man over, he reported that Goon was gone – not in his uniform either.'

'Don't say *he's* disappeared in his pyjamas too

213

– like the prince!' said Fatty, still more startled.

'I don't know,' said the Chief. 'Nobody would kidnap Goon, I should imagine – not out of his own house! It's most extraordinary. You are sure you don't know anything about it, Frederick? You usually seem to know a good deal more than most people.'

'No, sir. Honestly, I didn't know he had gone – or was meaning to go anywhere,' said Fatty, very puzzled. 'I can't make it out.'

'Well, I can't stop for more now,' said the Chief. 'Ring me if you have any ideas. Good-bye.'

And before Fatty could ask him or tell him anything more, the telephone went dead. Fatty stared down at it. He was most surprised at this news.

Goon disappeared! He must have gone after I left him. It was dark then, and he was in his uniform. He must have undressed. Gosh, don't say he's gone in his pyjamas too – this is all very peculiar! Fatty quite forgot that he hadn't finished his breakfast, and went out to get his bicycle to ride round to Larry's.

Larry was surprised to see him so early. 'No time to talk much now,' said Fatty. 'Come round to Pip's, you and Daisy. There's a lot of news.'

There certainly was! The others drank in all Fatty had to say about the boy in the caravan the night before, and what he had told Fatty.

'So you see, Sid was quite right when he told us about the boy who was hiding in the pram,' said Fatty. 'And now we know why he hid – and why he pretended to be the prince, and everything.'

'But we don't know where he's been hidden – the real prince, I mean,' said Pip.

'Well, I may even know that,' said Fatty, and he told them what the boy had said. 'He said his uncle, Old Man Tallery, was in Raylingham Marshes,' he went on, 'and as he was mixed up in the kidnapping, and produced his nephew, Rollo, to impersonate the real prince, it's very likely that the prince is there too. There's probably a good hide out there, in those marshes.'

'You did awfully well last night,' said Pip. 'What time did you get back?'

'Late-ish, in the dark,' said Fatty. 'And I hadn't a lamp on my bike – and what do you think! I was caught by Mr Goon!'

'Gracious!' said Bets, alarmed. 'Did he go round

and complain to your parents?'

'Of course not. He didn't know it was me. You forget, I was disguised as a tramp,' grinned Fatty, and then told them how Mr Goon had taken his bicycle and how he, Fatty, had got it back again. The others roared with laughter.

'No one will *ever* get the better of you, Fatty,' said Daisy, with the utmost conviction. 'Any more news? What a lot you've got.'

'Yes. I've kept the spiciest bit till last,' said Fatty. 'Mr Goon has disappeared! Nowhere to be found this morning, so the Chief Inspector says – and, he's left his uniform behind. Where, oh where, can he be?'

Nobody knew. They were all astounded at this last bit of news. 'Another spot of kidnapping, do you think?' asked Larry.

'I don't know *what* to think,' said Fatty. 'He certainly didn't appear to have any plans for going anywhere last night when I went to fetch my bike.'

'Of course, if you'd mentioned Raylingham Marshes to him, I would have thought he might be there,' said Bets. 'Just to get in before *you*, Fatty. But he wouldn't know, of course.'

Fatty sat up straight. 'Bets, you're a marvel!' he said. 'Hit the nail on the head, as usual. I *did* tell him the place, of course – but what with one thing and another, I'd forgotten I'd mentioned it to him. That's where he is!'

'Do you think so *really*?' asked Bets, her face glowing at Fatty's praise.

'Of course,' said Fatty. 'But goodness knows what has happened to him. Got a timetable, Pip? He wouldn't bike all that way, and the buses wouldn't be going at that time of night. But there might be a train.'

There was, of course. 'That's what he did!' said Fatty, jubilantly. 'As soon as I'd gone, he must have got out of his uniform and put on his ordinary clothes and rushed out and caught that train – and gone hunting for the prince in Raylingham Marshes!'

'Without saying a word to anyone!' said Pip. 'What a man!'

'What are *we* going to do about it?' asked Daisy. 'Anything?'

Fatty considered. 'I don't think I'll tell this idea to the Chief. He wouldn't want to send a posse of men searching marshes for Mr Goon unless he was dead certain he was there. We'll go ourselves!'

'What! All of us?' cried Bets, joyfully.

'All of us,' said Fatty.

'And Ern too?' asked Bets, pointing down the drive. Everyone looked and groaned. Ern was coming up the drive – by himself, fortunately.

'Well, I suppose Ern may as well come too,' said Fatty. 'The more the merrier. We'll be a company of kids out walking – looking for unusual marsh flowers and marsh birds.'

'I'll look for the Marsh Goonflower,' said Bets with a giggle. 'And you can look for the Clear-Orf Bird, Pip.'

'Hello, hello, hello!' said Ern, appearing round the hedge. 'How's things? Any news?'

'Yes, a lot,' said Bets. 'But we can't stop to tell you now, Ern.'

'Spitty,' said Ern, looking disappointed. 'What's the hurry?'

'You can come with us if you like and we'll tell you on the way,' said Fatty. 'I hope you haven't got Sid and Perce parked outside the front gate, Ern, because we are *not* going to take them too.'

'I'm alone,' said Ern. 'Perce has gone to buy some more rope for the tent – it flopped down on us last night. And Sid's gone to buy nougat.'

'*Nougat*!' said everyone astonished. 'But why not toffee?'

'Sid seems to have gone off toffee all of a sudden, like,' said Ern. 'Funny. He's never done that before.'

'Well, nougat is almost worse – so gooey,' said Bets. 'Spitty!'

'Now don't you catch Ern's disease,' said Pip. Ern looked startled.

'What disease?' he asked. 'I haven't got no spots nor anything.'

'We haven't any time to waste,' said Fatty. 'We'll go and buy sandwiches and buns and drinks down in the village. There won't be time to prepare food ourselves. We'll take the bus to the east side of the marshes and then walk.'

They left their bicycles at Pip's and went to buy their food. Soon they were on the bus to Raylingham. Fatty forbade them to talk about anything to do with the mystery. 'Someone might be on the bus that knows something about it,' he said. 'We don't want to give any information away.'

They got out of the bus at the edge of the marshes. They had talked so loudly about flowers and birds all the way that the conductor felt sure they wanted to search the marshes for them.

'You'll be all right so long as you keep to the paths,' he told them. 'See that one there? That leads right to the centre of the marsh. You'll notice other paths going off here and there, but be careful not to choose too narrow a one.'

Off they all went. Was Mr Goon somewhere there? Surely he hadn't fallen into the marsh in the middle of the night, and sunk down and down?

'Till his head's just above the surface of the marsh!' said Bets, with a shiver. 'Only his helmet showing.'

'He's not wearing his helmet,' said Fatty. 'Cheer up. It would take a long, long time for an enormous weight like Mr Goon to sink down and down and down! This is not a terribly *marshy* marsh – not in the middle of summer at any rate!'

But when Pip slipped off the path once, he

soon found himself up to the knees in muddy water! He didn't like it at all, and got hastily back on to the path.

'I shan't go looking for Goonflowers just here!' he said. 'I don't feel they'd grow very well!'

23. THINGS BEGIN TO HAPPEN

The marsh was a strange place. It was intensely green and it was also full of the most irritating flies. Ern nearly went mad with them, and the others nearly went mad with Ern's continual slapping and grumbling!

'Look – there's a house or something over there,' said Fatty, suddenly. 'On that high ground, see – where there are trees.'

'How nice to see trees again,' said Daisy. 'I was almost beginning to forget what they looked like. Ern, stop slapping about. You keep making me jump, and it's too hot for that.'

'Let's take this little path,' said Fatty, stopping where a narrow path curved off the main one they were following. 'It seems to go round the back of that copse of trees – it looks almost a wood really – and we could reconnoitre without being seen.'

'What's "reconnoitre",' said Bets at once.

'Spy round – have a snoop,' said Fatty. 'If Raylingham Marshes *is* a hide out for Old Man Tallery and the prince and his kidnappers, we don't want to be caught.'

But they *were* caught! They stole down the narrow little path that skirted the copse, looking carefully down at their feet to make sure they were going to tread safely, when two men rose up from beside a turn in the path. They had been lying behind great tufts of rushes, and couldn't possibly be seen.

The children stopped, alarmed and shocked at such a sudden, silent appearance. The men looked quite ordinary country men, though both had very dark eyes, and a rather odd accent when they spoke.

'Hello,' said Fatty, recovering. 'You startled us!'

'Why do you come through this dangerous marsh?' asked one man. 'It is not fit for children.'

'Oh, we're on a walk,' said Fatty. 'A nature walk. We're not trespassing, you know – this marsh is common ground.'

'But you *are* trespassing,' said the other man, and his dark eyes snapped at Fatty. 'This land belongs to that farm over there. See it?'

'Yes,' said Fatty. 'Well, we're doing no harm. Now we've come so far, we'll go right on to the other side.'

'Not this way,' said the first man, and he planted himself in Fatty's way. 'You can go back to the main path. I've told you, you are trespassing.'

'What's up that we can't go this way?' said Fatty, impatiently. 'Anyone would think you had something to hide!'

'I say – look!' said Larry suddenly, and he pointed up into the sky. 'What's that? A helicopter, surely! Gosh, it's not coming down into the marsh, is it? It will sink!'

One man said something savage to the other in a foreign language. Both glanced up at the hovering helicopter. Then the first one pushed Fatty firmly back.

'I'm having no nonsense,' he said. 'You'll do as you're told, all you kids. Go back to the main path and, if you're wise, keep away from this marsh, see?'

Fatty stumbled and almost fell into the water on one side of the path. Ern, angry that anyone should have dared to touch his beloved Fatty, gave the man a violent push too. He lost his balance and went headlong into the marsh!

'Shut up, Ern,' said Fatty angrily. 'What's the sense of doing that? We shall only get into trouble! Turn back, all of you, and go to the main path!'

The man who had fallen into the marsh was extremely angry. He clambered out, calling orders to the other man, still in a foreign language.

'You can come along with us,' said the second man to Fatty, grimly. 'You hear? Walk in front of us on this narrow path. We'll show you that we mean what we say when we tell you you are trespassing!'

The helicopter was still hovering over their heads. The men suddenly seemed in a great hurry. They made the children squeeze by them on the narrow path till all of them were in front. Then they made them march ahead quickly.

Nobody said anything. Fatty was thinking hard. That helicopter was about to land. Where? There must be some small landing-place cleared for it somewhere near. Who was it going to take away? The prince? Then he hadn't yet been spirited away. Those men had been on the watch for anyone coming through the marsh that day – something was going on, that was clear.

In silence, the two men hurried the children along. Bets was frightened and kept close to Fatty. Ern was scared too, and forgot all about slapping at the flies. And all the time, the helicopter hovered about overhead, evidently waiting for some signal to land.

Round a corner, they came into a big farmyard. Pigs were in a sty, and hens wandered about. It looked very homely and countrified all of a sudden. Ducks quacked in a pond, and a horse lifted its head from a trough where it had been drinking, and stared at the little company.

A very big farmhouse lay back from the yard. Its tall chimneys showed that it was old – probably built in Elizabethan times. There was a small door in the wall of the farmhouse not far from them. The men hurried the children over to it, opened it, and shoved them all in, giving them a push if they thought anyone was not quick enough.

Down a long passage – up some narrow, curving stairs, along another passage, with wooden boards that were very old and uneven. The passage was dark, and Bets didn't like it at all. She slipped her hand into Fatty's and he squeezed it hard.

They came to a door. The man in front opened it. 'In here,' he said, and in they all went. Fatty put his foot in the doorway just as the man was about to shut them in.

'What are you doing this for?' he asked. 'You know you'll get into trouble, don't you? We're only kids out on a walk. What's the mystery?'

'You'll be kept here for a day or two,' said the man. 'There are reasons. You came at an unfortunate time for yourselves. Be sensible and nothing will happen to you.'

He kicked Fatty's foot away suddenly and slammed the door. The six children heard the key turning in the lock. Then they heard the footsteps of the two men as they hurried away down the passage.

Fatty looked desperately round the room. It was small and dark, lined with oak panels. There was one small window, with leaded panes. He ran to it and peered out. A sheer drop to the ground! Nobody could climb out there with safety.

'Fatty! What's all this about?' said Ern, in a frightened voice. 'Sawful!'

'Shall I tell you what I think?' said Fatty, in a low

voice. 'I think Prince Bongawah was taken here and hidden, when he was kidnapped from his car. And I think he's been kept prisoner here till arrangements could be made to spirit him away somehow – and that's what that helicopter is arriving for! It will land somewhere here, the prince will be hurried aboard – and nobody will ever hear of him again!'

Bets shivered. 'I don't like you saying that,' she said. 'Fatty, what are we going to do? Do you think they'll hurt us?'

'No,' said Fatty. 'I think we're a nuisance, but I think they really do believe we're only six kids out hiking. They've no idea we're hunting for old Mr Goon, or that we know anything is going on here.'

'But what are we going to *do*?' said Bets again. 'I don't like this place. I want to get out.'

'I can hear the helicopter again,' said Pip. 'It sounds nearer. It must be coming down.'

'Do you suppose Mr Goon is a prisoner too?' said Larry. 'We haven't seen or heard a sign of him. Perhaps he didn't come to Raylingham Marshes after all.'

'Perhaps he didn't,' said Fatty. He went over to the door and tried it. It was locked. He looked at the door. It was old but very stout and strong. Nobody could possibly break it down!

'Do your trick of getting out through a locked door, Fatty,' said Daisy suddenly. 'There's a good space under the door – I believe you could manage it beautifully.'

'That's just what I was thinking,' said Fatty. 'The only thing is, I need a newspaper – or some big sheet of paper – and I haven't brought a newspaper with me today. Very careless of me!'

'I've got a comic,' said Ern unexpectedly. 'Would that do? What you going to do, Fatty?'

'Get through this locked door,' said Fatty, much to Ern's amazement. Ern fished in his pocket and brought out a crumpled and messy comic, which he handed to Fatty.

'Good work,' said Fatty, pleased. He took the comic and opened out the middle double sheet. He slid it carefully under the door, leaving only a small corner his side. Ern watched, puzzled. How was that going to open a locked door?

Fatty took a small leather case from his pocket and opened it. In it were a number of curious small tools, and a little roll of wire. Fatty took out the wire and straightened it.

He inserted it into the keyhole and began delicately to work at the key. He prodded and pushed and jiggled it – until, suddenly, he gave a sharp push and the key slid out of the keyhole on the other side of the door, and fell with a thud down to the floor.

Ern stared open-mouthed. He couldn't for the life of him make out what Fatty was doing. But the others knew. They had seen Fatty doing his locked door trick before!

'Hope it's fallen onto the paper,' said Fatty, and bent down to draw the sheet of paper back under the bottom of the door. Carefully he pulled it, very carefully. More and more of the comic appeared and, oh joy, at last the key appeared too under the door, on the second half of the double-sheet! There it was, on their side of the door. Fatty had managed to get it!

Ern gasped. His eyes almost fell out of his head. 'Coo – you are a one!' he said to Fatty. 'You're a genius, that's what you are.'

'Be quiet, Ern,' said Fatty. He slid the key into the lock on his side of the door and turned it. The door unlocked. Now they could all go free!

24. FATTY DOES SOME GOOD WORK

'Listen,' said Fatty, in a low voice. 'I don't think we'd all better go out. There's such a crowd of us, we'd be sure to be spotted. What I propose to do is this – get out by myself and have a really good look round. If there's a telephone, I shall immediately use that to get on to the Chief Inspector, and warn him to send men here at once.'

'Ooooh, *yes*!' said Bets, delighted at the idea of rescue.

'Then I shall snoop round to see if I can find the prince – though I'm afraid I won't be in time to stop the helicopter from going off with him, if they mean to take off again at once,' said Fatty.

'What about Mr Goon?' asked Larry. 'Will you look for him?'

'Well, I'll certainly keep a look out for him,' said Fatty. 'But, at the moment, the most important thing is to get in touch with the Chief, and also see if I can hold up the prince's flight. Now all you have to do is to keep quiet and wait. I'll have to lock you in again, I'm afraid, in case someone comes along and finds the door unlocked. But you know how to get out if you want to, Larry, don't you? – so you'll be all right.'

'Suppose someone comes and sees you're not with us?' said Bets, in sudden alarm.

'I don't expect they'll notice,' said Fatty. 'They haven't counted us, I'm sure! Well – slong!'

'So long!' whispered the others. 'Good luck!'

Fatty disappeared down the passage, after carefully locking the door behind him and leaving the key in the lock. He was very cautious. By good chance they had come at a most important moment, and Fatty did not mean to throw his chance away!

The telephone! That was the most essential thing for him to find. Where would it be? Downstairs, of course. In the hall, probably, which would make it very awkward indeed to talk into. He would certainly be heard.

A thought struck Fatty. Sometimes people had a

telephone in their bedroom. His mother had, for instance, so that if she happened to have a cold, she could still telephone her orders to the shops, or talk to her friends.

There *might* be one in a bedroom. Fatty decided to look. It would make things so much easier if there were.

He peeped into first one room and then another. Two of them were most luxuriously furnished, considering this was a farmhouse. Fatty stood at the door of one, his sharp eyes looking all round.

Then his face brightened. A telephone in pale green stood beside the big green-covered bed at one side of the room! Gosh! Could he possibly get to it and telephone unheard? He tiptoed across the room, first shutting the door quietly behind him. He took up the whole telephone, and crept under the bed with it, hoping that his voice would be muffled there.

He lifted the receiver and put it to his ear, his heart beating fast. Would the operator answer?

With great relief he heard a voice speaking. 'Number please.'

Fatty gave the number in a low voice. 'It's the

Chief Inspector's number,' he said urgently. 'Put me through quickly, will you?'

In under half a minute, another voice spoke. 'Police station here.'

'This is Frederick Trotteville speaking,' said Fatty, keeping his voice low. 'I want the Chief Inspector at once.'

There was a pause. Then came the Chief Inspector's voice and Fatty's heart lifted in joy.

'Frederick? What is it?'

'Listen,' said Fatty. 'I'm at the farmhouse in the middle of Raylingham Marshes. I'm pretty certain the kidnapped prince is here too. There's a helicopter hovering about, and I think maybe we've come at an important moment – when the prince is about to be spirited away. We're prisoners, sir, but I managed to get to a telephone. We're all here, Ern too. Can you send men along?'

There was an astounded silence. Fatty could picture the Chief's astonished face. Then his crisp voice came over the wires. 'Yes. I'll send some. Hang on till we come – and see if you can stop the prince from being taken away! If anyone can, *you* can, Frederick! Good work!'

The telephone went dead. Fatty replaced his receiver with a sigh of thankfulness. Help would come sooner or later. Now he was free to do a bit of prowling round and see what he could find. If only he could find out where the prince was!

Fatty crawled out cautiously from beneath the bed and replaced the telephone on its little table. He tiptoed to the door. All was quiet. He opened it silently and peered out into the passage. No one was in sight.

Better look for a locked door, thought Fatty. That's the only bright idea I've got at the moment. Let's think now – the farmhouse had two wings to it and I'm in the middle. We must have been locked up in one wing. Maybe the prince is in the other.

He leaned carefully out of a window to have a look at where the other wing of the house stood out. He at once noticed a barred window. Ah, surely that would be the room!

He drew in his head, and made his way down the passage. Was there any way of reaching the other wing except by the stairs and the hall? There might be.

Fatty came to the head of the stairs. Down below he could hear the murmur of voices coming from some room – and then his eye caught sight of something through the landing window.

It was the helicopter! With its vanes whirring, it was slowly descending! Fatty watched it disappear behind a big barn-like building. There must be a landing-place there. He frowned. There was no time to lose now. The prince might be hurried off immediately!

He went to the back of the landing and found a tiny, narrow passage there. Perhaps it ran to the other wing! He followed it carefully and quietly and, as he had thought, it did run to the other wing of the house.

Now to find the locked room with barred windows! thought Fatty jubilantly, and then shrank back in fright as he heard the sound of a door being shut and locked, and a man's voice saying something loudly.

Fatty crouched behind a curtain covering a window, hardly daring to breathe. Footsteps passed by him, and went on to the big landing where the stairs were. When all the sounds had gone, Fatty came out again. He tiptoed quickly along the passage, passed two open doors – and then came to a shut one!

It was locked! But, fortunately, the key had been left in the lock. Fatty turned it, opened the door, and looked in.

A dark-faced boy with a sulky, scowling expression looked up. He was about Pip's size, and in build and colouring was very like Rollo, the gypsy boy.

'Are you Prince Bongawah?' whispered Fatty. The boy nodded, staring in astonishment at this big boy in the doorway.

'Come on then – I've come to save you,' whispered Fatty. 'Hurry up.'

The boy ran to the door and began to jabber in a foreign language.

'Shut up!' said Fatty urgently. 'Do you want to bring everyone up here! Come with me and don't make a sound!'

The boy followed him, suddenly silent. Fatty locked the door behind him. Then, very cautiously indeed, his heart thumping hard against his ribs, he led the boy down the narrow passage, across the landing where the stairs were, and along the passage that led to the other wing.

He unlocked the door where the others were and pushed the boy inside. Everyone stared in astonishment at Fatty's grinning face and this newcomer, so dark and foreign-looking.

'I've found the prince,' said Fatty jubilantly. 'And I thought the safest place to hide him would be here. He can get into that cupboard. Nobody would dream of looking for him in a room where *we* are supposed to be prisoners!'

'Oh, Fatty – you're full of good ideas!' said Bets. 'Poor prince! He must wonder what's happening.'

The prince spoke beautiful English, and gave them all a little bow.

'I have been a prisoner for many days,' he said. 'I have been unhappy and afraid. You are my friends?'

'Oh yes,' said Bets, warmly. 'Of course we are. You'll be safe now Fatty has got you!'

'I found a telephone and got a message through to the Chief,' said Fatty, unable to stop grinning. 'Golly, what a surprise for this lot when they find the police coming through the marsh and surrounding the farmhouse!'

'Honestly, you're a genius Fatty,' said the admiring Ern. 'I think you ought to be made a Chief Inspector at once, I do!'

'Did you find Mr Goon?' asked Daisy.

Fatty shook his head. 'No – didn't see or hear a sign of him. I'm beginning to wonder if he came here after all.'

'Well, it's a good thing we *thought* he did!' said Bets, 'or we shouldn't have come ourselves! And then we'd have missed all this!'

'Did you see the helicopter come down?' asked Daisy. 'We suddenly saw it landing behind that big barn.'

'Yes, so did . . .' began Fatty, and then stopped speaking and listened. The others listened too.

They could hear shouts – and banging doors and running feet! What was up?

'They've discovered that the prince isn't in his room!' said Fatty, beaming. 'What a shock for them! *Now* there'll be a rumpus! Helicopter all ready to take him off – and no prince to be found! Get into that cupboard, Prince, and keep quiet. Don't make a sound.'

The prince disappeared into the cupboard in

239

double-quick time. Bets shut the door on him. In silence, they listened to the excitement going on elsewhere.

Then footsteps came hurrying down their passage, sounding loudly on the wooden boards. Their door was suddenly flung open.

A swarthy-faced man looked in, his eyes blazing.

'He might be here!' he shouted. 'These kids may have got him with them somehow. Search the room!'

25. A VERY EXCITING FINISH

That was a real shock to everyone! Bets went pale. Only Fatty didn't turn a hair.

'What's up?' he said. 'Who do you think we've got here? You shut six of us up, goodness knows why, and there are six still here!'

The man shouted something at Fatty in such a savage voice that Fatty decided not to say anything more. Three other men crowded into the room and began to look everywhere. In less than a minute the cupboard was opened – and the prince was discovered!

The swarthy-faced man pounced on him and shook him! He screamed something at him in a foreign language and the boy cowered in fright. He was dragged out into the passage. Fatty followed, protesting.

'I say, look here! I say, you know . . .'

The dark-faced man turned on him, his hand lifted – but before he could strike Fatty, a loud voice shouted down the passage.

'The police! The POLICE are coming! Tom's just seen them coming over the marsh. Someone's split on us!'

Then there was such a babel of noise and excitement that it was impossible for anyone to be heard. Fatty took the opportunity of pulling the prince back into the room, pushing all the other children in too, slipping the key from the outside of the door to the inside – and locking them all in!

As he turned the key, he grinned round at the six frightened faces. 'Cheer up! No one can get at us! We're locked in again but the key's our side all right!'

Bets was crying. 'Oh Fatty, I didn't like that man. Are we safe now? Can they break the door down?'

'They won't bother to try,' said Fatty. 'They'll be too anxious to save their own skins! We can just sit here and listen to the fun – and come out when everything is quiet!'

'There goes the helicopter again!' said Pip suddenly, and sure enough it was rising quickly over the barn. Evidently it had been warned to go.

'But it didn't take *me* with it,' said the prince exultantly, and went off into a stream of what sounded like gibberish to the children.

Not much of the excitement could be seen from the window. Two policemen suddenly appeared and made a rush for the house. One man suddenly ran helter-skelter across the farmyard and disappeared, followed immediately by a burly policeman. Yells and shouts and thumps and crashes could be heard every now and again.

'I'm rather sorry to be out of the fun,' said Fatty regretfully.

'Well, I'm not,' said Ern, who was looking extremely scared. 'Fun! Not my idea of fun. Sterrible!'

After about half an hour, silence reigned. Had all the men been rounded up? Fatty and the others listened. Then they heard a most stentorian voice.

'FREDERICK! WHERE ARE YOU? FREDERICK!'

'The Chief Inspector!' said Fatty thankfully, and ran to unlock the door and open it. He too yelled at the top of his voice.

'HERE, SIR! WE'RE ALL SAFE AND SOUND!'

He turned back to the others. 'Come on,' he said, 'it must be safe now. Come on, Ern. Your legs too wobbly to walk?'

'Bit,' said poor Ern, staggering after the others.

The Chief Inspector met them all at the top of the stairs. He ran a swift eye over the lot. 'All of you here?' he said. 'Who's this?' He pointed to the prince.

'Prince Bongawah, sir,' said Fatty. 'I got him all right. Did you catch everyone, sir?'

'I think so,' said the Chief Inspector. He pulled the prince to him. 'You all right?' he said. 'They didn't do anything to you, did they?'

'No, sir,' said the prince. 'It was my uncle who kidnapped me. I was . . .'

'We'll hear your story later, son,' said the Chief Inspector. 'Well, Frederick, that was a spot of good work on your part. Though how in the world you managed to smell out this place – and get here on your own – and find the prince – and telephone me in the middle of everything, I don't know! And taking the whole of the Find-Outers with you too – except Buster. Where is he?'

'Had to leave him behind, sir,' said Fatty,

regretfully. 'I was afraid he'd fall into the marsh and drown. Pity he's out of the fun though. He does love a scrap.'

'We've got some police cars on the edge of the marsh,' said the Chief Inspector. 'At present, two of them are taking some of the men to the police station but they'll be back soon, and then I'll take you home.'

'Let's have a wander round the place then, sir,' said Fatty. 'It seems odd to have a farm in the middle of a marsh.'

They all went thankfully into the open air. A frightened woman peeped from a doorway at them.

'Who's she?' asked Fatty, surprised.

'The housekeeper', said the Chief Inspector. 'We left her for the present, as someone's got to feed the hens and the pigs and ducks.'

They wandered round the farmyard and then round to the back of the big barn, behind which the helicopter had landed. A big flat space had been cleared there for the landing.

They looked at the cleared space and then walked round it to a group of sheds nearby. They talked cheerfully as they went, all of them feeling very happy to think that everything was over.

A sudden noise made them stop. 'What was that?' said Larry. 'It sounded as if it came from that shed. Is there some animal locked in there? A bull perhaps?'

The noise came again – a loud banging noise, then a series of thuds. The door of the shed shook.

'Better look out,' said the Chief Inspector. 'Sounds rather like a bull in a temper.'

Snorts and groans and yells came next. 'It isn't a bull,' said Fatty. 'Sounds like a mixture of a man and a bull! I'll look and see – through a window, not through a door!'

The window of the shed was very high up. Fatty ran a ladder up against the wall of the shed, went up it and peered through the window. He came down again, grinning.

'Friend of yours, sir,' he said cheerfully, and unbolted the door from the outside. It burst open and out came a big, dirty, perspiring, maddened creature, his fists up, and hair standing on end.

'*Goon*!' said the Chief Inspector, almost falling backwards in his amazement. 'GOON! What on earth – is it *really* you? GOON!'

Yes, it was Mr Goon, and a sorry sight he looked. He was filthy dirty, very angry, and looked as if he had been sitting down in all the messes he could. Straw was caught in his up-standing hair, and he panted like a dog. He stared in astonishment at the little company before him, and quietened down at once when he saw the Chief Inspector.

'Morning, sir,' said poor Goon, trying to flatten down his hair.

'Where did you disappear to without leaving any message as to your whereabouts?' asked the Chief Inspector. 'We've been hunting for you everywhere.'

'I – er – got a hunch that something might be going on here,' said Mr Goon, still sounding out of breath. 'Caught the last train, sir, and somehow I got lost in these here marshes. I found myself sinking down, and I yelled for all I was worth.'

'Oh, Mr Goon! How dreadful for you!' said kind-hearted Bets. 'Did someone rescue you?'

'Rescue me!' snorted Goon, sounding rather like a bull again. 'Yes, they pulled me out all right – and pushed me into that cowshed and bolted me in! What for? They should all be arrested, sir! Mishandling the police! Punching me in the back!'

'Don't worry, we *have* arrested them all,' said the Chief Inspector. 'You missed that bit of fun.'

'Coo, Uncle – you don't half look funny,' said Ern suddenly, and went off into a loud guffaw. His uncle appeared to see him for the first time.

'ERN! You here too! What you doing here, mixed up in all this?' shouted Goon. 'I'll teach you to laugh at me!'

'Behave yourself, Ern,' said Fatty, severely. He felt sorry for poor Mr Goon. What a hash he had made of everything – and yet he, Fatty, had given him all the information he could!

'It was jolly brainy of Mr Goon to come here, sir, wasn't it?' he said innocently to the Chief Inspector. 'I mean, he got here even before we did. It was just bad luck he fell in the marsh. He might have cleared the whole job up himself if he hadn't done that.'

Mr Goon looked gratified. He also felt suddenly very kindly towards Fatty. He wasn't such a toad of a boy, after all!

The Chief Inspector looked at Fatty. 'Brains are good, courage is excellent, resourcefulness is rare,' he said, 'but generosity crowns everything,

Frederick. One of these days, I'll be proud of you!'

Fatty actually blushed. Mr Goon had heard all this, but hadn't understood what the Chief Inspector meant at all. He came towards them, brushing down his clothes.

'So, it's all over, is it?' he said. 'What happened, sir?'

'You'd better go and wash,' said the Chief Inspector, looking at him. 'You've no idea what you look like, Goon. And if you've been shut up all night, you'll be hungry and thirsty. Ask the woman at the farmhouse for something to eat and drink.'

'I could certainly do with something,' said Mr Goon. 'You'll call me when you want me, sir?'

'I will,' said the Chief Inspector. 'We're just waiting for the police cars to come back.'

'Slong, Uncle,' called Ern, but his uncle did not deign to reply. He disappeared in the direction of the farmhouse – an ungainly, peculiar-looking figure, but not at all downcast. Hadn't he got there before that boy, anyhow? And hadn't that boy admitted it? Things weren't so bad after all!

'It was a peculiar sort of mystery this time,' said Bets, hanging on to the Chief Inspector's arm.

At first, there didn't seem to be any clues or anything – nothing we could get hold of – and then it suddenly boiled up, and exploded all over us!'

Everyone laughed. 'Bets quite enjoyed this mystery,' said Fatty. 'Didn't you, Bets? I did too.'

'So did I,' said Ern, thoroughly agreeing. 'Not half! Spitty young Sid and Perce weren't in at the finish.'

'Yes. SPITTY!' agreed everyone, chuckling, and the Chief Inspector smiled.

'Well, let me see – when do you have your next holidays?' he said. 'At Christmas time? Right. Here's to the next mystery then – and may it all end as well as this!'

The MYSTERY series
the Five Find-Outers and Dog

The Mystery of the Burnt Cottage · *The Mystery of* the Disappearing Cat · *The Mystery of* the Secret Room · *The Mystery of* the Spiteful Letters · *The Mystery of* the Missing Necklace

The Mystery of Hidden House · *The Mystery of* the Pantomime Cat · *The Mystery of* the Invisible Thief · *The Mystery of* the Vanished Prince · *The Mystery of* the Strange Bundle

The Mystery of Holly Lane · *The Mystery of* Tally-Ho Cottage · *The Mystery of* the Missing Man · *The Mystery of* the Strange Messages · *The Mystery of* Banshee Towers

Enid Blyton